C.R.I.M.S.O.N.

A Novel

R. H. KREBS

P
Prescience Publishing

C.R.I.M.S.O.N.

C.R.I.M.S.O.N. ordering information can be found at:

http://www.CRIMSONtheBook.com

C.R.I.M.S.O.N. may also be ordered from Amazon.com
and is available at booksellers everywhere.

Because of the dynamic nature of the Internet, any Web
addresses or links contained in this book may have changed
since publication and may no longer be valid.

Cover art by Dave Peeters including photos and images
http://www.davepeetersphotos.com

Prescience Publishing

ISBN-13: 978-0615435695
ISBN-10: 0615435696

Printed in the United States of America

To my wife, Renée
Her eyes have captivated me from the beginning.
Her faith in me is greater than my own.

And

to our precious gifts from God, Rachelle and Kimberly

Acknowledgments

I would like to first give thanks and praise to God for His grace and blessings. The homeschool families and support systems that have grown and flourished in this country have provided a means to allow us to raise and educate our children in a manner in concert with our Christian beliefs.

I would like to acknowledge the Christian homeschool speech and debate leagues throughout the country and the young men and women who compete in these leagues. Additional thanks goes to the homeschooling parents and team coaches who work tirelessly to help improve the skills of their students. And the alumni who move on to college and law school, but still have time to teach, support and encourage the new team members.

Finally, I would like to acknowledge a few special people and families: Coach Nogy and the families of Saddleback Christian Academy's Speech and Debate team, who have worked to constantly improve the speaking, reasoning and persuasion skills of so many students. They have inspired the next generation of leaders.
Also my wife Renée and Mrs. Virginia Thompson for their editing expertise, and Jessica Glasner who read it first and insisted I publish C.R.I.M.S.O.N.

Forward

A few years ago I was asked to be a judge at a speech and debate tournament that my daughter had entered. The tournament was sponsored by a Christian homeschool speech and debate league.

At the time it looked like our nation was falling further and further away from the intent of the Founding Fathers. Our Christian roots were being "uprooted", purged from our society. I wondered, 'where are the next generation of leaders? Where are the energized young men and women of integrity and morals, committed to preserving this nation and what it was originally founded on? Do they even exist?'

But then I judged a few rounds of Lincoln-Douglas debate and listened to some of the speeches. I was completely awestruck! I realized that the next generation is not all playing video games and watching TV reruns on youtube. There are some who were striving, studying constitutional law, understanding the concepts of John Locke, quoting Thomas Jefferson and John Adams.
Not only did they have a firm grasp of these things, but they were amazing speakers, fluent, articulate and persuasive, and to top it off, they were having a great time doing it. On that day, I determined to help support these young people, leaders of tomorrow, and the clubs and leagues that provide the structure so they can thrive.
One word of caution for parents: With these skills, your children will be more difficult to argue with.

C.R.I.M.S.O.N. was written for young adults to realize they have the potential with God's help to change things for the better. I hope to encourage them to understand the foundations of our great nation and to inspire them to stand for these ideals in the face of continuous assaults from many who no longer believe in Truth.

C.R.I.M.S.O.N. was also written to provide a more realistic representation of the Christian homeschool culture. Dispelling so many inaccuracies about the families that homeschool and the way in which we live and support one another. There are many dedicated homeschool moms and dads that have determined to sacrifice their time, luxuries, and in some cases, careers to provide their sons and daughters with the best education that focuses on essential knowledge and supports and integrates that knowledge with the values they hold dear.

Finally, C.R.I.M.S.O.N. was written as an entertaining, exciting and thought-provoking thriller that young as well as older adults will enjoy. The novel is written in two books, "On a Mission from God" introduces you to the main high school characters in the story and lays the foundation for other books to follow. The second book, "So Help Me God," continues the story and God's exciting and challenging plan as the characters make their way through college and into their careers, battling deadly adversaries at every turn.

I sincerely hope you find C.R.I.M.S.O.N. a story that inspires, enlightens and entertains.

– R. H. Krebs

Table of Contents

Prologue

C.R.I.M.S.O.N.
Book One – On a Mission from God   1

The Main Characters in Book One, Acronyms   2
Chapter One – The Vision   3
Chapter Two – The Meeting   19
Chapter Three – The New Kid in Town   36
Chapter Four – The Key   48
Chapter Five – Getting Serious   61
Chapter Six – The Hard Case   72
Chapter Seven – Interesting Distractions   83
Chapter Eight – The Competition   101
Chapter Nine – Back on Track   126
Chapter Ten – What a Knight   139
Chapter Eleven – The Ice Queen   160
Chapter Twelve – Unintended Consequences   174
Chapter Thirteen – Revealing Secrets   191

Table of Contents

C.R.I.M.S.O.N.
Book Two – So Help Me God   209

Chapter One – Seasons of Change   213

Chapter Two – My Plans are Not Your Plans   231

Chapter Three – The Breach   246

Chapter Four – A Tango in Paris   255

Chapter Five – The Best Laid Plans   279

Chapter Six – In from the Cold   297

Chapter Seven – A Blessing and a Curse   311

Chapter Eight – Trust   321

Chapter Nine – Just Dinner   336

Chapter Ten – Know it All   358

Chapter Eleven – Engagements and Arrangements   365

Chapter Twelve – Changing of the Guard   382

Chapter Thirteen – The Revelation   398

Epilogue

Prologue

"We the People of the United States, in Order to form a more perfect Union, establish Justice, insure domestic Tranquility, provide for the common defense, promote the general Welfare and Secure the Blessings of Liberty to ourselves and our Posterity, do ordain and establish this Constitution for the United States of America."

– Preamble of the United States Constitution

Standing on the platform in the Rose Garden, I prayed silently before the President spoke. Our journey was not over but God had been faithful and unerring throughout; and if those who stood with me today knew what had taken place, only a few would have considered it possible, but none would have believed it actually happened.

C.R.I.M.S.O.N.

Book One

On a Mission from God

The Main Characters in Book One:

The Families in CHESS (ages represented as the book begins)

The "Vision" Families
Mr. David & Mrs. Emily Reinhart, Sarah(12) and Joshua(16)

Dr. Daniel & Dr. Rachel Simmons, Dean(5), Catherine(7), Andrew(9), Laura(10), Ashley(13) and Zachary(13), Dan Jr.(16), Elizabeth(17)

Pastor John & Mrs. Barbara Miller, Rebekah(13), Robert(17)

Mr. Harold Stanton & Mrs. Jackie Stanton, Jenna(14), Ben(16)

Mr. Samuel & Mrs. Lisa Chung, Steve(16), Leah(18)

Mr. Doug & Mrs. Cathy McClaren, Bethany(7), Kristen(11), Mark(13), Alison(15)

Other CHESS families
Mr. Jack & Mrs. Yvette Petersen, Jeff(16), Lisa(20), John(23)

Mr. Rob & Mrs. Tracy Nichols, Jonathan(9), Jennifer(18)

Point men and women who were in CHESS
Aaron Morris(21), Jillian Holladay(22), John Petersen(23)

Other debate families
Mr. Ruben & Mrs. Angela Perez, Christopher(8), Jason(10), Marc(12), Cassandra(18)

Acronyms:

CRIMSON: Christian Reasoning Influencing Mankind, Serving Our
             Nation
CHESS: Christian Homeschool Educators of Santa Sonoma
CHAF: Christian Homeschool Aid Foundation
HGCF: His Grace Christian Fellowship
TPM: Thursday Prayer Meeting

Chapter One

The Vision

*"I tremble for my country when I reflect that God is just;
that his justice cannot sleep forever."* – Thomas Jefferson

Doors opened, doors closed … All part of God's plan for our
lives. That's what Mom called it …I just called it *The Move*. I
frowned as I watched the pine trees blur by as the black S Class
smoothly wound its way up the San Bernardino switchbacks.
The move had brought lots of changes for me this year: a new
home, new friends (a few anyway), new homeschool group, new
church. I thought about my friends back in Tampa where I grew
up. I missed them, but if they could be here in Southern
California they might see why we moved. The muted rumble of
the big Mercedes V8 was all I had heard for the last fifteen
minutes. I should have brought my iPod, I thought. But I hadn't
because of the rules of the retreat, and I had secretly hoped this
could be an opportunity to get to hang with my dad.

"Are there going to be any of my friends at the retreat?" I asked,
finally breaking the silence.
"I heard the McClaren boy might be coming, but I didn't have a
lot of time to get many details. We are fortunate we made it in at

all. If the Tanners hadn't cancelled at the last minute..." he trailed off.

Oh well, I thought, at least I get a whole weekend with my dad, and I would try to connect. It was funny how the timing had worked out. Dad had a free weekend for once, and then we got the call from Pastor Miller about the Tanner's canceling.

My dad was David Reinhart, CEO of Prescience, Inc. He had started the company with a little money and a lot of hard work, and then in a stock market frenzy it had gone public. I knew the story well as my mom taught Sarah and me all about how capitalism worked by using my dad's company as a perfect example; come up with a good idea, work hard, get some funding, hire smart dedicated employees, work even harder and you can succeed beyond your wildest dreams. She said it was what made this country great, along with the fact that America was blessed by God because we trusted in Him.

The squeal of the Michelins brought me back to the silence and the blurring landscape... I thought I'd let Dad concentrate on his mountain driving since the tallest hills in Tampa were about the size of a standard speed-bump here in California. That had been one of the best parts about the move; Southern California was amazing in its range of stuff to do, we had only been driving for a little over an hour from our new home and we were in the mountains. Last year when we made a house hunting trip to the area, Santa Sonoma was just being built out. It was one of those planned gated communities built in the rolling hills overlooking the ocean. Compared to my older home in Tampa, it looked like a Disney set, with large homes influenced by what my mom called "the craftsman" style. All I know was everything was new, younger than my sixteen years. Our house had a great back yard with a basketball/tennis court and a pool. I think Sarah had spent the first week completely underwater only coming up for air and meals. She had no problem adjusting, already had a new best friend and a dozen other "tween girls" who were constantly at each other's homes or on Skype.

I decided to try again, "What's going to go on up there, do you think we can try snowboarding?"

"This is a Christian Men's retreat," my dad replied with emphasis. "It's a time to put all the distractions of life down for a couple of days and focus on The Lord and His Word. But I did hear there was a stream with fish in it. We could try to rent some poles and learn to fish?" then after a bit, "This will be a great opportunity to meet the other dads," he said lamely.

I sighed. He was trying, but we both knew we would not be fishing this afternoon or tomorrow. No cable, no sports, no iPods, no internet and maybe I was the only one under the age of thirty up here.

"The other dads..." I thought. I had met a couple of them at our first debate club meeting. There was Ben's father, Mr. Stanton; he wore a suit and got there in time to pick up Ben after the meeting. He was tall, tan, 'imposing' was the word that came to mind. I think he was a lawyer of some kind. And then there was Mr. Chung, Steve's dad. He was an engineer, quiet and thoughtful, always had his laptop with him, and he had judged a few practice rounds.
But it was mostly "The Moms" who ran things. And some of them were *intense*. I mean, a couple of the guys already had their

cases polished before the beginning of the homeschool year; I doubted that happened on its own.

"The Moms..." They were everywhere and had everything planned, scheduled, organized and categorized. Homeschooling was a challenge for my mom, but really she had it easy; it was just Sarah and me. Many of the other families in our group had four or more kids and the Simmons' family had eight! Mrs. Simmons had helped Mom during orientation to CHESS (Christian Homeschool Educators of Santa Sonoma). CHESS was our group for the homeschoolers in our area, about forty-five families and growing. It was easy to see why. Santa Sonoma and its surrounding areas were pretty affluent, and to say the parents were not impressed with the local unified school district was an understatement.

I came out of my daze as the trees started to slow down and turning into a small but well paved road, there was the large hanging carved wooden sign, Pine Crest Resort. Ahead was an older two story lodge well placed within the pines and a few smaller buildings. My dad stopped by the first one and gave the attendant the email. "Just pull up by the lodge and you'll be in the Pinion Room. I think you'll find it has plenty of space and a nice view over the stream in the back." The attendant smiled and handed him back the email along with a yellow flyer with the resort rules.

"Better grab your jacket," Dad said as he opened the door and a blast of cold October air hit me.

'You're not in Tampa, anymore.' I thought, as I looked at the tall pines and smelled the air, clean and fresh and *cold.*

He pulled the suitcase out of the trunk, and I got my duffle bag out and followed him inside. The Pinion Room was upstairs and had two queen beds, a table and chairs, and a bathroom.

"Want to see who's here and get some lunch?" Dad asked as he hung his jacket in the closet. I was always ready to eat and maybe one of my new friends had showed.

Downstairs we met the rest of the men for lunch; it was make your own sandwiches and there was friendly chaos as everyone just dug into the cold cuts, bread and condiments. Now it became clear that no one my age was here this weekend. Everyone sat around the big dining room table and Pastor Miller led us in a prayer, asking God to bless this time together and that He would provide us with the strength and motivation to continue His purpose in our lives. I was thinking about the sandwiches my dad and I had just made. It was almost 1:00 p.m. and I was starving. Luckily Pastor Miller was not longwinded, and after the Amen's, I got down to the task at hand, making fast work of two roast beef sandwiches and a quart of milk before I started to slow down. I was still filling out my six foot frame and there might be a couple of more inches to grow, as my dad was 6'3". I often heard how I looked just like him, the dark hair and straight nose. Except for the eyes, gray-green like my mom's.

Then Pastor John Miller began a round of introductions. Sandy haired and average build, his easy smile and manner was offset by piercing blue eyes. He was an associate pastor for men's ministries in His Grace Christian Fellowship, a mega-church in the southland that had grown from a home Bible study about fifteen years ago to over 10,000 members. They had a large campus just a little east of Santa Sonoma. Everyone just called it "HGCF."

He and his wife, Barbara, had a son and daughter in CHESS. His older son, Robert, I knew from a few of the activities I had been to, and I was taking a Biology class at the local community college with him.

Really, I think this introduction was mostly for our benefit because it soon became clear that everyone else knew each other. Still, it did provide a nice jumpstart to help us get acquainted.

There was Dr. Daniel Simmons. He was the head of genetic research at DNACOR, a Biotech firm and his wife Rachel was a psychologist. The Simmons family had eight children, including a pair of twins. He ticked them off on his fingers, but I missed some as I finished my sandwich. Elizabeth and her brother Dan Jr. were veterans of C.R.I.M.S.O.N., our debate team. I'd seen Mrs. Simmons at the last few C.R.I.M.S.O.N. meetings, very involved, overseeing activities and greeting new members, always with a smile.

Then there was Mr. Doug McClaren; he was in real estate, his wife's name was Cathy and they had four children, all in CHESS, with his oldest being Alison, and on it went. I couldn't catch, nor did I expect to remember everyone's name. I was too nervous thinking about what I was going to say, as my dad was finishing his introduction...

"...we just acquired Apex Technologies last year; and so, in order to help with the transition, I decided to move out to Santa Sonoma. And I want to thank you all for inviting us up here this weekend and look forward to becoming better acquainted."

"Hi...I'm Josh Reinhart and I'm a junior. So far I like it here in California...thanks," I said, glad to have that over with.

"Decided on a University yet, Josh?" Mr. Chung asked.

"Not yet," I replied as I sat down with the final sandwich and another glass of milk.

Since homeschooling allowed kids to take classes and study at their own pace, many homeschool teens had skipped a grade and sometimes more. I would be seventeen when I entered college and twenty when I started Law School. At least that was the plan.

"He's considering Baylor, Wheaton, and John Adams University, Pre-law," my dad filled in the details.

"What about USC?" Mr. Stanton questioned, "Great law school. You know, David, I could put in a couple of calls."

"Thanks, Harold; I'll keep that in mind," my dad replied.

Everyone knew Mr. Stanton was a USC man. He had the license plate holder, the bumper sticker and you couldn't miss his USC ring. I heard from Ben that the Trojan football games were big events, setting the mood at their household. I guess it was fortunate they were expected to go to the Rose Bowl this season.

The afternoon was scheduled with a Bible session - Ephesians 6 - Putting on the Armor of God, from 2:00 – 3:30 p.m. After a break for free time (and snacks, I hoped) we were back together for worship from 5:00-5:30, then dinner at 6:00 p.m. I had heard it would be steak with mashed potatoes and gravy, plus dessert.

Just before dinner, Dad caught me looking a little bored, sitting on the bed. "How's it going?"

"Fine, Dad, sorry I only allowed you eight points," I grinned back as he scowled.

It hadn't been a fair match. First of all, my dad was almost fifty and while he was in reasonably good shape, I shot hoops all the time, and then there was a little matter of being at 5000 ft. I thought as I chuckled to myself.

I really did have a pretty good time this afternoon, the Armor of God study was OK, too. During the break my dad and I played one-on-one using a hoop that someone had mounted on one of the out buildings long ago. I went easy on him as he hadn't played in years, and I didn't want to be the cause of any major injury. Even singing the worship songs with the men turned out better than I thought, as they had used a CD player to help accompany our seven voices. "Better Is One Day" had sounded pretty good and even when we finished with "Amazing Grace" without the CD our voices rang out strong and true.

"Glad you're enjoying yourself. These are some great guys, don't you think?" he asked.
"Yeah, they've been really cool." I felt gratified that there had been no condescension, as I was afraid would happen; I was just one of the group.

Pastor Miller was calling us back to the dining room for prayer before dinner, and I could smell the steak and gravy as we came down the stairs. It seemed like the mountain air made everything taste better, and made me more of a bottomless pit than usual. My appetite earned me a few looks and grins as I loaded my plate for the third time.

Tonight there was going to be the big prayer meeting. I didn't have any idea what to expect, except that it started at 7:30 p.m. and there was no end time.

Up in our room I sat on the edge of my bed and nervously spun the basketball on my finger. On one hand, I felt proud to be included with the men at the prayer meeting, but I also had no idea what I would pray about or what I could add to the meeting. One thing for sure about homeschoolers, by the time we were in high school we had been in lots of Bible studies and prayer meetings. But this was a little more intimidating; these men represented the core leadership families of CHESS, and I was trying to make a good impression for my dad's sake, and, I had to admit, mine as well. I was just starting to fit in at CHESS, and I could imagine nodding off and snoring while Mr. Stanton was praying. That story would pass through the CHESS Facebook network before I even got down off the mountain. I was trying to come up with something interesting to pray about tonight when Dad came in.

"Guess you liked the dinner, but you should leave a little for the rest of us," Dad chuckled as he tried to make conversation. "I'm glad you're going with me tonight, you can really get to know people when they pray and ask for prayers. It will be interesting," he waited for a response. I put the ball down between my feet and gave him my best "interested" expression.

"Yeah, should be fun," perhaps not the word I was really thinking. "When do you think it will end?" I asked.

"I wouldn't think it'll be too late, probably be over by ten," he said.
Ten! What can possibly take two and a half hours with only six (or seven including me) men, I thought to myself as I replied with a controlled, "Oh." But my face must have given me away.

"Son, it is important to meet and get to know these men. We will be involved with their families for at least the next six years; so I know you will make me proud, you always do," Dad stated, closing the subject and just raising the pressure three fold.

As usual, I thought, as I let out a sigh. I was used to the pressure. My dad thought of me as his "first born" in the Biblical sense of the word. I was to accomplish great things and carry on the Reinhart name, etc. Of course, at sixteen, most of what I had accomplished was studying hard and getting straight A's. I had been in Toastmasters and then the debate team back in Tampa. I also had a nice jump shot from the key and could play guard or forward, but whether I made it on a team around Santa Sonoma was yet to be seen.

The "first born" was definitely focused on getting the grades and extracurricular credits, like being part of the math team and learning guitar and piano. But it was not all work and no play. Back in Tampa, I hung out with a dozen or so teens most of whom were from my homeschool group or church; they were a lot of fun. We did the normal stuff: go to the movies, or down to the pier and the beach, listen to music. I played hockey and basketball. Last year a few other guys and I formed a band and played at some church events. Then there were the Bible studies and of course the obligatory cotillion every six weeks or so. We were supposed to learn the finer points of etiquette and some ballroom dances, but I think we were lucky to keep from embarrassing ourselves. I had to admit, that even though we had to dress up for cotillion, it wasn't all that bad, and eventually, I actually stopped maiming my partners with my size 11Ds. Moms all seem to be big on cotillion; it must be some inner desire to see their son dance like Gene Kelly, or maybe they just remembered that when they grew up there were no boys to dance with. Dating?...not even in the picture.

There was a nice blaze in the big fireplace as we met the rest of the men in the main room of the lodge. We all sat around a large coffee table in some old leather couches and chairs. I sat between Dad and Mr. Stanton and eyed the pad of paper and pencil in front of me. Pastor Miller sat in a chair at the end of the coffee table and once everyone had settled in, he started the opening prayer. It was pretty generic, except that he made a point of thanking God for each of the new members of CHESS, including myself, Sarah, Mom and Dad. Somehow he remembered all the members of the eight new CHESS families by name. We then took the pad and wrote down a list of things we wanted to pray about, family, friends, and neighbors. After that we were to think of things to pray about for our city, state and so on all the way up to our country's leadership and finally the world.

Now I knew why it was going to take two and a half hours. No one seemed to be surprised at this, so I guess it was typical for this men's group. I started writing down things and covered about half a page, looking up I saw that some men were on their second page. After about ten minutes, everyone seemed to have exhausted their written prayer requests. This was going to be brutal! Pastor Miller then explained that we would start with each man asking for prayer, describing his notes on the first page. Then pass the page to his left so that the prayer warrior, (Pastor Miller called us that), could effectively pray out loud for him. Mr. Stanton started and after describing a number of needs and praise reports, he passed his first page to Dr. Simmons. I was surprised at how humble Mr. Stanton's list was. He had such a powerful self-assured presence about him, but his prayer requests were concerns we all would have. A praise report about how well Ben's leg that had healed after last year's skiing accident; a prayer for his wife's mother who was just diagnosed with Alzheimer's; and so on. Dr. Simmons began praying for Mr. Stanton and we prayed along, mostly in silence, but occasionally, others would affirm with a "Thank you, Lord" or "Yes, Lord."

Then it was Dr. Simmons' turn. I found out that Dr. Simmons had a heart condition and it was genetic. He did not pray for himself, but for his children and his childrens' children for generations (those were his exact word).

There was so much information about the CHESS families and their trials, concerns and successes. Many prayers that God would lead and influence their sons and daughter for His purpose. Prayers for salvation for a relative who was not yet a Christian. And so it went.

I was the last to describe my list. I asked that God would continue to help me in all my endeavors and that our move out to California would work out well and allow me more time with my dad. I did not look at him when I said it, but when Mr. Stanton prayed I thought I heard Dad murmur "Yes, Lord."

We took a break; it was 9:35 p.m., the time had flown by, and then I remembered that there was more praying to come. After everyone settled back with fresh coffee and some donuts, Pastor Miller organized the prayers for the city, state, country, and the world. He quickly summarized them, and passed them out to us.

It could have been a current affairs, political science and history lesson all rolled into one. How did these men know so much about what was going on in the world, I thought as they prayed? They must have been surfing the net for hours to come up with all this stuff. These men were some serious "prayer warriors." I felt like I was at the NBA finals of prayer meetings.

Finally, as we all stood around the coffee table, Pastor Miller led us in a closing prayer to thank God for His presence here tonight and to ask for His direction for each of our lives. And that He would provide each of us with a vision to embolden us to be mighty warriors for God referring back to Ephesians. "Amen," I called out. It was 11:05 p.m.

I was exhausted, but it took me a while to settle into the unfamiliar bed and I listened to Dad talking enthusiastically about the prayer meeting until I finally fell into a deep restful sleep......

"NO!" I heard myself shout, or was it still in the dream....
....As the flag stopped waving, the colors began to fade to a monotonous dark gray. I heard a low but clear voice say, "All that is necessary is that good men do nothing." I felt a great foreboding. Then seven small stars, more like pinpoints of light, shone in a circle where the fifty used to be. One thin ribbon of bright red emerged, shining as it moved left to right bisecting the field of dark gray where one of the original red stripes had been. I jolted awake, sitting up in a sweat, my pulse hammering in my ears. It was unlike any nightmare or dream I had ever experienced. The final image of the gray flag with the pinpoints of light shining brightly and the red ribbon burned in front of my eyes. I shut them tight, but it was still there. It was as if I could reach out and touch the fabric. My dad had stirred as well, but as I looked over he had dropped back into a fitful sleep.

After a time, I don't know how long, my heart rate became more normal and I felt very thirsty. Getting up, I pulled on my sweat pants and went to the bathroom. My hair and the front of my t-shirt were soaked, so I splashed some water on my face and then dried my hair and change into a new t-shirt. I decided to go down to the kitchen and get a drink of water, and as I descended the stairs I noticed the lights were on. As I turned the corner, Mr. Stanton was drinking something from a mug. I must have startled him, because he looked a little wide eyed.

I nodded to him and went for a plastic water bottle. It was 3:20 a.m.

"Couldn't sleep?" he asked, but his voice was not the usual smooth legal tone.

"Yeah, I had an odd dream that woke me up," I lied, calling that nightmare an "odd dream" was like calling T-Rex an interesting reptile.

"Me too," he said as he went for another gulp out of his mug. He was flushed, and I wondered if I looked as shook up as I felt.

"Well, goodnight, Josh," he said a little more nonchalantly and headed out of the kitchen.

"'Night," I replied; my mind was still on the image of the nightmare. I drank down half the bottle of water and brought the rest upstairs.

As I lay there, a shiver went through me, thinking I might have a repeat of the dream if I went to sleep; but finally I dozed off and was aware of nothing until my dad's hand shook me awake.

"Josh, come on, you're going to be late for breakfast. It's almost 8:00."

"OK, Dad," I groaned. I felt like I had about two hours of sleep; I needed more rest.

As I got dressed, I asked Dad if he slept OK last night.

He looked at me and raised one eyebrow. "As a matter of fact, I had a very strange dream," he said. "It woke me up. I can still remember it clearly."

"Was it about the flag?" I asked. I hoped the combination of curiosity and fear wasn't too evident in my voice.

His eyes went wide, "Yes, Son," he said quietly. "Tell me about yours."

"The flag had turned all gray, and then there were seven small stars and one red stripe," I said as my heart raced, seeing the image again like the first time last night. The look on Dad's face confirmed that he had seen it too.

"Exactly. Did you hear the voice?" he asked.

"All that is necessary is that good men do nothing," I quoted and stared at him, because I had never seen my dad stunned before.

"We had the same dre… nightmare," he finally said. His voice cracked.

We were very late for breakfast, but as we got down to the kitchen, Mr. Stanton was giving everyone one of the pads from last night and asking us to describe the dream we had.

"David, did you have a dream last night? I know Josh did." Dad replied to Mr. Stanton that he had, and so we both were handed paper pads.

Evidently, everyone had experienced a vivid dream of some kind last night a little after 3:00 a.m. and he wanted unbiased descriptions from each of us. Well, Dad and I already knew we had the same nightmare, but to humor Mr. Stanton I drew my dream - a gray flag with seven pinpoints of light and the red stripe. Then underneath I wrote: "All that is necessary is that good men do nothing." with an arrow to a bubble that said *I heard this.* Then I wrote, *first our flag went completely dark gray, and I heard the voice, then the seven lights appeared, and finally the stripe appeared from left to right.*

Everyone was finished, and we all turned in our pads to Mr. Stanton. His mouth was a tight straight line as he looked at each pad describing the same dream. Then he spread them out on the kitchen table. Everyone had heard the voice; everyone had seen the flag go from red, white and blue to dark gray. And everyone had seen the seven pinpoints of light and the red stripe appearing from left to right. There was no denying it.

Mr. Chung spoke first, "This is highly improbable. What do you think, Dan?"
Dr. Simmons just shook his head slowly, and eventually said, "I don't know."

Finally, Pastor Miller spoke. "It's a vision," he said quietly. "A vision for us... for the seven of us, just like we stood around the table for prayer last night." After an outburst of discussion, the Pastor spoke again. "We need to pray about this."

Chapter Two

The Meeting

"The Constitution... is a mere thing of wax in the hands of the judiciary which they may twist and shape into any form they please." – Thomas Jefferson

Coming down the mountain Sunday afternoon was not the uncomfortable solitude I had experienced coming up. Dad and I, spurred on by the Vision, were trying out theories and ideas. Whatever came out of this, it was exciting to be discussing something we both had in common.

"I don't think we should talk about this right away to anyone until we understand it better ourselves.... it's not that your sister and Mom will think we made it up, it's just that I feel I don't have a clear idea about it yet.... I just don't think.....maybe after Thursday...," Dad was shaking his head as he drove.

The seven of us had spent all of Sunday morning trying to understand what had happened and what it meant. I pretty much kept silent while the men gave their opinions and theories. One thing was known for sure, we had all had the same dream, or "vision" as Pastor Miller called it. I don't mean approximately the same vision, but the *identical* vision. We compared them and each detail matched. From the timing of the voice, how the pinpoints started small and then shone, the red ribbon going from left to right… exactly the same.

"…. are we going Thursday?" I really didn't hold out much chance of this; maybe the first few meetings…but beyond that…

After we had prayed about it, Dr Simmons had made a suggestion. He said that we should not ignore the Vision, but we should meet for a "prayer meeting" regularly to discuss it. This had started a round of discussions that finally ended with a decision to meet at HGCF on Thursday from 7:00-9:30 p.m. And we had all agreed to keep the Vision to ourselves, at least for a little while.

"We all had the Vision and I think it must be important for each of us, especially you and me…," then he fell silent. I could see he was hesitating, trying to formulate the sentence.
"You know your mom is always saying that with God there is no such thing as coincidence…Josh, you and I were supposed to be at that retreat and have the Vision," his voice was quiet but resolved.

Well, that settled it, Dad and I would be going to the Thursday night "prayer meeting." We both knew it would not be your basic men's prayer meeting, and it was meant to determine what we were going to do about the Vision. In a way, I thought, this could be exciting. I was now part of a secret club, and we were going to meet regularly and decide to *do something*. That was assuming we actually did something as well as pray.

"Why did you think the flag turned gray?" I really wanted to hear this one from Dad. I knew what I thought about this, and it was partly because Mom was always looking at current events....She was a crazed internet surfer and talk radio listener. I mean, Worldnetdaily short cut was on the desktop start page and so was Drudge and Townhall. Then there were the conservative talk radio stations programmed in her car radio.

So I was always getting the latest in how or why "our Founding Father's would be spinning in their graves" as she put it. She said that they were trying to remove God from all areas of our nation and it was getting worse. I had to admit that it seemed like there was cause for concern, given the tone of recent events and court cases. But Mom also said that she felt that God had His hand on America and evil would not prevail. She said all you had to do was look at the life of George Washington to see that the U.S. could not have come about without help from The Almighty.

"I think it means this country is in trouble; ...it means that if we don't do something like the voice said, we will lose what we have....the way we live will be different... our freedoms... I don't know... but something bad is going to happen," he trailed off, lost in thought.

"You think the seven of us can really do anything about it?" I waited, holding my breath.

"Yes, Josh, we *must do something* before it's too late." I saw his features set hard in his face as we wound down into the San Bernardino foothills. I had seen that face before. When he was making a big decision, like last year during the acquisition or just before we decided to move, the same hard features. He was thinking and cementing his resolve.

At that moment, a lot of different feelings welled up. Pride that my dad was the kind of man he was, excitement because I was going to be part of the *do something*, nervous and anxious because I did not know if "the first born" would live up to his expectations, worried about what could be the *something bad*. Mostly, I felt heady anticipation because Dad and I were in it together.

"Josh, I want to be clear, we are not going to tell Mom or Sarah just yet. There will be time for that after we get some things sorted out," he said as he took his eyes off the road and glanced at me, breaking into my thoughts.

I nodded, "OK Dad, I understand."

Mom and Sarah met us as we drove into the driveway. It was clear Mom had missed "her men." She gave us both big hugs as Sarah was showing off a new pair of shoes she had found at the mall. "Missed you guys, did you have fun?" Mom asked as I started unloading the car.

"It was interesting." Not exactly a lie, trying to seem casual. I was glad the trunk lid was up so she couldn't see my face. I can't say that I never lied to my parents, but I couldn't remember the last time. Dad had his suitcase in one hand and his other arm around Mom as they walked in the house. How were we going to get away with it? I mean, Sarah maybe, but Mom? She ran the place, and more importantly, I was with her most of the day for school. This was going to be more difficult than I first imagined. But Dad had given me strict instructions, so I was going to have to find a way.

"So your dad says the men at the retreat were great and had lots of good prayer," Mom was checking the table settings for dinner. Marisa, our maid/cook was just putting the finishing touches on the chile rellenos. They smelled wonderful, another reason I liked the move, homemade Mexican food.

"Yeah, there are lots of things about CHESS that need praying about." Oh Boy! As soon as I said it I realized that was the wrong thing to say. I think she had been suspicious how the weekend went, but now I had just waved a red flag in front of a bull.

"Like what? Who needs prayer? Is someone sick, having family problems? You know we have a women's breakfast every month, we could pray too." How do I get out of this one I wondered as I sat down at the table?

My mom was a graduate of Florida State University with a degree in Communications and Marketing. In fact, before she quit to homeschool me, she worked as marketing VP at Prescience. She was insightful, smart and quick on the uptake. But most importantly, she fervently believed she could impact lives with her prayers.

"I don't know if I can remember all that we talked about." Which in a way was true, although it wasn't going to put her off. I had just piqued her interest more intently than an hour on the cell with Mrs. Simmons. "Did you know that Ben Stanton's grandma has Alzheimer's?" I figured that was a safe one to toss out there while I thought of how to get out of the coming flood of questions. Here I had not been home more than two hours and already my firewall was starting to break down. This was not good.

"Oh, I heard about that last week, it's a real shame, and only in her seventies, too. What else?" She zeroed in on me as she sat down at the table, while telling Sarah to ask Dad to come eat. He had been smart, begging her indulgence right after we got home, claiming he had been away from his email too long.

This time I needed to give up something that would satisfy her at least through dinner. As my dad sat down, I looked at him for help.

"This looks great, Marisa." He caught my eye and then remarked on the Mexican banquet. "When did you first learn to cook?"

Marisa blushed a little, and in her slight accent explained that she had been taught by her mother from the age of five. She placed a pitcher of sun tea on the table and hurried back to the kitchen.

We all held hands as Dad prayed over the meal and thanked God for keeping us all safe while we were apart and continuing to watch over us. As we all began to pass the salsa and pitcher of tea around, Mom began the interrogation again. "What were some of the other prayer needs from the retreat?" This question was directed at me, but I hesitated long enough to allow Dad to field it.

"Well, lets see, there was a prayer request for Leah Chung to perform well at the state violin recitals... and Ted Johnson is still out of work. Emily, you remember, we met him at orientation; he and I were about the only men there. It's been a couple of months now, so the Johnson's could use our prayers and a good lead on a job. I think he said he was in sales or marketing, so maybe you can check out some of your old cronies."

"Honey, you know, I might be able to help. I'll get out my contact list and see what I can do. It will be fun catching up with some of them." Mom was satisfied for now. It was interesting watching Dad maneuver around her. I often wondered if she could sense he wanted to change the subject, and she submitted to this because she understood he was the head of the family and had immense respect for him. That was the way it was in our family. Mom ran things on a daily basis; but when it came to bigger decisions, Dad made them (with her input, of course).

We all enjoyed Marisa's cooking and, after my third plateful, were deciding on dessert when Dad dropped the bomb. "Josh and I are going to be attending a men's prayer meeting this Thursday night over at HGCF. Some of the guys at our retreat invited us; and we had such a good time this weekend, we thought we would try it out."

"Really? I think that's a great idea." Mom was always for anything that got Dad and I together. Though I think she was just a little skeptical about how long it would last; she wasn't about to show it.

"It will be weekly, so I thought it should go on the calendar," he replied. Nothing happened unless it was on Mom's calendar.

And that was it; no more questions about the weekend, except who had attended and what the main topic was. But I felt that Mom might be waiting to talk to Dad without Sarah and me around. But for now, I wouldn't need to worry about accidentally mentioning anything even close to the Vision.

The first part of the week went by fast as I anticipated Thursday night. I did hear Mom talking to one of her new friends on the cell about the prayer meeting. "...can you believe it, David was always too busy to commit to a prayer meeting, and weekly at that. ......no, I think its great, I just hope he can find the time....I know what you mean, David is a workaholic too, and I want them to have as much time together before Josh goes off to college.... OK, I will see you there, ... sure, feel free to call anytime Rachel, Bye." So "the Moms" were already wondering about the "prayer meeting." I hope we could get things sorted out *this* Thursday.

Wednesday night was the CRIMSON meeting. As we pulled into the parking lot of a local church, it looked like a minivan convention, and we just added to their numbers. I couldn't wait to get my license so I could add a little diversity to the scene, as my dad had hinted at a new car. The CRIMSON debate team for Christian homeschoolers was made up entirely of CHESS students. C.R.I.M.S.O.N. stood for: **C**hristian **R**easoning **I**nfluencing **M**ankind, **S**erving **O**ur **N**ation. There were debaters ranging from twelve to eighteen years old, and this was the fourth meeting of the new school year. Luckily, the first big tournament was more than two months away giving me some time to work on my cases. Those with completed cases were going to get some practice rounds in tonight. Mom came ostensibly to watch the activities, but truthfully I think it was to catch up on the latest CHESS news as a number of the Moms were here to judge along with Mr. Chung and Mr. McClaren. Sarah and I joined a group of about twenty students that were there to discuss the upcoming debate tournament and work on their cases. I had a fairly decent affirmative case or "Aff" in debate-speak, but my negative case needed a lot of work. Our debate coach, Mrs. Stanton, was already taking names of people who wanted to debate tonight.

She looked up as we walked in. "Josh. Nice that you could join us; how are your cases coming?"

"I guess I could try out my Aff," I said after a little hesitation, having just written my six minute affirmative constructive speech a week ago supporting the resolution with the value of 'Liberty.'

"How many years were you in debate in Florida?" Mrs. Stanton pressed.

"Two," I replied.

"OK, how about doing a round tonight? I need someone to match up with Rebekah," she requested, firmly.

I blushed a little at this; I couldn't help feeling slightly embarrassed as I looked at my opponent: a very petite thirteen year old girl complete with the obligatory braces with blue bands to match her eyes. She gave me a shy smile from behind long blond hair. I think she had been at Sarah's swim party last week; she was Robert Miller's kid sister.

"I guess so," I finally said waiting for the couple of giggles from 'Bekah's friends to subside.

I took a seat by Ben Stanton and tried to get into the flow of the discussion about making sure the debaters were following the set format for the Lincoln-Douglas debates. The L-Ds were one-on-one "value" debates with the affirmative debater supporting the resolution with an affirmative constructive speech and his opponent negating the resolution with a negative constructive, each speech was followed by cross-examinations and then rebuttals. They were very structured and strictly timed. Some of the younger team members in the room were just there to be timers. It was a good way for the beginning members to see debates in action.

The next topic was the upcoming tournament. This was a four day statewide competition for Christian homeschool debaters and the winners in each category of debate would automatically go to the nationals. This was no small feat as there would be over 300 debaters all trying to advance. There would even be scouts and recruiters from some of the most prestigious pre-law colleges in the nation looking for talent to bolster their collegiate debate teams. The competition was fierce and Mrs. Stanton was making a point that we had to turn it up a notch if CRIMSON was to perform up to "nationals" standards. She knew what she was talking about, having coached many CRIMSON debaters to nationals over the years. And two years ago, two students placed 2nd and 4th raising CRIMSON's status as a team to beat. As she put it "every other team in the league had developed briefs and tactics aimed specifically at CRIMSON." I got the feeling last year had been a tough one for the team, a 'rebuilding year.'

"OK, here are your room and judge assignments; first name is Aff," Mrs. Stanton called out.

"Ben and Robert, room 102, Mrs. Simmons. ….

Josh and Rebekah, room 105, Mrs. McClaren…"

As I followed Rebekah into the room, I noticed her four inch thick notebook with debate written in large blue script and lots of flower doodles around it. I had my two pages of Aff stapled together. Once in the room I stood waiting for Mrs. McClaren to prepare her debate judging sheet and ballot.

"Is the judge ready? Timer ready? My opponent ready?" I asked ceremonially and then began my first speech.

"Tonight, I will show that, as the judge, you must find for the affirmative, affirming the resolution: The U.S. Constitution

should be strictly interpreted as the Forefathers envisioned and should not be re-interpreted to allow for the needs of today's changing society."
"First I would like to provide some definitions: Strict interpretation.....

... And for these reasons I strongly recommend the judge cast an affirmative ballot," I said in my closing argument.

After forty-five minutes of mental root canal, the embarrassing ordeal was over. Possibly the only thing I was happy about was that there were just three people in the room to witness my dismantling. Little Miss Rebekah had ripped apart my arguments like a tree shredder. They lay in tatters as I finished my final rebuttal. She had pulled cases out of the air that I had never heard of, Constitutional cases back in the 1800s, and statements from the framers of the Constitution. Not just in the Constitution itself, but drawing from many other documents and historical precedents for her Neg case. Quoting verbatim on her feet without a script!

As her blue eyes flashed and her clear high voice emphasized each of her own points, she simultaneously showed that my contentions and examples were seriously flawed; I really felt I'd been set up. Who was this 4ft. 10in. buzz saw with braces? I looked ridiculous beside her as she had to crane her neck to look up to my 6ft. height and ask if I was ready for cross-examination. You got to be *kidding* me.
Mrs. McClaren, keeping a pretty good straight face, completed her ballot and handed it in to Mrs. Stanton. I had no doubt of the score: Blond midget buzz-saw 1, 6ft. new guy hoopster 0.

I couldn't get out of the room fast enough, so I simply shook Rebekah's hand, mumbled "nice round" and went out to join the high school guys helping take down the folding tables and chairs. At least I could be of *some* use.

As I got ready to leave, little Rebekah came up to me and with that same shy smile asked if she could have a copy of my Aff. I was surprised; but thought, maybe I didn't do as bad as all that, and she wants to get some ideas for her own case. "Sure, but its still needs some work," I agreed, and gave it to her.
"Thanks," she said, almost a whisper, then she put it in her huge notebook and slipped back to join a couple of tween girls who were watching her return, giggling about something.

"How'd you do tonight?" Mom asked as she started out of the parking lot.
"OK, I guess," I lied.
"I heard you got crushed!" My helpful, supportive sister added with a laugh.
"Can we get something to eat? I'm starving; drive-thru is fine," I tried to change the subject.
Mom took pity on me, "Sure, what do you feel like?"
"How about *Toxic* Taco," I offered. *[the chains real name being Takeout Taco]*
It wasn't until Thursday night that I found out that the "Dads", a group not generally known for their connectivity, had been racking up the cell minutes. These were some very capable men who knew how to run things, invent things and make things happen. So by the time Thursday night rolled around, a lot of planning had already been done.

My dad and Dr. Simmons both had lots of experience in running experimental projects and they had developed a framework for the "process" of determining the "what should be done with respect to the Vision" plan. I had grown up hearing words like "brainstorming", "process", "framework", etc. These were part of Dad's daily vocabulary. Lately, though, there had been some new entries, "encryption", "trusted computing group", "lockdown", "network access control." Security was a very big part of Dad's recent conversations. His efforts in internet security meant he was always being called to Washington for some hearing or other. Luckily, Prescience had two corporate jets, one based near D.C. for just such trips.

Dad had access to a very secure encrypted server through Prescience, so he had set up a secure database and data storage area for the Thursday Prayer Meeting's use. It was better than keeping multiple copies of stuff on everyone's PC. It looked like a stripped down version of Facebook to the user, and used the most up-to-date NSA-type encryption with a secure backup vault. Best of all it would seem like just another Prescience development project (there were hundreds).

Prescience, Inc. had started out as an internet search engine company with a predictive search algorithm that was the trade secret and the crown jewels of the company. Developed by my dad, Anticip8 had been nothing less than revolutionary in the way it searched out information for its users. While how it actually worked was only known to a few, essentially it was able to predict what you wanted to know before you asked for it and provide it in a file structure on your PC. By the time you wanted to know something, your desired data was already available on your desktop. Anticip8 was 97% accurate, and so for a license fee that varied from home use to large corporate and government

contracts, Prescience became an indispensable tool of modern
life.   It spawned a large number of associate application
programs, and Prescience, Inc. achieved Fortune 100 status
within three years of going public. "Pi", as Dad like to call it,
had been an all consuming passion. But recently, he had begun to
realize that Sarah and I would be grown and gone before he knew
it. So he was trying very hard to make time for us. I know it was
difficult for Dad because, truth be known, he was happiest
developing a new product or application for Pi.

As we entered the room at HGCF, I could see some men were
already in deep discussion. Dr. Simmons followed us in. Now
that we were all together again, the Vision became very fresh in
my mind. From Sunday till today, it had to take a back seat in
my thoughts from time to time, but now it was reinforced by the
other men who had experienced it. We all wanted to talk about it
and about what we should do. Pastor Miller finally got the group
to quiet down for prayer and then asked my dad to take the lead.

"First, I want to say that I look forward to discussing what we
should do with respect to the Vision we all experienced.   Dr.
Simmons and I have been working all week on a framework and
process to come to some decisions.   We thought we should
employ a brainstorming method, but we must keep our sights on a
godly effort. I also thought that I would offer a place to keep all
the records of the group.   I have a secure server and project
management system that we can use at Prescience.   It will allow
us all to communicate and develop the project in one place, and it
is very secure and continually backed up."
"Do you think we need a central secure site for this?" Mr.
McClaren asked.

"I think we have no idea where The Lord will lead us in this endeavor, and so I think it is only prudent to start out with a secure depository for our communications and ideas," Dad replied, "I cannot stress enough that it will be 100% secure and encrypted; only this group can get access."
"I think it's a good idea," remarked Mr. Stanton, "PCs are always getting viruses or hard drive crashes."

That pretty much settled it. So Mr. Chung offered to be the scribe for the meeting as he had brought his laptop.
Then Dr. Simmons took the floor, "At DNACOR we use brainstorming all the time. There are only a few rules to brainstorming: 1. All ideas are initially allowed; 2. Respect each others right to speak, try not to interrupt; 3. Wait till the end to sift through the ideas and pick out the best ones." Then he wrote the problem statement on the big white board.
What do we do as a group about the Vision?

Right away there was chaos, but Dr. Simmons raised his hand, "one at a time, *please*; Harold, you have something to say?"

Mr. Stanton responded, "I looked up the phrase and it is a portion of a quote from Edmond Burke: '*All that is necessary for evil to triumph is for good men to do nothing.*'
I think we are being called to do something or evil will triumph."

"The flag turning gray is obviously bad or evil," replied Mr. Chung. "I hate the way the colors faded to gray, like the life went out of it."
"The fifty stars are no longer there either, so that could mean there are no more states or states rights, same with the stripes –

they were representing the thirteen original colonies," added Mr. McClaren.

The brainstorming had begun and ideas started flowing fast and furious. I could hear the constant rapid clicking of Mr. Chung's keystrokes. Finally, the deluge reduced to a stream and then a trickle. The men were exhausted, out of ideas. I looked up at the clock, 10:15! We had been at this for almost three hours.

I looked at the large list. It ranged from simply gray represented bad or evil, to a possible split in the nation north and south divided by the red ribbon. Some thought there could be a natural catastrophe or a terrorist event. Someone thought the nation was already gray ever since God had been taken out of our public schools. I decided to keep my mouth shut.

Pastor Miller suggested a break, and everyone went to get a drink and eat what was left of the donuts. When we got back together, Dad spoke first as he walked to the white board.

"I want to see if we can come to at least one conclusion and decision tonight, so let me try something and see what you think." Then he wrote on the white board as he spoke.

"We all agree that something bad or evil will happen to our nation, and we must, as a group, do something about this." He wrote *Our Nation is becoming bad or will experience something bad, destructive or evil.* There were murmurs of agreement amongst the men.

"We also said we wanted to keep a godly influence or focus on this meeting," he continued, and wrote *Need Godly Influence.* I heard a few 'Amens' around the room. *"So how do we cause godly influence to save our nation from its path of evil or destruction?"* he wrote this exact question on the board.

You could have heard a pin drop as I saw the men stop and look at my dad and the board. Now I knew why he was where he was, why he ran Prescience, why he was so successful. He had taken a long list of diverse opinions and ideas from a room full of accomplished men and distilled and summarized our task down to one sentence. Pastor Miller interrupted my thoughts with a request to pray silently about this question.

After a little while, Mr. Stanton spoke. "It's the courts," he said it as a matter of fact. Then he went on, "Our courts have gradually removed God from the fabric of our public institutions. From the lower state courts all the way up to the Supreme Court, their decisions have allowed godly influence to be undermined and removed from public society."

Dad simply wrote down *The Courts*. And then he said, "Even if there are other places like our schools and our elected officials, I have to agree with Harold, the courts are the most influential and have the most direct, immediate impact."
Mr. Chung spoke up, "There is no doubt; if we could get more Christian men on our courts, things would change. It's just how do we do this?"

It was almost 11:00 p.m. and we had done a lot of work; Dad was still up at the board and wrote one more sentence. *Ideas on how to get more godly men on our courts:*

"I suggest we call it a night and let's go off and think about ways to influence our courts. Add your ideas to the database and we can talk about them next week. And I think we should still keep this quiet," Dad said to a few nods and no one's objection. With that Pastor Miller closed the meeting in prayer.

Chapter Three

The New Kid in Town

"Far from being rivals or enemies, religion and law are twin sisters, friends, and mutual assistants. Indeed, these two sciences run into each other. The divine law, as discovered by reason and the moral sense, forms an essential part of both." – James Wilson

"Sure, let me check ,... Mom!... Some of the guys from CHESS want to come over and shoots some hoops." I got the nod from Mom, and so I told Ben to come on by and bring his friends. It was Friday about 3:30, and I was just finishing up my chemistry problems. It had been a pretty stressful week, and I was glad to put down the books and get into my sweats. Sarah was already alternating between the pool and the spa I heard her laughing with Ashley Simmons.

I was getting warmed up, shooting around when Ben, Robert Miller and Steve Chung came through the back door.
"Sweet. Two on two. You guys need to warm up?" I asked as I tossed Ben the ball. It was a nice warm October day with a slight breeze to take the edge off the sun.

"Let's just shoot a few and then pick teams," Ben replied as he missed his first shot from the key.

Steve and Ben against Robert and me; a pretty good match up because I had heard Ben say that Steve, while shorter then the rest of us, was very quick and deadly from the outside.

"First to 21 wins; gotta win by 2. Call it," As I tossed a coin. …

"19 – 16 skins," I said as I took the ball out and passed it to Robert; but Steve was too fast and picked it off, dribbled around Robert and had the easy lay-up.

"Sorry, Robert," I said. I was going to have to pay closer attention and get the ball up a little higher so Robert could use his height to keep Steve at bay.

"19 -18 skins," Ben stated as he passed it into Steve.

This was about the best time I had had since moving to Santa Sonoma; a tough game of hoops with what were becoming good friends. I was the new kid, but they treated me like I had been in CHESS for years.

Ben missed off the rim; I pulled down the rebound and passed it out to Robert, this time he had to jump for it, but brought it down for a single dribble and then passed it back into me for the six footer that was nothing but net.

"Yes!, 21," I yelled and it was high fives from Robert.

"Nice game," Steve grinned and Ben tossed me the ball.

"You're quick, man," I said to Steve, "and sneaky, too." I grinned back.

"How about some drinks?" Mom called out from the patio. She had some glasses full of ice and the sodas from the patio 'fridge. How do moms do that? Know just exactly when to have stuff ready, as Marisa followed her out with a huge bowl of chips and salsa.

"Yes, Thank you." "Thanks, Mrs. Reinhart." "Thank you, Mrs. Reinhart." "Thanks Mom, thanks Marisa." She went back in to chat with Mrs. Stanton, who had brought the guys over.

Let's face it, when you're homeschooled by your mom, you better have decent manners, or you'll get signed up for *two* cotillions.

What a great way to go into the weekend; we were all replaying the game as we devoured the chips and drinks. Robert mentioned that there were usually some guys looking to play after school at the local courts, and with one or two more players we could form a decent team. Perhaps this was going to be a good move after all. Finally, Steve said he had to get back, something about seeing Leah perform. Mrs. Stanton offered to take Steve home as it wasn't far out of her way.

Mom asked Robert if he needed a ride as she was taking Ashley home anyway. So with the two girls chatting away in the very back of the mini-van, Robert and I talked about a number of things: who we could get for our team, how I liked it here, getting my drivers license, where Robert wanted to go to college... We pulled into the Simmons' driveway and Ashley gave Sarah a hug and jumped out of the sliding door of the van. Her mom was out front expecting her and walked up to say hi and talked to my mom for a minute. I caught the tail end of the conversation, something about "... the prayer meeting ran awfully late...I know... well, thanks for bringing Ashley home... anytime." Then we were off, this time we had to head inland some to an older community of more modest homes where the Millers lived.

"Can we use the courts there?" I asked Robert as we passed by the sprawling HGCF campus.

"Sure, I don't see why not. Maybe next time you can come up here for some full court games," Robert replied.

"Do I turn here, Robert?" My mom shot a look over her shoulder.

"Yes, Mrs. Reinhart, just turn at the next right."

We turned down a street lined with huge eucalyptus trees, and Robert pointed out his house on the right.

"Is your Mom at home?" Mom asked as she was getting out.

"I'm pretty sure," Robert said as he was exiting the mini-van.

Sarah and I got out too; I had never been to Robert's place, and Mom seemed to be interested in taking a few minutes to talk to Mrs. Miller.

"Hi Emily; so nice of you to bring Robert home," Mrs. Miller said as she came out the front door. She had been baking by the looks of it, with her apron still on and white flour dust here and there.

"Want to check out my new laptop?" Robert said leading me into the house. "I just put a bigger hard drive in for all my music." As I was turning down the hall I heard a squeal and saw a flash of blond hair as a bedroom door slammed shut. "...I loaded some new software on it so I can make my own movies with audio clips.... check it out," he went on.

After a while, Mrs. Miller poked her head in the door, "Josh, your Mom is ready to leave, but I'm sure you guys will be seeing each other soon."

"Sure, thanks Mrs. Miller." I followed her out of Robert's room. As I walked to the van, Sarah was talking to my nemesis,

Rebekah, who refused to even look at me; I wondered what Sarah had said.

Mom was already in the mini-van and called out to Sarah, so I got in and asked if we could come back soon; Sarah seconded the motion. As we drove off, I saw Robert looking pained while Rebekah's blond hair shook as she was obviously giving him a piece of her mind about something. *Good luck, man,* I thought as I had only been sliced up by the cordial side of her verbal swordplay.

The weekend went by in a blur of activities: church, sports and some homework that needed to be done for my Biology class. Monday it was back to it, up at 8:00 and listening to history tapes while eating breakfast. Then we had Bible study, followed by Pre-Calculus and Literature (currently famous Asian historic authors). Lunch was a nice break, but then came Latin and Chemistry.

On Tuesdays, it was the same except that I went to the local community college for a Biology class. Wednesdays, there was a break from the Literature, replaced with Writing.

Sarah had joined a swimming club, the Aquadors, so she was in the local Olympic pool every other day for an hour in the afternoon.

Wednesday night. CRIMSON. I had not looked at my case, except for printing a new copy of my Aff. Mrs. Stanton would not be pleased, the tournament was a little more than six weeks away and I still had just an Aff case, and a poor one at that, remembering what happened last week. I took my seat and waited for the inevitable.

"I thought we would try to get in two rounds tonight," stated Mrs. Stanton.

"Who wants to debate tonight?" Only about half the students raised their hands.

"OK, this is not a democracy, even if you have a rough Aff or Neg case, you need to debate. As you know, we have less than two months to get ready for the tournament.

So, *who* wants to debate tonight?" She asked again. This time nearly everyone raised their hand including me.

Mrs. Stanton broke into her easy smile now. "Thank you.... Mrs. McClaren, could you pair up the students and assign judges?"

"Before we start, I have a couple of topics. First and foremost, this is not all about winning trophies; it's about being 'salt and light.' Our Lord asked us to go out into the world and represent Him by our actions and words. The better you are at debate, which is really the art of representation, persuasion and critical thinking, the better witnesses you will be, helping people see the truth about God. That is why I want you to practice your cases each week and work on them during the week."

"Elizabeth, how often do you practice your debate?"

"Probably three times a week, and I worked on my case at least an hour each day," Elizabeth replied. She had placed 12th in the nationals last year and was probably CRIMSON's leading debater.

"If everyone will work on your cases for at least half an hour a day and practice your debate twice a week, we will be awesome witnesses for God, and the trophies and nationals will come along for the ride," Mrs. Stanton challenged us all as she looked around the table. "Also try to befriend some of our competitors, remember they may be your debate partners in college. I want CRIMSON to be known as a friendly team that goes out of its way to encourage others. God will bless us for it."

She continued "Secondly, we all need to help each other, and the veterans need to come along side the newer debaters. This is a team, and while you might face each other in a final round, I want each team member to be as well prepared as possible. We have a website where cases are posted and a lot of us are on Facebook, so if you see something in the debate rounds tonight that could help your teammates, get with them and discuss it." This set up a brief discussion around the table.

"Mrs. McClaren, how are you doing?" Mrs. Stanton inquired.
"I am just about done; I have two more to go. Mrs. McClaren looked up from her paper at me, "Josh, do you have a Neg?"

"I have an outline, but it's really rough." Great, after that speech by Mrs. Stanton, I get called out as the laggard.

"That's OK Josh, I'm pairing you with Alison for the second round. Her Aff needs a little work, too." Alison blushed as her mom just embarrassed her, and for *my* sake. I was going to have to buckle down if I was going to stay in CRIMSON.

The debates went OK, and I actually felt pretty good about my Aff round tonight against Ben. There was no question my negative constructive was a disaster, so I promised myself I would work on my cases at least a half an hour a day.

It was pretty late as the two rounds ran long and then Mrs. Stanton wanted to talk to the debaters. Mom and Sarah were waiting in the mini-van as I walked out to the parking lot. I heard some soft footsteps behind me, and as I turned, she was right there.

"Oh,.. Rebekah," I was caught off guard.

"Hi," she said as she looked up at me with large blue eyes and that shy smile, "I wanted to return your Aff case. I made a few notes on it." She handed me a plain 9" x 12" manila envelope.

"Er.. Thanks, but you didn't have to do that," I said waving my two page Aff copy.

She just looked at me for a moment, her smile disappearing as she bit her lip; then she looked down and said quietly, "Guess I'll see you next week." She turned and walked away.

For a moment, I just stood there trying to figure out what I had said wrong as her long blond hair receded in the shadows. Then Mom called out, "Josh, it's late."

When we got home, I went up to my room and tossed the envelope and my Aff on my desk with the rest of my school work. I was tired. Debating the last round with Alison had been tough because both of us were not prepared. I could see that even our judge, Mr. Chung, was embarrassed for us both.

I wasn't going to go through that again, so I opened up my school work calendar on my laptop and entered CRIMSON in a half hour slot each day. I printed out the new schedule and replaced the one on the bulletin board. Then I went to bed and immediately to sleep.

Thursday's Prayer meeting started out with a bang. Both Dr. Simmons and Mr. Chung wondered if they shouldn't tell their wives about the Vision. Their argument was that now that we were going to undertake some action shouldn't the wives be told, and then there would be added support and prayer. Dad and Mr. Stanton argued that we really did not have a concrete action list, and until we did, telling the wives would only increase the opportunity for the plans, when we had them, to deteriorate into so much talk. There was proper time to tell the wives, but we were not there yet. Ultimately, the group agreed that, at least for the next two meetings, the Vision would be kept under wraps.

As the men settled down, Dad went forward with the night's agenda. "During the week, Doug pulled together a demographic study of the current judgeships that need to be filled throughout the country. There are nearly *fifty* circuit and appeals judgeships waiting to be filled. Here is the breakdown," he remarked as he pulled up the spreadsheet from the TPM database and projected it on the white board.

Dad sat down and Mr. McClaren began, "Really, these are the courts that impact society the most, because the Supreme Court takes just 2% of the cases that are brought to it from these lower courts, so we need to determine how to secure these judgeships. Currently there are thirteen judgeships open on the appeals courts, and most appeals courts are considered conservative in their value stance, having mostly Republican appointees, except, of course, for the 9th Circuit which rules over the western region including California." There were some murmurs and comments about the outrageous actions of the 9th Circuit Court from the room as Mr. McClaren continued using the laser pointer. "You can see by this column that the 4th Circuit Court has four openings, and currently the judges are split five Republican and five Democratic appointees. So the balance would be changed depending on who was appointed, and this circuit covers Virginia, Maryland and the Carolinas. That means it often rules on national security cases because the CIA is in Langley. I plan to do a more in depth analysis of each appeals court and the lower courts. Where their values lie and how many judgeships are available, or are expected to become available, in the next several years."

The last two words had just sunk in.

"Several years?" asked Dr. Simmons.

"This is going to be a long process. It will take time and a lot of our energy and commitment to redirect the future away from the gray flag," Mr. Stanton stated this matter-of-factly and all but Dr. Simmons nodded.

"I guess I just didn't consider the scope of what we are trying to do. Maybe we should consider other avenues to impact the Vision," Dr. Simmons replied.

"Dan, how long does it take to bring a new drug to market, ten to fifteen years, right? Well, this is going to take the same kind of planning, commitment and effort." Pastor Miller wanted to make a point. "Remember, that God gave us this Vision; and we will also have His help in executing it, as long as we are in His will. Just look at William Wilberforce; he underwent a dramatic conversion to Christianity, and then spent the rest of his life fighting to abolish slavery. He succeeded just three days before he died."

"So, you're saying this may be a life-long endeavor?" Dr. Simmons was still not convinced of this course of action.

"Can you think of a better one? Dan, we are talking about changing the course of this nation and history. And remember the alternative – the gray flag. There is no quick fix for the road this nation is currently on; it took a long time to get us in this mess, and it will take a while to get out of it." I could see Dad was trying hard to maintain a unanimous consensus.

"OK, David, I see your point; I just hadn't actually thought about how long this will take. We could be talking ten, twenty years." Dr. Simmons sounded like he would join the rest of us on this for now.

"So where do we start?" Mr. Chung asked the obvious.
"Is there a list of possible candidates for these positions? They're political, right, so maybe the Republican party can get us a list," Pastor Miller offered.

"That's a good idea, John; I can check with our lobbying team in Washington to find out." Being CEO of Prescience did have its advantages I thought.

"What about lower down the food chain, there should be local judges, Superior or State Supreme Court judgeships we can work on," This came from Dr. Simmons, who was making an effort to come on board with the plan.

"There are always judges up for election on the ballot, we should contact the ones who can help us with the Vision," Mr. Stanton replied.

The ideas were flowing fast and furious and Mr. Chung had to ask for a break more than once to get all of them into TPM.

Then Pastor Miller hit upon something that everyone had overlooked. "How do we know that the men who are running for these judgeships are the *right* men? Even if we succeed in filling some of these openings, how do we know these are the men who will make the hard, godly rulings?"

Silence filled the room for more than a few moments, finally Dad spoke. "John, I guess we will have to trust The Lord to show us their true nature. Otherwise, how are we going to do it? We'll have to look at their track record and see how they have ruled in the past. Maybe interview them if we are going to support them."

The Pastor had brought up a very serious issue, and it wasn't going to be solved tonight.
This time the meeting ended about 10:00 p.m. Again, I had just listened.

On the way home, I couldn't get two things that Pastor Miller had said out of my mind. "How do we know if they are the *right* men?" and "Wilberforce spent the rest of his life fighting to abolish slavery." To me the statements seemed connected: Finding the *right* men who would fight for the rest of their lives to save us from the "gray flag." It wasn't just the seven of us. There had to be more committed to the plan.

Chapter Four

The Key

"A good moral character is the first essential in a man, and that the habits contracted at your age are generally indelible, and your conduct here may stamp your character through life. It is therefore highly important that you should endeavor not only to be learned but virtuous."

– George Washington

This Saturday was the cotillion, and Sarah was bugging Mom about a new dress and shoes, especially shoes. I guess there was no reasonable way out of it, but at least I had a dark suit already. And Ben, Steve, and Robert would be there.

Saturday afternoon, Mom and Sarah were at the Mall and Ben and I were just shooting a few hoops. "Does your Dad go to that new prayer meeting on Thursdays?" he asked. "Yeah" I replied, technically telling the truth but not wanting to give up anything more. "Mom says there must be lots of things in need of prayer because the meeting goes awfully late," Ben continued.
"Yeah, I guess so. Hey, you want something to drink?"
"Yeah, a soda's fine." We grabbed a couple of sodas from the patio 'fridge.

"You want something to go with it, chips or something?" I said. Anything to change the subject. We went into the kitchen and found some pretzels in the pantry. As Ben munched away, I asked, "Have you found anyone who wants to join us to get a team together?"

"No, seems like all the really strong players are already taken," He replied.

"Yeah, I was afraid of that." I seemed to have succeeded, but that had been too close. Mom had not questioned me about the prayer meeting since we started, and I think it was her way of saying "if it gets you and your dad together, I am not going to question it." But I couldn't help but think she was trying to find out more via "the Moms."

****

We pulled into the new Civic Center parking lot a little early, just in time to witness the strange transformation of friends from casual jeans and t-shirts to this. Dark suits and ties for the guys, the girls in dresses, high heels, white gloves and hairdos. Sarah couldn't stop talking about seeing her girl friends and showing off what she had found at the Mall. I was glad when she ran ahead of us. Yup, "the Moms" were in full force tonight. This was their thing, and like many, Mom had brought a camera to document her triumph and my torture. She would send photos back to grandma, as if that is how I always looked; dark hair combed, shoes shined, suit pressed and a smile brought to you by thirty months of orthodontia.

I guess this was the price you paid for having a great mom who cared so much about you that she was willing to spend eight to ten hours a day to make sure you were taught what mattered. Mom had insisted that she be allowed to homeschool us when

Dad had suggested the best private schools in Tampa, or even private tutors.

She was definitely in her element tonight. One thing Mom knew how to do and that was 'work' a room, or in this case a large foyer. She had seen and talked to almost every mom and a few dads, and provided the proper comments about most of the cotillion participants. All the while she snapped photos discretely. Sarah, not worried about discretion, called out to Mom that she wanted photos with all her friends: Ashley, Kristen and another girl I didn't know.

I worked my way over to Ben and Robert who were talking about using the HGCF courts after church. ".... There are usually some courts available right after service, but we will have to grab 'em quick."

I was just watching everyone file into the ballroom, hoping against hope that the San Andreas Fault would break loose. No such luck, so I put on my name tag and entered the room. This was the older cotillion group, eighth through twelfth grade, and the range of heights was striking, which made for some comical dance pairings. The grand march was starting. This was a diabolical mechanism designed to pair up the dancers supposedly at random. But you could count on it to match up the shortest young men with the tallest young ladies and vise versa. But I was lucky this time and ended up with a reasonably tall partner. Hannah was a sophomore; it was her third year in cotillion which was great as she actually knew how to follow my lead, and I didn't step on her once. The fact that she had a nice smile and could hold a conversation while we danced was definitely a plus. Unfortunately, cotillion was designed, I was certain, for maximum embarrassment. That must be why at the end of the dance, the girls all shifted partners by one. This time I ended up with Ashley Simmons, and during the entire time, she chattered on nervously as if I was Sarah. She and I couldn't really dance together but it was rather amusing, for everyone else that is. Finally the dance coordinator announced that the girls were to shift partners by *two*. Naturally, another petite girl. As I looked down on an array of loose blond curls, a familiar smile and startling blue eyes looked up at me. *Oh, just perfect!*

"Rebekah,...Hi."

"Hi Josh."

I took her gloved hand and started the Waltz. She was a pretty good dance partner and had every step down precisely; except that, even in heels, she was nearly a foot shorter than I was.

"You're a very good dancer; how long have you been in cotillion?" I figured I'd try a compliment to help smooth whatever feathers had been ruffled recently, I'm sure there had been some, but I would be the last to know.

Rebekah looked up at me with a smile, "Since 5th grade; I like the Waltz. You know the Waltz was originally an 18th century folk dance called the "Lander" and "waltzer" comes from "volver" which..."

"...is Latin for revolving," I finished her sentence. I felt like I had to put at least one point on the board.

"How long have you been studying Latin?" she asked, even though I could see she was bemused by my interruption of her treatise on the Waltz because a little crease appeared between her eyebrows.

"About two years," I replied; this was all very interesting – NOT.

"I like the Samba," I said, filling in the silence, "but I'm not very good at it yet." It was all I could think of at the moment; keeping the subject on dancing seemed safe enough, trying not to rile her unintentionally as I had in all the other times we had met. She had the most striking blue eyes I had ever seen; they were kind of disturbing when she focused up at you.

"The Samba is a lot of fun. It's like the Carnivale dances in Rio de Janeiro, but it's been changed through the years to contain elements of the Maxixe and Carioca…ever see Fred Astaire in the movie 'Flying down to Rio,' they do the Carioca in it…. So how long have you been in cotillion, Josh?"

What *is* it with her, I thought; she's a miniature walking encyclopedia.

"My mom has a real thing about cotillion," I said, "so I have been going for about four years. She insists that I know etiquette and can hold my own on the dance floor." I smiled down at Rebekah, keeping on my best behavior.

"You don't like cotillion." It was a statement not a question from my partner.

"Oh, it's OK I guess. I just think it was designed to embarrass us," I chuckled a little as I thought how comical we must look trying to dance together.

Rebekah's eyes flashed ice blue as she flushed, "Are you embarrassed dancing with me?!"

"No! ... No, I meant 'us' as in 'all of us.'" I said as I waved my hand in an arc pointing to the room full of dancers. Phew, I thought, that was close. Nice save, Josh.

Her eyebrows narrowed, and she looked up; her blue eyes had laser lock on me. She said with a tight smile (I had seen *that* one before in our debate), "Perhaps *we* should all work harder to be better dancers, then *we* wouldn't need to be embarrassed."

I was now concentrating on not accidentally stepping on her, and really I was at a loss for words. She had seen right through my "nice save" and had in one concise sentence made three things very clear. She danced quite well, thank you very much, even if she was only thirteen and just over five foot in heels. Secondly, if I was embarrassed it should not be on her account; it was my *issue*. And three, she was much too smart to fall for my clumsy attempt to cover up my gaff. Well, I had done it again and could only be glad she had her white gloves on because my palms were sweating like crazy. Just then I was saved by a very attractive brunette who stepped in behind Rebekah and asked if she could have the next dance; it was now ladies choice. As Rebekah looked back and up at her older replacement and then back to me, I couldn't say whether it was anger, or disappointment, or something else. "Of course, Jennifer," she hissed, turned on her heel and walked straight off the dance floor.

I watched her go, looking over Jennifer's shoulder, and then had to refocus as my new partner said. "Josh, right? I'm Jennifer Nichols." She held out her hand and we began the swing. In heels, Jennifer almost met me eye to eye. We didn't do too badly, and I was even able to slip in a joke that she laughed lightly at with a brilliant smile. "You've just moved here, from Florida?"

"Yes, from Tampa, because of my dad's business," I replied.

"Do you like it here?" she asked.

"Sure, so far everyone in CHESS has been great." Except perhaps for a certain small blond Merriam-Webster, I thought. "How long have you been in CHESS?" I asked Jennifer.

"Oh... Since I was little, but I'm graduating this year. Your dad is president of Prescience, right?" I guess information like that would travel pretty fast.

"Yeah, he founded Prescience... So what are your top choices for college?" I asked; a lot more interested in talking about Jennifer than my dad.

"Oh, I don't know; I would like to go to Cal State, but it's pretty expensive. I'm trying for some scholarships." She blushed a little.

I knew that this was generally the case. Homeschooling families put their beliefs and children's education ahead of financial gains and because mom stayed home, they were almost always one income families. It was easier in Tampa, but I didn't know how the families managed to make ends meet in Southern California. The dance ended and I looked around to see if Rebekah was still in her seat, but I couldn't see her in the room. It was men's choice and while I didn't want to dance with her after my gaff, I did feel bad that I had, once again, upset her. The music for the next dance was beginning and Jennifer looked at me expectantly, I smiled, why not.

****

On my way home, Sarah was all about "did you see what Ashley had on, she's always trying to look older than she is…"
"Did you have a good time tonight, Josh?" Mom asked.
"Mostly." I didn't want to give her too much encouragement, as I was sure *she* had a great time.
"He danced *twice* with Jennifer Nichols. She's a senior, you know," Sarah gushed.
I blushed a little, "Yeah, she's nice, and the dances were fun."
"She's tall. You like her, *don't* you?" Sarah nearly had me engaged.
"I just met her tonight," I said with my best nonchalant tone.
"Did you find out where she is going to college?" Oh, oh, now Mom was joining in the inquisition.
"She said she didn't know; it depended on scholarships. It's too bad that some of the really smart kids won't get the college of their choice if they don't get some financial aid."
"See, he *does* like her. He just said she was really smart," Sarah said and then sat back smugly.

"Can we get something to eat? ... I'm starving," I sighed, employing my standard escape hatch.

The CRIMSON meeting went much better this time with my Aff looking better and my Neg case more than an outline. I debated Alison again. This time my Aff was a good match for her Neg case, and we got encouraging comments from our judge. At the end of the night, Mrs. Stanton requested everyone sign up if they were going to be debating in the upcoming San Diego tournament. I got to the sheet toward the end and there were twenty one names on it. I thought to myself, 'this is one obsessed group.'

Mrs. Stanton was very pleased, and after a closing prayer she said, "Remember, one hour a day now and practice three times a week. Finally, and this is *very* important, I need some young men to step up and take leadership roles. I am your coach, but CRIMSON is *your* team, not mine. So see me after or email me, to find out what's involved. God is doing a great work here and the young men and women of CRIMSON will be the leaders of your generation; watch and see."

It hit me like a lightning strike. CRIMSON! CRIMSON will be the godly leaders.

I physically trembled. After the initial impact of the revelation, the more I thought about it the more sense it made. This solved the big issue posed by Pastor Miller; how do we know we have the right, godly people. And it solved the mystery of the red ribbon in the Vision. It might take twenty years to accomplish, but isn't that what we had discussed last Thursday? There was no time limit on the Vision. And it must be why *I* had seen the Vision. So many things fit; as if it were designed...I couldn't wait to tell Dad. I pondered exactly what to say all the way home.

Dad was still up in his office on the computer. I knocked and heard "Yes."

I burst in and as the door closed behind me, "Dad, I think I have the key to the Vision!"

My dad looked up from his monitor with a quizzical smile, "What's your idea, Josh?"

"It's CRIMSON, Dad. It all fits...The ribbon...why I was shown the..."

"Josh, slow down... remember ... point by point, like I've taught you."

I took a deep breath, and my pulse slowed just a little as I began again.

"OK...First, remember the problem Pastor Miller posed last week about 'how do we know we have the right men?' Well, CRIMSON is full of lawyers-to-be, and we know them. These are some of the smartest kids in CHESS from strong Christian families. They will be the right men and women."

"Second: The one part of the Vision that could not be explained was the red ribbon. It represents CRIMSON, and it starts in the west coast and will move east."

"Point three: It's the only explanation why I had the Vision. I mean, I am the only student, why else would God have shown me the Vision?"

"And four: You said it will take a long time and a lot of commitment. So even though they are not lawyers yet, in twenty years many CRIMSON students could be judges and national leaders. Even Mrs. Stanton thinks so."

My dad frowned and held up his hand, "You didn't tell Mrs. Stanton about the Vision?"

"No, Dad, but she gave me the idea by saying CRIMSON students would be leaders," I said quickly, not wanting to lose my next few points.

Dad lowered his hand, "Go on."

"Point five: CRIMSON will help train more students to be godly leaders; it's been growing, and with our help it could become much bigger." I paused a moment, forming the next point in my mind.

"Point six: Remember the seven points of light? Well, the other five families are deeply involved in CRIMSON; Mrs. Stanton's the coach, and Mrs. McClaren is her assistant, Mr. Chung is always there, and so are the Millers, and the Simmons'. But the Tanners are *not* in CRIMSON, and we replaced them at the retreat at the last minute." It was all I had... but it was good, somehow I knew I was right.

My dad sat back for a minute and looked very intently at me. Finally he said, "You make a very compelling argument." He came around the desk and put his arm around my shoulder. "I'm very proud of you, Son. Now let's get some sleep, and we'll present it to the TPM tomorrow."

I didn't get much sleep, and I sure couldn't concentrate on my studies the next day. More than once my mom caught me "day dreaming", which wasn't the case, but I couldn't tell her how pre-occupied I was with events of last night and what was to come.

Dad and I finally arrived at HGCF, and I had butterflies the size of B-2 bombers in my stomach. But Dad said, just do exactly what I had done last night. Once everyone had settled in and we prayed, Dad stood up and asked for their attention.

"Josh has a proposal he would like to share with you. I want to make it clear that this is all his idea; I just provided the slides... Go ahead, Josh."

I stood up as my dad sat down by his laptop and I addressed the first slide.

THE KEY TO THE VISION

Shown on the screen.

Silence filled the room, as I remembered, 'point at a time, point at a time.'

"I propose that CRIMSON, our debate club, is the key to the Vision." That ended the silence. Everyone was talking at once. Finally, my dad stood up and held up his hands for the men to quiet down. "Please, let's hear the proposal and then we can discuss it."

I went through my points as I had with Dad last night.

At the end of the presentation, I saw some nods and some smiles. I also saw some questioning looks and one very hard stare.

That stare belonged to Dr. Simmons. "I have eight children, four in CRIMSON, and I don't know if I want them to be involved with the Vision."

Mr. Stanton spoke up. "Dan, you didn't disagree with Josh's proposal, you simply said you didn't know if you want your children to be involved in the solution to the Vision. We can get back to that, but first I would like to hear what people think about the proposal on the table." He looked over at me and winked.

"I think it makes sense," said Pastor Miller. "Where else can we be sure we have the right godly judges and leaders. The time is not an issue to God, He is not temporal. He sees the end from the beginning."

Mr. Chung spoke up next, "It makes sense to me, except how will we know we are making progress? It will take at least six or seven years for the current students to even start passing the bar."

My dad interjected, "According to Josh, some CRIMSON alumni are already graduating into law school, so we might begin by concentrating on them."

"Just how do you propose to implement this? Can six families really change the course of this country?" Mr. McClaren questioned.

As Mr. Stanton ripped pieces of paper from a legal pad he looked around the group. "We ought to first determine if this proposal has merit or not. Let's run this like a jury. Everyone take a piece of paper. Take a couple of minutes and remember the question is: Yes or No, does this proposal have merit? In fact, is this proposal the best idea so far in solving the Vision?"

I held my breath and tried not to look too nervous as I turned in my vote. The votes came back quicker than I would have thought, and Mr. Stanton tallied, "5..6..7 its unanimous."

"But now we have lots of implementation issues. Now we'll need everyone in CRIMSON to know about the Vision," Mr. Chung stated.

"I'm not so sure we do," Dad replied, "I would still like to take some time to develop at least a framework of a plan. Before we share the Vision and the idea that CRIMSON is to be the vehicle to solve the problem of the gray flag, we should at least be able to show that we have given this considerable thought."

I knew my dad was still cautious about sharing the Vision. I had seen him work late into the night on the finishing touches on a proposal because he had told me that the key to corporate success was thorough preparation. In the business world, coming to the table without a well thought out plan would not succeed. And we were talking about our families and their children's futures, not just a business deal.

"Can you all keep the Vision private just a little longer so that we can at least have a plan to share with those we tell? I know it has been hard keeping this secret from our wives and others; but without a plan, we will not look united nor in control."

I saw most of the men nod in agreement, and Dr. Simmons, the man I most worried about, kept quiet. My dad had held the tenuous consensus together once more.

We spent the rest of the meeting discussing and developing a framework of the CRIMSON plan.

My role (and unknowingly my entire future) had completely changed tonight, from quiet observer to the inside man. I was now very central to the plan, being both a member of CRIMSON and part of the seven devising the framework for using the debate club as the generator of young godly leaders. The men considered me an essential part of the group, having provided the key to the Vision. One thing was clear. I needed to become much more than a debater; I needed to be a leader. Tomorrow I would email Mrs. Stanton and request to take on a leadership role within CRIMSON.

Chapter Five

Getting Serious

"Nothing is more essential to the establishment of manners in a State than that all persons employed in places of power and trust must be men of unexceptionable character."
— Samuel Adams

The next morning, Mrs. Stanton must have been online because she replied immediately to my email. '*I'm very glad you want to sign up, Josh. You will need to understand what is involved, but I am sure you're up to it. Please get to debate thirty minutes early next week so I can go over it with all the new leaders. See you there. Mrs. Stanton.*'

The other thing I needed to do was get to work on my case, so I started searching my desk for the copy of my Neg as I logged on and accessed my CRIMSON folder on my laptop. Then I saw it, the corner of a manila envelope sticking out from a pile of books. I pulled it out and opened the clasp. Sliding out the contents, heat flowed into my face. "A few notes" *Right.* More like six pages of finely written red script in almost perfect handwriting. Not only was my two page Aff covered with red ink, but the additional four had topic after topic carefully underlined with

associated examples, quotes and their references including foot
note numbers. "Good grief," I muttered. I couldn't help but be
impressed by her critique, which, while not mean-spirited, was
very frank and incredibly detailed. She had signed the last page
with a practiced flourish.

Rebekah

This was followed by a note: *Maybe we can discuss these ideas at
the next CRIMSON meeting.* I frowned and then gave out a short
sardonic laugh. Absolutely, I thought, just what I had in mind,
discussing the bloody carcass of my case with the little blond
piranha in braces that had perpetrated the massacre in front of the
entire CRIMSON team.
Sometimes it was hard to remember that Rebekah was only
thirteen.
I stuffed the sheets back into the envelope and went downstairs to
look for a snack.

****

The weekend was mostly going through routine activities while
my brain was frequently occupied with thoughts about the
CRIMSON plan. But the best part was a strategy session with
my dad on Saturday night in his office. I brought in my laptop
and we worked for a couple of hours on the framework for the
CRIMSON plan, accessing the TPM database. He was sending a
lot of broadcast posts to the other five men, partly because this
Thursday was Thanksgiving and we would not be able to meet,
but he wanted input and ideas from everyone. It was great just
being with him, but also to be working on a secret project

together that involved a goal of impacting our nation; that was really hard to get my head around. Because I was on the inside of CRIMSON, I was finally able to contribute, and Dad was very interested in my ideas about which students were good candidates and how we would influence them and their families to join our cause to overcome the gray flag. Some would be easier than others; and yet, even if we were successful with half of the current membership we would have produced about a dozen leaders to turn this country around. We needed to also involve some of the CHESS/CRIMSON alumni, college students who were headed toward law school or public policy leadership. I listed all I could, but we needed to get a comprehensive list so Dad sent the TPM group an inquiry. These CRIMSON alumni would spearhead the assault on the gray flag. How many we could recruit for our cause was yet to be seen. Most of these college students were at John Adams, Baylor or Wheaton.

These Universities had great biblical world view pre-law programs designed to produce the type of individuals who would impact our legal system and government. I mentioned that the San Diego tournament was a step to the nationals and that the best pre-law colleges were looking to recruit for their debate teams and it was important that CRIMSON place high in the competition.

Dad looked at me and said, "What are you doing about this?"

"I'm working hard on my cases and I think I will do well. I've signed up to be part of the CRIMSON leadership team, too," I said after a moment.

Then Dad said something I would never forget. "Son, you will be a leader in this cause, and it's important that you lead by example. I have no doubt you will get into John Adams, and you will excel. But first things first, you need to score high in this tournament and get to the national tournament. However you accomplish it, your case can't just be good, it must be the best."

I went to bed that night with my dad's words in my head; "the first born" syndrome had struck again, except this time there was a concrete goal and a cause.

What I needed to do in the short run was clear; in the next few weeks I must get my debating skills and case up to "nationals" standards. I finally fell asleep fitfully dreaming of standing by a podium, ".... Judges ready?.. My opponent ready?" (Rebekah nodded with that tight, knowing smile).

****

This week would be a short one, with the Thanksgiving holiday leaving just three days of school. Wednesday, I had Mom drop me off at CRIMSON at 5:30 while she and Sarah went last minute grocery shopping. As I walked in, Robert, Ben and Dan Jr. were already there. I expected Robert, as he was the senior, and Ben because his mom was the coach. Dan Jr. was a surprise. I wondered if Dr. Simmons had strongly suggested he sign up. Mrs. Stanton asked us to gather around.

"You four will be the core leadership for CRIMSON. Before we get started, Robert, will you lead us in prayer?" Robert was a lot more comfortable with this than I would have been, and asked God to bless CRIMSON and the leaders, that we would strive to always act in accordance with His commandments, and that any reward that would come from our accomplishments bring honor and glory to Him, in Jesus' name. " Amen," we concluded.

Mrs. Stanton asked us to take a seat and she handed each of us a sheet of paper.

It contained several points, many that were obvious, and some that were not.

- Dress always respectfully and conservatively, setting the example for all CRIMSON.
- Open the debate meetings in prayer, rotating each leader, (I was next alphabetically).
- Always encourage the other debaters, never a disparaging or discouraging word, even in jest.
- Always keep your speech clean, no innuendos, and no signs or signals.
- Treat all members with respect, but especially the young women, even in a tough debate.
- During tournaments always gather the group together for prayer before each round. Asking God to bless the round and all the glory to Him.
- Offer help and tutoring to the less experienced members of CRIMSON.
- Look for possible recruits to join CRIMSON from the CHESS organization, and possibly outside.
- Be early to CRIMSON meetings and help set up and also tear down tables, etc.
- If someone is struggling with their case, or even has other personal problems, be a strong understanding friend.
- The leadership will meet once a month for half an hour before the regular meeting to discuss how things can be improved.
- The leaders must have their cases in perfect shape as an example to all the other members.
- NEVER compromise CRIMSON's integrity.

Mrs. Stanton waited for any questions from us after she had read off the list. I raised my hand and asked about new members. "Who can we recruit; can I recruit from other debate teams?" "Absolutely not. Stick with CHESS if possible, and only recruit outside of CHESS if the person has no other team affiliation," came the reply. There were no other questions, even though I was puzzled by exactly what the last bullet meant. Mrs. Stanton said how proud she was of each of us. I could see she had a little glisten in her eyes. The other CRIMSON teens were starting to come in, and we got to work setting up the tables and chairs.

Our first Thanksgiving in California. Mom had tried to make it as normal as possible. Her parents even flew out from Florida to be here for the occasion. Unfortunately, Grandpa Reinhart was not able to fly out due to his heart condition, but we had an hour long SKYPE call with him and he looked pretty happy. Marisa had made some traditional Mexican dishes, roasted calabaza, a spicy butternut squash cake, and also a pumpkin cheese cake flavored with Mexican cinnamon or canela. But the main event, Turkey with traditional dressing and all the other fixings, was as it had always tasted. I had my fill of tryptophan as I had seconds, and thirds of the succulent bird along with all the gravy on my mash potatoes and some calabaza too. Topping that off with pumpkin pie and also some cheese cake, I was ready for a nap as I tried to hold a coherent conversation with my Grandpa, but he and I both dosed off in mid-sentence.

That Monday was a big event in my life, and I guess for everyone my age. I got my drivers license! I couldn't wait to take the mini-van out solo. Ok, it was just a mini-van, but I had freedom, no more little sister in the back seat. But Mom said she had an errand to run, and Sarah had Aquadors; so I was left alone, supposedly working on my case. It was hard to concentrate on studying as I planned out where to drive to first. I called up Ben and we talked about getting together the next day, just so I had an excuse to drive somewhere. I heard a car door close and the 'beep' of a security lock as I was studying. Mom had just left, so who could this be in the middle of the afternoon. I open the front door and just about fell over.

There stood my dad in front of the most beautiful sight in all the world, a shiny black BMW three series, tinted glass, custom wheels, my dream car. "Catch!" he said with a huge grin as he tossed me the keys. Luckily my reflexes were more on automatic as my mind was taking in the all the possibilities. I hugged my dad and looked over his shoulder at the automotive sculpture. "Want to take it for a drive?" he asked as he walked toward the passenger door. I looked at the key and pressed the unlock button; the satisfying beep-beep let me know I had done it right. "Oh, Yeah!" I finally managed to speak.

As I got into the black leather driving environment, I adjusted the seats and the mirrors; with seat belts and an ear-to-ear grin firmly in place I turned the key. Then it was off to the Rancho Santa Fe scenic drive. The strong 3.0 liter just ate up pavement as it hummed through the gears. Both Dad and I were having the time of our lives, cruising California's hillsides and beachfronts. Dad said my plates were coming and they said JSH S BMR. I would have to add the apostrophe myself.

Nothing could ruin my week now; even my obvious loss to Elizabeth Simmons at debate was overshadowed by the excitement of driving myself to CRIMSON in my new car. I had given what I thought was a pretty good prayer to open CRIMSON this week and even thought I had seen Rebekah give a shy smile.

Robert, Ben, Dan Jr. and I were all congratulated by the CRIMSON team and we told everyone we would be available for any help we could provide. At the end of the meeting, most of the guys were out drooling at my BMW. I was showing off all the features and then it was time to get in, open the roof to the stars, turn the key, and wave as I cruised out of the parking lot. No more mini-van for me.

The distraction of my new car was not very conducive to stepping up my studies or improving my case. But I secretly thought my dad had felt I needed a test of maturity. Could I hold my level of commitment to CRIMSON with the beautiful black distraction out in the garage? I decided I would prove to him that the "first born" had what it took. So I worked on my case Thursday afternoon instead of taking a drive. Elizabeth's negative had shown some gaping holes in a few of my Aff's arguments. The tournament was just after the holidays and I was running out of time. Luckily my other studies were in good shape, but to get my debating skills and case up to "nationals" standards would take a miracle.

I decided to get out the manila envelope and seriously study the contents. Putting my ego aside, I had to admire the depth of knowledge and logical structure of the arguments and examples written on those six pages. But what about my Neg? Well, first things first, I would work on my Aff until it was "the best." I spent the afternoon revamping my Aff using Rebekah's notes.

I got to her signature and read the post script: '*Maybe we can discuss these ideas at the next CRIMSON meeting.*' That had been three meetings ago. No wonder she had not made any attempt to engage in conversation, or even look at me for that matter. She had expected some response to her extraordinary review of my case and she had been rightfully disappointed by my oblivious behavior.

The TPM went very well this time; we were men on a mission. And once these guys got going it was pretty impressive. We had the entire roster of CHESS sorted by who was in CRIMSON, who were likely to be in CRIMSON in the future, and who were the CRIMSON alumni. Also, where those alumni were and what they were doing. Then there was an idea I had suggested to Dad last week, that he donate six laptops to CRIMSON to be checked out by some of the students whose families were not able to provide them. Dad had brought them to the meeting and Mr. Stanton said he would get them to his wife, as an anonymous donation.

Mr. Chung had set up a database program inside the server to allow for cross reference of all the students of interest and the possible judgeships that needed to be filled. These were long range plans and goals, but we had to start somewhere and begin planning the future.

The next day, I could see I was not going to get my case in shape without some help. I considered Robert or even Elizabeth, but finally had to admit that the one person who knew most about my case was Rebekah.

Time to eat a little humble pie, I thought, but she had offered to help and my case needed help, that was for sure.

"Miller residence."

"Hi Mrs. Miller, this is Josh Reinhart," I replied, hoping this was really a good idea.

"Hi Josh, I'm afraid Robert's not here right now, but I'll let him know you called," she assumed understandably.

"Well, actually I wasn't calling for Robert,... I was calling to talk to Rebekah."

"Oh,...Ah... Just a moment, let me see if she's available." Mrs. Miller hesitated, I could hear her call out, "Rebekah... it's Josh Reinhart for you."

After a few moments I thought I heard her in the background 'Josh Reinhart? for me?' Then Rebekah was on the phone.

"Hi Josh,… this is a surprise," she actually sounded pleased at my call.

"Yeah,..ah, Rebekah, I was wondering if you had time to help me with my debate cases," the first swallow of pie didn't taste too bad.

"So you *finally* read my critique." Man, was there anything that got passed her, I thought, as I could imagine that she was smiling that knowing smile on the other end of the phone… caught again.

"I had a few questions on a couple of your points and examples." I decided to ignore the jab.

"I really would like to discuss your case, but I have my skating lesson this afternoon…" Of course, why had I expected she would not be busy?

She ice-skates?.. I smiled at this image of a diminutive fairy flitting around the rink. Back to the mission, I had to persevere for my case's sake.

"Oh…Well, how about tomorrow?" Maybe Saturday's were better.

"I've got piano 'till 4:00, but after that I have some time."

"Great…could I come over after 4:00?" I said with some enthusiasm.

There was a pause on the line, "….you want to come over here?" Her voice sounded guarded, why she paused was hard to say, I wished I could see her face.

"If it's Okay?" I replied a little puzzled.

"…Just a minute please, Josh, I'll ask." Another pause, and I could hear parts of the discussion on the other end of the phone.

"….he wants to go over his case….Yes, Mother, he wants to come over after piano tomorrow." I heard her explain my request to Mrs. Miller, then another pause.

"Josh, why don't you come over after 4:15? I'll have until 5:30," Rebekah finally answered.

"Great,.. Thanks, Rebekah, I'll see you tomorrow." That had gone well, I thought.

"Bye, Josh," she almost whispered.

Chapter Six

The Hard Case

"Liberty must at all hazards be supported. We have a right to it, derived from our Maker. But if we had not, our fathers have earned and bought it for us, at the expense of their ease, their estates, their pleasure, and their blood."

– John Adams

As I pulled up to the Miller's house I thought I glimpsed a flash of blond hair from the front window. I shut the door and engaged the security system on my black Beemer with a "beep." I walked up to the front door with my laptop and the manila envelope and rang the door bell.

The door opened and Mrs. Miller greeted me with a warm smile. She was in her baking apron, and I could smell something wonderful as I stepped in and she led me to the dining room.

"Rebekah will be here in a minute. Please have a seat." Then Mrs. Miller stepped into the kitchen as I sat down at the round table with four chairs. I spread out Rebekah's critique and powered up my laptop feeling a little uncomfortable waiting for a thirteen year old girl to help me with my most important assignment.

After just a couple of minutes, Rebekah came into the room carrying her ever present huge notebook. She was in some jeans, but had a fancy frilly blue top on that accented her already startling eyes. "Hi, Josh," she smiled that shy smile and I stood up realizing all my cotillion training wasn't totally wasted. She sat down in the nearest chair as she put her notebook on the table.

"Thanks for letting me come over; I really need your help if I am going to break in this next tournament." I figured I might as well get this out of the way as I sat back down.
"What part of your case do you need help on?" she still had to look up at me even when we were sitting. I imagined her feet were not quite touching the floor.
"Pretty much all of it." I looked down at the six pages of red ink, my hands framing the pages, and then looked at her with a slightly hopeless crooked smile.

Rebekah laughed. A high lilting laugh as she smiled more broadly, this time showing the blue spangled braces, and her eyes sparkled. I had never heard her laugh before, smile yes, but never laugh. I wondered if she saved it for rare occasions. It did make me chuckle and some of the tension of the last few minutes flowed out of me. This might just work out okay, I thought.
"It isn't all that bad," she smiled looking at the papers. "Your case is fundamentally sound, it just needs good support and some strong examples."
"I also need work on my cross-ex and refutation skills." She might as well know what I'm asking of her.
She looked up and locked me in that laser blue stare. "I can't do all that in an hour," still smiling, but with an unstated question.

"Well, I was hoping this would be just the start of some study sessions." Oh man, I could tell by her expression that I might have assumed too much.

"Why don't you ask one of the *senior* girls to help you?" Her blue eyes went icy and her smile had disappeared. *Ouch*, just when I thought things were going well.

"Rebekah, I really need *your* help. You're the best debater in CRIMSON, even better than Robert or Elizabeth. You also know my case like no one else, probably better than *I* do." This must be what they mean by sacrificing for a cause, but I had been sincere, regardless of her age or size, I had debated the others and there was no comparison. Her technique and her depth of knowledge were astounding.

She softened at this, and I actually saw a little blush. "I'm sorry Josh. It's just that so often, people don't take me seriously...because... I'm short." She looked down at her hands.

...and young, I thought, finishing her sentence in my head. I too had thought she was just a little know-it-all; but now I could see that she was trapped, at least for a few years, in a tween's body with an adult mind. If this was going to work I would have to make a concerted effort to treat Rebekah like an adult, and try to get passed the braces and her 4'10" stature.

"Oh, believe me, I take you seriously." I grabbed a few of the red pages and shook them, and we both laughed. I sighed as I sat back in my chair. Back to the task at hand.

Just then, Mrs. Miller appeared with some hot cranberry scones and tea. The smell was amazing. "How about a break?" she inquired.

"Thanks, Mrs. Miller." Yeah, I could use a snack, my stomach was vying for attention.

As I ate, Rebekah critiqued my Aff case, each contention, my points and each sub-point. She made recommendations and I was typing furiously while chewing.

I didn't notice at first, but gradually it became apparent that she had not looked once at the papers on the table. How did she do it? Amazing, I thought.

Five-thirty came fast and I had hoped to get much further, but it was a start.

I was getting ready to go, standing with Rebekah in the Miller's front room, having already thanked Mrs. Miller for her hospitality and the scones.

"Is it possible we can have another study session? My Neg is a mess," I asked, hoping it would not be met with the same response as before.

"Let me ask, .. Mother, I have next Saturday afternoon open, don't I?"

"I don't have anything scheduled," came the reply from the kitchen.

"How about the same time next Saturday, Josh?" She smiled up at me as she opened the door. As I started to walk out, "I like your car," she said with a blush as I passed. That put a smile on my face; so she had noticed.

As I started to pull away from the curb, I saw Rebekah with her mom standing behind her in the doorway. The nationals might just be possible after all.

I was pretty sure I would need more than just another hour and a half of Rebekah's time, but like most homeschoolers, she had lots of extracurricular activities besides her studies. She had been pushed ahead and was now taking freshman AP classes at the very least. That had to mean she was always busy, but I needed to somehow get more of her time. I decided that while it was best to do debate prep face to face, the phone would have to do.

"Hi, Mrs. Miller, its Josh Reinhart, can I speak to Rebekah, please?" It was Tuesday about 6:00 p.m.

"Just a minute, Josh…."

"Hi, Josh, did you have a question?" Rebekah's clear high voice came on the phone.

"I have lots of questions; do you have some time to talk?" I asked.

"Dinner's not for another hour, so I guess I can for a while," she replied.

We talked about my negative assertion, and I had the phone on speaker so I could type while talking.

"I hope you don't mind helping me, it's just that I had a couple of ideas I wanted to get your opinion on."

"I don't mind, Josh, but does this mean you won't be coming over on Saturday?" she asked quietly.

"Oh, no, I still want to come over Saturday if that's all right?" I needed as much help as I could get.

"Okay, I just wanted to make sure."   She seemed tentative. Maybe I was asking for too much of her time; but I plowed ahead with my questions, and by the time she had to go and set the dinner table, my Neg looked pretty good.

"Rebekah, you are *amazing.*" I really meant it; forty five minutes and my Neg was starting to show real promise. There was a pause at the other end of the phone.

And then quietly, almost a little sad, "Thanks, Josh, I got to go now," and hung up.

I looked at the phone for a moment and then shrugged; I would never be able to figure her out, I frowned and hung up.

Armed with my new Aff and my improved Neg, I felt good about coming to CRIMSON this week. Mrs. Stanton and Mrs. McClaren set the assignments for two rounds, one Aff and one Neg. I was matched up first with Ben and my Aff took his Neg with relative ease. Then I was up against Robert for the second round. He was a very polished debater, and I lost due partly to my unfinished Neg and partly due to my debating skills, or lack there of. I didn't see much of Rebekah because the two rounds had taken up nearly all the time. When I did see her walking to the second debate room, she didn't look happy and I hoped it didn't have anything to do with me this time. I asked Robert what the problem was and he said that it probably had to do with a conference his parents were attending in New York a week before the tournament. I decided not to press my luck and bother her tonight. I figured I could find out more details on Saturday.

I drove Dad to the Thursday prayer meeting which provided some interesting diversion from all the debate focus. It was also helpful to get a constant reminder of why I was working so hard. It was important to establish as many of the CRIMSON team members into the nationals as possible. And if some did not get to the nationals, at least they should be noticed by the collegiate debate scouts. Mr. Chung and Mr. Stanton had started charting some possible career paths that could lead eventually to judgeships for our four point men (actually three men and one woman), as we called them. These were the four most advanced alumni from CRIMSON; two were law school students and two were entering law school next year. John Petersen, a second year law student, was already interning for a senator and looked to be interested in staying in politics. The group felt he would be a promising candidate. The Petersen's had a daughter in nursing school and Jeff who was a sophomore in CHESS, but was not in

CRIMSON. It was suggested to me that I might try to recruit Jeff into CRIMSON. At some point the TPM would need to recruit his brother, John, for a "Point Man" assignment, and this would be easier if we also recruited Jeff. I said I would work through the CRIMSON leadership team, and we should have a list of possible candidates from CHESS to recruit, not just Jeff. So Mr. McClaren was assigned to generate that list for the next meeting. This was starting to get exciting, as I felt like a spy master, recruiting for a secret mission. "The name's Reinhart, Josh Reinhart," I said to myself with a smile as my BMW shot down the freeway.

Friday night, Ben, Robert and I went to the Mall Cineplex to see the latest 3D blockbuster. It was great to forget about studies for a while, and as we dropped by Antonio's Pizza beforehand we talked about anything but school. Robert said he was hoping to be able to buy a used car soon, as he had been saving up. I know he was envious of my Beemer, especially since it was just *given* to me. I told him that as soon as I had a year of driving with my license he would be the first to get a ride in it. Unfortunately, till then Mom had to take us because I was restricted to older passengers. She and Sarah were shopping and would pick us up after the movie. Dad, as usual, was working late. I asked Ben if he knew Jeff Petersen. Ben said that Jeff was into hockey, and he wasn't sure he would have much interest in CRIMSON. I then thought I would see if Robert or Ben knew of other possible new recruits for CRIMSON. Robert said that at the beginning of each school year the applications for new members goes out to all CHESS families, but many felt it took too much time out of their schedule or that it was too expensive because of traveling and staying at the tournaments.

I filed away the idea that maybe financial aid could be something Dad could help with, like the laptops, to allow families to get involved with CRIMSON that couldn't afford it.

On our way home, I asked Mom how the Millers could afford to be in CRIMSON and also piano and ice skating for Rebekah.

"Mrs. Miller teaches a class in both Biblical History and Home Economics. So she earns some extra money that way. Also, I think Mrs. Koffman, who manages the local Ice Castle and skating school, has two children in Mrs. Miller's classes, so she sees to it that Rebekah gets lessons and ice time."

"The Moms Network at it again," I said shaking my head.

"You have no idea. There's constant bartering and trading of time, talent and services. It makes you feel like you're part of a very big close-knit family."

The Moms could never be underestimated, I thought. I wondered when we would let them in on the secret I had been hiding all this time. How much stronger the TPM would become with their help. It had to happen pretty soon.

****

"Hi, Josh. Come in," Rebekah held the door open as I stepped into the Miller's home. She gave me her shy smile and led me into the dining room. She had on a very pretty black sweater with gold threads that offset her blond hair.

"Thanks... I like your sweater." I figured I could start this Saturday on the right foot. Never hurts to give a compliment. I could hear her mom in the kitchen.

"I... ah... thanks... I just came from my piano recital, but I changed into some comfortable jeans." The compliment must have caught her off guard, so she explained to cover it.

"I play a little, what's your recital piece?" I asked.

"Today, I played Polonaises opus 71 No. 1 and 2 by Chopin," she replied.

"Whoa! That's out of my league, how long have you been playing?"

"Since I was seven," she blushed a little and then sat down at the kitchen table.

I put my laptop down and brought out a large folder that I kept all my notes in.

"You seemed a little upset at CRIMSON last week. Did something happen?" I thought I would see if there was anything I had unknowingly done wrong.

"Well... I have to go with my parents to this Pastor's conference in New York, and I will miss the last week before San Diego.... It's not *fair*, Robert gets to stay here because he's eighteen, ...and was invited by the Stantons but..." she trailed off looking down at her hands.

"Sounds like it might be a fun trip, New York at New Years, and all..." Ooops, I would have to start engaging my brain before I spoke around her.

"It may sound like fun to *you*, but I don't see why *I* can't stay here. I have lots to do and it cuts into my debate practices," she fired back, blue eyes flashing.

"Speaking of that, do you want to try a round today?" Let's try changing the subject and get down to the business at hand.

She paused and her eyes narrowed before she spoke, "...you want to debate *now*?"

"Sure, even though I beat Ben last week, I could use the practice."

"Josh, are you *sure* you want to do this?" For some reason, she was hesitant.

I decided a different tactic. "Don't worry; I'll go easy on you." I smiled but she didn't. Did she actually think I was serious?

"You will go easy on *me*? You *arrogant...*" She flushed, eyes flashing. I kept my grin firmly in place, but held my hands up defensively, leaning back in my chair, hoping she would not gun down an unarmed man using the two blue lasers at her disposal. "Oh...sorry," she murmured after a moment looking down again.

Now I had really embarrassed her. If I was going to get anything out of this session, I had to do some repair work and do it fast. "Just kidding, just kidding. Look, I know you can easily dismantle my case, but I was hoping to get some pointers on cross-ex and refutation. And I do need more practice rounds. So will you please forgive my bad jokes and help me so I have a chance to break in San Diego?" I gave her a crooked smile.

She finally looked up, "I'm sorry, it's just I'm upset about this trip, and... OK, let's do a round.... Mother, can you help us do a debate round, we need a judge."
Mrs. Miller came in, taking off her apron. "Sure, I got about an hour before dinner will be ready. Where's the timer?"

Rebekah's Aff case was brilliant and my cross-examinations were futile. After the voting points, we looked at each other's flow sheets. Mrs. Miller gave us her score sheet and went back to preparing dinner. You could see what had happened in the debate by analyzing the flows. Any way you looked at it, Rebekah had ruthlessly cut me to ribbons. I felt a little discouraged that I didn't even put a dent in her Aff.
I don't know whether she was making sure I had no illusions about who was the tutor and who was the pupil or if it was something else. I tried to make light of the devastation.

"Next time, you should field your varsity team," I said ruefully. I guess I thought my Neg had been in better shape. She had just shown me I was not ready for San Diego, let alone the nationals.

"Josh, I'm sor... *you're* the one who wanted to debate, remember?" She blushed a little and looked down at her hands. I could see that she had not meant to damage my Neg or my ego to the extent that she had. It was just, in the heat of the debate, she could not pull any punches.

"That's OK,... like I said, I need the practice." I put my Neg back in my folder and shut down my laptop. I had to admit, my mood was turning dark.

"Rebekah," her mom called from the kitchen, "it's time to get ready for dinner. Josh, you're welcome to stay and have dinner with us; there's plenty of pot roast." It smelled delicious, and I was starving; but I thought I had outstayed my welcome, at least as far as one Miller was concerned.

"Thank you, Mrs. Miller, but I do need to get back. I've got lots of homework." This sure was true, given what had just occurred.

Mrs. Miller led the way to the front door, and Rebekah was slow getting up from the table. I stepped outside and thanked Mrs. Miller for her invitation and hoped I could get a rain-check; I couldn't see Rebekah. As I drove away, the Miller's front door closed.

I opened the sunroof to the remains of a beautiful Southern California sunset, and I decided to take the long way home and enjoy the 'superb German handling', as the commercials promised. There would be plenty of time to think about debate and what had just happened at the Miller's.

Chapter Seven

Interesting Distractions

"The sacred rights of mankind are not to be rummaged for, among old parchments, or musty records. They are written, as with a sun beam, in the whole volume of human nature, by the hand of the divinity itself; and can never be erased or obscured by mortal power." – Alexander Hamilton

Saturday night I called Dan Jr. up to see if I could drop by.

"Come on over; Elizabeth and I were about to meet some of the team at Starbucks."

"Great! How 'bout I meet you there?" It made more sense, and I could be free to leave when I wanted to.

I put on a favorite sweatshirt and headed out, but Mom called to me, "Could you bring back a chocolate chip Frappuccino with whipped cream? And get back in by ten, OK? And drive careful."

"Sure, Mom, Bye." I was out the door and in the sanctuary of my car in no time.

I thought back to this afternoon and my debate disaster with Rebekah. I replayed the entire episode in my mind. She started out OK, my compliments on her sweater, piano, then New York.

Now that was where the root of the problem must lie. She felt that if Robert could stay home, then she should, too. But she was only thirteen, and I'm sure her parents thought she was too young to leave for ten days. Or maybe no one had offered to let her stay with them, like the Stantons had for Robert. 'Ouch,' I thought, it was possible that she did not have that many friends. Any girls her age would probably not be very interesting to her, and she might seem to be a know-it-all to them, as well as anyone else, for that matter. Rebekah was not easy to get to know; it certainly took work. I'm not sure I would be making the effort if not for my goal to get to nationals. But once you did get past her sharp edges, she was interesting in a way, like playing with a chemistry set. If you didn't have your wits about you, explosions were inevitable. Perhaps that was it. She was the most accomplished CHESS teen I knew, regardless of her age, and yet I did not see her with friends except on the fringes of a group of girls at CRIMSON. I was pulling into Starbucks before I knew it. It was amazing how I could think things through more clearly in my Beemer.

As I walked into Starbucks, I saw Dan Jr. and Elizabeth, as well as Ben, Steve and Alison. I walked over to a couple of couches and chairs that the CHESS students had staked out as their territory. It was a fun crowd and the caffeine and sugar swung the energy meter to the redline. A few more students came in, and I recognized Jennifer from cotillion. She walked over and gave me a friendly smile. "Is this seat taken?" she asked expectantly with big green eyes.
"Please," I said as I stood up, and then we both sat down. She was in tight jeans and a short tan jacket over a mint green top that accented her eyes. I wondered whether her eyes were really that green or if she had colored contacts.

"Is that *your* BMW?" she gestured out the window.

I guess word had gotten around. "Yeah, I just got it."

"Maybe you could show me before you leave tonight," she flashed a great smile.

"Sure, it's got all the gadgets, even a USB port for my playlist."

'The name's Reinhart, Josh Reinhart,' I thought with a smile.

"I bet it has an *awesome* sound system," she said enthusiastically and sipped her drink.

"Yeah, it has thirteen speakers for surround sound." This evening was turning out better than I'd thought.

"How've you been, any progress on the college front?" I asked.

"I got accepted to UCSD, and I'm trying for a scholarship," she said looking down into her drink.

"Do you know what you are going to major in?" I was interested for a couple of reasons. First, just on a personal level I'd like to get to know Jennifer better, and second, in case there was some opportunity for recruitment.

"I am looking at being a communications major; I'd like to work in films as a writer or in the news business," she responded.

News and media are important tools in swaying public opinion, thinking about the TPM, but only for a few moments. I was enjoying just having a normal conversation with a very pretty girl at a café. Not that it was going anywhere, but I could still enjoy the evening.

I checked my cell phone to see that it was 9:30, so I asked Jennifer if she would still like to see my car. We walked out to the parking lot and I opened the passenger door for her. Then I got into the drivers seat. Turning on the accessories, I powered up the audio system and asked her what she would like to hear. "Do you have any 'Skillet?'" she asked.

I scrolled through my play list and found a song she liked. It did sound great.

"That's awesome, Josh," she said as she moved in her seat to the music.

It was really too bad I couldn't give her a ride in my car, but that was the law. I was imagining cruising with the roof open and enjoying the music with her. But...

"I wish we could listen to more, but I need to get back," I said lamely. She stepped out of the car and gave me one more smile as I held the door and we walked back to Starbucks.

As I drove out of the lot, debate was the last thing on my mind, a Switchfoot praise song filling the BMW's cabin.

I made it home just at 10:00 p.m. Mom greeted me and then asked about her Frappuccino.

"Oh, ...I'm sorry Mom, I completely forgot," I flushed, I had obviously been preoccupied.

"That's okay; I'm trying to cut back on the sugar anyway." I could tell she was a little disappointed, but was going easy on me.

****

Dad and I got together up in his office again on Sunday night. It seemed to be a time that both of us were available, and it was starting to become a regular event.

After a while, the question I was afraid of was asked. "How's your case going?"

"I think it's pretty good. I've won with my Aff in practice rounds every time," I replied, stressing the positives.

Dad could see I was holding back. "What about your negative case?"

"I've been working hard on it, but it is not as strong as my Aff."
An image of my Neg case pages torn to shreds and a knowing
smile flashed by.

"Is there anything I can do to help you, Son?" Oh, boy. He is
really serious about seeing "the first born" get to the nationals.

"I don't think so Dad, I have plenty of help. Robert, Elizabeth,
and some of the others and Mrs. Stanton's a great coach." Oh,
and did I mention the 4'10" debate-obsessed walking law library
I've been working with every week.

"Josh, I know with Christmas coming up it's tough to stay
focused, but that *is* going to be the difference between the teams
that just show up and those who win," Dad reinforced.

"Yes, Dad… I know CRIMSON will do great." No pressure,
Josh, I thought, just quit goofing off and get it done. I would
have to give *her* a call tomorrow.

"Dad, you know in the last meeting we discussed recruiting more
teens into CRIMSON in order to get more lawyers, what about
other majors." I decided to try to change the subject.

"I guess you lost me," Dad replied.

"Well, not everyone wants to be a lawyer, but there are other
ways to influence public opinion. The news media for instance,
or even Hollywood," I replied as I thought of a pair of smiling
green eyes.

"I see what you mean; but that significantly broadens the scope of
our efforts, and I think to start with we should try to stay focused
on CRIMSON and future lawyers. Perhaps as we move forward,
we can start working with other ways to impact the gray flag. For
now, I think we have a good game plan and we should stick to it."
That was my dad; that was how he had been so successful; focus
on one important thing and make it happen. I had to admit, it
made sense; we were only a small group, and we had decided that
our primary target was the court system.

"I did get some information on Jeff Petersen, but I don't think he's really interested in joining CRIMSON," I offered changing the subject.

"Have you talked with him?" Dad looked up from his monitor.

"Not yet, I need to meet him. Ben knows him a little; Jeff's into hockey."

"Maybe you should check out the local ice rink," Dad gave me a wink.

"Good idea," I replied.

I couldn't help smiling as I thought: 'Josh Reinhart, your assignment, if you decide to accept it, is to seek out Jeff Petersen and recruit him for CRIMSON. As always, if you are caught or killed, the TPM will disavow any knowledge of your action,' as a famous spy theme song ran through my head.

Having finished my chemistry problems at about 3:30, I had the rest of the afternoon to become 'Josh Reinhart, agent for the TPM.' The hockey practices were from 5:00-6:00 p.m. so I thought I would get over to the rink and brush up a little on my skating. I had played hockey growing up, but decided basketball was my sport a couple of years ago.

The Ice Castle parking lot was filled with minivans, SUVs and kids everywhere. It would have been a tough DMV driving test. Try to park your car while dodging multiple minivans backing out, and *do* use every effort to avoid running over any of the Sasha Cohen wanna-be's and their over-indulgent moms.

I paid for an hour of ice time and laced up my skates. It had been at least two years since I had skated, but after a few minutes I was moving pretty well. The ice was fairly crowded and there were skaters of all sizes and skills: little tykes who were just beginning, girls skating in groups laughing and trying to help each other, college hockey veterans zooming around the rink. I was concentrating on getting comfortable on the ice, trying some moves, gaining confidence and speed, when I caught a flash of bright blue and blond out of the corner of my eye, but then it was lost at the other end of the rink. The rink started playing a popular new song, and everyone was moving in a large chaotic donut with only a few skaters in the donut hole, reserved for the elite, by some unwritten rule. A girl commanded the center, as she landed a double axel, her cobalt blue and black outfit shimmering and her blond hair tied in a tight bun with a blue ribbon. I stared as her routine culminated in a scratch spin that made her appear to be a blue and blond blur, finishing with arms held high and a broad smile as if for Olympic judges. Wow!, '10.0, 10.0, 10.0, 10.0, 10.0,' I thought to myself. As I skated closer, my eyes widened and my stomach tightened when I realized who had provided the mesmerizing show.

Rebakah! Just then she recognized me.

"Josh!" she stared back at me, and whether her cheeks were red from the skating or from embarrassment was hard to say.

"Hi...ah.. I didn't expect to see you here," was all I could think of as we skated to the boards and stopped.

"What brings you to the rink?" she asked, as her eyes narrowed. I could see she wasn't buying my honest statement about not expecting to see her.

"I actually wanted to talk to some of the hockey players, and I thought I would warm up a little before they take the ice," I replied.

"Oh," she said looking down. She seemed disappointed about something.

I couldn't tell what she was thinking at this point; Rebakah was so hard to read.

So perhaps more honesty and a compliment....

"I couldn't believe what you did out there. Are you thinking of the Olympics?" I gave her my most encouraging smile and I gestured toward the donut hole.

"No, I just really enjoy it. I feel like I'm flying out there." She gave me one her rare, honest laughs and her blue eyes sparkled.

We started skating around with the rest of the crowd. She was so different on the ice. So much more relaxed and comfortable; she asked if I was interested in hockey, and I said no, I just wanted to talk to Jeff Petersen. She knew him and said she would introduce us. She did appear to fly on the ice and she literally skated rings around me. We laughed and joked; best of all, there was no mention of debate. The public session ended and the Zamboni came out; and for once, the ice was the only thing that needed smoothing over.

"Jeff, this is Josh Reinhart, he just moved here recently. He's in CHESS."

"Hi, I'm Jeff, Jeff Petersen." He was in his hockey gear and pointed to a big 'PETERSEN' on the back of his jersey.

"I've got to start my private lesson now, so I'll see you later," Rebekah waved as she headed toward the gap in the boards. I watched her go, still thinking about her prowess on the ice, but then was brought back to reality by Jeff's question.

"Are you interested in joining the team?" He naturally thought I was there about hockey. I smiled.

"No, actually I was wondering if you would like to join CRIMSON."

"I don't know; isn't the debate season already half over?" he said.

"Yeah, but the good thing about that is that you can start out learning the ropes this year and by the time you get into competition next year you're already a veteran."

"I know John thought it was great, but I don't know if I have time with hockey and all," Jeff replied.

"Well, why don't you come to one of our meetings? We have a great group. We meet on Wednesday nights, so do you think you could you make it?"

"Let me check with Mom; things are getting pretty crazy with Christmas."

"Yeah, I know what you mean. Can I check with you after the first of the year? I think you'd really like it. We have a lot of fun," replying enthusiastically.

"Sounds good. I got to get ready for practice now; nice meeting you, Josh." Jeff headed off and I went to see if Rebekah was still on the ice, but I didn't see her. Stomach growling, I entered the snack bar; I spotted her toward the back unlacing her skates; her mom was with her.

"Hi, Mrs. Miller" I said.

"Hi, Josh. Rebekah said you were here."

"What did you want to talk to Jeff about?" Rebekah asked.

"I wanted to see if he was interested in joining CRIMSON," I replied. "He said he'd think about it."

"His brother John was a one of the best CRIMSON has ever had. He's in law school now," her mom stated.

"Speaking of that, is it possible I could come by this Saturday for a little more practice?" I looked at Mrs. Miller first, and then I saw Rebekah look at her mom in an odd way.

"Josh, we have to get ready for this trip to New York so I don't think we can this time. Why don't you call and do some over the phone this week."

"Alright, if that's OK with Rebekah?" I smiled and cocked my head hopefully.

"Sure, why don't you call me tomorrow night and we can work on your Neg," Rebekah replied with a smile and then shook her head once as she focused on her skates.

"Great! Nice seeing you, Mrs. Miller. I'll call you tomorrow, Rebekah. You had some amazing moves out there today." I smiled and walked out to my car, trying to sort out the afternoon. Rebekah had been a completely different girl on the ice, and we actually had fun for a change. I didn't quite understand that odd glance between Rebekah and her mom, but at least I had arranged for some more help on my Neg. And then there was the real reason I went to the rink in the first place: Jeff seemed somewhat interested, or at least he didn't say no immediately. If I could get him to come to one of the meetings perhaps he would join. First things first, CRIMSON had to score high in San Diego. And "the first born" had to at least break at the tournament.

It was the last CRIMSON meeting before Christmas, and then we would be going to San Diego. I arrived early and helped set up. Ben led us in a great prayer asking God to help us improve our skills and also to help each other tonight. My Aff was performing well, and I easily won my first debate; I had to admit a lot of credit had to go to Rebekah. Rebekah was matched with Elizabeth and then Dan Jr.; it was obvious, Mrs. Stanton felt that she belonged in the top tier at CRIMSON. My second round was against Elizabeth, and my Neg still needed work. But after our debate, she offered to show me some presentation skills that had worked well for her in competition. As I stood at the podium, she walked out in front and moved from side to side making her points as she smiled using hand movements and held eye contact with each of the imaginary judges. Then she asked me to try it. Since there were no judges, we had to act out in front of two empty chairs. I walked out in front of the podium and used my current closing arguments and voting issues speech while smiling and making eye contact with the empty chairs. It was somewhat comical, and as Elizabeth held my arm to show me how to make my point, we both laughed at our debate charade. Just then the door to the class room opened and Rebekah stepped in. I turned in time to see her eyes flash and her face color as she set a manila envelope on my seat, turn and exited the room without a word.

I thanked Elizabeth for her help and went out into the parking lot just in time to see the Miller's minivan taillights fading down the road. I got into my BMW and tossed the manila envelope onto the passenger seat and frowned at it; it felt like more than one or two pages. I turned on my favorite CD, opened the top and drove home. Is it possible that I could do well in San Diego with my Neg seeming so weak? There were six initial debate rounds before the break to the outer rounds and three were Negs.

That didn't bode well for my chances to break. I needed to pray for a miracle.

When I got home, I went straight to the kitchen, starving as usual. There was a nice plate of spicy chicken, courtesy of Marissa. As I ate the cold chicken leg, I decided I'd take a look in the envelope. I slid the papers out, and this time the near perfect script was in a light blue.

Hi Josh,

I felt I didn't really help your Neg much in the round we had at my house and our phone call just didn't get my points across very well. Here is your Neg, but I hope you don't mind that I've added a few things. You can call me if you have any questions,

Behind that page were five pages of what I would call 'The Josh Neg Remix.' It did have a vague resemblance to my Neg, but as I continued to read, I just shook my head. She had redone it completely, and it was the best Neg I had seen in CRIMSON. God does answer prayers, I thought, and mine were delivered in the form of an over-achieving tween genius. I decided to forget my version and begin to concentrate on her Neg remix. I would need to study it hard over the next couple of weeks to be ready for San Diego, but with it I felt like I had a chance.

I called Rebekah the next day, mostly to thank her for the new Neg. But her mom said she wasn't available, however, she would make sure Rebekah got my message.

It was almost time for the Christmas break and tonight was the last TPM meeting this year. We decided to take a couple of weeks off, mainly because some of the men would not be available, including Pastor Miller. It had only been about two months since the Vision and the seven of us felt we had made some good progress. But laying the framework for the mission was just the start, next year we needed to show some concrete progress in securing judgeships. The Moms would need to be told soon, and this would change the entire chemistry of the group, but perhaps for the good.

****

Sunday the Stanton's threw a Christmas party for the CRIMSON team and their families. It was a casual affair and people brought salads and desserts, while there was all manner of main dishes. It was a lot of fun seeing all the CRIMSON families together, and it was a big group, including nearly all the debaters and many of their siblings and parents were there. When I looked at it from this perspective, the task of halting the gray flag seemed a little less daunting. These would be some of the leaders of our country in a decade or two, and I was excited to be part of it. Robert was staying with the Stantons, but the rest of his family were on their way to New York. I asked him how things were, and he said that Rebekah had been more difficult than usual. I could imagine that Robert had to master the fine art of walking on eggshells ever since he got to stay here and she did not.

"Your sister takes this debate stuff pretty seriously, doesn't she?" I already knew the answer to that.

"'Seriously' is not the word for it, more like 'fanatic.' She's a perfectionist in everything she does, but when it comes to debate, she takes it to a whole 'nother level." Robert was in a good mood; essentially on his own for two weeks, even if he was staying with the Stantons.

"I think I know what you mean, but she's helped me a lot with my case," I replied. More like she rewrote my entire Aff and Neg, I thought.

"Oh, don't get me wrong. I love my sister more than anything in the world, but she can be a real pain sometimes. You're about the only one who has accepted her help. She tried to help some of the other debaters, but most of them wouldn't put up with her, no matter how smart she is," he chuckled. I guess I could understand how the others might not have taken the effort; Rebekah was very sensitive about being taken seriously and woe to anyone who treated her lightly.

"Just how smart is she?" I tried to sound nonchalant, but I was curious having only really seen her in action a few times. I figured Robert ought to know.

"With Rebekah, it's hard to say. You know she skipped into high school and she says she'll be in college at seventeen, perhaps earlier. There doesn't seem to be any subject she can't just study a little and then she knows it. It's pretty tough being her big brother, let me tell you. It's like driving while looking in your rearview mirror constantly, just knowing that Ferrari is back there waiting to blow by you at any moment." He shook his head, but you could see that big brother was very proud of his little sister, for all her difficult personality.

"Does she want to be a lawyer?" I asked.

"Ya *think*? She wants to be a Constitutional expert. Do you know she has it memorized?" he replied.

That's not all she has memorized, I thought with a smile. Robert was probably not paired up in debate with Rebekah much, so he wouldn't necessarily know all the cases or reference material she could cite verbatim.

I decided to change the subject, as it seemed Robert was getting bored discussing his genius sister. "I talked to Jeff Petersen the other day about joining CRIMSON, and he said he might come by on a Wednesday night to check things out. I've got to call him after Christmas."

"That's great. If he's half as good as his brother, he could be a real asset to the team." Robert was always supportive. I really appreciated his upbeat personality.

"How do you think we will do in San Diego?" I figured he would have a pretty good idea having been in CRIMSON for four years.

"You know, I think we have about six or seven strong debaters, including you, but you never know. It can be so subjective sometimes. You'll think you won hands down and you lose, and then you think 'I really blew it' and you win. The best you can do is be as prepared as possible and practice, just like Mrs. Stanton says. And at least she has us prepared this time, so we should do well."

We worked our way over to the spicy chicken wings and each took more than we should have.

"Do you know the Nichol's family?" I asked casually.

"Sure, Jennifer is a senior, she goes to cotillion; you must have seen her," he replied.

Oh, yeah, she's hard to miss, I thought.

"We had a couple of dances. What's her dad do, do you know?" I asked.

"I think he is in construction; it's a tough time for anyone in that business right now," Robert replied between wings.

"Yeah, Jennifer is trying to get a scholarship to UCSD; if not, she will have to go to a community college," I said, and then realized I just gave Robert a perfect opening.

"I thought you didn't know Jennifer?" he smiled and raised his eyebrows.

"Well, we did get a chance to talk while dancing." I decided not to mention the BMW music episode.

"Sorry I can't tell you more, but it sounds like you don't need any help," he chuckled.

I had to smile. Robert may not be a genius like his sister, but he was quick on the uptake.

"Hey, there's Jeff Petersen," I pointed with a chicken wing toward the foyer to a small group that had gathered around the new arrivals. Then I realized they were actually gathered around an older and taller version of Jeff. That must be John Petersen, I thought.

"Do you know Jeff?" I asked Robert as I started working my way over to the group.

"No, but everyone knows John. He was the star debater for CRIMSON for three years running. He's in law school now; Virginia, I think."

Having made it to the group, I asked Jeff, "Could you introduce me?"

"Oh, Hi… Josh, right? Sure. Josh, this is my brother John," Jeff said.

"Josh Reinhart, nice to meet you John." I gave him my best business handshake and smile, having to look up just a little as John must have been 6' 3" or so.

"Nice to meet you Josh…Reinhart; you're not the son of David Reinhart, president of Prescience?" John asked.

"The very same, would you like to meet him?" I replied.

"Very much. I'm a big fan of your dad's software; it's helped me tremendously at John Adams and Virginia Law," John replied, suddenly a lot more interested.

"I hope to get into John Adams myself. I hear you're interning for a senator."

I had to make the most of this meeting. I caught Dad's eye and motioned with my head to come over.

"Yes, Senator Harcourt, but we're in recess right now so I'm visiting," John replied.

Dad stepped up to the group, and I gave my best formal introductions.

"Dad, I would like to introduce you to John Petersen. John, this is my dad, David Reinhart."

"Very nice to meet you John; Virginia Law, right?" My dad had already made an impression on our first 'Point man.' "Tell me, what's it like working for Seth Harcourt?" He released his handshake.

"You know the Senator?" John replied, more impressed.

"Yes, the Senator and I had a number of interesting exchanges during the judicial hearings dealing with internet security while Prescience was under investigation by his sub-committee two years ago. You could say we are well acquainted," Dad smiled and was showing the power behind the persona. It was clear that John understood. That investigation had completely exonerated

Prescience, and Dad had wiped the Senate floor (figuratively, of course) with the good Senator from Michigan.

"I would like to continue this discussion, but it looks like I will have to wait my turn," Dad smiled as he motioned to others in the group, including Elizabeth, Leah, Alison and Mr. and Mrs. Stanton. Yes, John was quite the favorite. My dad stepped over to freshen up his Sprite.

But I was interested in making one more point with John. "Jeff is thinking of joining CRIMSON, even though it's mid-year," I interjected.

"Is that right?" He looked at his younger brother. "Of course it's up to you, but I think you'd be making a mistake not being part of CRIMSON. Mrs. Stanton's a great coach and this year's team seems pretty strong."

"That's just it, I would be starting in the middle of the year, and hockey takes up a lot of my time." Jeff was obviously a little nervous about discussing this right now. He gave me a wary glance before looking back at his brother.

"Like I said, it's strictly up to you," John said. But I could see Jeff was going to get a cross examination when they were alone. He was all but in I figured; mission accomplished.

Now if Dad could get better acquainted with John, we could be two for two tonight. I smiled to myself; this wasn't as difficult as I thought.

"Jeff, let me introduce you to my good friend, Robert Miller," I said, releasing some of the pressure off Jeff, and also giving him another contact in CRIMSON.

"Jeff Petersen. Nice to meet you. You must be Rebekah's brother." Jeff shook Robert's hand, as John was already in conversation with the Stantons.

"You know Rebekah?" Robert inquired.

"Yeah, from the rink, everyone at the Ice Castle knows who Rebekah Miller is," Jeff answered and took a sip of his soda.

Everyone knew Rebekah? I had to admit I was surprised at that statement. There were so many mysteries about her, and I had only discovered a few.

The party had been a big success; as the evening progressed Leah played a few of her concert pieces on violin. Then we all sang carols as Steve accompanied us on the Stanton's baby grand. Finally Ben played some of the soundtrack from Narnia. I had to say, I was glad no one asked me to play as I was a little intimidated by the musicianship on display. I did wonder, though, if the best pianist in CRIMSON was on her way to New York.

Chapter Eight

The Competition

"On every question of construction carry ourselves back to the time when the Constitution was adopted, recollect the spirit manifested in the debates and instead of trying what meaning may be squeezed out of the text or invented against it, conform to the probable one in which it was passed."

– Thomas Jefferson

The sun was just up on the first day of the San Diego tournament, and I had been laying there for a half an hour. I was thinking, this is the first real test of the "first born" since the Vision. Had I worked hard enough? Would the CRIMSON team do well? Will I satisfy my dad… and myself?

Suddenly, the "Get Smart" ring tone on my cell phone went off. "Hullo, …could you please repeat that?" There was a lot of noise on the other end.

"….. Rebekah?!" I suddenly became a lot more awake as I strained to hear the distraught voice on the other end of the line.

"Josh, we're stuck at the airport!" I could hear her voice crack as she tried to keep her composure.

"We've been here since *yesterday* and we're delayed until late today!" Rebekah's voice pitched higher than normal and finally broke as she sobbed out the last few words.

"...I'll miss... the....the tournament," I could barely make her out over the terminal noise.

"Rebekah, please... calm down. I can barely understand you." My bedside manner was not very well developed, but I had to at least get her to speak clearly.

She stopped sobbing for the moment, but now her voice had a desperate edge on it.

"I'm going to *miss* it, Josh. I'm going to miss it and no one can do *anything* about it! I *hate* this stupid trip!" The anger and despair were evident over the noise this time. I could imagine everyone diving for cover behind airline counters as the blue lasers blasted gaping holes through everything in sight; no airport security was equipped to handle an enraged Rebekah.

"Wait... just let me think; you're in the New York airport, right?" I had the threads of an idea...

"Yes, *Kennedy* Airport..." she finally exhaled.

"What time is it there?" I asked.

"About 4:30 in the morning. We've been up *all night*." At least now she sounded like she wasn't going 'psycho.'

"OK... Just hold on, I have an idea, this might take a minute." I ran up to my parent's room.

"Dad, Dad... are you up?" I knocked and whispered through the crack in the door.

"I am now. Come in... What's wrong?" Dad replied. I guess I must have looked more concerned than I thought, and I still had my cell in my hand.

"Rebekah Miller is stuck in New York; she'll miss the first day of competition. It means she has no chance to break!" I guess I sounded a little upset, as Dad held up his hands.

"I'm sorry Josh, but what can I do?"

The threads were starting to weave a fabric of possibilities in my mind.

"Doesn't Prescience have a jet in Maryland?" I asked, calming down a little so I could make my case, point by point.

"Yesss," he said slowly. "It's for our Washington and New York lawyers and lobbyists." He nodded to the phone in my hand, "Who's on the phone?... Rebekah?"

I nodded and then got my next two points out.

"What if the Millers could get to Maryland, could they use the Jet and get here in time?"

"Josh, tell Rebekah you'll call her back." My dad was out of bed now and putting on his robe.

"Rebekah, OK, I'm working on something... I don't know, but I will call you back in a few minutes.... This is your mom's cell. Right?..." I hung up the phone.

"Josh, the jet is for corporate use and ..." he stopped and looked at me. "Your timing is good, Son. I'm appearing in front of a technology subcommittee in D.C. next week...." he trailed off and thought for a moment.

"This is about CRIMSON and the Vision isn't it?" he said. As I nodded, he asked, "How good is Rebekah?"

"Rebekah is our best debater, by far. And she helps others on the team, too. CRIMSON will not be the same without her." That was no lie; she was better than everyone else, I knew that. The fact that 'the others' was currently just me still counted, and CRIMSON would certainly be different without her.

"OK, hang on a minute while I make a call," he was already heading toward his office as I followed, my pulse now racing.

"Hank, this is David. Yeah, sorry for the wake up call and please give my apologies to Brenda. Can you have Pi-squared ready to fly to San Diego this morning?".... "That's correct, as soon as you can... how long will...An hour and a half... How long is the flight time?...4 hours and 50 minutes ...Clear skies, OK,... Yes, get her ready ASAP; I'll call you back in a couple of minutes... Thanks Hank." Dad hung up the phone.

"Call Rebekah back and let me talk to Pastor Miller," Dad said as he scribbled a few notes on a pad.

"Rebekah, it's Josh, could you put your father on please?.. Yes, I will,... My dad wants to talk to him." Rebekah sounded exhausted but she was calmer now. I handed the phone to Dad.

"John, this is David Reinhart. What a pain for you and Barbara... and Rebekah.... You say your flights delayed due to fog, but can you get a train to Baltimore?".... "John, I think I can get Rebekah to the San Diego Tournament if you can get to Baltimore by 8:00?...Yes,...I'll hold."

"Josh, when do the first debates start?" Dad asked.

I had to run back to my room and get the San Diego schedule.

"She'll miss the first two rounds at 9:15 and 11:00 a.m., but the third round isn't until after lunch, it starts at 1:30," I reported.

"It's OK to miss the two rounds?" my dad was doubtful.

I nodded, "She'll forfeit them, but if she can win the rest she can break into the outer rounds." If anyone could do it, Rebekah could. No one was more obsessed. I shot a little prayer skyward, "Lord, please help her."

"Hi John, ...right, Baltimore Amtrak station: arrive at 8:30. That's cutting it close but I think you can still make it. I'll have a driver meet you there. Look for a man holding a sign that says 'John Miller' and he'll take you to the Pi-squared, it's Prescience's corporate jet. That should get you into San Diego at about noon. I'll have my limo service pick you up, so you should get to the tournament before 1:00," Dad ticked off the instructions.

"No, ..John, I want to do this. It's important for CRIMSON and the Vision; besides, I need the jet out here next week anyway....Don't worry about that. You better get moving if you're going to make that train. God bless you too, John and yes, we will be praying for you." He hung up the phone.

"That was awesome, Dad!" I was astonished at how fast it was accomplished.

He smiled broadly "Josh, I need to make a few more arrangements, but this is what we are talking about when a Reinhart says *'commitment'* – doing what it takes."

I sat and watched as he made the limo arrangements for the Millers. He was just my dad most of the time, but I was starting to see that he had power and resources far beyond most people.

Finally, he made one more call. "Hank, this is David again...You're going to be taking on three passengers: Pastor and Mrs. John Miller and their daughter Rebekah. Yes, Baltimore to San Diego. ... And please give them the VIP treatment. They have been stuck in Kennedy Airport since yesterday, and finally had to take a train to Baltimore to meet you. Yes, expect Raymond to meet them in San Diego. ...Sure, go ahead and get her prepped for the flight back to D.C. on Monday. .. Yes,... and Hank, thanks for your extra effort on this... and fly safe."

It was 7:45 a.m., and I had to get ready myself, so I jumped into the shower, adrenaline pumping.

"Josh, call for you. It's Rebekah Miller," Mom yelled through the bathroom door.

"Tell her I'll call her back," I yelled back.

But with all the excitement and getting ready, it slipped my mind, until I saw Robert at the tournament. He had a garment bag over his shoulder and a small case in his other hand.

"Man, how lucky can she get, private jet, limo ride, *everything*." He was pretty envious, and a little bummed out for missing all the VIP treatment. I couldn't feel very sorry for him, given that he had stayed with the Stanton's for the last two weeks, which was like staying at a resort, I was sure he got the VIP treatment there, too.

"Would you do me a big favor and please don't say anything about the jet. My dad had to pull some strings to make it happen and he wants it kept quiet, OK?" He could see I was serious and assured me he would.

"Only, next time it's my turn to ride in the jet," he grinned.

My first two rounds went very well; my new Neg arguments were strong, and I found plenty of weaknesses in my opponents' cases. I went to lunch feeling I had won easily. Mrs. Stanton caught me in the lunch room.

"Hi Josh. How'd your rounds go?"

"I think they went pretty well; I guess we'll see." I didn't want to sound as confident as I was, just in case the community judges didn't see the rounds the same as I did. Community judges, recruited from the surrounding area, were often inexperienced at judging debate, but they were essential. Without them it was impossible to fill the 1500 judge slots at a tournament. And as Mrs. Stanton often said, "It's *your* job to convince the judge."

"Have you seen Rebekah? I think she 'no-showed' the first two rounds..., that's just not like her." Mrs. Stanton looked concerned.

You got that right, I thought. Can you say "obsessed?"

"No, I haven't. Have you checked with Robert?" It was only 12:30 and all would become apparent soon, I hoped. The plan just *had* to work, and then it was up to the 4'10" law library to do the rest.

A crowd of debaters was forming as we hung around the plaza between the two buildings being used for the competition, waiting for the pairings for the third round to be posted.

Rebekah was matched up against Aaron Baker. He was well known to CRIMSON as a tough competitor; he almost always broke and even won one tournament last year. I had seen him earlier working at his laptop, sitting on the wall by the commons. I hoped Mrs. Stanton wasn't too put out by Rebekah's two no-shows, as she must know about the delayed flight by now.

Just then a long black Lincoln limousine pulled into the campus parking lot and up to the plaza curb. Everyone just stopped and stared including me, as Robert strolled as casually as he could toward the passenger door. The driver came out preparing to assist the occupant; I recognized him as my dad's driver, Raymond, dressed impeccably as usual in a black tuxedo. Rebekah, dressed in jeans and a blue blouse hesitantly stepped out of the elegant ride as Raymond held open the door. She blushed as a few 'Oh, My *Gosh!*' and ''Bekah!'s were heard from the crowd. Robert had reached her, shielding her using the garment bag as they walked into the building heading toward the ladies bathroom.

I couldn't help but chuckle at my private knowledge, as everyone stared first at her and then back at the limo. But Raymond was already pulling away from the curb, and while there was no sign of the Millers, I knew they must be behind the privacy glass. Surprised conversations broke out all over the plaza and for a short time ''Bekah', Debate Diva, had eclipsed the drama of the competition.

It was 1:30 p.m., time for round three. I drew a girl who was not in the CRIMSON database but she was not well prepared and my Aff contentions were hardly refuted. Finally, the round was over and I was hoping I had gone at least two for three.
As I was walking out of the classroom into the commons, Mom and Sarah were waiting.
"Did you see 'Bekah's limo?' Sarah gushed, "That was *wicked* awesome!"
Mom gave her a sideways glare that Sarah ignored, being in full animation mode by then. "She looked so *glam* with the driver holding the door and the windows all black. She's *so* lucky."
"How did your round go?" Mom asked as she handed me a snack and some Gatorade.
"I'm pretty sure I won; so I think I'm at least two for three, but I want to work on my Neg before the next round." This was partly true, but I also didn't need to get drawn into a discussion about 'Bekah's limo.' "I'm going to find the guys."
"OK dear. You sure look sharp in that suit." She gave me a proud smile and watched me walk into the grassy area covered with debaters. Moms always took every opportunity to compliment their sons when we were in suits; it must be a side-effect of the Cotillion gene.
I spied Ben and Steve and walked over as the discussion was in full swing, "... and then I got killed in my last round," Steve grimaced. "That Perez girl is *dangerous*. She's even better than last year and is running a very clever Neg, so watch out if you go up against her." Ben and I looked at Steve's flow, and I asked Ben,
"How'd *you* do?"

"OK, I think, it's hard to tell, first time judge, so you never know," he replied.

"I'm hoping the same, but..., you never know," I said in sympathy. But remembering what Mrs. Stanton always said, 'You have to be able to persuade the man in the street.'

Some of the other members of CRIMSON were gathering, including Robert.

"Hey everyone, can we pray for our results and the upcoming round's efforts?" he suggested. We all fell silent as Robert led us in prayer to The Almighty, who deserved all the glory. "Amen," I said, thinking of all the miracles God had performed today already.

After the prayer, I asked Robert where his sister was.

"I haven't seen her since she showed up in the limo." He still seemed a little jealous and asked Alison, "Have you seen 'Bekah?'"

"Not for a while. I saw her walk across the grass after the third round with her rolling case and notebook, but she didn't look up when I called to her. I guess she was in a hurry," Alison replied.

No telling with her, I thought.

The posts went up for round four pairings. Sometimes you could get a sense of how you were doing at the tournament depending on the power matching criteria for the preliminary rounds and the pairings. In CRIMSON's region, the debate director chose to power match high-high toward the end of the prelims and low-high for the out rounds, so after this fourth preliminary round the students with more wins start to be paired against each other.

Occasionally, there were 'byes' because of an odd number of students, or a student had to drop out for some reason. This was the case with me, as I received a bye in the fourth round: an automatic win. 'All Right!' I thought, I might have three wins already, raising my hopes to break in the tournament.

As I stood in the crowd, looking over the heads of smaller competitors, the pairings also provided one very interesting match-up. Cassandra Perez and Rebekah Miller.

"Whoa, this ought to be good!" I chuckled to myself. I've got to see this. I had heard about Cassandra Perez. According to the guys, Cassandra was poised, talented and very competitive. A senior now, she had taken many rounds from CRIMSON over the last four years; went to nationals the last two.

But I bet she had never faced anyone like Rebekah, even if she was just thirteen.

Yeah, this should be quite a show. I smiled to myself.

I went over to the classroom early and sat in the back. A community judge was seated in the first row, preparing his debate flow, speech points sheet and ballot with uncertainty. He was middle aged with glasses and a receding hairline, wearing non-descript clothes and shoes. 'You never know' I thought, shaking my head a little.

Just then, Miss Perez swept into the room, there was no question it was her. The first thing that struck me was her large hazel green eyes set perfectly in her striking Latin features. Dressed in a deep red suit and gold blouse, she was tall, slim and well,.. stunning. To call Cassandra poised was a serious misrepresentation; she had a catlike grace to her movements that made it hard not to stare. I bet the girls must dread getting matched with her. Following her into the room, a younger brother rolled in her debate gear. One of her *many* minions, I imagined with a smile.

Everyone, including the judge watched Cassandra glide from the door to the podium, where she turned, gave a knockout smile to the judge and sat down all in one fluid motion. The performance was punctuated with ankles encased in dark nylons crossed demurely over black patent high heels. From where I sat in the back watching Cassandra and then the judge, this contest was over before Rebekah even showed up.

"Wow!" I whispered to myself.

At about two minutes till 4:00 p.m. Rebekah sped into the room drawing her rolling case behind her. Cassandra stood up to greet her and shake hands emphasizing the difference in size and age. As Rebekah turned and saw me, there was just a hint of a frown, then she gave a nice smile and swept everyone with those bright blue eyes as she walked forward until she stood in front of me.

"Could I please speak with you a moment?" she almost whispered and headed outside.

'Finally, a nice word about my part in the private jet and 'Bekah's Limo' episode,' I thought as I followed her outside.

"Josh, would you please not watch this debate?" she said with a quiet, but deadly serious tone, and no hint of a smile.

"Uh... Sure... If that's what you want?" I replied to the unexpected request. I had again been caught off guard, as this was not quite the 'nice thank you' I had expected. I should be getting used to it; mental note to self: With Rebekah, always expect the unexpected.

"Thanks," she said quietly as she turned back into the room. As the door closed, I heard Cassandra begin, her voice conversational, yet in control,

"...is the timer ready, is the judge ready; my opponent? Then let's begin."

I walked off to the refreshment area. I was trying to decipher what had just happened, but it sure wasn't obvious to me. One thing that was obvious, Ben and Robert had been holding back with respect to Cassandra. I shook my head trying to dislodge the image of her catlike entrance just now, but it seemed to be stuck on replay.

As I sat eating an apple and some chips, I was glad the first day was almost over.

It seemed like a few days ago that Rebekah's cry had broken into my consciousness, but it had only been this morning. I tried to sort out the day, filled with surprises.

I had (along with Dad's help) come up with a plan to get Rebekah to the tournament against all odds. But now the odds were stacked even more against her. After seeing Cassandra Perez, I felt really sorry for Rebekah, I was afraid my great idea and everyone's effort were for nothing. No wonder she was so serious just now. The math was undeniable, if she loses just one round she would not break, and after seeing Cassandra and the judge, Rebekah was likely to lose this one. I said a little prayer that the judge would score on the merit of the debaters and not the obvious mismatch in appearance. "Let him judge fairly and wisely, in Jesus' name, Amen," I whispered.

It was a beautiful crisp evening in San Diego and the moon was almost full. The day's four rounds were over and I saw Pastor and Mrs. Miller with Robert from across the grass park, but no Rebekah. Perhaps she knows she won't break and just doesn't want to face anyone.

Everyone was gathering to see the results from the first day. I passed by the door to the Tab (tabulation) room, imagining it looking like the Houston space center before a Shuttle launch. Everyone feverishly working at their laptops. A handmade sign was short and to the point: TAB ROOM - GO AWAY.

The Millers came up from behind me in the crush of the crowd waiting for results, and Pastor Miller gave me a strong hand shake and Mrs. Miller whispered thanks for getting Rebekah here today as she gave me a quick hug.

It must have been beyond tense at the airport when Rebekah realized she was not going to make it to the tournament. I asked Mrs. Miller where Rebekah was and she explained that Rebekah was working on her case in a dorm room. They had arranged to use the room of a daughter of one of the HGCF congregation so Rebekah could have a quiet place to rest and prepare between rounds. I guess this was news to Robert by the look he gave his mom.

I spotted Ben and Steve and waved at them to make their way over to us. Too late. The tab room door opened, and the crowd tightened up as the day's results were posted. Being tall has its advantages. I was able to see the scores of the first page of results, Elizabeth had gone 4-0!, and Ben, Robert, Dan Jr. and I had gone 3-1. "Yesss!" I said as I turned to give Robert a high five.

CRIMSON was starting to shine, I thought. Looking closer, Cassandra Perez had also gone 3-1 and so had Aaron Baker. As the next page was posted, there was a lot of 2-2s, there was Steve and Alison, and right at the bottom of the page was the answered prayer, **Rebekah Miller 2-2**. She had done it! Rebekah had taken Cassandra! I turned to see that Robert was already letting his parents know.

Where was Rebekah? Didn't she want to know? This morning she had been without hope, fogged in at Kennedy Airport, and tonight she could still break in the tournament, having bested Cassandra and Aaron.

Tomorrow will tell, but it looked very promising. Elizabeth had no doubt made it to the out rounds, and all I had to do was win one of the next two rounds to break. This was true of a lot of the CRIMSON team, and even the 2-2s had a chance, including one small blond law library recluse.

It was late, almost 10:30 p.m. when I caught a ride back to Santa Sonoma with Ben. Mrs. Stanton couldn't have been more proud. "Three – One, you both were awesome today!" she exclaimed as Mr. Stanton chuckled, "I'm going to have to make some room for you two in my firm."

"There's still tomorrow, Dad," Ben remarked.

"Yeah, and 'you never know,'" I replied as we both smiled at each other.

"And Rebekah beat Cassandra Perez; can you believe it, Mom?" Ben was pumped, too.

"Don't *ever* count Rebekah Miller out.   She has more determination than anyone I've seen since I have been coaching," Mrs. Stanton replied.

"More like "most obsessed person" you have ever seen…" Ben chuckled good-naturedly.

As the big silver BMW rolled out of the parking lot, I glimpsed the Millers alone in the plaza, looking at the results, dimly lit by the moon and a few lights. And there was Rebekah, in the middle of the little group hug, or more likely a family prayer.

"It's past 11:00 Josh, time to get some sleep," Mom called through the door.

"All Right." It was hard coming down from the adrenaline rush of the first day at San Diego. But she was right; I had to get some rest before tomorrow. All I needed was one more win. I thought again of that little huddle in the plaza, heads bowed, definitely a prayer. Not a bad idea…

"Heavenly Father, Praises to You for making all the miracles happen today; thank You for Mom and Dad and Sarah. Thank

You for the Millers, the Stantons and the McClarens. All the CHESS families and for CRIMSON. Please bless them. Guide my path, Lord, and give me a blessed day tomorrow, giving all the Glory to You, in Jesus' name, Amen," I whispered.

As I fell off to sleep, I was left with an intriguing image in my mind – Cassandra and Rebekah stood on either side of the podium. One graceful, warm and stunning; the other intense, crystalline, and brilliant.

The schedule for the second day of the tournament was really hectic with two more prelim rounds, then the L-D break announcements, then the start of the semifinal out rounds that consisted of three play-off rounds. This would leave three more play-off and final rounds and the awards ceremony for the third day.

On my way back to the plaza, I felt pretty good about my two rounds, but it was difficult to tell. I was now being power matched, and the competition was much tougher. One out of two was all I needed to break as I had been told that almost always any 4-2 would break into the outer rounds.

As I crossed the grass, thinking about a snack and the break announcement, I was approaching a group of debaters sitting on a number of blankets spread out under a large tree. Their rolling cases and other debate gear scattered around. They were from a competing club, all in the usual black suits except one, in elegant maroon, her dark hair in waves flowing down her back. As I passed by I recognized John Hall, as I had just debated him this morning.

"Josh Reinhart, right? Meet some of our team." He waved me over and stood up.

"Hi,.. John, isn't it? Great round this morning," I replied as we shook hands.

"Thanks, Josh. This is James, Karl, Jordan, Brittany, Alan and Cassandra; why don't you join us?" he called out their names. I may have made eye contact with everyone, but I only remembered Cassandra's.

"Hi, I'm Josh... What's your club's name?" I asked as I squatted down between Alan and Cassandra.

"We're REASON," Cassandra said in a musical voice. "And you're from CRIMSON."

"That's right. How'd you know?" She had amazing hazel eyes that in the sunlight looked almost light green with flecks of gold, but in the shadows became more hazel; and her hair was a gloss black frame of waves and curls. I tried to be casual.

"I make a point of knowing all my opponents, but you're new, as well as the little girl I debated yesterday." She gave me that knockout smile.

"Rebekah," I informed her; she seemed to dismiss it as if she felt she had won their round. Cassandra had reason to be confident, she had the reputation and the skills.

"Did you start debating this year?" she asked. *Ouch!* Did I look like a newbie?

"No, I debated back in Florida. We just moved out here this year. I'm in CHESS."

"What do you think of the debates out here on the West Coast?" Alan asked. He was stocky with short hair; maybe he played football or soccer.

"The style is a little different, more memorization and the cross-ex is harsh." I looked back at Cassandra for a reaction, and because I found it hard not to, I had to admit. But hey, didn't Mrs. Stanton want us to be friendly to the other debaters?

"The *suth'n* style must employ *bettah mannahs* and chivalry, what do you think, gentlemen?" Cassandra smiled as she drawled for affect. The REASON team chuckled at this and added a few remarks, I started to blush, but 'chilled.' I felt I had to come back with something to defend my honor as well as CRIMSON's. So I stood up and decided to have the last word.

"I've always felt that debates can be won while still being chivalrous. What's the point of debating a lovely opponent if you can't dance with her afterwards?" Giving her my best grin, and a gallant bow, "Nice meeting you all," I said as I swept my imaginary Musketeer hat over them.

I turned and walked off toward the snack area. Exhaling, I smiled to myself. Well Josh, you made an impression, perhaps good, perhaps bad, but you made one. She was one lovely opponent, that's for sure. Were those golden green eyes watching me walk away? I'll never know.

By the time I got to the snack area, my stomach was wrestling with my emotions for attention. I got some Gatorade and a few granola bars. Alison, Steve and Ben were there, and the plaza was filling up in anticipation of the break announcements. Pretty soon the entire CRIMSON team was there, with the exception of the elusive Miss Miller. Was she too shy? I couldn't imagine what was with her. Mom, as well as Sarah and some other CRIMSON parents and siblings, created a casual double circle around the team, hands on our shoulders; and Robert asked for us to pray. "Father in Heaven, we know You are in control with plans for our lives, so whatever the outcome of these debates, win or lose, we will bless Your Holy Name. We thank You for Your Grace and Love, in Jesus' name, Amen." That was for sure, plans for my life and the lives of the CRIMSON families, I thought, as I felt Mom's hand upon my shoulder.

The tournament director stood up on the platform with a microphone,

"The time you all have been waiting for is just about here. As soon as I get the sheets from the tab room we will announce those who have made it into the out rounds. As always please use the forensic, or one clap cheer for each name or we will be here all afternoon." The tab room director stepped up to the podium and handed the director a stack of papers, to the cheer of the crowd.

He held them up and there was some shushing, but then the crowd fell silent.

"Advancing to the out rounds for Lincoln Douglas debate at the San Diego Tournament are:"

And the list began,

"Tom Alvarez – ANTHEM, … Aaron Baker – QUADRANT, … John Hall – REASON, … Michael Johnson – RESOLUTE,…

Rebekah Miller – CRIMSON, ..." A loud clap and a cheer went up loud enough for the director to give a scowl our way. Rebekah had 'broke!' For some reason I was more excited for her than the possibility of my own success. Maybe because I knew how much it meant to her. I took a look around, no Rebekah.

"Robert Miller – CRIMSON, …" Yes! I thought.

"Cassandra Perez – REASON,…" No surprise there.

"Josh Reinhart – CRIMSON,…" Oh Yeah! I had reached my first goal. It was a small goal, but a step in the CRIMSON plan.

"Daniel Simmons – CRIMSON,…

Elizabeth Simmons – CRIMSON,…

Ben Stanton – CRIMSON,…"

It was high fives and hugs all around the CRIMSON circle, as the others were read. We knew we had a good chance to place high in this tournament. CRIMSON was *back!*

I had my own reasons for wanting the CRIMSON team to do well, and while I couldn't share it with them, I felt the plan was starting to develop momentum.

The large sanctuary of a nearby church was filled to capacity with all the debaters and their families awaiting the final awards ceremony. The debate director waved the crowd down into their seats.

"Before I announce the four finalists in this week's tournament, you all should know that this is the largest we've ever had, and the level of competition has been equal to anything I've seen at state or nationals. So just breaking into the outer rounds should be considered a great achievement. In fact, we are awarding a spot to compete at the California state championships for all those who did break."

The crowd exploded into sustained cheer and applause. I was going to state, and more importantly, so were many of the CRIMSON team.

"I have been holding back the Championship trophies for the best debater and also for the team championship until now. So gentlemen...."

Two men brought up the trophies, as the crowd stirred and more than a few "Oh My Gosh" was heard. They were both huge, each one over three feet tall.

"Now it's late, and we have just a couple more things to do tonight," he smiled as the crowd hushed.

"The four finalists in the San Diego Lincoln Douglas Debate Tournament are:

Aaron Baker – QUADRANT,

Cassandra Perez – REASON,

Elizabeth Simmons – CRIMSON, and …

Rebekah Miller – CRIMSON.

Each section of the sanctuary cheered for their champion as the names were read, and Rebekah was no exception with lots of "'Bekah!"'s added.

As Rebekah walked up onto the stage, along with the other three finalists, it was clear what a distinct disadvantage she had overcome. She really looked like a girl next to Aaron, Cassandra and Elizabeth. But she was not being judged now.

Aaron took fourth place and walked over to receive his trophy and a great round of applause.

"Cassandra Perez, third place" A rousing cheer and applause rang out from the REASON section of the sanctuary. As she glided off stage she gave a glorious smile and waved to the crowd. Could she look any better? I thought.

An all CRIMSON final! This was about as good as it gets. Glory to You, Lord, I shot a little prayer up to heaven. I saw Robert and the Millers and the Simmons' down in front to the left of the stage. They must all be holding their breath like I was.

"In case the first place winner cannot fulfill her obligation to represent this tournament at the nationals, the runner up will go in her place," the director said and then paused, prolonging the tension.

"Second place ... Elizabeth Simmons." Rebekah had prevailed! Rebekah's hands went to her face and for once she was speechless. Elizabeth gave her a long hug and when they separated both were in tears.

"First place and Champion of the San Diego Lincoln Douglas Debate Tournament, Rebekah Miller."

The crowd cheered wildly and gave a standing ovation as Rebekah, straight backed and head high, walked across the stage to accept the trophy that seemed nearly as tall as she was. "'Bekah!" echoed through the building as she held the trophy with both hands and turned to face the crowd. Blushing and smiling, with a few tears glistening from those sparkling blue eyes.

She had done it! She had persevered and with a great deal of help from The Lord, took first place and was headed for nationals. As she came off stage, she huddled with her family for a moment of prayer, and then Pastor Miller came to my row and motioned to me. I came out to the isle; he gave me a great hug and whispered, "Josh, thank you for all you've done ... and for caring about Rebekah."

"Can I ask you all to take your seats and settle down; there's one more small item to attend to. The overall Team Champion." The tournament director motioned for a few moments to get everyone's attention.

"When I call out the Team, will the team leaders please come up to accept the trophy?"

"The overall Team Trophy for the San Diego Lincoln Douglas Debate Tournament goes to ..... CRIMSON!"

The whole crowd jumped to their feet again and cheered. I made my way up to the stage along with Robert, Ben and Dan Jr. We each held a corner of the Trophy over our heads as the applause rolled over us. "God is Awesome!" Robert exclaimed, as we smiled for pictures. I motioned to Rebekah, who was still down at the left of the stage to come up and join us. She shook her head 'no', but then we all waved for her to come on stage. She blushed bright red as she stepped back on stage carrying the other huge trophy. She stood in front of us as we were flooded in camera flashes. God had been faithful to us and His plan; I was sure more than ever that CRIMSON was the key.

Finally, the crowd started to file out and we all went to get the manila envelopes that contained the ballots and comments. These would tell the story behind the story. How well we argued each round and influenced the judges. Where we excelled and where we needed work. In many ways the contents of the envelopes were much more valuable than the trophies. I couldn't wait to see the ballot from the Cassandra/Rebekah round.

The word went out that, even though it was late, the McClaren's had invited the CRIMSON team back to their house for a celebration party. Pizza and hot wings were on their way. As I drove through the neighborhood, there was no mistaking the McClaren's house, even if I had not known. Still lit up for Christmas, there were a crush of minivans parked on the street and people were filing in. Even after midnight on a tremendously emotional and exhausting day, I don't know why I questioned the nearly unanimous attendance. These were the hard-core CRIMSON. All the members who broke, and many that did not were up for it. As we walked into the family room, the party was in full swing. Spread out over the kitchen island, the pizza and wings were already well on their way to extinction. Right in the middle of the dining room table the Team Trophy was gleaming under the chandelier, being inspected by Ben, Dan Jr. and Alison. I wondered whether the owner of its twin would show. Surely, even the shy recluse would come to share the great victory with the rest of CRIMSON.

She can't miss *this*, I thought almost aloud. She had secured her hard won reward, a first at San Diego and a spot at nationals. She was the star, at least for now.

The doorbell rang and in stepped Robert and behind him, almost hidden by the huge trophy, was Rebekah, blushing and smiling as she was mobbed by the team. I held back a little to appreciate the scene. The petite girl with long blond hair and laser blue eyes had, against all odds, won the tournament. I smiled as I felt an odd pride; I suspected it was knowing I was slightly responsible for the victory. "'Bekah", "'Bekah", "'Bekah" was the chant as she blushed completely. It felt unusually warm in the house.

The McClaren's very large backyard was done in tropical landscaping including a natural rock pool and grotto. I walked on a gravel path that wandered through the empty side yard covered with dimly lit palms and large ferns. It was a cool clear evening and I was enjoying the quiet and the stars, trying to dissipate some of the stress of the past three days. The "first born" had done well. Certainly CRIMSON had taken the competition by storm, capturing first, second, and fifth place, not to mention the overall team trophy. I had added to that by scoring a very respectable sixth. Everyone had worked hard and God had blessed us as well; surely the victory was ultimately His, I thought, Thank you, Lord!

I heard a crunching sound and turned to face the girl who had been my nemesis, tutor, answered prayer to my part of the secret mission, and hopefully, my friend. "Rebekah." I smiled.

"Hi," she almost whispered, looking up and then back down at her hands.

"I wanted to talk to you alone," she looked back up, this time with something unsettled behind her clear blue eyes, evident even in the dim lighting.

"Josh, I owe you so much…the private jet, the limo, all you did. The nationals, I can't tell you how I really feel,… it's… it's like a dream. I hope you understand why I couldn't thank you 'til now. … I just couldn't stand the … the distraction."

"It's all right, you deserved it. *All* of it." I could see she was having a hard time with this. The last thing I wanted her to feel was guilt.

"No, .. No, I didn't. I was hurt and upset and then we had to go to New York and you shouldn't have been the focus of my..." her voice broke off but her lasers had locked on and would not release.

I could see I needed to supply some reassurance.

"Rebekah, don't you realize? You're important to... it's important for me to help you. It's more than that, but I just can't tell you." I had already said too much. I was tired; I didn't want to cause her to be more upset. I wished she would end this. I had gotten my "thank you" and now much more than I had expected (as usual).

Although they never released me, her eyes did soften a little, and she still had more to say.

"I'm sorry I have been so ...difficult....and you've been.... really great... I can't expect you to always..." she trailed off, her blue eyes glisten just before she looked down.

I heard the ground crunch and looked up as Rebekah turned.

"There you are! They want some pictures with the trophies. Your fans await and the Moms must document," Robert said lightly. "You too, Josh."

The private moment had vaporized. I had mixed feelings as I watched her long blond hair sway as she followed her brother toward the back door.

In a way, it had been the first time Rebekah and I had actually been alone and able to talk seriously. And yet, both of us had held something back; I couldn't possibly tell her about the Vision, and she was being cautious for some inexplicable reason, mysterious as usual. While it was important to me that we be good friends, I will never understand her, I thought, perhaps that was the way it was with genius, or maybe just the way it was with women. I promised myself I would replay our conversation and try to make sense of it some time when my mind was clearer. My stomach growled, and I wondered if there was any chance a pizza slice had survived till now as I headed back into the house.

Chapter Nine

Back on Track

"For no people will tamely surrender their Liberties, nor can any be easily subdued, when knowledge is diffused and Virtue is preserved. On the contrary, when People are universally ignorant, and debauched in their manners, they will sink under their own weight without the aid of Foreign Invaders." – Samuel Adams

It was Tuesday afternoon and time for a man and his car to bond. A beautiful, sunny winter day with some wispy clouds, I needed to clear my head and get out on the road. There was so much to consider, my work on the CRIMSON plan, Rebekah's win, the Moms and the Vision,…and Cassandra… Yes, there was plenty to dwell on, and things were starting to get pretty complicated. Dad would be back on Wednesday, and I wanted to have things sorted out and restore my focus.

Number one on the list: The CRIMSON plan, it was underway. John Petersen had been introduced to Dad and recruitment or at least influence had begun. I was confident that with a little more effort Jeff would join CRIMSON.

When the Moms would be let in on the Vision was anyone's guess, but I had to think it would happen soon. I would leave that one up to Dad and the other men.

Rebekah, now there was an enigma to say the least. I was still confused over our last conversation at the McClaren's; but I would have to watch it because she had a way of extracting information, and that was something I just could not let happen with regard to the Vision and CRIMSON.

And then there was Cassandra. Admittedly, I had only seen her twice and spoken briefly to her, but I regarded those instances as much more than casual meetings. Realistically, that was the most any rational person could have labeled them, 'casual.' But as I am periodically reminded by Mom, a young man's mind is not always rational. The fact was I didn't even know her email address or cell number. But I was sure we would meet again at the next tournament, perhaps then I could get to know the graceful Miss Perez a little better.

****

As I cruised along my car radio had scanned to the oldies station... and Brian Wilson's lyrics.

'It starts with just a little glance now. Right away you're thinking 'bout romance now...'

I jerked back to reality as I nearly blew a stop sign, seriously testing my Beemer's brakes. Man, thinking about certain things could be hazardous to your driving record. Realizing I was just passing the Ice Castle, I decided I could use a little cooling off.

Skating around the rink, thinking hard about the CRIMSON plan, it occurred to me that I needed to invite Jeff to a CRIMSON meeting. Didn't he have practice today? I looked up to get the time off the big score board when a blue flash skated around me, turned and faced me while skating backwards.

"Hi!" She gave me one of those rare smiles and her blue eyes were full of mischief knowing she had surprised me out of my skates (and thoughts).

"Rebekah, ...Oh, that's right, this is your day." I was caught completely unaware.

"Catch me if you can!" she called over her shoulder as she flew off through the relatively light crowd.

Catching her was out of the question, but she did allow me to get within a few feet and then cut in the afterburners, leaving me in her shaved ice. Man, could she skate. I just shook my head.

Finally, she came back to face me and I motioned to the boards.

"How long *have* you been skating?" I asked after catching my breath.

"About five years on and off." Her eyes were very bright today, and she looked a little older with her hair up.

The announcer asked for the ice to be cleared for the Zamboni. As we skated off the ice I offered, "Can I buy you a soda?"

She smiled and blushed a little, "No, I can't have sodas," as I saw the braces.

"Gatorade?" I asked. I could use a drink after the game of ice tag. She nodded looking up.

I held the door as we entered the snack bar. It was half full, but there was a booth in the back away from the moms and their high pitched kids. I placed a Gatorade with a straw in front of her and sat down to face her taking a big draw on my drink.

She took a sip and then looked up, "What brings you out here, Josh?"

"Oh, I happen to be out for a drive and when I passed by I thought it would be nice to do a little skating." I sure didn't want to tell her about cooling off after the almost-blown stop sign and the lovely reason behind all that. I smiled to myself; stay cool Josh.

"Hmm," as she finished another sip her eyes locked on, "Can I ask you something?"
"Ah.. Sure.." Did I sound a little hesitant?
"The other night, at the McClaren's, what did you mean when you said, "I was important to…?" she blushed a little but still did not drop her eyes.

I really wanted to tell her that she was an important part of an intricate long term plan to save our nation from some terrible fate. When I thought about it, it sounded corny, unless of course you'd seen the Vision, then there was nothing corny about it. I could see this conversation would lead to nothing good.
She immediately saw the hesitation in my eyes, and she looked down at her drink.
"Rebekah, you are very important to CRIMSON. You proved that at San Diego." This was true and I was sincere, but there was so much I couldn't talk about.
"Oh…" Her shoulders dropped a little.

This was definitely not a conversation I wanted. I couldn't tell her the real reason, and she was much too perceptive for me to stay on this topic long without slipping up like last time.
"You know Robert, Ben, Dan Jr. and I are trying to lead CRIMSON, but *you* are the true star. You're our Kobe Bryant." I immediately regretted the analogy as she shook her head; but it wasn't far off, she was the key player on the CRIMSON team.
"I don't feel like a star … No one in CRIMSON likes me…" she would not look up now. This was going from bad to worse.

Where was the playful Tinker Bell zooming around the rink just a few minutes ago? Her mood swings were murder.

"That's not true, *I* like you... You *are* pretty amazing. In fact, can I ask *you* a question?" I wanted to change the subject fast.

"I guess..." She looked up again, but no smile.

"I noticed that every time we work on my case you never look at the papers or your big notebook. Robert says that once you've studied something for a little while you know it cold. How do you do it?"

"I have a ..... I concentrate," she creased her brow, and I could tell she was holding back. But she wasn't about to be derailed.

"Josh, No one else could have managed it. But you were the *last* person I wanted to call,... let you see me so upset.... Why was it so important for me to make the tournament? Why was it so important to you?"

Oh Man, I thought, just like they say 'no good deed goes unpunished.'

New defense on the court. "You won, didn't you?" I grinned trying to lighten up.

She frowned, "You said yourself 'It was more than that'...Something else is going on. Getting to the debate tournament meant the world to me, but you and your dad made an *extreme* effort to get me there. To any reasonable person, I wasn't worth it. It must have cost *thousands*." She was very serious now. She had the blue lasers dialed up to full power and I felt the truth being drawn out past my defenses. I had to give her some kind of answer.

"You're important, that's all... can't you just accept that?" was all I could think of. Just great, Agent double oh Zero. Keeping secrets was a lot harder than it looked.

"Hi, sweetheart. How was your practice?" Saved by the buzzer, or in this case her mom. The spell was broken.

"Hi, Mrs. Miller," I looked up and realized I had been holding my breath.

"Josh and I *were* having a discussion," Rebekah hissed.

More like an interrogation under the hot lights. She didn't lose laser lock even as I stood up for Mrs. Miller, providing an escape route. More cotillion training, I would have to remember to thank Mom one day.

"You're not going to answer me, *are* you?" she challenged even as I stood to leave.

"I'm on a mission from God." I gave her my best mischievous grin over my shoulder as I walked out of the snack bar. Well, at least it was the truth.

After I got into my ride I realized I had forgotten all about Jeff. Little Miss Sherlock Holmes had completely distracted me from my mission. Well, she should be leaving the rink soon with her mom, so I just waited watching in my rearview mirror for her. She should be out any minute.

A knock on my window made me jump. How did she sneak past me? As the window rolled down I smiled "Yes?..." Before I could even be courteous, she slipped a folded sheet of paper through the half opening and was gone. Her face still set in that serious expression, blue lasers threatening to burn holes in my leather seats if she had paused any longer. Unfolding it, I wasn't surprised.

I know there is something going on and I WILL figure it out.

Why did I have to make friends with an obsessive compulsive little genius, why not a nice normal sweet-natured …

I walked back into the Ice Castle to find Jeff. He was just getting ready to take the ice. I let him know that tomorrow at 6:00 p.m. the CRIMSON team would be meeting, and I was sure he would find it interesting given it would be the first meeting after the San Diego victory.

When I got home, I felt like I had sorted a few things out but created a very serious situation regarding Rebekah. I would simply have to avoid her from now on until the Vision could be revealed. I could just see it now, trying to explain the Vision one-on-one to Rebekah. Good luck with *that*.

"Did you have a nice drive: did you see anyone you know?" Mom inquired.

"Yeah, it was a great day for it. I did see Jeff Petersen and invited him to CRIMSON tomorrow," I replied. And Oh yeah, did I mention my nearly fatal disclosure at the hands of a blue-eyed inquisitress who has sworn to rip the vital secret from my brain or die trying.

"After San Diego, I'm sure a lot of students will want to join. I still can't believe little Rebekah Miller is going to the nationals. But they say she is very advanced for her age," she replied. "Well, come and sit down. Marissa almost has dinner ready."

"You know, she has so many cases and historical documents memorized; it's unreal," I said, although I really didn't want to get into it.

"Rebekah is very special according to Mrs. Simmons. The Millers are very protective of her," Mom replied. "What you did for her made a big impact."

And created a big problem, I thought.

"I knew she could win, and Dad needed Pi-squared out here anyway. I did it for the team," I said lamely hoping to lower my mom's antennae. The last thing I needed now were *two* smart women trying to figure out what I was doing.

"I think it's amazing how it all worked out, like God had His hand in it." She was right about that, I thought.

"Have you spoken to Rebekah since the tournament?" Oh, here we go.

"Yeah, she thanked me at the McClaren's party." Just keep to the facts, Josh.

"I think she kind of likes you … maybe a little crush perhaps."

OH, now that's *just* perfect. I wonder if this fabricated rumor was the current chart buster on the CHESS Moms Network. If only Mom had seen her in action this afternoon, that would have laid that idea to rest. But Mom just looked up with a little smile.

I shook my head, "Really, Mom. I think she just feels grateful about getting to the tournament, that's all." Come *on*. This had to end soon.

"Well, it was a very nice thing you did for her and her family; and I'm very proud of you." She put her arms around my shoulders as she went back into the kitchen to check on Marissa.

Wednesday night, CRIMSON. I was early as usual, joining Robert, Ben and Dan Jr. We were all in a great mood, recounting San Diego and some of the high, and low points of the tournament. Mrs. Stanton had set the team trophy in the middle of the long set of tables, and as we all stood around admiring it, Dan Jr. asked us to assemble for a prayer.

"Amen." I was so glad that the guys understood that God had plans for all of us and CRIMSON. As a few late members were coming in, Jeff Petersen was with them. I came over and asked him to sit with Ben and me. Mrs. Stanton had everyone quiet down and asked Jeff to stand up and tell us a little about himself. Then she asked everyone to pull out their ballots. She wanted to review them and get details of the how CRIMSON had done against the competition. Rather than start with Elizabeth or Rebekah, she started with Alison and Steve. While it made sense to focus on the less experienced debaters to strengthen the club, I was hoping for a review of Rebekah's ballots (actually, just one ballot). Remembering my promise to myself to steer clear of her, I couldn't just ask to see them. Besides, Rebekah was hardly acknowledging my presence, as she sat at the other end of the room. Going over the ballots, Mrs. McClaren was noting who had not entered their debate flows into our computer database. This was one way CRIMSON would stay on top, with all our competitors' cases in the database we were able to study them and determine their weaknesses and develop counter arguments.

It wasn't a secret, and other clubs had them, but ours was the largest and most complete database simply because our club had the most members and debated nearly everyone. Rebekah would have been a big surprise to the other teams. It was her first tournament, so the other teams had nothing on her. She would have appeared like CRIMSON's secret weapon, the stealth bomber of homeschool debate; I let my mind play with this analogy a while. It fit pretty well; no one saw her coming, and she obliterated the competition before they even had a chance to react. And whatever means she used to know all those cases and historical references, it was like a new technology in the debate wars. Even Elizabeth was no match for her. Once Rebekah was engaged on a mission, destruction was inevitable. And now she was on a new mission. Man, this did not bode well for my efforts to keep the Vision a secret. I would really have to watch out.

Jeff seemed to enjoy himself, and he also was getting plenty of assistance from the feminine side of our debate team. I figured, with his older brother's influence and all the attention as a new member, my job was accomplished. I also had avoided a certain blond investigator the whole night. In fact, she hadn't said a word to me, or even looked my way. Perhaps because a number of the team members wanted to hear about some of her rounds, she was finally getting the attention she honestly deserved. I hoped it would make her feel more accepted and less defensive ...and happier.

Wednesday night and Dad was back from D.C. I guess it had been an eventful trip as he asked me to come up to his office after dinner.

"How are things around here? Looks like Mom's a little nervous about testing this year."

"It's the SATs. This is my first real SAT exam for college, and she's a lot more worried about them than I am. I got straight A's for this semester," I replied. I wasn't too worried about the SATs. I was sure Mom had been about the best teacher I could have, and I had worked hard.

"Well, this year has had its share of disruptions, but high SAT scores are a must to get into John Adams." He was stating the obvious; perhaps he had a lot on his mind due to the trip.

"Yes sir." What more could I say, he always expected straight A's.

"Did you see John Petersen?" might as well see if I could change the subject.

"I took him to dinner one night. He's definitely ambitious. Harcourt's got him working on some environmental bill," Dad replied, glad to get off the personal stuff.

"Did you talk to him about the Vision?" I asked.

"No Son, we need to get a consensus of the TPM before we disclose the Vision to anyone. I was just laying groundwork.

John has my contact information, and I let him know that I could help him land a good position when he got out of Virginia Law."

"I'm pretty sure Jeff will join CRIMSON. He was there last night and seemed to have a good time," I added, wanting to score a point or two.

"Nice job... By the way, good call on flying Rebekah Miller out to San Diego. ...took the whole tournament and going to nationals...How old *is* she?"

"Thirteen... I thought she could do it; the rest of CRIMSON was awesome too." Hope he leaves it at that, no need to get into the details of the Rebekah situation.

"Dad, I was thinking; many of the CRIMSON students will need financial aid to afford the good schools. They have the grades, but can't afford the tuition. Can we help them somehow; a scholarship program or something?"

"I was thinking about this just the other day. I need to get hold of my accountant and see what can be set up. I want to keep it anonymous, so don't mention it to anyone,.. clear?"

"Sure Dad, that's great!"

"The TPM needs to get back to work. I want to focus on our point men. We've got Petersen in the works, but we need to get the others going. I want to map out a longer term strategy with names and goals. This has got to be in place soon, before we can tell anyone about the Vision." He was typing into the TPM database as we spoke. "Anything else happen while I was gone?"

"Nope," I shook my head. Well, let's see Dad...remember that little debate obsessed genius Rebekah? She's made it her life quest to find out about the Vision, after I almost spilled the beans. And, oh yeah, ever since the tournament I can't keep my mind off this incredible looking lead debater from REASON. Then there's the Moms Network. ... Nope, nothing's happening.

"Well, I think we should call it a night. We both seem a little tired." Dad got the hint.

At the TPM, the men were getting back up to speed after having taken a few weeks off. My dad had contacted them all through the database last night and set the agenda for tonight's meeting. Mr. McClaren and Dad had created a power point presentation entitled "CRIMSON PLAN."

On slide one was the general goals, and then on slide two was a chart.

There were four CRIMSON grads that were in law or pre-law programs on the left side of the chart and then there were over a dozen high court judgeships at right. Presented in this way with a big gap in the middle really brought home the magnitude of the undertaking. The obvious question was how do you get the grads from where they were today to our goals.

Then there was another chart that was more detailed that showed CRIMSON's twenty eight members set in columns according to graduation year, and on the right side of the chart were a list of about twenty colleges that were thought to be preferred targets. Some of the junior and senior CRIMSON students were in light green boxes indicating that they had determined to go into pre-law. There were a couple of lines drawn from senior names to colleges. While his name was in a green box, Robert Miller had no line to a college. Elizabeth (no green box) had her line to Wheaton (pre-med, under her name). Too bad, she would have made a fine lawyer for our cause. My mind wandered as I looked at the chart, I wondered where Cassandra was going to college...I knew so little about her...

"Josh, you can help us fill in information for the second chart. Who's really interested in getting into law school and who isn't. We already have the info about our children in the chart," Mr. McClaren said, pulling me back to reality.

"Sure, I can help there." I notice that Rebekah was not in a green box. Did Pastor Miller have any doubt she was going to be a lawyer? Perhaps he didn't want to draw attention to her, as she would certainly be the only green boxed thirteen year old.

The meeting closed out without mention of the Moms. There was still too much work to do, and I think most of the men realized that their wives were too busy right now with the second semester underway. Perhaps after testing in the spring.

Chapter Ten

What a Knight

"If passion drives you, let reason hold the reins."
                                    – Benjamin Franklin

It was Sunday afternoon, and I was just relaxing out on the patio munching on some chips and guacamole. Another perfect day in paradise.

My cell phone rang its "Twilight Zone" ring tone, an unknown caller.

"You've got Josh."

"Hi Josh, this is Cassandra Perez," her musical voice set my pulse rate up a notch and my mind froze, inundated with a dozen thoughts. She continued, "I wanted to see if you were serious about your offer," her voice recalled that knockout smile.

"Cassandra. Hi…ah..offer?" Once my mind's transmission shifted out of park I replayed our first, last and only conversation.

"Suh, it's not very gallant to raise a lady's expectatshuns, and then not follah through," she flirted with a stern southern drawl and mercifully gave me the hint I needed.

"…dancing?" It was the only thing that made sense.

"Mahy, mahy… what a lady has to do these days to jog a young man's memory," she replied, still in Southern Belle mode; then more directly, "Josh, would you come to my cotillion as my guest?"

Ah, I had to smile. Cotillion. Why were moms always right... Ok, chill Josh.

"Fahgive me, it would nevah be mah intentshun to cuhrtail a lady's expectatshuns, but could I impose upon her for a few details about the ball?" I might as well play along.

"Next Saturday night at the Mission Center Cotillion. It'll be a Latin dance theme; I hope that fits your style," she had dropped the accent, but I still had to focus on what she was saying. My mind was not exactly in 'rational mode.'

"Oh, I think I can manage," I replied.

"I'm so glad you can come; I'll see you there, Saturday, 6:30." Her voice was amazing even through the myriad of cell tower connections.

"I'll be there on my trusty steed M'lady." So I mixed centuries, it was the best I could do under the circumstances.

As I shut the cell phone, I noticed my palms were sweating. Come *on*, Josh, get a grip! ... Cassandra called *me*... I must have made an impression. I smiled again at the cotillion connection. I would have to brush up on my Tango and Samba... and perhaps a trip to the mall for a new suit was in order. At least I had the presence of mind to save her number.

The week went by pretty fast, and I tried to focus on school, SAT prep and the TPM. At the CRIMSON meeting, Jeff returned and asked Mrs. Stanton if he could officially join. I had accomplished my first assignment on the CRIMSON plan. There seemed an infinite number of tasks left to be done, but at least it was a start. Rebekah was still not speaking to me, which was fine as I was trying my best to stay out of her way. All in all, this had been one of the more uneventful weeks since I had arrived in California, but that was about to change.

****

The Mission Center was a little more than thirty minutes north up the 5 freeway in the historic town of San Juan Capistrano, where the Mission itself was established on the west coast in the same year the Declaration of Independence was signed. The Mission San Juan Capistrano anchored the downtown area, and the beautiful rolling hills around the Mission were now covered with homes ranging from upscale to true mansions.

I drove my BMW into the parking lot just as the last lights of sunset were fading. The center was obviously new but retained the historic mission style with arches made of brick and stucco. Minivans were already dominating the parking lot, and my black beemer caught some attention from the teens heading toward the center. I looked to see if Cassandra just happened to be among them, but no luck. Closing the top, I check myself in the mirror, popping a mint, "Just relax, she invited you," I said to myself.
I walked through the entrance and was glad to see my dark suit, shirt and tie would not stand out. A typical cotillion crowd, I thought, girls all dressed-up excitedly talking in groups, guys uncomfortable in suits wishing they were somewhere else, and the obligatory fastidious moms.
I scanned the room, checking out each group of attendees, and I was receiving the same treatment from more than a couple of the girls. This could be an enjoyable evening, if I could just turn down the angst meter. The corsage box was starting to feel awkward; it was like carrying a blinking neon sign, "NEW GUY, NEW GUY."

Just when I was considering tossing it, I spied her across the room as she turned and gave me a dazzling smile. She was wearing a gold gown that fit like a glove down to a flair to allow reasonable dance moves. It cleverly met all the cotillion dress guidelines while deliberately providing an enticing visual display. Her jet black hair was up, but in loose curls, revealing an elegant neckline.

Watching her as she crossed the room towards me, I was struggling unsuccessfully to remember the classic line I had planned for this moment. I hoped my expression didn't give away my thoughts or nervousness as the room telescoped in on Cassandra.

"Josh, I'm so glad you could make it." There was nothing like that voice, and as I kept thinking each time I saw her... 'could she look any better?' I paused as there was a lot of creative brain activity, but it was definitely not focused on my speech center.

She gave me a look of anticipation with those amazing hazel green eyes ...tick...tick...tick...

I recovered just in time, "Mayhm, it was necessary, as I must always defend the Reinhart word of honor, but in this case the pleasure's all mine." I handed her the corsage.

She played along for a moment. "Whah, thank you, Suh." She gave me that knockout smile and slipped the corsage on her wrist. "Let me introduce you to some of my friends," as she led me toward the ballroom entrance. I was sure thankful the center had good air conditioning.

The first dance was a waltz just to get the dancers warmed up (like I needed that). As I took Cassandra's hand and slipped the other around her back, I really wasn't prepared for the full court press on my senses. She stepped close, and her perfume and the warmth of her in my hands short circuited all my well rehearsed 'cool.' Luckily, I could waltz without thinking.

"How do you like our ballroom? We had a lot of fun decorating it in the Latin theme," she threw out some small talk. I had to believe that this was something she was used to doing: bringing her dance partners back to reality. I hoped I wasn't *that* obvious.

"It looks great, especially the banners." I really didn't want to talk about the decorations. "Do you live near here? It's the first time I've been up this way."

"I live in Aliso Viejo. It's about ten miles from here," she replied. "That's right. You're new to the area; Florida, right?" she questioned as we came back together after a turn in which I was able to appreciate a 360 degree view of her. She was, no other way to put it, dazzling; and she knew it.

"We moved out to Santa Sonoma because of my dad's company, Prescience." I hope that might help even her home court advantage. She was quite aware I was completely entranced by her, evidenced by her little knowing smile after the turn.

"Reinhart…" she paused, "Your dad's not David Reinhart, as in *The* Prescience David Reinhart." Her eyes widened and I almost stepped on her, not due to my misstep. Score one for the visiting team.

"Guilty as charged," I gave her my best smile; I was finally starting to relax a little. "We moved out here because of the Apex acquisition."

She covered her astonishment with her favorite weapon of choice, that knockout smile, and asked another question, "Do you plan to follow in your father's footsteps?" But I could see her eyes were not as playful as they had been. If I had to guess, her considerable mental abilities were fully engaged. At that moment, I wished I knew what was going on underneath those raven curls.

"I hadn't really thought that far ahead, but I do plan to go into law. What about you?"

"I've been accepted at John Adams and will be starting pre-law next year." She was proud of it and I didn't blame her; I was hoping to get into John Adams myself.

"I've been looking into a number of schools. John Adams is one of my top picks."

Now I hoped we (I, mostly) had gotten past the initial awkward stage because I really wanted to know more about my lovely dance partner. I mean, I still had a long ways to go, and I knew there was no way I could get serious about any girl right now; but Cassandra wasn't *any* girl. As we completed the waltz, she was, without question, the most captivating partner I could imagine.

The music changed to a Tango. *Now* I needed to seriously focus, hoping my practice sessions with Mom had brought my Tango up a level or two. It was tricky because the cotillion version, while still following all the Tango steps, was performed with a few inches of discretion separating the dancers. Cassandra and I moved well together; she was nearly my height in heels, and her natural grace followed my lead with ease. I was actually starting to enjoy myself, and her musical laughter at a couple of my comments set my pulse rate up.

Toward the end of the dance another couple got too close, and in order to keep them from colliding with her, I had to guide Cassandra away with a very strong lead. To keep her from tripping, I drew her close, taking her weight against me for a few heartbeats. Her eyes widened and caught mine as we separated, but then a smile crossed her lips.

"You're more than 'managing' the Latin style," she breathed.

Oh Man.... I felt a strong flush coming and tried to hold it back; Chill, Josh, Chill.

"I...I think you're taking it easy on me. Your cotillion seems more focused on Latin." Did that sound casual enough? I hoped the blush didn't get past my collar. She *must* be aware that she had just raised my temperature about ten degrees above normal. 'Young man spontaneously combusts at local cotillion, film at eleven.'

Time for a break, and I was grateful to have more than a few inches distance between me and my beautiful host. I offered her a glass of punch and some cake; I was starved of course, but at the moment my stomach was no match for my emotions.

As we sat down in adjacent folding chairs, she raised an unexpected subject. "You placed pretty high at San Diego, especially considering it was your first California tournament."

"I was fortunate to get a 'bye' and I do have a *very* good coach," I smiled at this as an image of a little blond girl with a huge notebook crossed my mind.

"Hmm... CRIMSON has a pretty strong team this year with the addition of you and that new girl.... 'Bekah?'"

"Rebekah Miller... She just started this year," I replied

"San Diego was her *first* tournament?!" Her eyes widened, "How old *is* she?"

"She's thirteen, but she's a fast study," I replied, no question about that.

"How well do you know her?" She asked,

Oh great! How did we get on to the subject of Rebekah?

"Not that well, you probably know Robert, she's his younger sister." Down play it Josh. But really, did anyone know Rebekah well?

"Hmm...It's amazing she won San Diego considering she only broke four-two." Cassandra replied.

She must know that Rebekah had won their round, I thought. Why was she so interested, there must be some way to get off this topic. 'Hey Josh, how'd your dance go with Cassandra? Oh just fine, we talked about Rebekah the whole time.'

"Yes, she's pretty good. What about you, will you be trying out for the John Adam's debate team?" Hope this does the trick.

"Actually, I got a collegiate debate scholarship to John Adams. I'm really looking forward to debating at the college level." Given Cassandra's obvious physical attributes, it was easy to forget that she was very intelligent *and* ambitious.

"That's impressive. Guess you'll be very busy for the next few months... with graduation and preparing for J.A. and all." I wondered what it took to get a full ride debate scholarship to John Adams; I had no idea.

"*Very*, but I'm still going to states and I hope to get a rematch with Elizabeth Simmons," she replied, her eyes flashed, flecks of gold catching the light.

No doubt about it, she was hard-core debate, competitive as they come. I mean, she already had a debate scholarship to one of the best law colleges in the nation, but wasn't satisfied till she had avenged her loss in the homeschool semi's.

This was all very interesting, but I really didn't want to spend the rest of the night talking about debate.

"I hope the fact that REASON and CRIMSON are competing teams won't affect our friendship; Shakespeare would not approve." I gave her a sideways glance, and my best grin.

"Are we *friends* now, Mr. Reinhart?" She playfully lifted one eyebrow as she over-emphasized 'friends.'

"I hope we can have a few more dances to be sure, *Miss* Perez."
She was no longer in competitive debate mode, and I was hoping
for a little more time to get to know her warmer graceful side.

"Hmm...that would be nice. Unfortunately, I'm not allowed to
monopolize you. But I hope you'll come back another time."
She gave me a smile that lit the ballroom with those hazel green
eyes. She seemed genuinely disappointed to end our dance time.

I had forgotten that this was 'cotillion rules' and different
partners were required.

As she got up and the new dance began, I watched her head off
toward another dark suit. Then I focused back on my new
partner, one of Cassandra's girlfriends I had met earlier. I found
out one thing right away, it was hard dancing the Rumba, when
your mind was still on the Tango.

I had to admit I wasn't paying much attention during the next two
dances, not that my partners weren't interesting and attractive,
but my thoughts were otherwise occupied. More than once I was
caught watching Cassandra across the ballroom.

The cotillion was drawing to a close and I was formulating
multiple options to assure I got at least one more conversation
with her.

The final dance was a Conga line as we exited the Ballroom, and
I lost track of Cassandra as the dancers scattered. Looking
around, I saw that she was surrounded by the same circle of
friends, 'holding court.' I casually joined them, but definitely got
a sharp glance from a couple of the guys, and one giggle out of
my last dance partner. As she saw me come up to the group,
Cassandra flashed the formal smile.

"Josh, I hope you enjoyed yourself, and perhaps you can come
back and join us another time."

She was all graciousness, in hostess mode. But the warm, natural Cassandra I had held on the dance floor had retreated behind the knockout smile and smooth manners. When she had phoned, she had said "come to *My* cotillion", and she wasn't kidding. Amongst this group, she was the Cotillion Queen and had an image to uphold. I, on the other hand, was the presumptuous knight-errant from a foreign land, especially as far as the local "knights" were concerned.

"I had a great time and would *definitely* look forward to another dance lesson." No reason to give these guys any hope of brushing me off. After a little more formal conversation, I was trying to decide if I might have overstayed my welcome, as it was clear that Cassandra's Rumba partner felt I had.

"M'lady, I will take my leave, but your Cotillion Court and Ball have been most enjoyable." I gave a slight bow to her; might as well play out the scene. I hoped for a glimpse of the warm Cassandra, but I had to settle for a flash of humor in her hazel eyes.

"I'll walk you out," as she gave a sideways glance to her friends.

I crooked my elbow and she took my arm as we walked to the door (take that, Mr. Rumba).

"Josh, you definitely don't need lessons, but I wouldn't mind dancing again sometime." She released my arm.

As I turned to face her, she gave me that wonderful warm smile, topped off with those amazing eyes. She must know what affect they had on all her "knights." I had thought of a number of clever things to say, but all that came out was, "I'd like that a lot...Can *I* call *you* this time?"

"Please do," she replied.

"I will...you have the Reinhart word on it, M'lady." I looked back into her eyes and gave her my best parting smile. Nice try, Josh. I was sure my face gave away any attempt at being nonchalant. My thoughts about Cassandra had not changed since the first time I had seen her. She was simply… stunning.

I turned and stepped out into the cool California air. Wow! What a night.

I really don't remember much of the drive back to Santa Sonoma. My mind was trying to sort out the evening; what had actually happened from what I imagined had happened. The Tango incident was undoubtedly distorted in my mind, but the last few minutes with her were not. She had purposefully stepped out of her circle to offer me a chance to see her again. She had an image to maintain, but one on one she had me at "Please do."

Passed the San Onofre check point, from here the traffic was light and very fast. I had to keep watching my speed, which was no small feat as my mind was focused on the night's events. It was good to be back in my think-tank/BMW. I had about twenty minutes of uninterrupted contemplation to do. One thing was certain, regardless of how impractical or unlikely, I wanted to spend more time with Cassandra. She filled my imagination, and that was difficult to ignore. I'm sure others would just see it as an infatuation, a 'crush', like Sarah might have on a teen idol. But this was not the case; I had worked hard all night to keep it light… Reinhart… Josh Reinhart… *Right*… Who was I kidding? She had mesmerized me from the first time I saw her enter the classroom in San Diego. I really had nothing to compare it to.

I could hear Dad now, 'Come on… Focus, Josh; you have commitments and priorities. And he was right; realistically, I couldn't stand the distraction. (Man, that phrase sounded familiar.)

For all I knew, she just considered me another one of her court, like many of the guys at cotillion, at her beck and call. It sure didn't feel like that when we danced, but I had to admit my experience in these things was limited (more like non-existent). For the last fifteen minutes my mind had been arguing the negative contentions; you don't have time for this – focus on school and the CRIMSON plan, she lives too far away, she'll be going to college and you'll still be in high school, she may be just adding you to her collection of beaus, Mom and Dad are *sure* not going to go for it, and on and on. But emotionally, I felt a strong affirmative case for seeing her again and soon. (Josh, what have you gotten yourself into?) I had to just shake my head and smile.

I couldn't take her anywhere in my car, curse the DMV laws, but I had to admit there was good reason for them. I can just imagine taking both our lives in my hands trying to concentrate on driving while the warm and lovely Cassandra was gracing my black leather passenger seat. I already had evidence that I could blow stop signs just thinking of her. So there had to be a place we could meet (like cotillion). I thought about my cotillion but I was sure that might get rather awkward, especially with two completely obsessed debate furies demolishing the formal but friendly atmosphere. No, it would have to be somewhere up in her area, somewhere we could meet where at least I could start out feeling comfortable.

I was driving back in familiar territory, and my off-ramp was coming up. Luckily, I hadn't attracted the CHP, and I was just about home. The night was still young as they say, and I was famished. I pulled into 'Toxic Taco' near the Cineplex, and rather than possibly spilling hot sauce on my brand new interior, I went inside to order.

As I stepped up to the counter, I realized I had made a big mistake.

"Hey, Josh. We were trying to get you all night," it was Ben and Dan Jr. sitting in a booth nearby. I still was in my shirt and loosened tie, cell phone off due to cotillion.

"Hey," I gave it my best casual greeting.

"Come on over and join us. What's with the tie?" Dan Jr. inquired.

Luckily, I had to give my order: two volcano burritos and some chili fries...To Go. I hoped they would drop the questions, but I could see that wasn't happening.

"Did you have to go to a funeral or something?" Ben inquired.

"No, I just had to do something for cotillion." Now this was technically true, and I sure wasn't going to give out any more details.

"Cotillion, ugh, I'd rather go to a funeral. Your Mom makes you do it?" Ben didn't want to talk about that.

"Yeah, something like that. What are you guys doing?" I stood sipping on my drink, trying to change the subject.

"We just saw the Bond flick that's out this weekend; it was pretty cool; I think Dan Jr.'s in *love* with the new 'Bond girl.'" Dan Jr. turned red, and we all had a laugh.

If only they had seen the 'Bond girl' I had been dancing with tonight, I thought with a smile. I could just hear Ben now. "No way, Cassandra Perez! Dude, she's the competition; almost won at San Diego. She's *all* about winning. I wouldn't trust her; I mean, she might just be trying to get our cases."

I went and got my burritos and fries.

"Sorry I missed it guys, but I got to go. .. early church tomorrow." I made my lame excuse and got out the door.

I hadn't even considered how I would tell anyone about taking Cassandra out. This was just getting more and more complicated. My stomach grumbled as I drove home, munching a few fries.

I guess I should have figure that Mom would have been waiting for me to get home. For one thing, she was bound to be just a little worried as I had not driven this far before, and of course she was bursting with curiosity about how it went with cotillion.

I had barely set my food down in the kitchen and started to eat when she came in and tried not to appear on pins and needles. I figured I would keep my mouth full of burrito, and then I wouldn't need to say much.

"How'd it go? Did you have a good time?"

I finally swallowed and had to say something, "It went fine, Mom," and quickly took another bite.

No way that was going to satisfy her.

"Well, were the dances fun? How were the other teens?" She waited patiently as I finished my next bite.

"The dances were fun, and it was a lot like our cotillion." Except there was one major difference; there was no one like Cassandra at our cotillion.

"Oh, ...how did you do on your Latin dances, did you Tango?" As I chewed I tried to see if there was a good way of answering her question. I guess I could just come out and say that I danced the Tango with the most drop dead gorgeous girl on the planet, and even when she fell against me for a few moments, we hadn't missed a step. Nope, don't think so. How about 'I danced two dances with Cassandra, Queen of the ball, and stared at her the rest of the time; so I can't remember how I did the Rumba or the Cha Cha.' Nope, not going there either.

"Our practicing was a great help; I thought I looked pretty good out there. We did the Cha Cha, Tango, the Rumba and finished with a Conga line." Just the facts, Josh, just the facts.

"Well, its sounds like you had a good time. Cassandra, the young lady who invited you, was she nice?" she was really fishing now. Working on my second burrito, I thought about this for a moment. Was Cassandra nice? I guess that depends on the context. Cassandra could appear very nice, superficially, as long as she was in control, Queen of Cotillion. In reality, she was very smart and ambitious, so she could be nice if it suited her. She sure *felt* nice. She had been nothing but nice to me, so I guess she was..."nice" (so many other words came to mind).

"Yeah, she was nice, even invited me back sometime," I replied.

"Did you dance with her much?" OK, her we go. She had waited till I was finished with my burritos to get to the main line of questioning.

"The standard two dances." Trying to downplay this before Mom got some idea in her head. She would be right of course, but I wasn't playing this game for her benefit.

"Just two? I thought she might have cut in for one more." She was in scrutinizing mode now.

"Just two; then I danced with a couple of her friends." I hope I don't have to give much detail on those dances, I barely remember what the girls looked like. Mom seemed disappointed, no real story here.

"Well, as long as you're home safe and had a good time. I'm going to bed now. Don't stay up too late; tomorrow's Church." She must be tired; she gave up much too easily.

I finished the chili fries and downed the last of my soda. It would be an hour or so before my adrenaline level would return to something close to normal. I was still trying to think of a place I could legitimately take Cassandra.

I finally got to sleep about midnight, with a final image of
stunning green eyes laced with gold, and her musical reply
"Please do" in my head.

****

A bright warm Sunday morning, Church. I drove out to HGCF
and would meet my family there. The 10:30 service was
convenient in that I had hoped that Robert would like to shoot
some hoops or maybe we could join a pick up game after the
service. Mom, Dad and Sarah sat together, but I chose to sit with
Robert and a couple of other high school guys. The sanctuary
could have been used as a basketball stadium; there must have
been seating for five thousand. While Our Lord was here in
spirit, the ladies baking club fed 'the five thousand' out in the
huge patio. The worship team – nearly all professional
musicians, played contemporary praise songs, and it was an
emotion filled environment. I enjoyed worship. Singing His
praises, giving love and thanks to The Lord.
The bulletin indicated today's message was from 2 Kings 19.
Lay out your troubles before God, just like Hezekiah had done
with the letter from the Assyrians. The battle belongs to The
Lord; He will show you His will to Glorify His Name. This was
a good theme for me today. I had lots of battles, and I sure would
like God to fight them for me. He had given me the Vision, and a
mission - the CRIMSON plan. But there were so many other
battles going on. What was I supposed to do about Cassandra;
how can I legitimately spend time with her (OK, call it what it
was..."date" her)? It was certainly against my parents wishes.
(The 5th Commandment's promise flashed in my mind). I knew
my mom had let me go to her cotillion, but she *sure* was not
going to like the plan I was formulating in my head to see

Cassandra again. And then there were my efforts to get to Nats. How was I going to do that without a certain blond genius who was bent on using all her considerable mental capacity to extract my secret? I couldn't get close to her, let alone ask for her help on my cases, as I was afraid of dropping enough information for her to piece it together. Then there was just the incidental things like SATs, schoolwork, and coming up with something brilliant for the TPM.

As I sang the songs, I could see Rebekah two aisles over and down closer to the front. She was with her mom. That was Rebekah, no friends to sit with, on the aisle so she could see the podium better. Her father was giving the sermon today and I was actually looking forward to it. I had always been impressed with Pastor Miller. He seemed very smart and there was no doubt in his 'Calling.' He could display passion when it suited him, but more often he used his incredible ability to quote anywhere in the Bible at will to support his very logical and well thought out assertions. Pastor Miller had us all over the Old and New Testaments, quoting as easily out of Habakkuk as John, it was a real challenge keeping up with him. He spoke standing away from the podium, only going back there for a sip of water. I could have joined the teens in their study group, but today I decided to stay in the sanctuary, not surprisingly, so did Rebekah. I could just see her from where I sat, being attentive to her father. I had always thought there was a special bond there, something they shared that was just between them. I was about to go back to the outline in the bulletin, when she glanced up in my direction. She had caught me staring, and she fired a single burst from her lasers before quickly turning away, a flush forming on her cheek.

After church Robert and I went to shoot some hoops. The courts at HGCF were pro; full courts with glass backboards and not only nets, but *unripped* nets. A couple of other guys from church had decided to join us for a full court game of shirts and skins. Robert and I were skins and it felt good to be without my shirt on this unseasonably hot day.

"16, 14, Skins," I wiped the sweat from my hands on my jeans and tossed the ball into Robert over the other defender. He took a couple of dribbles but was getting double teamed, so he released to me as I ran under the pass and dribbled for a nice easy lay-up.

"18, 14, Skins," I shouted back to the others down court as I retrieved the ball and turned. At first I saw the Miller's minivan and then its recent occupant. Rebekah was standing with her back to me at the other end of the court talking with her brother, blond hair swinging. The game had been interrupted. I jogged back up the court to see what was going on.

"Ask Mom for a couple more minutes, please," I heard Robert say.

"Time out, Skins." I said as I made a "T" sign with my upraised fingers into my palm just in time for her to turn to face me. This time I caught her staring.

"Hi, Rebekah. Game called on account of 'Moms?'" I smiled. She flushed completely, glared and then turned quickly back to face her brother.

"Mom says we have to go *now*, otherwise Dad will be late for the seminar." She would not even acknowledge me.

Just then, I heard Mrs. Miller call out of the van, "Robert, we have to go, *Hurry!*"

"Sorry guys, I got to go. Maybe we can pick it up another time. See you Josh." Robert grabbed his shirt and jogged toward the car, leaving Rebekah to catch up.

I held the ball, watching them leave and chatted about playing some one-on-one; it seemed a shame to waste the beautiful weather and the court. Just as the sliding door closed I caught a glimpse of blond locks and brilliant blue eyes.

****

It was Tuesday after dinner, and it was time. I said a little prayer and picked up the phone.

"Hi Cassandra…This is Josh." I hoped I sounded confident, at least my voice cooperated, no sign of the nerves I was feeling.

"Josh?...Oh, Mr. Reinhart…I was wondering if I had misinterpreted our last conversation," she sounded a little petulant …. Interesting. It had been just over a week since cotillion. I guess she was used to a much quicker reply to her requests. Well, my delay was partly due to my inability to come up with an ideal venue for our next meeting, and also due, I had to admit, to being nervous.

"M'lady,..please forgive my inattentiveness, but I hope you would allow me to accompany you to the Ice Castle next Saturday evening," I said it so formally; I hoped she understood that I was "in character."

"Hmm…Mr. Reinhart, I must consider your offer in light of my other activities that day…" There was a pause as she must be checking her schedule or something. Her formal use of "Mr. Reinhart" was either playing along or I was about to strike out. Her voice still held that musical quality. I heard some muffled voices in the background but could not make it out, partly due to my pulse pounding in my ears. I'm sure it was seconds, but it seemed like an eternity, 'Say "Yes"…' my thoughts prayed.

"Sir, before I accept your invitation, I must know one thing: How well do you skate?" I didn't understand how this had any bearing on the situation, I obviously must be able to ice skate or I wouldn't have suggested it. I decided to answer honestly.

"I skate better than I dance, M'lady, if that's your concern?" I hoped she could imagine my smile through the phone. There was a pause…She liked to maintain the tension, the control. I decided to play my whole hand.

"I would also like to offer dinner after skating, if I may be so bold, M'lady."

I notice that the Aliso Ice Castle had a nice Chinese restaurant in the same parking lot. My plan was that we would have dinner after skating, a chance to get to know each other a little. She still held the pause and finally….

"Josh...I don't… Skating does sound *interesting*, and dinner afterward would be nice." she sounded hesitant and I had no clue why; but she had said yes, and that was the important thing.

"Great…I'll meet you at the Aliso Ice Castle on Saturday 6:00; I'll be the one in shining armor." I hoped my slight attempt at humor had covered my nervous excitement.

"Hmm, OK… 6:00 at the Ice Castle; Bye Josh," she still sounded unsure, but...

"Bye Cassandra." My pulse rate was through the roof, I was taking Cassandra out… Oh Man, I had to make sure it was perfect.

To say that I was a little distracted for the rest of the week was an understatement. I was sort of on autopilot as I worked through my studies and CRIMSON; there were bigger things on my mind. What did I want to know about her, what music did she like, what was her family like, how did she get to be 'Cassandra?' And most of all, did she really like me or was this just a courtesy date on her part. I thought she had seemed a little hesitant on the phone, but I was pretty nervous and maybe it just sounded that way to me.

The conversation with Mom went about as expected. After all, I couldn't have expected her to say 'Oh, Honey I'm so happy; it's about time you started dating, and who better to do that with than a girl from a competing team that we hardly know.' No, I guess not. It started with a little bit of misinterpretation... 'Oh, going out with her cotillion group again'...then surprise and a little concern. 'Oh, just you and Cassandra ice skating and dinner,... how well do you know her?'...and of course why dating was not a good idea, especially now 'You don't have time for this, your studies, CRIMSON, SATs'....to the review of the rules. 'You know you should have checked with me' ... to 'When will you be back?'... And finally, 'Please, just be careful.'
In the back of my mind, I couldn't help wondering, 'is the 'first born' being tested again?'

Chapter Eleven

The Ice Queen

"Great ambition, the desire of real superiority, of leading and directing, seems to be altogether peculiar to man, and speech is the great instrument of ambition." – Adam Smith

Driving up the 5, I tried to relax and enjoy the occasional ocean view, but the anticipation was a constant interference. Had I made the right choices, going against my parents wishes? Was tonight going to go as I had planned; and most of all, how would Cassandra be tonight – warm and stunning or queen of her castle? Aliso Viejo was a real life version of "Pleasantville", a carefully master planned community nestled in the rolling hills between the beach and the older Mission Viejo community to the east. There was a wide range of homes from McMansions to dense apartments. But what struck you most was that it was so clean and organized; the entire town screamed, "Stay off the manicured lawn!"

The Aliso Ice Castle parking lot was a clone of the obstacle course I had to negotiate down south. I noted the Peking Dragon restaurant and the ubiquitous Starbucks as I looked for a spot that would give my BMW a fighting chance against door dings. Crossing the lot with my skate bag, I hoped I had achieved the desired look, cool and casual, but with class – Reinhart, Josh

Reinhart, I chuckled. I wore my favorite jeans and a new casual sport coat over a long sleeve black knit shirt. I was early, but there was no way I wanted to keep Cassandra waiting, and it gave me a chance to familiarize myself with the place. Six o'clock came and went as I stood outside the rink realizing I had no idea what her car looked like. I hoped she was claiming a woman's prerogative to be fashionably late as I scanned the cars coming into the parking lot.

Just as my stomach was getting that sinking feeling, a new black panel van with "Perez Electric - commercial contractor" in gold lettering cruised into the lot and pulled into the drop-off area just in front of me.

I stepped forward and opened the door to be greeted with that knockout smile.

"Hi…ah.. could you introduce me?" I motioned to her mom in the driver's seat.

"Mother, this is Josh Reinhart," her mom smiled, I could see where Cassandra got her eyes.

"Nice to make your acquaintance, Mrs. Perez. I planned to have dinner at the Peking Dragon after skating; I don't think we will be out too late." It never hurts to get on the good side of the mom.

"Nice to meet you, Josh. Cassandra says you're in CRIMSON," she replied.

"Yes ma'am. Thank you for driving Cassandra." I gave her my best 'nice, responsible young man' look.

"I'll text you when I'm ready to be picked up," Cassandra said to her mother, then turned and stepped out of the van.

It had just been two weeks, but seeing her again set my pulse way up. She wore a short leather jacket over a white top and tight jeans that ended in black heels. She caught me staring and smiled.

"Ah...you ready?" I exhaled, picked up my bag and opened the door to the rink. Stupid question. The real question was 'are you ready, Josh?' The cold air hit me as we stepped into the rink, thank God for that, I thought.

"What size skates do you wear?" I noticed she didn't have any with her.

"Size 7, I think... Josh, I should tell you I haven't skated very much," she replied.

"Oh, you'll pick it up right away, anyone who can dance the way you do," I smiled, this was what I had hoped, an opportunity to get her out of her element. A chance to get past that self-assured mask she put forth to the world, I was hoping to see the warm, real Cassandra tonight. It had taken me quite a while to determine to take her ice skating; it was the best plan I could come up with.

I got a nice pair of size 7's and sat down opposite her on the benches.

"M'lady, if I may be so bold?" I offered to lace up her skates, and she presented me with a very pretty ankle to hold. I slipped on a skate and started to lace it up. It was an interesting situation to say the least, and I missed a lace loop and had to go back.

"I'm really glad you decided to come skating, I was afraid your hesitation was for some other reason." I began lacing the other skate.

"Hmm...I'm looking forward to this; I always wanted to ice skate, just too busy."

I finished lacing her skates.

"How do they feel?" I asked as I pulled my skates out of their bag.

"Good... Those are nice. How long have you been skating?" She asked noticing my skates.

"I played hockey back in Florida, but I quit to play hoops - easier on the teeth." I gave her a big grin, hoping for that warm smile and receiving a 'Hmmm.'

The Zamboni had just finished, and the evening crowd was beginning to take to the ice. We were at the break in the boards.

"Are you ready? You can take my arm if you like," I offered. If *you* like? more like 'if *I* like.'

We got on the ice and Cassandra was pretty unstable at first. I had to grab her waist a couple of times to keep her from falling, and she flashed those hazel eyes, but I hoped my smile didn't show all the way to my face (I had gotten her out of her element). But soon she was moving along on my arm and we laughed about it. We did get going a little too fast, and she let out a tight scream of fear and fun as I had to grab her waist once more.

She was very determined, and soon we were just holding hands; sometimes I would skate backwards with her facing me as we worked our way around the rink.

A couple of times I almost ran into some skaters, as I was definitely not paying attention to them. Even unstable on skates, she was captivating, more so because I was seeing a little of the real Cassandra as I guided her around.

"I think I can go on my own if we can slow down just a little." It was not a request. Perhaps I had presumed too much.

"Sure." I released her, and she gave me a sideways look as I skated beside her.

She continued to skate without my help for a while until a young girl cut in front of her. Cassandra tried to stop but caught her toe pick and started to fall forward. It actually happened in a blink of an eye, but I saw it all in slow motion; Cassandra falling, arms out stretched, green eyes wide, black tresses flying. I was just able to come around her waist with one arm and as she fell I lifted her off the ice. She turned to me with a look I hadn't seen before, her face flush, fear,.. anger,.. perhaps gratitude, then everything went cold. I set her down, and with my arm still around her for support, we skated to the boards as the rest of the crowd past by, oblivious.

"You OK?" I asked, concerned; that was close.

"Yes… Thank you." There was no mistaking the look that said, 'please remove your arm from my waist or I will break it off.' Why was she angry with me? What was I supposed to do, let her do a face plant on the ice? I removed my arm as we stood at the boards catching our breath.

"Well, that was exciting," she said with a frosty laugh, flashing the knockout smile as she breathed out, eyes still as cold as the rink surface.

"Are you ready for dinner?" I figured we had had enough excitement on the ice for one night.

"Yes, I think I'd like to go eat now." She stayed on the side moving toward the break in the boards. I skated with her. Well, I hoped the dinner would go better than the skating. Man, I was starved.

She was a lot more relaxed once she was back in her high heels. We walked out of the rink and over to my BMW.

"Josh's Beemer … must be nice," she quipped at my license plate as I dropped my bag into the trunk.

"You like my trusty steed, M'lady?" I grinned, I had detailed my ride before driving up, and it gleamed with the reflection of the last twilight and the lot lighting.

"Hmm-mm," she smiled back and was starting to thaw out as we walked toward the restaurant.

A nice Chinese lady led us to a round table toward the back. I sat next to her and decided to open with something innocuous.

"So how long have you lived in Aliso Viejo?"

"About five years, but I've lived in Orange County all my life. Mom and Dad are originally from Argentina," she replied.

"Your dad has his own business, electrical contractor." Assumption made from the panel van.

"My dad and my uncle. It's not Prescience, but they built it up from nothing. Twenty years of sixty hour weeks," she sounded a little defensive.

"I admire that a lot. Prescience wasn't always big. Dad started it from almost nothing." It was true; I understood the sacrifices made for entrepreneurship.

"Hmm...I don't think you can make the comparison. Dad works hard just to keep the business going. If he couldn't work, the business would fail even with Uncle Javier."

I could see I wasn't going to get anywhere with this, and besides I really did not want to talk about the great capitalist experiment.

"I bet he expects great things from you. You're the oldest, right?"

"You have *no* idea. I'm expected to be a great lawyer someday, and failure is not an option," her eyes flashed.

I laughed, "I call that the 'First Born Syndrome,' I get that all the time from my dad. Sometimes it seems no matter how well I do it's not enough."

"Hmm...I know what you mean, Debate, French, Calculus, Biology....; but I want it, too. When I first started debate, it was like I had found my mission in life. I love the competition." Her eyes went into that intense green with golden sparkles mode.

"From what I hear, your competition wished you didn't." That brought a low laugh that sent my temperature up a few degrees.

"San Diego didn't quite go as planned," she smiled but the voice was rueful.

"You got 3rd, and you're already on the J.A. debate team." What more did she want?

"I'm not qualified for Nats yet," she replied, mouth set, eyes flashing.

What was it with me? Did I have a big neon sign on my forehead 'obsessed, hardcore debate girls only - apply within.'

The Chinese lady brought us our drinks and some noodles.

"There's still states and the at-large slots," I replied. 'Competitive' was not the word.

"That's just it, REASON is not that strong this year; John is pretty good, but I have to carry the team. CRIMSON really surprised me. Is your coach using some new drills, some new debate methods?" I was surprise she asked so directly.

"Mrs. Stanton hasn't changed any of her teaching or coaching methods for a while. She simply asked us to work hard. And some of us have taken it more seriously than before." This was certainly true, and I saw no reason to introduce Rebekah into the conversation even though it was essentially her cases that I was using. Not to mention that she was undoubtedly the best debater in the state, with her own methods. Our stealth bomber.

"I would *just* like to get to Nats in my senior year." I could see she was serious, but I didn't really want to discuss debate all night.

"Do you think about anything else?" I grinned to make sure she saw it.

"…Occasionally," she smiled back knowing she sounded a little obsessed.

"Do you like any sports, other than ice skating?" I smiled.

"*Funny*," she flashed, then, "I like to watch my brother's soccer games, but I'm too busy to play any sports. What about you, other than hockey?"

"It's been a while since I played any hockey, but I do play some basketball, just games with the guys at my house," for once we weren't talking debate.

"My brothers have a hoop on the garage, is that what you mean?" she replied.

"Something like that." I didn't need to get into a discussion about the lighted basketball court in my backyard leading to the obvious differences in our dads' entrepreneurial successes. "How about your dancing, cotillion?" smiling, remembering the Tango.

"I like it, but sometimes the group gets a little boring." She looked up from her drink. Could the Queen be bored with her own subjects? I guess so.

"They all seemed nice to me... mostly." I grinned, more memories.

"Hmm...You mean Eric."

"I got the feeling I'm not his favorite person," still smiling, this could be fun.

"I think it might have been something to do with our Tango," she brought it up. This was getting more interesting by the minute. I needed to stay cool.

"You mean he didn't like my 'Latin Style?'" I smirked.

"You know what I mean," she flashed me with the eyes, but no smile.

"Do you go out with him or something?" *Sooo not* cool, Josh, but it just came out.

"Josh, I really don't have time to date...and no, I only dance with Eric at cotillion," she smiled that knowing smile. I must have really sounded pretty lame there. Oh, well, she already knew I was new at this.

"I don't have time for this either, according to my parents, but I gave my word..." Perhaps not the best way to have phrased it.

"And *that's* the reason why you *finally* called?" No smile, green eyes flashing. Oh Man, could she really not know how I felt about her. She was very touchy about this 'delay in calling back' thing. I needed to set this straight.

"Cassandra, I spent days deciding where to take you before I called." There, flush the cool 007 attempt, if it was ever there. I looked straight into her eyes.

"Oh..." she softened "You're kind of a planner, aren't you. Spend a lot of time thinking things through." She gave me that warm smile I had been waiting for.

It took a moment to get my thoughts back in gear.

"Yeah, I guess... There was a lot to consider, mostly how to manage my parent's reaction." That was the truth, too; Mom was less than pleased.

"They didn't approve?" I couldn't be sure if she meant approve of her or what.

"They don't think dating is a good idea for me, especially right now." Now that was an understatement. I had no idea how I would arrange another chance to see her again.

"So you asked me out even though your parents objected?" Smiling, one eyebrow lifted, now she was interested.

"I decided in this case to ask for forgiveness, rather than permission." I grinned at her looking up from my drink.

"Hmm...do you do that often?"

"I can't remember the last time." Then quickly, "How about your parents?" Let's get off me for a moment, good grief.

"Hmm... Well, legally they can't say much as I *am* eighteen, but I respect them and we did have a short discussion." She was *still* homeschooled, I thought.

"Was that the reason for the hesitation and muffled discussion on the phone." I wanted to understand if there was a problem.

"You caught that, huh... To answer your question – partly." Not giving me much go on. She was not going to be as candid with me without some prodding. I sensed she had played this game before, unlike Mr. Open Book here.

"Did you not want to go out?" Might as well get this out in the open, if she'll oblige.

"I'm here and I'm glad I decided to come, but I'm not sure it was a good idea." Now that was perfectly clear... as mud. What is it with women?

"Can I get three minutes to cross-examine that last contention?" I gave her my best mischievous grin; let's get back to debate, it was a lot simpler and safer.

"I stand open for cross-ex, Sir," she smiled; her eyes sparkled ready to play along, some tension dispelled.

"Ah... you said you are glad you came."

"Yes."

"But you also stated you weren't sure it was a good idea."

"Yes."

"What's your concern? Why wasn't it a good idea if you're glad you came?" There, hopefully I could get an answer that could be understood by something other than the demented maze of the female mind.

"Josh, I'm concerned you may expect me to accept another date and I may need to disappoint you." She looked down at her drink. *Ouch!!* Well, that was clear enough. My smile faded. I'm sure my future disappointment already was evident on my face.

"I guess I'll have to plan it so that you can't resist," I said, trying to make light of the blow I had just received to my guts.

"I'll be looking forward to what you come up with. And I didn't say 'I would' I said 'I may'...And I think your three minutes are up," she smiled that warm smile she knew I wanted to see. Letting me down easy.

"M'lady, you seem to have many suitors, are there any of particular interest?" I retreated back to playing my part. The chivalrous Knight-errant. It was a comfortable defense.

"Your question is impertinent, *Sir*," she frowned and turned her head in a staged manner. But as I told you I don't have time to date and therefore I *may* need to disappoint you," smiling again as she looked at me across her drink.

So it wasn't me, per se; she was just too busy, period. I could live with that. My heart came up a few inches off the floor. I was pretty busy myself.

"Now will *you* stand for cross examination, Sir?" She was back in a playful mood, and I was relieved. Getting to know the real Cassandra had to be done in small amounts, sort of like getting a tan. Too much at once and you would come away painfully burnt.

"Sure... I stand open ... remember, three minutes." I replied, a little guarded.

"You're a junior, right. Seventeen?"

"Yes. And I will be in August." I hoped that had no bearing on anything.

"Hmm...What's it like to be the son of David Reinhart?"

"I guess I don't know what you mean. He's my dad."

"I mean, what's it like to be the son of a multi-millionaire CEO legend? I'll bet there are some great parties," she smiled, but held a steady hazel gaze.

"Oh, ... you know, I don't think of him that way; just lately I've noticed the wealth and power he controls. All I want is to spend more time with him. He's always away on business, Washington, or back to headquarters. This year I've gotten more time on his schedule, he's making a real effort now, knowing I'll be in college soon." And knowing we have the country to save, I thought. I paused and then continued.

"And I got a lot of plans to make this country better somehow. I don't like the direction its going and I think we need to get back to some fundamental truths. All that power and money is useless unless it can make an impact." Wow! Where did that come from? It was true, but the last thing I needed was to discuss the CRIMSON plan even in general terms.

"Hmm...You don't seem like the devil-may-care rich kid I thought you'd be. I figured you for a guy who's never seen hard times and never will, so it doesn't really matter what happens." She was looking at me with those large eyes, green with golden specs. "But I can see you're deeper than that." Then she turned serious, "Josh, I want to be in a position of power too some day; and I want to use my skills for more than just making money."

Well, I had wanted to know more about Cassandra, but this was a pretty deep discussion for a skating date and some dinner. I decided the best way to keep from slipping up about the Vision was to change the subject, a little diversion.

"Don't get me wrong, there are some *great* parties, too," I said as we laughed, a little uneasy about the direction the conversation had been heading.

She texted her mom as I paid the check, knowing my first evening with Cassandra was coming to an end. I thought it had gone reasonably well, except perhaps for my 'I got a lot of plans to make this country better' speech. I even remembered to help her with her jacket as we stepped out into the cool night air. Standing outside the restaurant, I thought I heard my name being called from across the parking lot.

"Josh! Josh Reinhart!" I look toward the sound to see Jeff Petersen in his hockey jersey coming toward us. *Just* what I needed.

"Hey, Josh! I thought that was you. What are you doing here?" as he appraised Cassandra with obvious approval.

"We were skating, what about you?" Try to be cool, perhaps this will not get back to CRIMSON. Right, I imagined Facebook adding a dozen more data servers to help manage the overload of traffic.

"I have a league game here tonight. Introduce me?" He was not going to let this juicy piece of news get by without all the details. 'Josh Reinhart, leader of CRIMSON was seen outside of the Aliso Ice Castle tonight with Cassandra Perez, lead debater for REASON. Well, Josh and Cassandra, what tangled web of deceit and treachery are you cooking up within the Christian Homeschool Debate League? This is Gina Gossip, more hot rumors at eleven.'

"Jeff Petersen, Cassandra Perez," I said as low as possible.

"Hi Jeff." I don't think she was too excited about this either.

"Cassandra. Hey, our game starts in about ten minutes. You're welcome to watch." Was he *kidding*? I didn't think Jeff knew Cassandra, but she was known by everyone else in CRIMSON. This was not good.

"Ah ..Thanks Jeff, but we've got to get back. Have a great game." Please let this conversation end, right here and now.

"Sure, see you at CRIMSON." Arrghh!

After he was outside of earshot, Cassandra turned to me in a low voice,

"He's in CRIMSON?" She was concerned, too. Probably thought this would get back to REASON somehow.

"Yeah, he just joined so he didn't recognize you, but everyone else will."

I couldn't believe the timing. Five minutes either way and this would never have happen.

"I'm sorry, Josh. This is going to be difficult for you, isn't it?" She actually seemed concerned for me; I warmed up inside.

"No... Well, maybe a little. I mean I *am* a CRIMSON team leader, and you *are* the lead debater for REASON. But can't a guy ask a girl out to skating and dinner without causing an international incident in the Homeschool Debate League?" We both chuckled, knowing it could certainly cause ripples in our little world. Perhaps I was making too big a thing of it. All in my mind. Maybe Jeff would forget about it after a great hockey game. Who knows?

Cassandra gave me a terrific smile, and her perfume closed the gap between us.

"Don't you think most desirable things are worth a little trouble?" And then, "Besides, I'm sure you can handle it." She stepped in and took my hands which were pretty warm after all this. My heart came way off the floor and pounded in my ears once again. She gave me her warm smile and those big eyes. I was completely mesmerized by her musical voice. I was fully aware she knew she had that effect on me, but it didn't change anything. "Call me with that irresistible plan of yours," she whispered.

She turned, and I could see the black van pulling into the parking lot. She waved to her mom.

I watched as the van drove out of the lot. Then I walked back to my "trusty steed." 'Desirable' and 'Trouble' having a wrestling match in my head. The next few days might get very interesting, but one thing I was certain of, I would find a way to see Cassandra again. 'Trouble' had lost tonight, but was definitely looking for a rematch.

Chapter Twelve

Unintended Consequences

*"Men must be ready, they must pride themselves and be
happy to sacrifice their private pleasures, passions and
interests, nay, their private friendships and dearest
connections, when they stand in competition with the
rights of society."* – John Adams

In the next few weeks "busy" was not the word for it. CRIMSON
was preparing for the next tournament, my midterm exams were
coming up, and I was now in serious "SAT prep" mode. Mom
had added an extra hour labeled 'SAT' to my already hectic
schedule each day and one more on Saturday. There was no way
after the last dozen years of homeschooling me she was going to
drop her guard and back off now. Expectations for the 'first
born' just got set higher if that were possible. I barely had time
to turn around, but I did call Cassandra back (*within* the week this
time) and let her know it was not possible for me to see her right
now due to my schedule. She said she understood and that she
would probably have had to turn me down in any case as things
were getting super busy for her, too. I figured I would see her at
the tournament and I would have to be satisfied with that for now.
One bright spot in all of this was this was evidently Jeff had

failed to mention Cassandra, either because he forgot, or he decided it wasn't his business. Either way, I prayed thanks to The Lord for His everlasting kindness.

At the CRIMSON meetings we were all focused on the upcoming tournament. The first hour was spent on technique, practicing cross examination and refutation, followed by a practice round. The CRIMSON team was operating like a well oiled machine, partly due to an unlikely situation. Since her victory at San Diego, Rebekah had developed a following of sorts. Some of the younger, less experienced debaters hung out at her end of the table. Even Jeff Petersen was getting the benefit of her extraordinary expertise and in return she was getting some much needed practice in social skills. That was not to say that from time to time some of her charges didn't have to duck out of the way of the blue lasers or a sharp remark, but she was beginning to fit in. I, on the other hand, was still on "ignore", and although I would catch her glancing at me under her hair from time to time, not a word had been said other than an occasional terse "hello." This certainly suited my desire to avoid Rebekah in my attempt to keep the Vision secret; but I had begun to enjoy our rather challenging relationship (sort of like blue laser tag), and I had to admit I missed it. I also wondered what was going on in that very creative and complex mind. Was she actively trying to figure out my secret, and if so, how and how close was she to finding out? I was caught on the horns of a dilemma as they say and the painful analogy was appropriate. On one horn, I was curious about what she was up to; and on the other horn, I didn't trust myself to keep the secret from her. I had been reading "The Art of War" as part of my History / Literature studies and Sun-tzu stated that "If you know your enemy and know yourself you will not lose 100 battles." While I would never consider Rebekah my enemy, she *was* trying to unravel a secret that was vital to me. Sun Tzu also said, "If your opponent is temperamental, seek to irritate him" (or her in this case). Maybe I should take old Sun Tzu's advice, the former, knowing Rebekah, might truly never be accomplished, but I had no problem succeeding in the latter, in fact I had a gift for it. Maybe at the next CRIMSON meeting I would see what I could do.

The TPM was working on the details of the influence plans for the point men and women of CRIMSON. Dad had met with two of them. Jillian Holladay was a first year law student at Georgetown. Her family was in CHESS and their youngest daughter Carrie would be eleven next year. The other was Aaron Morris, in his final year at John Adams; he was headed to Harvard if he could afford it. Aaron was an only son, and so his parents were no longer active in CHESS, but they had formed long term friendships with the Stantons and Petersens. In both cases, a meeting with David Reinhart, CEO of Prescience was an opportunity the two law students had been excited about. Dad had indicated to Jillian that he was sure next year she would be in line for an internship with a congressman he knew. And Aaron was given assurances that he should not be overly concerned about his financial needs. There was no doubt that the CRIMSON plan was underway. The rest of the week passed without much excitement just a torrid schedule of study.

How's the investigation going, Miss Sherlock? ☺ *Josh.*

Rebekah crushed the note with one hand as her head jerked up from her debate notebook where it had been placed. She colored noticeably as she fired both lasers at full power down the table. They drilled into me, but I held my grin and composure, sitting back in my seat trying not to chuckle. She finally looked away, answering a question about the second amendment in an overly sharp manner. This might be fun; she had treated me like I was non-existent for the last few weeks and I had missed her intriguing personality and those blue eyes. OK, now to see if old Sun-tzu knew what he was talking about. Leaving CRIMSON, I noticed a folded piece of paper on my windshield. In her usual perfect script came the answer.

Things are going quite well, thank you. All will be known soon.

P.S. How are you enjoying your prayer meetings?

Oh Man, that last bit about the TPM got my attention. I wondered if I would have gotten that hint without my aggravating note. If Rebekah ever figured out the CRIMSON plan or found out about the Vision, I was not quite sure what I would do, but at least I had gathered some intelligence.

****

My meeting with Dad on Sunday was full of excitement. I hadn't seen him this enthused since the roll-out of a new killer-app for Anticip8. He said that tomorrow the "Christian Homeschool Aid Foundation" would be announced.

It had taken his lawyers a while to set up the anonymous charitable organization and get it properly funded (by Dad, of course). Even though it would appear anonymous, Dad had total control of where the scholarships and financial aid went. The announcement would indicate that there would be at least six undergrad scholarships available and four additional law school scholarships. Then he talked about the CRIMSON plan, and he was very encouraged by his meetings with Jillian and Aaron. He expected Aaron to receive one of the law school scholarships. Jillian was on her way to getting into the D.C. scene as well. Yes, it would all take time, but the seeds were getting planted; we had to trust in God that the trees would grow and be fruitful (as Mom would say).

The next day CRIMSON was abuzz with the news. Scholarships were available to homeschoolers setting a course for the legal profession. "CHAF", as it was instantly tagged, was lighting up the email and chat boards across the Homeschool Debate League. The CHESS Moms Network was probably overtaxing the cell towers around Santa Sonoma. Mrs. Stanton was inundated by calls from perspective CRIMSON members, 'when were sign-ups? Can I join now? How much time does it take? … and what about expenses?' I could see that CRIMSON was going to get a lot bigger, and it would be a lot more work for the leaders. Mrs. Stanton was having a hard time getting the team to focus on the tournament next week, but she was almost as excited as the team members about the possibility of some of her students getting to go to the colleges of their choice.

In stark contrast to the jubilant tone of the meeting and all the excitement, Rebekah held a very dark expression. She was slicing up her unprotected minions with laser blasts and scathing comments. Her attitude was so toxic that by the end of the meeting only a couple of her group would sit by her. She acknowledge my "Hi" with a hissed "…You!" blue eyes glistening, glaring; then she stomped away. Wow! She was really angry and upset about something. I didn't think it had anything to do with my note last week; I had no clue. Even if she had found out something about the CRIMSON plan, it shouldn't have caused this severe reaction. Perhaps Robert knew; I hadn't seen her like this since she was in Kennedy Airport, and I had actually only heard her then. I knew Rebekah was volatile, but this time she was just this side of going nuclear. I saw her in the parking lot, followed at a safe distance (no need to start World War III), and watched her get into the back of the Miller's minivan. As the door slid closed, I saw the small blond girl bury her face in her hands, rocking forward in pain. I was struck by a wave of concern and puzzlement; I mean I still considered Rebekah my friend, and it was hard to see her in such a state. I wondered if someone in her family had died, or ... I'll have to give Robert a call.

Another note on my car, I would have to tell her there was such a thing as human conversation. I got in my car and opened the note. No question it was from Rebekah, but the handwriting wasn't quite the perfect script I was used to seeing, and the note was somewhat crumpled and there was no flourish or signature.

I thought you were the one I could trust.
I wanted it to be true so I could share things with you. I was a fool.
You're a leader in CRIMSON, they look up to you. How could you do it?

Josh, your secret is safe with me but others know, too.

Oh MAN! This was *not* good. Had Rebekah figured out the CRIMSON plan? I guess that could cause the reaction. If she didn't know about the Vision, it would seem a little devious; perhaps even sinister to be planning out the team's entire career paths and lives for them. Others know? What others? I had to talk with Robert, first thing tomorrow.

"Hi, Mrs. Miller, it's Josh Reinhart. Can I speak to Robert please?" I hadn't called the Miller's in a while, I hoped he was home, I figured lunch time would be good.

"Just a minute, Josh.... Robert, it's Josh." I could hear some conversation in the background, sounded like Rebekah's voice, something like "....not here.....", then Robert came on the line.

"Hi, Josh. What's up?" Robert was so straight forward, I hoped he could help.

"Can I talk to you in private?" I didn't want anyone to hear even his side of the conversation, especially Rebekah.

"Sure, hang on while I go outside," he replied, and then, "Ok, go ahead."

"Have you noticed Rebekah acting strange lately?" Might as well get it out in the open.

"You mean strange–ER?" he chuckled. "Come to think of it, she has been more prickly than usual for the last day or so, and very emotional. Cries for no reason."

"Well, did she say anything, about CRIMSON ....or me?" I had to know what this was about.

"Well, I did hear her say to mom, 'I would rather drink battery acid than talk to him', but I don't know who she was referring to. You think it's you?... Why?"

Obviously, Robert was more in the dark than I was.

"I don't know, but she has been ignoring me and then last night at CRIMSON she was really upset, and if looks could kill, I would be buried already." I couldn't tell him about her note, but any extra information would be helpful. There was a pause on the other end, then Robert sighed.

"Josh, you *do* know she likes you, right?" Oh great, now my friends are spreading this.

"You're *kidding*.   She's barely spoken to me for a month. Besides she's only *thirteen*." I couldn't believe I was having this conversation.

"Who is spreading this? I mean, I like Rebekah, but I don't '*like*' her,… you know what I mean." How did we get on *this* subject?

"Look Josh, ever since San Diego, it's all over CRIMSON, didn't you know?" Robert was acting like it was old news. Was I that dense? It would explain some things, but I would have to recalculate with this new information.

"OK, even *if* the rumor is true, does this explain her latest behavior?" I was still worried about the CRIMSON plan and the Vision.

"Well, I don't know. You tell me, what could make her so upset she stays locked in her room with her law books for hours at a time? That's pretty weird, even for her." He was trying to help, but he didn't have much more to offer; besides I was starving.

"Well, the tournament *is* next week… hours huh?   ….Well, thanks. And if you think of anything call me." I was hungry and just a little confused.

I hung up the phone and went into the kitchen to see what was in the 'fridge' to warm up.

I can just hear all the little 'tweens' giggling behind my back.

" 'Bekah is 'crushing' on Josh, *everybody* knows it."

Everybody, that is, but the big dumb hoopster…

As I sat down to some barbequed chicken, I tried to rethink all the conversations and incidents over the last couple of months in light of this new information, assuming it was even true.

In some ways it certainly would help explain a few things: The way she kept glancing at me under her hair. Her temperamental nature when I didn't take her seriously. Even the time we debated at her home and she had not seen me out after shredding me in front of her mom, seeming to be upset with herself. And most of all, our strange conversations after her victory at San Diego and at the Ice Castle.

I went into my room after downing a half quart of milk. I found the folded note from last night and re-read it. One thing Rebekah was and that was concise. She could pack more meaning into a few words than most people could in a paragraph. So I needed to carefully study this note, it was the only other piece of evidence I had. I sat down at my desk and after reading it over a few times, assuming my new information as a basis, I formulated some questions.

I thought you were the one I could trust.
I wanted her to trust me, I needed her help.
I must have broken a trust of some kind. Had I promised something or someone?
I wanted it to be true so I could share things with you. I was a fool.
She felt foolish because I had not been trustworthy? She had tried to share things? What things? Every time we talked she was always holding back. OK, so was I, but that was different, that was the Vision.
You're a leader in CRIMSON, they look up to you. How could you do it?
I did something against CRIMSON? And the team? WHAT? CRIMSON was so important to me right now, how could I damage it? What had I done?

Josh, your secret is safe with me but others know, too.
What secret? What others?

I stared at the note; I knew Rebekah was trying to determine what I was doing about the Vision, but what if this note had nothing to do with the CRIMSON plan or the Vision. What if the note meant something else entirely, but still involved CRIMSON.

I decided to start with the easiest question. What Secret? Unlike most sixteen year olds, this could be more complicated than expected. I got out a legal pad and listed the secrets I knew.
The Vision,
The gray nation
The CRIMSON plan,
The Point men
The TPM
CHAF
Rebekah's cases that I used as my own.
The private jet to San Diego for Rebekah.
Rebekah likes me. (Rumor – not a secret).
I believed in Rebekah's abilities before anyone else in CRIMSON
Rebekah has a secret or talent that she won't tell (not my secret, but her's)
Rebekah is trying to figure out my secrets (I think this is a secret).
I need to be the best debater I can be, go to Nats at least, and lead by example.
I am leading CRIMSON because of the plan, not necessarily because I wanted to.
I spend too much time thinking about girls (specifically, two: Cassandra and …. yes, Rebekah) and not focusing. (this is a confession, not a secret)

The date with Ca

I stopped writing and sat back in my chair.

What an *idiot*!

Rebekah had found out about Cassandra!

I mentally plugged my date with Cassandra into the equation that consisted of Rebekah's note.

The only possible answer came back: Josh, you are an IDIOT.

It all fit, in Rebekah's eyes I had betrayed CRIMSON and the Team by taking Cassandra out. Other's know… at least one, Jeff. And finally if the rumor was true, I had hurt Rebekah, unknowingly, but still ….

No wonder she was upset. But how could I explain that I hadn't done anything but taken Cassandra out ice skating and we had dinner. No big deal (Liar). OK, so yes, the date was a big deal (to me at least), but I didn't betray anything, and it's not like I had breached some contract or trust. I hadn't even set up another date. (but you tried…).

I was trying hard to justify my actions, and the more I thought about it, I did look like, well,… a traitor. Certainly from Rebekah's point of view, but even from the CRIMSON team's for that matter. What would Mrs. Stanton think? I wonder if she knows? It was just some ice skating and dinner….

****

The second tournament of the season was underway up in Anaheim and all of California Homeschool debate was there. I hadn't been able to talk to Rebekah, and Robert had not given any indication that he knew about my date with Cassandra. But I had seen the REASON team crossing the quad, and did catch sight of their lovely black haired competitor. I would try to meet up with her later.

It was the second day and the breaks were being announced. Things had gone well for CRIMSON. Robert, Ben, Dan Jr., Steve and I had all broken, along with Elizabeth, Alison and, of course, Rebekah. In the first set of Octo rounds, we lost Ben, Steve and Alison. I was not really prepared for what happened next as the pairings for the next elimination rounds were posted.

Robert Miller vs Dan Simmons
John Hall vs Rebekah Miller
Elizabeth Simmons vs Michael Johnson
Cassandra Perez vs Josh Reinhart

OH GREAT! I could feel a full body blush burning up into my face, no stopping it.
Rebekah was standing a little in front of me, and she turned back with a glare that in another reality would have severed my head from my body. Her lips barely moved, but I thought I heard "…fool." I didn't know if she was describing me or herself. Certainly, I had been proved a fool for not considering this very real possibility. Can you say "Conflict of interest?" Except for Jeff, Rebekah might still be the only person that knew about my date with Cassandra. She had made it abundantly clear what she thought about me in that regard. She walked off without looking further at anyone with her head down. I asked if anyone had a flow of Cassandra's new Aff, and Steve gave me his with, "Good Luck, you're going to need it." Evidently, his debate with her in prelims had not gone well. What a mess! I couldn't just fall for some nice uncomplicated communications major, or someone

unrelated to CRIMSON. NO-oo, it had to be the top REASON
debater. The one person who had sworn revenge for her 'poor'
3rd place showing in San Diego. I had never debated Cassandra
before, but then my mind flew back to a cross-ex over Chinese
noodles on a very different topic, when I was trying to determine
if I had a chance with her.

Using her musical voice and that knockout smile, "I now stand
open for cross examination." The three judges, two men and one
woman, were ready. I began by attempting to pull apart
Cassandra's definitions. She answered coolly and with resolve,
continuing to smile at the judges. Not much luck there, perhaps
another approach. "Do you think slavery was a justifiable
practice?"

"What do you mean by justifiable?" she replied dodging,
delaying.

"Do you think slavery should be allowed legally in the United
States?" I rephrased. She was not going to be drawn in.

"No, I think slavery is wrong, and I believe that many of those
who drafted the Constitution wanted to abolish it," she answered.

"Was slavery allowed in the United States after the Constitution
was ratified?" I pressed.

"Yes. Although within the Declaration of Independence we can
see that the Founding Fathers wanted to declare all men free," she
continued to attempt to support her position.

I pulled out another brief, another approach.

"Do you think men and women who meet the standards of the
state in which they reside should be able to vote?" I asked.

"....Yes," she finally answered warily.

"Do you believe in the tenants of The Bill of Rights?" I asked.

"Of course, The Bill of Rights is a cornerstone of our laws."

Hmmm, a straight forward reply. Time to set the trap.

"But isn't it true that it was necessary to modify the original Constitution with The Bill of Rights and then later to achieve the abolition of slavery and allow women to vote." I thought this should be a straight forward yes or no, but now I found out why Cassandra had gone to Nats the last two years. She began without notes, with great confidence,

"Again, The Bill of Rights is not a modification of the Constitution, rather an extension of the original. And as far as the abolition of slavery, again I assert that many framers of the Declaration of Independence and the Constitution determined that slavery should be abolished. Likewise, I believe that women were also considered within the Declaration of Independence as its states: 'We hold these truths to be self-evident, that all men are created equal, that they are endowed by their Creator with certain unalienable Rights, that among these are Life, Liberty and the pursuit of Happiness. — That to secure these rights, Governments are instituted among Men, deriving their just powers from the consent of the governed.' It is *obvious* that *women*, as well as men, are *the governed,* and therefore the *government's just powers* are derived from the *women's consent* (or vote) as well as the men's. I think this is clear by the text and this is the intent of the framers of the Declaration of Independence as well as the Constitution." Concluding, she flashed her signature smile at the judge and then at me, as the timer signaled my cross-ex time was up.

Sorry Josh, no simple 'let your Yes be Yes and your No be No.' She wasn't about to give on any point, and her tactics were excellent, using up much of my three minutes of cross-ex time with *her* speech and arguments.

"....I have provided strong voting points supporting my negative arguments and have shown inaccuracies and inconsistencies in my opponent's case. Therefore, Judges, I strongly urge you to cast your ballots in favor of the negative. Thank you." I sat down.

Had I done my best? Was I influenced by my feelings for her? Yes, I had to admit, my pulse had raced when she had stepped into the room in a perfectly fitted black suit, with a gold blouse, flashing me her warm smile with a "Josh, how nice to see you again." Graceful as ever.

She sure hadn't taken it easy on me, not that I had expected anything different. She was very well prepared and had me stumbling a couple of times trying to defend my position. The fact that during the round on two occasions she had given me that warm smile, flashing those big green eyes in gold speckled mode, hadn't helped. She was using all her considerable skills to win this tournament.

After leaving the room, I figured I lost either way. If I won the round, it was unlikely Cassandra would even answer my calls. And if I lost, I had to wonder if I had been compromised by my feelings for her, even subconsciously. And to top it off, at least two people in CRIMSON would feel I had dropped my guard and damaged the integrity of the team.

I was never more nervous than waiting for the final round postings; they finally came.

Cassandra Perez vs Rebekah Miller
Robert Miller vs Michael Johnson

I had lost, I felt a terrible knot in the pit of my stomach, a jumbled mixture of emotions, none praise worthy and no small amount of shame. The "first born" had failed the test.

"Rebekah...," I was just able to get it out as she turned toward me.

"I'll take care of *this*," she hissed as she pushed passed me through the small crowd.

I turned to watch her leave, blond hair swaying, on a mission. The CRIMSON stealth bomber had just been launched with orders to destroy the competition with "extreme prejudice."

****

"Runner up in the Anaheim Lincoln Douglas debate tournament.. Michael Johnson - RESOLUTE," The tournament director stood at the microphone.   The CRIMSON team cheered wildly, Rebekah had taken first again.

"First place and representing the Anaheim tournament at the Lincoln Douglas debate national invitational tournament," he paused for affect, "Rebekah Miller - CRIMSON."

CRIMSON just kept cheering, "Bekah, Bekah...," as the little debate genius collected another gigantic trophy. She held it up for photos, but there was little or no smile and not one tear from the brilliant blues. Ice was flowing in her veins.

I had not gone to any final rounds, but I heard from those in attendance that Rebekah had taken no prisoners. In fact, at one point in the round, she had actually broken Cassandra's cool, polished demeanor causing her to utter under her breath "... you little..." before recovering her poise. Rebekah, on the other hand, had been a master surgeon, slicing and dissecting her opponent's contentions, with dozens of references to back up her position while demolishing her opponent's. They came so fast and furious that some in the audience thought she might lose some points due to possible inaccuracy, because not once had she glance at her big notebook. Yes, Rebekah had "taken care of this" and, in addition, had dispatched Michael in the final round with ease, like he was some collateral damage from the previous debate round.

I clapped like a robot. My mind was focused on what I had (and had not) done. I had lost an important friend and ally. I may have lost the respect of my team and even my parents. I had put my personal desires and feelings above my commitments and my better judgment. The CRIMSON plan was in jeopardy and with it the key to the Vision.

Josh Reinhart .... Supposed Great CRIMSON leader, ...Secret agent for the TPM... Savior of the Gray Nation...First Born of the Reinhart Clan....what a joke.

I collected my ballots. There would be another late night victory party and I was expected to attend. I told Mom I wasn't feeling that great and I would be home soon, keeping my appearance to a minimum. She said she understood (although I doubt if she understood completely) and told me how proud she was of my seventh place trophy. As she left with Sarah, I wondered if she had figured it out. Did my face betray my true feelings? It was hard to say.

Lying in bed that night, I prayed. It was a humble prayer; I questioned whether God even had the right man for this immensely important job. I asked God for help and that He would guide me. I asked Him to direct me to those from whom I should take counsel. And finally I prayed that a little blond girl would someday think highly of me again, or at the very least not hate me. I finally fell asleep, exhausted.

Chapter Thirteen

Revealing Secrets

"I am not influenced by the expectation of promotion or pecuniary reward. I wish to be useful, and every kind of service necessary for the public good, become honorable by being necessary." – Nathan Hale

The Ice Castle parking lot was the usual menagerie of minivans and SUVs; but I had decided to park across the street and walk a little, trying to reduce the tension. This was not going to be easy. The café was busy, but I spied her blond hair toward the back. I prepared for the onslaught as I sat down across from her in the booth.

"I don't remember inviting you to sit with me." Her lasers blazed and her mouth was set in a tight thin line.

"Rebekah, please, just listen. I got a couple of things to say, and then I'll leave you alone." She was about to say something and then just drilled me with her eyes, arms crossed in front.

"I know you think I betrayed CRIMSON and the team. You think I abused our friendship and destroyed any trust we had." I figured I would lay it all out, no sense in trying to be tricky or charming... never had worked with her anyway.

"OK, yes, I took Cassandra Perez ice skating and we had dinner. But I never discussed anything of importance regarding CRIMSON. I would never do that, I told you, CRIMSON is too important to me."

"Why *her*, Josh? Why Cassandra? You can't trust her; all she cares about is winning," Rebekah fired back. I guess if blue eyes could turn green, I would have witnessed it right there. And *Rebekah* never cared about winning? I decided to drop that contention; no sense pouring gasoline on a forest fire.

"She invited me back to her cotillion, and I said I would call her. I gave my word."

This excuse had sounded lame the first time; now using it on Rebekah, it sounded ridiculous.

"*Back!*" Even upset, she didn't miss anything.

"Yeah...ah...After San Diego, she invited me to cotillion. I went once, and then she asked me back." Why did I feel like a grave digger ...I was just getting myself deeper and deeper.

"So you just *couldn't* wait and *had* to ask her out." She was ice cold as she looked at me and then dropped her eyes examining her glass. She had cut right through to the heart of the matter. Yes, I hadn't even thought about waiting six weeks till the next cotillion. I could feel a strong flush rising into my face.

"Yes, but I didn't give anything away, it was *just* dinner," was all I could say.

"Did she ask about CRIMSON.....about ...me?" She still wouldn't look up.

"Actually she did. She couldn't understand how you could have won the San Diego tournament. I think she thought it was a fluke." Man, I sure didn't want to get into this.

"A *fluke*!... you know I work harder than anyone, Josh, *you know*. What *did* you tell her?" I could tell by her voice she was powering up the lasers.

"I didn't tell her anything...like I said. She seemed a little disappointed about that, hurt feelings. I think she's used to getting her way." Arrgh! Too much information Josh, just keep it simple.

"And what about...my..." Rebekah shook her head

".... Don't you see? It's how it looks," she pleaded as she looked up; she was mad and hurt, now she was going to let me have it, blue eyes glistening.

"When Jeff told me, I couldn't *believe* it. I knew it was a lie. I told him you would never do a thing like... like that. I told him, '*Not* Josh, he's got too much integrity. You can trust *him* .... ' But Jeff described her too accurately;... Said you seemed to be enjoying yourself. He was *so* smug, and I .... I looked like such a fool." She looked down at her drink.

She had believed in me; gone out on a limb for me at CRIMSON, and I had chopped it right off. She had put me up on a pedestal, and I had fallen flat. Josh Reinhart, black-hearted scoundrel and Benedict Arnold of the Homeschool Debate League.

"You're not a fool...I wasn't thinking ..., I told you, your important to me."

"You say that... but you *like her*," she retorted, voice cracking.

"I thought so,.... I don't know, *maybe* I do, but I've decided not to see her again. Even though I didn't betray anything, I have too many important commitments I can't afford to jeopardize. Leading CRIMSON, my rep with the team... and you, my studies ...SAT's." Reputation and trust, two of the most fragile things in life, and I had thoughtlessly shattered them both.

"Josh... I ..." It was almost a whisper, her shoulders shaking a little. I waited but nothing ...

"Look, I don't expect instant forgiveness. I understand if you don't trust me now, but maybe I can win your trust back someday." It was a true prayer.

I got up to leave, "Rebekah, you're the last person in the world I wanted to hurt; I hope you can believe that." I walked past her and she just looked straight ahead as I saw a tear fall.

I had said my piece and walked out of the café. The icy air from the rink hit me full in the face, which was still flush. With just a few small choices, I had sure created a lot of trouble. All I had really wanted was to take Cassandra out on a date. Was that such a crime? It wasn't like she was Mata Hari. On top of that, I hadn't betrayed anything, or *anyone* for that matter. So why did I feel so guilty?

I got behind the wheel and drove off without looking back at the rink. I'd had enough of this, from now on I was just going to focus on what I had to get done. One thing was for sure, women were simply more trouble than they were worth.

****

The rest of the school year was just insane. SATs, finals, the national debate tournament, TPM, the CRIMSON plan ....   I committed myself to excel in the SATs, and Mom was more than happy to oblige putting on the full court press 24/7.

CRIMSON was in a state of constant effort especially for those members going to Nats – Robert, Elizabeth and Rebekah. My trip to Nats would have to wait till next year. Unlike Cassandra, I had not amassed enough points to garner one of the four at-large slots available in our region. Sixth and seventh places were just not good enough at this level of competition. In some ways I was relieved; SATs were my main focus, and I just didn't need the distraction and stress of going to Nats and experiencing the levels of rampant tension sure to be present. And while Cassandra got her wish and was going, nothing had prepared the California Homeschool debate community for Rebekah; she had won every debate she had entered and took the state finals undefeated. Word was out that there was a 'phenom' coming out of California to Nats. The entire universe of debate chat boards was buzzing. She would no longer be completely stealthy; everyone had heard of 'Bekah Miller. But unless they had seen her in action, she would still surprise any opponent with her less than five foot stature and her brilliant mind. There were no traditional debate weapons to match CRIMSON's little blond genius.

My difficult decision to not contact Cassandra, even to congratulate her, was made a little easier because of my hectic schedule. I also took solace in the fact that she was probably busier than I was getting ready for Nats and preparing to attend John Adams. This was fine for now, but during the summer it might be a different story. I was still periodically tempted to pick up the phone and call her, but to what purpose? An awkward congratulations to her for defeating me at Anaheim and winning a slot at Nats. Then exchanging pleasantries before both saying we were too busy to even talk much more right now. Just because I wanted to hear that voice again. Nope, better to leave it alone for now. And next year didn't hold much promise either, she was off to J.A. and collegiate debate; and I would still be trying to make it to Nats and playing blue laser tag with Miss Miller.

This summer wasn't all play and no work either; I was signed up for a six week summer camp at John Adams. It was a way to get acquainted with the University before my senior year, to determine if that was where I really wanted to go; and also to get more prepared for what was going to be a challenging academic environment. And then CRIMSON would start up in mid-August, with forty-one members, by far the largest team in the nation. The success of this year's team and the promise of CHAF had done the trick; all part of the CRIMSON plan, but that meant more work for the "first born."

****

"Honey, won't you give me just a little hint about tonight?" Mom was trying her best to get some preview of the TPM meeting tonight. To say that she was excited was an understatement. She had been on pins and needles ever since Sunday night when Dad had told her that all the wives were requested to attend the men's prayer meeting this week. Amazingly, the actual purpose and activities of the TPM had remained secret for these seven months. Perhaps because the Moms were just too busy with homeschooling to play detective or perhaps it was God's timing; either way, the Vision would be a big surprise tonight. We walked in with Mr. and Mrs. Stanton, and for once the Moms didn't huddle together, but each sat with their husbands after some brief greetings.

Dad and I had spent the last two Sunday evenings preparing a slide presentation for this special night. He stood up and raised his hand for silence.
"First, I would like Pastor Miller to open with prayer." Dad sat down and Pastor Miller rose.

"Heavenly Father, Glory to You and thank You for bringing us together. May You impart Your plans and vision to all of us tonight. Let our hearts and minds be joined together for Your purposes, Lord. Thank You for blessing all the men with their partner that completes and supports them. Bless this meeting and may our efforts all be for Your Glory. Amen."

Dad stood again and began.

"Tonight is a special night for the Thursday Prayer Meeting, and I am sure that all the wives are wondering why we have invited you to our meeting. In order to properly explain, I need to go back to last fall. It's important that you hear the whole story; and please, if you could hold your questions until I am done, I think that will make this go more smoothly." Some of the wives murmured to their husbands but then gave Dad their full attention.

"All the men in this room tonight attended the men's retreat last October. It started out like many of the retreats in the past; we had fellowship, worship, and a Saturday evening prayer session. That night as we slept, each of us was given the same Vision – a dream of sorts…" The room stirred as the wives shot glances at their husbands and more than one 'why didn't you tell me?' was heard.

"Please, let me explain," Dad paused before continuing.

"Harold… Thank you." My dad took a folder from Mr. Stanton and spread the pads of paper on the table.

"The next morning, before we had time to discuss anything, Mr. Stanton had us all draw our impressions of the dream separately, and here is the result." The wives looked at the pads and this time there was a lot more noise and exclamation. Dad let the affect of the shared Vision sink in and then asked for quiet again. It was interesting to watch him work the audience. I noticed that

Mom had not said a word; she was just watching very intently. She knew this was very important to him.

"As you can see, the dreams were identical." Dad put the first power point up, a small animation of sorts, showing the flag going gray, the seven points of light and the red ribbon flowing from left to right. Then the message, "all that is necessary...."

"This is the dream or Vision that we all saw. We prayed that Sunday morning and asked God for guidance and wisdom. God had called us to action for His purpose – the men in this room, your husbands and Josh, are the seven points of light." He let that sink in and then continued.

"We decided to meet again the next week, so the Thursday prayer meetings began what we call the TPM. At each meeting we do a lot of praying, but there is also brainstorming and planning. What did the Vision mean and what were we supposed to do? Some things were obvious: the graying of the flag was something very bad happening to our country. The voice told us we needed to act. The pinpoints of light – the seven men in this room," Dad paused again.

"Then there were the mysteries, the things about the Vision that were less obvious. Just what was going to happen to the country and what did the red ribbon mean, what were we called to do, what actions did God want us to take?" He took a long breath and started.

"We determined that the best way to influence the moral decay in this country was through the courts. We needed to somehow influence the higher courts in the land to take a more Christian world view, to reverse course from their attempts to remove all Godliness from our public society. We decided to target the Judgeships and public policy positions, to work to place strong Christian leaders into the open Judge posts and also influence

Washington policy. We needed to find strong Christian lawyers who could make the hard decisions for God, to reverse the graying of the flag." You could see the nodding and murmurs of agreement in the audience, wives and husbands. Dad was sure good at this; there was so much I could learn from him if I could just get more of his time.

"How were we to know we had the right leaders, certain of their conviction? And there was one more mystery, what was the red ribbon running from west to east about? Then Josh had a breakthrough." Everyone looked at me. I fought back a blush.

"He figured out that the source, the group of godly leaders that the Vision required, was to come from CRIMSON." The room erupted, and it took a couple of minutes to settle down.

Dad put up a new slide with the judgeships and possible candidates.

"Here is our current plan –"

More comments and hard looks from the wives, Dad held up his hands trying to calm everyone down.

"OK, I know you all have questions," Dad opened the floor.

"How do you know this is a vision from God and not something else?" Mrs. Simmons was the first.

"Part of this is on faith, but as we have prayed and progressed, God has opened doors and made things happen… we were called to act," Dad replied.

Mrs. McClaren was next, "Why did you wait to tell us until now?"

"We needed the time to be certain of what we were planning, to be sure of the Vision. We wanted to be sure we were on the right track before getting you involved."

"So you plan to use *our* children to fight this fight?" Mrs. Simmons, she had the most at stake in this with eight children in CHESS, and most were planning to be in CRIMSON.

"What we propose is to enable or support our most certain group of godly leaders, the young men and women of CRIMSON, to fully attain their potential and, with God's help, to change the course of our country. Many CRIMSON students want to pursue a career in law and public policy, and more importantly they are sold out to Jesus. So, yes, we are asking that our children join us in the fight to turn this country around and serve Our Lord in the process. But we are not proposing to force anyone to take a course of action that they are not already aligned with."

"Can you give us a real life example, not just slides and words?" Mrs. Simmons wasn't a psychologist for nothing.

"OK, for instance, many of you know John Petersen. He was a debate star in CRIMSON a few years ago and will be graduating from law school next year.

We have opened a couple of doors to offer him a position in Senator Bennett's office. He will begin to impact public policy almost immediately. John is very excited about the opportunity, and it is perfectly in line with his chosen career goals."

"But he doesn't know about this group or the Vision?" Mrs. Simmons questioned.

"No, but he will. You see, that's the beauty of the CRIMSON plan. We *know* John. We know he will be guided by his strong faith and influence policy with his Christian world view, regardless of his knowledge of the Vision. But we do plan to make him part of the Vision eventually.

Pastor Miller spoke up.   "Please understand the secrecy surrounding the Vision is due primarily to our plan's immaturity. We are stepping out in faith, and praying for God's timing to work all things for good, according to His will."

This seemed to settle some of the wives down a bit, they knew their husbands. These were strong Christian men, asking for support from their wives as they took these steps of faith.

Dad finally asked, "I have a question for the wives. We have shown you the Vision God gave us and laid out our plans. We know we are called to this and need your help in what promises to be a great endeavor. We are humbled by the calling, but we know that if it is our sovereign God's will He will accomplish it with or without us. Your husbands have done a lot of inspired work and planning to get to this point. Will you go home tonight and discuss this with them and then continue to join us each week as we try to save our nation?"

It was 10:30 p.m. and we were all exhausted as Dad drove home. Mom was silent the whole way. When we got home I grabbed a snack and went directly to bed. I had lots on my mind but it could wait. I was concerned about Mom's silence and the tension coming home was very unnatural. But I was beat.
There was a light knock on my bedroom door, then Mom looked in.
"You asleep yet?" She said in the near darkness.
"Almost," I sighed sleepily. She walked to my bed, knelt down and whispered, she hadn't done this in many years.
"Josh, I just want to tell you how proud I am of you. You have been carrying this around with you since school started, and somehow you have been able to keep it secret and still excel in all your work. I know it must have been very hard. Plus, Dad says you're playing a crucial role in the seven called by this Vision, and that it was you who initiated the CRIMSON plan. God is really using you, and I am so thrilled..." She kissed my forehead, and I could hear her choke up a bit. She stood up, "You get some sleep now."
She quietly shut the door, and I was out like a light.

****

They were not that uncommon, but occasionally God creates a perfect California summer's day and the postcard photographers work overtime. The CRIMSON beach party was greeted by such a day at Moonlight Beach in Encinitas. The team and their families staked out their turf early in the day that promised to end far into the evening. The fire pits were already smoking and smelled of hot dogs and burgers. Everyone could finally relax, the school year was complete, the SATs were done and the debate season was finished. Jeff was trying to teach me skimboarding, and after a little practice, I actually stayed up and sliced across the wet sand formed by the receding waves. I really couldn't hold a grudge about Jeff divulging my 'secret' date, and I still had my mission for the CRIMSON plan to consider. Robert, Dan Jr. and Ben had shown up in Mr. Stanton's BMW, and there promised to be an epic volleyball game later in the afternoon.

CRIMSON attendance was nearly perfect, apart from one major exception – Rebekah. The stealth bomber had failed to even do a flyover. Once again, I could not imagine why the star would be absent from her team. I had heard all about it from Ben, the diminutive blond girl with piercing blue eyes and amazing mental skills had taken the National debate tournament by storm. She had not lost a round and won the final in a unanimous seven-oh decision. It was unlikely that anyone would repeat this performance; and at thirteen, she was by far the youngest champion in the history of Nats. As for Cassandra, she had the misfortune of crossing wits with Rebekah in the first octo round after breaks, placing her well down in the standings (by her standards). So the driven Miss Perez would just have to be satisfied with her J.A. scholarship. Speaking of scholarships, the collegiate scouts were salivating over Rebekah; their enthusiasm only overshadowed by the offers of full-ride scholarships to Harvard, Stanford, John Adams and Georgetown. The fact that they might have to wait three more years was of no matter. I mean, how often does a "Kobe Bryant" or a "LeBron James" come on the scene?   But as the sun finally melted into the Pacific painting the wispy clouds a deep orange against the china blue sky, the Christian Homeschool Debate national champion had not been sighted.

I had wandered down the beach and was thinking back on the year. What a series of events had transpired. The Vision being the explosive catalyst that had triggered the rest: the TPM, the CRIMSON plan, Rebekah, the point men, CHAF, Cassandra. God had used me and others to accomplish more than I could have imagined, all to His Glory. I was humbled by the thought; I had made so many mistakes (and a few ill advised adventures into the realm of the fairer sex) but God had been faithful to me and to His plans to stop the graying of the flag. The CRIMSON plan was well underway. With Robert taking 4th and Elizabeth 7th at Nats, CRIMSON was viewed as the powerhouse team to beat; and with CHAF as the added inducement, we would field a team of over forty budding CRIMSON plan candidates next year.

I was throwing stones back into the waves enjoying the last of the sun reflecting off the clouds when I heard the sand crunching behind me. I could almost feel the lasers before I turned. She hadn't spoken to me since my confession of sorts at the Ice Castle some weeks ago, and I hadn't really expected her to break her silence today. But even my usual unintentional gaffs couldn't account for the storm that raged on her features.
"Josh, I need to talk to you. I'm going *away*." Her eyes were rimmed in red.
"Away? What do you mean 'going away?'"
"I'm going to *China*," she said it like a curse word.

"China?" Why was I always the one to deal with this? Maybe I should just forget law and become a psychiatrist. 'Ya, ich bin Dr. Reinhart, vut's on your mind?'

"My dad is called to a Missions trip to China, and *I* have to go." She was starting to tear up, trying to hold it back so she could continue.

"For how long?" I asked as calmly as I could. OK, Josh, you prayed she would trust you again someday, and this is a start so try not to put your foot in your mouth.

"A year, maybe more, I don't *know*! ...it depends..." she trailed off, looking down and wiping a tear.

"You mean you won't be in CHESS ...or CRIMSON?"

"NO!..I won't be here...I won't be *anywhere*! it's so *unfair*..." she was mad, and the tears kept flowing. I didn't know what to say.

"Rebekah... I'm sorry...I was hoping we could lead CRIMSON together next year."

"Sorry! You should be *happy*. You don't have to worry about me digging into your secrets anymore. You can *do* whatever you want...*date* whoever..." She had powered up the lasers and they caught me full force. I guess she hadn't gotten to the point of forgiving the knight-errant.

"What about Robert?" Let's try a change of subject.

"Oh, he's just *fine*...off to J.A. But *I* have to go because of my *stupid* age." Her age-old problem, adult mind in a 'tween's body. I felt very sorry for her, but...

"Will it be *so* bad? China might be interesting." Perhaps this was not what the doctor ordered.

"I'm not going on a *sight-seeing* tour. We're traveling to small villages out in the middle of *nowhere*. I won't even have email."

She was pretty distraught, but for a person like Rebekah, where research and books were everything, this could be a personal hell. "When are you leaving?" My guess was soon, otherwise why the rush to tell me.

"In about five weeks... It will be *awful*, I can't take my books ... I...I'll lose a year of my *life*!... Robert said you're going to John Adams camp next week so I ... I won't see you and... and I wanted to ... to let you know before you left," she looked down at her hands.

"Look, it's only a year; it'll go by fast, you'll see and then you'll be back," was my only reply, trying to ease her pain.

"And you'll be at J.A. with Robert and....and I'll *still* be in high school," she fired back.

"That would happen anyway until you catch up to us." And then pass us, I thought.

"But it'll be three years... and I'll be *alone*. I was just starting to fit in, to have some...some friends, you and....but now that's all *ruined*." She was sobbing now.

"You'll forget about... me." She looked up, the sunset reflected in those brilliant eyes glistening with tears.

"Rebekah...no one could ever forget you. You're too... unique." What could I say to make here feel just a little better? It wasn't working. She just sobbed.

"Rebekah... *I'll* never forget you." It was true, she was the most unusual and talented person I had ever known; if I lived to be a hundred, I doubt if I would forget her.

"Oh, Josh....it's so unfair...I may never... *see* you again." Then she gave me a strange look, a piercing gaze with her blue lasers that was like she was scanning my face; it held me for a few moments. I felt like I had just been faxed to some unknown number.

"Bye, Josh," she whispered, and then she turned and walked back up the beach.

I watched the orange glow of the sunset play in her hair swaying as she headed for the parking lot. She was not going to the party, and I understood. I thought about following her, but what would be the point. She had said her piece, and I had tried to understand and be understanding, but she was taking it to extremes again. Of course we would meet again. I would be going to college with her brother for one thing. And as he had said, she was like a Ferrari in the rearview mirror; just a matter of time before she would blow by us, three years tops and she'd be in college. I mean, she already could go to the school of her choice when she got out of high school. How strange it must be to be so brilliant and still be considered a little girl. What frustration she must constantly endure. And now this China trip had put a detour in her carefully crafted life plan. She would have to start over, being an outsider again. The little know-it-all who takes herself too seriously. I said a silent prayer, "Lord, watch over Rebekah. May her trip to China be a safe one; may your Holy Spirit work within her for Your purposes. ...And bring her back safely. Amen."

The final rays of light had disappeared, and I couldn't see her anymore. I sure didn't feel like staying at the party, but I was starving so I headed toward the glow of the fire pits down the beach.

'This is not the end. It is not even the beginning of the end. But it is, perhaps, the end of the beginning."

                                        – Sir Winston Churchill

C.R.I.M.S.O.N. Book Two – "So Help Me God" moves God's plan forward about ten years, and Josh is at the center of it. Find out more about the Vision, the CRIMSON plan, those who are being used by God and those who would do anything to thwart His plans.

C.R.I.M.S.O.N.

Book Two

So Help Me God

"Before God, I believe the hour has come. My judgment approves this measure, and my whole heart is in it. All that I have, and all that I am, and all that I hope in this life, I am now ready here to stake upon it. And I leave off as I began, that live or die, survive or perish, I am for the Declaration. It is my living sentiment, and by the blessing of God it shall be my dying sentiment. Independence now, and Independence for ever!"
– John Adams to the Continental Congress, July 1, 1776

"Do you swear to tell the truth, the whole truth, and nothing but the truth, so help you God?"
"I do." So now we get to see what the U.S. Senate thinks they know, I thought as I sat with Dad and our legal counsel.
"Could you state your full name for the record, Mr. Reinhart?"
"My name is Joshua David Reinhart," I said formally.
"And you work for Prescience, Inc.?"
"Yes."
"How long have you been employed at Prescience?"
"Eight years."
"Could you tell me what your duties are at Prescience?"
"I'm Vice President of Project Staging." This ought to be interesting. It was a title that allowed me to do my real assignment: to be my father's eyes and ears and his right hand

man. I could get away with almost any activity at Prescience in the name of "staging."

"And just what does that entail, project staging?"

"When new ideas start to become possible projects at Prescience, we begin work on them using a staging team. You could think of it as prototyping."

"So you get to see all the new ideas for products at Prescience?"

"Not *all* the new ideas. There is a filtering mechanism that weeds out bad ideas before I get involved." At this rate, this could be a very long hearing.

"But you get to see the ideas before they become products, in their early stages?"

"Yes."

"Mr. Reinhart. Can you tell us about the 'SAFE YOU' project? What does 'SAFE YOU' mean?" Now we're getting down to it.

"The SIAFU project" was named after the African 'siafu' ant. One of our programmers came up with the name." I hope they don't have to call in an entomologist to testify. Evidently this giant ant can bite with the equivalent force of 200,000 pounds per square inch, enough to cut mild steel; and swarms number in the tens of millions.

The beginnings of the project had started back in Apex which was one of the reasons for the acquisition. It was the basis for Prescience's new security and encryption technology. I began to reflect back to just before I had heard about SAIFU and hoped that very little would have to be revealed.

Chapter One

Seasons of Change

"For having lived long, I have experienced many instances of being obliged, by better information or fuller consideration, to change opinions, even on important subjects, which I once thought right but found to be otherwise." – Benjamin Franklin

The shot rolled off the rim, pretty much representing my first semester at John Adams. I had been close with a lot of things, but not right on target. Robert was now backing me up into the key as he maneuvered for what would be the final shot of our one-on-one game. He had called me to see if I could use some company and a break from my studies for finals. I could have easily said no, but needed some fresh air and also someone to hang with. Robert had been a good friend to me and helped me sort through the maze that was John Adams: the classes, the professors, the clubs, the study groups, the Bible studies, the debate team trials, and Who was Who on campus.

"21-14," he called as his five foot jumper was all net.

"Nice game, sorry I couldn't give you more competition," I replied.

"Hey, if a couple of those "in and outs" had stayed in, you might have won." I knew he was just being kind. My game had been going down hill since I entered J.A. Even the extra inch and twenty pounds was of little help.

"You want to get something at the commons?" He knew I was always ready to eat.

"Sure, and I'm buying, even if you are on scholarship." If Robert only knew that he was able to afford to be here because of the Vision and the CRIMSON plan.

"Sounds good to me." He grabbed the ball, and we headed for the lockers.

The café at the commons had everything a growing young man needed, burgers, fries, milk and soft drinks in mass quantities. I ordered the double-double cheeseburger, cheese fries, and a large milk and sat down at a table away from the crowd. Robert joined me with an over flowing tray of his own. He had ordered a massive pile of onion rings to add to the banquet.

"Hey, you said you were buying," he grinned. He knew I was good for it. A lot of students on campus knew about the "heir apparent" to the Reinhart legacy. Except it seemed like more of a hindrance than an asset. Even my beautiful BMW was less accepted here. Too ostentatious I guess. Hey, a guy had to have wheels. Perhaps it all had set the bar pretty high and made it more difficult to meet expectations.

"So how're thing's going?" Robert could see I was not enjoying my first semester.

"Oh, things are going. I'm pretty sure I aced my econ exam, but I got three more in the next four days." I kept it to school, but there were a number of other things on my mind. My disappointment in not making the debate team this semester was probably what irked me most. And there was always Cassandra.

"Look, Josh, almost no one gets on the team the first year."
Although Robert had, and of course there was Cassandra Perez;
but that was it for last year. I had spent my senior high school
year concentrating on CRIMSON. With CHAF and the efforts of
the TPM the debate team had become a powerhouse.

I had recruited a couple more top debaters; I had honed my own
debate skills, and done it without the brilliant Miss Miller. I
missed having her to critique (more like re-write) my cases, but at
least it was all my own work now. Finally making it to Nats and
finishing in the semis. Dad had been proud and I had to admit, I
felt I deserved to be on the John Adams debate team.

"I'm sure you'll make it. You have all the skills; besides, do you
really have time for it right now?" I knew what he meant; I had
been working about as hard as I could to get the kind of grades I
was accustomed to getting. To say John Adams was a very
competitive environment was a gross understatement. Just
getting admitted meant you were the top of your high school
class. So there was nothing but true red blooded American over-
achievers all now vying for top slots at J.A.

"It's just that I thought I would be added to the team because of
my good looks and charm, not to mention my connections." I
gave a rueful smile. Robert understood. I was the rich kid with
good skills, but sometimes that put me at a peculiar disadvantage.
Almost a reverse discrimination. Most of the students at J.A.
were either on some form of scholarship or had to go into serious
debt to pay tuition. I, on the other hand, had no such problems;
and therein might lay the problem, it was just a theory. But the
team and coach had voted, and I was not on the team.

"I didn't get you out of your room to get bummed about debate,
so what else is on your mind?" Did he really have to ask? No,
but I guess he just wanted me to open the subject. OK, why not,

he was a good friend, perhaps my best friend and he wanted to help.

"Have you talked to her lately? Is she still the princess of J.A. debate?" Cassandra had been automatically admitted to the J.A. team due to her debate scholarship. I hadn't actually talked with her much while I was still in CRIMSON and she was at John Adams, and I could see why. Even with all her drive and brains, she would need to be fully focused on studies and debate. And after all, I was just a high school senior. Plus I suspected, but had no proof, that she was busy utilizing her considerable charms on the male debate population. Why should she change her M.O. now as it had worked so well in high school? Was I a little bitter? Perhaps.

"Well, of course I see her every week at debate, and I guess you could say that she has worked very hard to endear herself to the coach and members of the team," Robert replied.

"You mean the male members of the team. I doubt the other gals were pleased when Cassandra showed up," I corrected him.

"No, probably not," he chuckled.

"Does she seem to have any particular targets, or does she spread her wit and charm around pretty evenly." Now that did sound a little sad. Come on Josh, you had two dates, well actually only one, and you're still affected by her. Give it a rest.

"She seems to be pretty even handed, accept for me, of course." I can imagine that, as far as Cassandra was concerned, Robert was persona non grata.

Being the brother of the one person who had single handedly demolished her hopes for a stellar last year in high school debate, Robert Miller would not be on her Christmas list.

"So the fair Lady Cassandra doesn't like you?" My mood was starting to brighten; maybe it was the onion rings.

"Let's just say that my family relations cause a bit of a strain," he grinned widely.

"Have you seen her since you've been here?" he asked more seriously.

"Oh, I have sat with her and some of the debate team at lunch a couple of times before they voted me out, but that's about it. Not since then." I hoped I kept the disappointment from seeping into my last words.

"You know I was aware you went out with Cassandra, but I felt it was none of my business…" Robert paused.

This was new, I wonder when and how he actually found out. Had Rebekah told him? No, that wasn't like her. She kept secrets and was very private about personal things, or so it seemed. Perhaps Jeff….

"But, I felt at the time it was…ah… not well thought out." Could he be any more diplomatic?

"What you mean is 'I was an idiot,'" I replied with a smile.

"I wasn't going to put it that way, but let's face it; you should have realized there was a good chance you would have to debate her in a tournament." At the time I hadn't considered that possibility. I had only considered those green eyes topping that warm smile and that musical voice. But that was nearly two years ago, and I had only spoken to her a half a dozen times in passing. However, I had to admit, she was still on my mind.

"And you should have realized that even if that didn't happen, it put you in a compromised position with the team… and caused a few other problems as well." He looked me straight in the eyes. For nearly two years, Robert had not brought up my relationship (if you could call it that) with Cassandra, but he had thought about it. He was a good friend, but it was also clear he was not happy with me for hurting his sister.

"I did apologize. I didn't intend to hurt Rebekah. I didn't even know she felt that way about me." I wanted him to understand. I wanted *everyone* to understand, but it had happened and that was that.

"Look, *you* didn't have to be around her for the weeks, months after that. She was like a porcupine, getting near her meant you were going to feel one of her barbs. And she would break down, sometimes for no apparent reason. As far as I know, she still feels bad about it. I hope she can get passed it, because it was no fun living in the same house with her. I'm sure my parents are having to put up with a lot of grief from her on this missions trip."

That I could almost guarantee. Given the drama and tears the last time I saw her at the CRIMSON beach party where she had informed me she had to accompany her parents to some God-forsaken village in China. Well, it wouldn't be God forsaken after Pastor Miller arrived, but Rebekah was no doubt going to provide an example of what the other, much warmer, place might be like.

"Have you heard from your family?" I was curious.

"I got a letter awhile back; I guess they are traveling a lot from village to village. There isn't much infrastructure, and I get the feeling they are pretty exhausted much of the time from working with the villagers. Otherwise they seemed to be fine."

That was it, only an occasional letter. Well, they had a true mission, and I wondered how God was using this apparent detour from the Vision to serve some divine purpose in China, other than the obvious: bringing Bibles and teaching the good news of the Messiah to the rural villagers.

"How *is* your sister?" This was my main reason for asking.

"Oh, she's doing alright I guess, the letter simply said she is growing up and sends her love." Either the letter was very short, or he was just not going to get into private family details. Deciding not to push it, I took an oversized bite of my burger and chewed for some time in silence. I was still bothered by the way things had been left. Robert was not comfortable with the silence, and he finally broke it.

"Have you heard much from Dan Jr. or Ben this year?" My good friends from CHESS, Dan Jr. had gone pre-law at Wheaton, same university as his sister, except she was pre-med, and Ben had gone to USC, where else, given his fathers background.

"I called Ben a month ago and he seemed excited, sounds like SC suits him; *he* got on their debate squad... Perhaps I should transfer." I shot a look at Robert; if Ben had gotten on the Trojan debate squad, I would have been a slam dunk there.

"Hey, if it's any consolation, I voted for you," Robert quipped. Well I hope so! That just meant that many others did not. I guess finishing 4th at Nats wasn't good enough, leading CRIMSON, great SAT scores and grades; what was the problem?

"I just don't understand it, but I guess I'll have to live with it till the next vote." That was coming up for next semester. I had applied again and expected to... I didn't really know what to expect.

"I'm sure you'll make it, we need some 'newbies' to abuse," Robert said it with an over emphasized grin, but I can remember being called that by someone else a long while ago. It wasn't true then, and it wasn't true now. I swiped the last onion ring off his plate before he could stop me.

"Wait till I get on the team, then we'll see who's the 'newbie.'" I could sense he felt uncomfortable discussing this any further. He changed the subject abruptly.

"Are you going home for the break?"

"No, I was thinking about going down to visit some of my friends in Tampa. Hey, why don't you come along? They won't mind, and it would get you out of here." I was sure Robert was staying because his family was still back in China.

"You sure it would be OK? I don't want to intrude." I could see him light up at the thought of escape.

"I'm sure it would be fine. I'll check, but you should plan on it. ....Road Trip!" I gave him a high five.

"OK, sounds great. And thanks for the lunch." He got up from the table, then,

"I'll see if I can put in another good word for you with Coach Grant. And maybe you should talk with *Miss* Perez about the team." He gave me a sideways glance and took off toward his class. I was left with that last statement stuck in my head.

Could Cassandra be why I hadn't been getting the vote? Was she getting back at me just because I hadn't really given her any attention since the last time we debated (and I lost). I just shook my head as I finished the last of my milk and dumped my tray. I would have to call her and try to find out, and soon. Great, I had three finals due and now this.

That evening back in the dorm, "Hi...It's Josh... Josh Reinhart," might as well get this out of the way so I could concentrate on my studies. I had considered trying to see her, but then spiked that idea. I had enough trouble concentrating without having to deal with her in person ....

"Oh...Josh....to what do I owe *this* honor." Oh Man, this is not starting out well.

"I'm calling because I'm up for the debate team vote in a couple of weeks and wondered if I could count on your support? I think my qualifications speak for themselves but evidently some don't."

"Oh... I thought the knight-errant had *finally* decided to visit my castle after so many crusades." She hit me with that musical voice, but I wasn't about to be sidetracked.

"While I would like to discuss that some time, right now I really could use your help with the team." I tried to sound relaxed; I hoped I didn't sound too desperate.

"Hmm...What makes you think I have any influence with the team?" You've got to be kidding me, with fifteen guys on the team... I thought.

"Oh, I suspect you have more pull than you know. I hear you've been doing very well in the tournaments." I was not going to let that one slide.

"Have you talked with Coach Grant?" She was really avoiding the question.

"I'm having a meeting with him this week, just before the break, but I can't imagine there's a problem." Coach Grant was straightforward; if you had the skills, could work hard and be an asset to the team, he wanted you.

"Hmm....I don't know... He's the one with the most influence on the team." For some reason, Cassandra was deflecting and avoiding my request.

"Ok, just so I'm clear. I need to get 17 out of the 22 team votes and Coach Grant's OK to be on the team. Right?" I knew she must know this, but I wanted to hear her reply.

"That's what I understand." We were now in cross-ex mode and she had gone very cold.

"So there are six people that voted against me last time, or the coach did." I was careful to be as nonchalant as possible.

"Do you know why this would be?" I decided to lay it out there.

"I don't know what was on their minds; it's a secret ballot, you know." Again a deflection; I could see I was not going to get much further with this approach, and my ear was getting very hot against the phone.

"Ok... Well, I hope you can put in a good word. I know I can be a real asset to the team." Put in a final plug and leave it at that.

"I'm sure.... Was there anything else, I really need to get back to cramming," was Cassandra's chilly reply.

"I know; I've got three more finals myself, but.... I would like to call you later." Perhaps I could salvage something out of this.

"I think that will depend on your definition of "later." By the recent evidence and application, it doesn't align well with mine. Good night Mr. Reinhart." The phone went dead.

Wow! I stared at the phone. There was no doubt where one of the six no votes had come from. But I was really surprised she would vote against me just because I hadn't called her recently (my ego wasn't that big). However, that meant five others had voted against me. And I can imagine there had been some lobbying going on behind my back, too. I would have to make a strong case to Coach Grant, and also call Robert for his support and influence. Cassandra or not, I was getting on that team.

****

Robert was fiddling with the CD changer as my beemer cruised west over the interstate heading toward California. I had finished my freshman year at John Adams and it had been difficult, but my grades had held up. I had made it on the J.A. debate team for next year despite the best efforts of a certain hazel eyed lady. I had tried to talk to her about it, but she would not return my calls. I wasn't surprised, but I just couldn't understand why Cassandra, with all she had going for her, would be so petty. I am sure it had damaged her standing with her teammates a little when I was confirmed over her objections. But that was water under the bridge as far as I was concerned and it was important to help and support each other in our efforts for another national title. John Adams had been the national champion moot court team for the last three years. Hard work and team work would be key to continuing that streak. Maybe she just didn't like me.

We were having too much fun on the trip back to Santa Sonoma for my serious topics, so I kept it light.

"Man, I'm dying for some of Marissa's tamales; I haven't had decent Mexican food since I left home," I chatted, as Robert finally inserted the Switchfoot CD he was looking for. Yup, the good residents of Virginia barely knew how to spell Chile Relleno. We were approaching Riverside, and I could almost taste Marissa's homemade salsa.

"I just can't wait to see my family; it's been almost two years," Robert replied.
I guess I never was concerned about Robert, he always was so even tempered and straightforward, but his parents and his sister had been in China for quite a while and not in the best of circumstances. They had made it home last month, and he was very anxious to get home. We had been on the road for a couple of days; and I had to say that, of all my friends, Robert was closer than anyone. He understood a lot of what I was going through, and my family's wealth did not seem to affect him at all.
"I'll bet your mom has baked you some of her apple blueberry scones." Mrs. Miller was famous for them, and I hoped to eat more than my share this summer.
"I hope I can make it for dinner, so drop me off first, OK?" Robert was excited.

I guess I was too. I had a summer to decompress and find out how things were going with CRIMSON and the Vision. I would need to get briefed on the news from my parents. There still were very few people who knew about the Vision and the CRIMSON plan, only thirteen as far as I knew. When that would change was anyone's guess.

****

I stepped out onto our patio and scanned the backyard. Sarah was holding court over her pool party. It was a warm Sunday afternoon, the sun sparkling off the water; I recognized a few of her guests, Ashley, Alison, Jeff and Andrew. On the grotto overhang, a sleek blond in a shimmering blue one piece had just launched herself into an exquisite arc. She entered the water like a knife, no splash, as if the surface had been sliced open and then sealed shut. I watched; rapt, waiting for her to resurface. She must be a new friend of Sarah's; I know I had been away for some time, but I *definitely* would have remembered. After what seemed too long, and I'm sure I must have been staring, she emerged out of the pool walking up the steps as she used both hands to slick back her blond hair from her face. The rest of the backyard disappeared out of focus, she was riveting. She wasn't tall; perhaps 5'4", but her slim tan form barely hid sinuous muscles. She bent down to retrieve and fasten a gauze skirt around her waist. Turning toward me, there was no mistaking the blue lasers that locked on in surprise. My mind took a moment to unravel the revelation – Rebekah?! I was glad to be in the shadow of the patio, so the relative darkness hid some of my surprise and slight blush as I am sure she had caught me staring.

"Josh!" she called out in surprise. Her bright smile, absent the hardware, combined with her brilliant blue eyes sent a thrill up my spine. Always the unexpected.

I was trying to sort out too many thoughts and emotions as I gazed at the lovely young woman dancing toward me. Recovering, I was just able to quip,

"Who are *you* and what have you done with Rebekah Miller?" I grinned broadly.

I felt a warmth; it reminded me of a night more than two years ago in a different backyard but with the same blue eyes. Between then and now, a lot of growing up had occurred. I had just finished a tough first year at John Adams, and added an inch and filled out my frame a little. But Rebekah! The time had added about six inches and considerable maturity; and while her mind had always been amazing, it now had some serious competition. She had, as Mom would say, 'Blossomed.' Grabbing a towel as she entered the patio, she patted her face before taking my hands in hers.

"It's *so* good to see you!" She looked up at me and for a moment I was frozen, my mind still trying to reconcile my last image of Rebekah with the poised beauty so near to me now. The last time I had seen her was two years ago, a young teen girl who had told me with tears in her eyes that she had to go to China with her parents. At the time I was leaving for the John Adams summer camp before my senior year at CHESS, it seemed like a long time ago. The scent of cocoa butter, the warmth of her hands and smiling blue eyes brought me back to reality.

"It's still me, Josh," she smiled, as if she read my mind.

We stood there looking at each other for a few heartbeats, or maybe more, I don't know. I really didn't want to break the silent communication between us. She was still the most amazing person I had ever met, and now...

The others at the pool had come over, and Rebekah dropped her gaze and my hands.

"Josh! I thought you were due in tonight." Sarah seemed happy to see me as she gave me a hug.

"We made better time than I planned. Where's Mom?" While the road trip had been a blast driving my beemer across the country with Robert, I was glad to have made it home for dinner.

"She's out shopping for your favorites with Marissa. You remember the gang, Ashley, Alison." She swept her arm over the group, lots of changes had occurred to the old CRIMSON team.

"Sure... don't let me disturb your party. I need to go get cleaned up for dinner." What I needed was a shower and time to think. 'Rebekah. How old could she be now...fifteen, almost sixteen?'

They went back to the pool, except Rebekah. She bent down to get a soda from the fridge. I couldn't take my eyes off her.

"I hope you're not going anywhere *this* summer," I tried to be relaxed.

"No...Why do you ask?" she smiled; she wasn't going to make it easy on me, lasers at full power.

"I'd like a chance to see you while I'm here, it's been a long time and I...I've missed our conversations." This was certainly true; I had missed the mental jousting, but that certainly wasn't 'the whole truth, so help me God.'

"How about meeting me at the Ice Castle next week, I still have ice time on Tuesdays," she smiled, blushed a little, and then dropped her eyes.

"Tuesday it is. Can I call you for the time?" I knew the time, but I wanted to talk to her before Tuesday. There was a lot of catching up to do.

"Sure, Josh…" she wasn't fooled, and then she looked back up, her blue eyes glistening.

"…I've missed you, too," she almost whispered and then turned back to the pool.

I watched her retreat and then went back into the house. Two years had made Rebekah more self-assured; she had been willing to say what I had just stumbled over. Yes, I *had* missed her, and she wanted me to know she understood that I wasn't just talking about 'our conversations'; there was much more to this than had just been said. It was a good thing I had the summer off, because I might need all of it to get this sorted out.

****

Sunday night I had a chance to get a full briefing from Dad on what had been going on recently with the Vision. The fact that the Moms were on board made a big difference in how the group operated. Before the men had to work at maintaining communication and using the secure server and information site, but the Moms had made it their own version of Facebook. There was constant chatter on the different subjects and forums, and consequently many new point men and women had been identified and contacted. The other major impact was a strong influence on the high school students already in CRIMSON. Once the Moms internalized the Vision and the CRIMSON plan, their students were encouraged and even maneuvered to do more work on debate. There was no problem getting help for Mrs. Stanton, and most of the time there were at least two dozen parents at the CRIMSON meetings. My senior year I had led CRIMSON to the nationals; we had three strong debaters, myself, Ben and Dan Jr. But now there was a possibility of four students qualifying for Nationals, and this was without the brilliant Miss

Miller who had missed all but the last month of school and the debate season. She might have been capable of winning at Nats, but she just had no way to qualify. The Millers were just settling in again, and Rebekah would be back in CHESS and CRIMSON, but now it was summer. We had one point man and one point woman out practicing law and working on national policy. John Petersen had become a key player in Senator Bennett's organization. And Jillian Holladay would be taking a position with an influential lobbying firm in D.C., having graduated from Georgetown. Aaron Morris had gotten into Harvard Law School partly due to a CHAF scholarship.

Then there was the next wave, the true CRIMSON leading edge, Robert, Ben, Dan Jr. and myself. All in pre-law, all with Vision parents, but I was still the only insider, as it had not been determined when to let the students know about the Vision. By the time I graduated law school, we might have twenty CRIMSON plan students in the pipe, maybe more. I could start to see how the plan could be coming together. With God's help we had created a Christian judge and policy-maker factory. I could see fifty, perhaps one hundred participants in the CRIMSON plan by the time I was a few years out of school. If a third of them made it to a judgeship or a place of influence in public policy, this country could be turned back from the brink of the gray flag.

As Dad and I finished talking about the CRIMSON plan, I could see that, while he was excited, he was also looking older and a little more gray was gracing his temples. He looked at me with tired eyes from across his desk.

"So, I understand you had a rather tough year. Like to talk about it?" 'Thanks, Mom,' I thought; but I guess I had to expect her to discuss things with him.

"Dad, I did great in my school work and pulled a 3.9 GPA, only one B+ for the entire year." I knew he knew this already, but I wanted to start from a position of strength.

"Son, I'm not talking about your grades; I'm talking about your ambitions, your desires." Of course, the 'First born' was expected to get perfect grades; why bother mentioning it.

"You mean not making the debate team this year. You know I'll be on it next year." Keep it positive, upbeat.

"Yes, but I heard that you might have made it this year, something about a team vote that kept you off. What happened?"

"I guess some of the team members had reservations about me at first. Coach Grant was very supportive and so was Robert, but there had to have been six members of the team who voted me out." There, is that what we need to discuss? I was getting tired and really, it didn't matter now. I knew who had been behind my delayed acceptance into the J.A. team. I knew and I still wasn't quite sure why she had done it. This conversation was not going anywhere, at least anywhere I wanted to go.

"Did you find out who voted against you? I'm sure Robert supported you."

"Yeah, Robert was great. In fact, he helped me a lot this year." It was late and I couldn't see any value in hashing over this.

"Dad, can we discuss this another time? I'm pretty tired and you look like you could use some sleep, too. Are you feeling OK?" I was a little concerned about him.

"Oh, I'm fine, the Apex integration is complex and taking longer than I thought but their security and encryption intellectual property are extraordinary and some of the people we acquired are first rate. You should meet this one guy, Hunter Erickson, MIT by way of West Point. Apex coerced him out of the NSA...." He started to light up when talking about his work.

Man, did he love his job. I guess that's why he kept at it 24/7, it sure wasn't for the money.

"Maybe I'll have your mom set up a party and invite some folks from work; you could invite some of the CRIMSON group, too," he was off on another subject.

"Sounds great, I think I'll turn in now …and thanks for the update." I shut the door to his office as he went back to his computer.

It felt great to be in my own bed, but the conversation with Dad played over in my mind. Cassandra, Cassandra… why had she done it? What had made her turn against me? I just couldn't figure it out, and I was tired of trying. Besides, I had a whole summer in front of me, and I would like to just forget about my freshmen year and enjoy just hangin' with my friends, and perhaps a certain young lady. I turned over and finally gave in to sleep; for once, I could wake up when I felt like it.

Chapter Two

My Plans are Not Your Plans

"There are two educations. One should teach us how to make a living and the other how to live." – John Adams

"Mr. Reinhart, when did you meet Mr. Hunter Erickson?" the Senator asked.

"I met Mr. Erickson in the summer after my freshman year in college," I responded.

"Mr. Erickson." He would have laughed at that. I don't think I had ever called him that; he was just "Hunter." I had been sent out for some extra food because the party was starting to run low, and I offered because I needed some fresh air. It was the first time I had met many of the Apex (now Prescience) employees, and the conversation had gotten pretty esoteric. As I was pulling out of our gate, I was nearly run over by a huge dark orange Hummer coming in. We both stopped before we exchanged paint.

"Hey, watch it!" I called out, how the driver heard me with the music volume pumped up and the rumble of his exhaust was beyond me. He looked down at me and grinned.

"Sorry Man, I'm late; I hope this doesn't mean the party's over. Hunter's the name."

"Oh, you must be Hunter Erickson. Glad to meet you; I'm Josh, Josh Reinhart." He had short-cropped blond hair and aviator sunglasses.

"Why are you leaving your own party?" he asked.

"I was going to get some more food. We were running low on drinks." And fresh air, I thought.

"Mind if I join you? I'd rather; I see these people everyday, and all they talk about is ciphers and Standards Committee meetings," Hunter replied,

"Sure, why don't you park, and I'll back up to pick you up," I suggested.

"I got a better idea. Park your Beemer and climb in," he motioned with his head.

"OK." I backed up till I could park, and then I trotted back and climbed up into the shotgun seat of the Hummer. And climb was no exaggeration; with the over size off-road tires and lift kit, let's just say I was glad I was almost 6'2".

When I sat down, he met me with a powerful handshake and a big grin.

"Your dad can't stop talkin' about you. He said we needed to meet, so I guess we're just following orders." He grinned again as the tires screeched while he backed the Hummer into the street and then took off.

"My dad told you about me?" I always thought when Dad was at work his mind was only on work.

"Yeah; John Adams, pre-law. On the debate team, super student, pretty fair b-baller," he rattled it off as he cranked up some hard rock.

"I hear you're the "super student." I figured I would repay the compliment.

"Oh, you mean MIT. Well, I had to do something after I got back from Iraq. And I got interested in data security and encryption."
He was pretty unassuming, considering his resume.
"And West Point, and NSA, plus a dozen patents in data security…" I smiled smugly, I knew about him, too.
"You know, now I have to kill you," he laughed; but I was pretty sure he had the skills to do that, too. He wasn't as tall as I was, but he was broader and more muscular, perhaps in his late twenties.
"What did you do in Iraq?" I was curious.
"I mostly worked in Command and Control. But I did get out in the field from time to time. That's when it got interesting." It seemed like that was a story for another time.
We pulled into the local market, and I hadn't realized how loud the trip had been until he killed the engine. We jumped out and went in to pick up more munchies and drinks.
By the time we got back to the party, we had discussed school, music, cars, basketball and laughed the entire way. We entered the party together, and Dad was there to greet Hunter with a slap on the back.
"I see you met Josh; well, make yourself at home. Emily!... Hunter and Josh are here."
I could see why Dad thought highly of Hunter. He was a brilliant guy, but you would never know it by his appearance. He was very unassuming and liked to keep people off guard with his ex-military jargon and air. He was the brains behind the Apex data security and encryption technology and tops in his field.

During the summer Hunter and I became fast friends; basketball usually one-on-one and sometimes pick-up games with the guys, a paintball outing and mostly just hangin' out. He even let me try his Kawasaki ZX a couple of times. One day I was polishing my rims and heard the familiar rumble of the orange Hummer. He jumped down and admired my beemer.

"Glad I got my shades on, otherwise I'd be blind." He motioned to my wheels. He continued, "You got time this afternoon?"

"Sure, what's up?" I stood up.

"Kind of a surprise. Ready to go?" He motioned to the Hummer.

"Do I need anything?"

"Nope." He jumped up into the driver's seat.

I got in the other side, "Where we going?"

"You'll like it, that's all I can say," he gave me his big grin and turned up the tunes.

We pulled into the parking lot of non-descript buildings and parked. Hunter pulled an aluminum briefcase and a black duffle from the back seat. He handed me the duffle; it was moderately heavy. We walked up to a door with block lettering.

Moving Target - Firing Range
Ammo and Guns–new and used

Hunter was right; as we walked in I could smell the gun oil and hear the sound of muffled shots, making me grin ear to ear.

"Hunter! Good to see you, Man. Who's your friend?" the man called from behind the counter. He looked ex-military, gray crew cut, rough tan face and a crooked nose.

"Josh, this is Joe Platt. He's the owner and has forgotten more about firearms than most people know," Hunter explained as I stepped up to shake Joe's hand.

"Josh Reinhart, nice to meet you." He looked me over, and then he eyed the case that Hunter carried.

"Got some new toys?" Joe asked.

Hunter unlocked the case and opened it as Joe's face beamed.

"New Kimber Raptors!" then he whistled.

"You gonna break 'em in today?" Joe had one of the stainless pistols in his hand, checking the action.

"Yeah, ... can we get Josh set up?" Hunter gave me a glance.

"No problem, just fill out these forms and sign your life away and we can get you started." Joe handed me a few forms and a pen.

"Kimber makes some sweet hardware, laser sight rail too. You need any ammo?" Joe asked.

"Yeah, but not your reloads for the 45s, how about some new Speer Gold Dot 185 grain, hollow point?"

"It'll cost ya; damn shortage, everyone is hording 'em." He walked back into a locked room and returned with a couple of boxes. "If you need more I can get 'em, but it'll take a couple of weeks."

Hunter paid for the shells, and I handed Joe my paperwork and I.D.

Joe gave Hunter some silhouette targets and handed me a set of earmuffs and some earplugs,

"Make sure you have these on before you go through the double doors. Have fun."

He gave a knowing grin to Hunter, and we went through the two sets of doors into the firing range. The smell of gun powder was strong, and I could feel more than hear some large caliber going off. We set up in one of the stalls and put a target out about fifteen yards.

Hunter dug into his duffle and produced a 9mm Smith and Wesson; he had a loaded clip and shoved it in. Then he showed me how to use the pistol, firing off a few rounds into the center of the heart of the target. A tight grouping of four shots.

He handed me the gun and nodded at the target.

"Squeeze firmly and smooth, two seconds between rounds."

I stepped up and held the gun as he had shown me; it felt good in my double handed grip. Sighting down the barrel at the center of the head, the gun went off and I felt the kick, not as much as I had expected; but more importantly, there was a satisfying hole in the target's head. Three more in ten seconds, and three more holes.

I finished off the clip and set the gun down, turned to look at Hunter; we both had big grins.

"Pretty good shouting for your first time. Ready to try some more."

"Yeah! That was awesome!... How do you load the clips?" I wanted to learn and I figured the more clips that were loaded the more shooting I could do.

"OK, here's the clip and you push in the bullets point first until it's full. I'm going to work with the Kimbers now, so you can reload these clips with 9mms." He took the boxes of new ammo and one of the new Raptors out of the case.

We spent the rest of the afternoon firing everything in Hunter's arsenal, from hunting rifles to the Raptors to a small, but deadly, Ruger LCR .38 caliber with an integrated laser sight. I couldn't remember having as much fun since my first drive in my BMW.

We came out of the air lock, and Hunter went over to Joe, who then went into his back room and brought out a few more boxes of ammo, plus a small holster. Hunter dropped them in his duffle and paid as I looked into the gun cases. There were some used models as well as new, they all looked interesting to me right now. I was hooked.

"Ready to learn more?" Hunter asked as we got back into the Hummer.

"Are you kidding, what's next? Can I buy one of these now?" Examining his Smith and Wesson; I was pumped. I could have gone through another couple hundred rounds right then.

"You need to get your handgun certificate, and then you need to select a handgun you want to become proficient at, then practice, practice, practice. Pretty tight grouping, this guy is *definitely* dead." We both laughed as he handed me a silhouette target with just my bullets in two groups, head and chest.

"How about getting something to eat, I'm definitely buying," I said. This was the least I could do. I had just been introduced to my newest hobby.

****

Activities with Hunter weren't the only distractions that summer. As I entered the ice rink, I was definitely nervous. It wasn't like a date or anything, but she was no longer just a little girl with braces either. Rebekah was already out on the ice moving at light-speed while setting up for a double jump. I watched her from the boards as she completed the move with perfect form (what else). Shaking my head, I wasn't caught completely off guard this time, but it was still hard to fathom the transformation. I skated up to her and she smiled that new bright smile.

"Stalking me?" she laughed, and with a twinkle in the blue lasers, darted off.

I decided to play along and chased after her, but again she would only allow me to get just so close and then effortlessly zip away. Man, she was fast, so fast in fact that I decided we might get called off the ice for our game of tag, so I conceded and pulled up to the boards. I watched her as she came back to me, all grace and looking very mature with her hair tight in a French twist and a new blue and gold outfit. That familiar warmth raised the temperature of the rink considerably.

She arrived a little out of breath with that special lilting laugh I had heard maybe two or three times before. "I hope you haven't given up chasing me," tilting her head and lifting an eyebrow.

We took a familiar booth in the back of the café, and I couldn't help but feel the uncomfortable memory of two prior meetings; one having to do with my secret about the Vision and her desire to find out about it, and the other my confession of sorts about Cassandra. Both were unpleasant and I just didn't want this to be a three-peat. Be smart Josh, I told myself. Remember, this is the most brilliant, insightful person you may ever know, so watch it.

"So, … tell me about China." I was naturally curious, maybe there was something in the water that had caused the apparent change in Rebekah.

"Josh, first I want you to know, I said "it's still me" the other day. And ….well, it's true and it's not. In many ways I *am* still the same person, but I grew up a lot in China."

"I can see that," I smiled after taking a sip of my drink, and she flipped her bottle cap at me. Only a faint blush and no lasers slicing up the café; she had learned to control herself.

"I learned that if I let others bother me with what they say or do, I've lost control and they win. When I was in China, I had to be careful about how I acted around the villagers. They were looking for weakness, and I was the obvious target. At first, I cried every night about how unfair it all was, but finally I realized that God had called us to do His will in China and I was a part of that. So I just decided one day to put my heart and soul into the task and forget about anything else for awhile. So even when Dad said it would be another nine months, I was okay with that. Plus I had begun to enjoy some things about what we were doing, pretty rewarding, actually."

I had been sipping my drink as she talked. Compared to this, my stint at John Adams was no big thing.

"Like what? You told me you were in the middle of nowhere," I recalled.

"But that was where we were needed, and we did reach a lot of people for The Lord. I taught Bible classes to the villagers, and many of them received Jesus as their Savior; *so* many blessings, it made being there worth it. But I learned from them, too; how to live more simply and how to develop the mind and the body together. I was careful not to get into their religions, but some of the exercises and practices helped me tremendously."

"So you've come back a *new* person." Did I sound a little disappointed?

"I couldn't help but change. Each new experience or person you meet changes you a little. Only God is foundational, never changing, everlasting," she replied with a smile, assured.

And then, "Are you disappointed?"

She sounded a little hurt, but had cut right to the core issue. Was I disappointed in the *new* Rebekah? Did I miss the temper tantrums and the flashing lasers? Who knows? If you answer this question wrong Josh, you might get to see the old Rebekah in action.

"Disappointed? No, not at all...well, maybe a little," I replied in all honesty. "I mean, I like that you've grown up to be so...ah...so *nice*," I could have used a number of other words, 'lovely, graceful... intriguing.' "And I'm glad China ended up being a good experience for you. But does this mean I'll never see those blue lasers again."

"My blue *what*?" she was no longer smiling. I realized as often as I had referred to them in my thoughts about Rebekah, I had never actually voiced my description of her disturbing blue eyes. Better get back on defense Josh, or you're toast.

"Oh, it's just something crazy I made up about your eyes," I replied with an honest smile. "You see, I used to imagine that they would power up into destructive blue lasers, capable of reeking havoc wherever you looked or...be used for irresistible interrogation." Josh, I sure hope you know what you're doing, I thought. Of course you don't, just telling the truth and probably digging yourself in deep. I could see I might get a sampling of the lasers right now.

"Was this to make *fun* of me?!" her eyes did flash.

"*No*. No... actually, it was an admiration. *Really*, you have the most amazing blue eyes I've ever seen. They've been...ah... disturbing me ever since we've met." I might as well lay it out there. She looked at me for a little longer, and then her smile returned and the lasers powered down.

"I like the 'amazing' part... not so sure about 'disturbing'... so I disturb you?" she tilted her head and looked me straight in the eyes. She was not going to give me an out. But she did give me a little smile.

"Ah....yeah... ever since our first debate. You made me realize I needed to stop just skating by on my reasonable talent and the family name." Maybe I could leave it at that.

"Well, your skating does need some work," she smiled again, but then it faded.

"So was that why you asked me to help you with debate?" she asked, her shoulders dropping a little.

"Well, partly... I wanted to become the best debater I could be in the shortest amount of time, and I knew you were my only real chance; plus, you seemed to be willing to help.... And when you weren't shredding me alive, I really enjoyed our tutoring sessions," I grinned, thinking back on the debate at her house that had not gone well at all. She blushed at this.

"Can't we forget that incident; it does neither of us credit," she mused.

That would be just fine with me. We had had an odd relationship, but now it might change. Did she still have a "crush" on me? I doubted this was the case in the true sense of the word. She was so mature for her age now and had become much more knowledgeable of worldly things; self-assured. On the other hand, I had not progressed very far in that regard. In comparison, my time at J.A. had been a rather cloistered experience due to my desire for academic excellence; and my other unattained goal... Cassandra. She had made my time at J.A. much more difficult and disappointing than I had expected. But somehow, I felt better about this just talking with the "new" Rebekah.

Rebekah's lasers were powering up as she could see I was ignoring her. I recovered just in time as something she said finally surfaced in my mind past the reminiscing.

"You taught the villagers...in Chinese?" I gave her a puzzled look.

She looked down a little and then back up. "Yes... a Mandarin dialect, a variant of Standard Mandarin."

"But you were only there for a little over a year," I looked at her, amazed.

"Yeah, I had to study pretty hard for the first couple of months. But, when all you hear is their language, it *is* easier to pick up," she replied as if it was like learning a piano piece.

"How do you do it? Chinese in two months, well enough to teach the Bible.... The entire Constitution, all the cases that were ever tried at the Supreme Court..."

"I told you before, I...I concentrate," she looked down. "And I don't know *all* the cases."

"You'll have to tell me how you do it sometime." I just shook my head and smiled as she looked up with those brilliant blue eyes, defiant but tempered with a little humor this time. I could see she wanted to tell me more, but not today. Her gaze held me as it had so many times before, but now there was more complexity, more wit and depth. The café went out of focus, and I felt my heart jump...

After a time, she blinked exclaiming, "Oh, I gotta go... my lesson...I'm late." She broke the close connection, but it had definitely been a two way street. I realized I had been caught up in those blue eyes. Josh, get a grip...this was *still* Rebekah.

"Wait... I'll call you?" I stood up as she was already out of the booth.

Looking up at me, she flashed a little smile and just gave a nod, then turned and danced out of the café through a slalom of young skaters.

****

"Mr. Reinhart, how did you come to be employed at Prescience?" the Senator asked.

"I joined Prescience in the middle of my junior year in college at my father's request." This had been the biggest change in my life; bigger than the move to California, and much more disruptive. I'll never forget my mother's voice; only once in my life had I heard it like that.

"Josh... it's your dad... he's...he's had a heart attack." Mom had called me in the evening after dinner. It was like getting kicked in the stomach by a mule.

"How bad?" I held my breath and shot a prayer skyward, 'Don't let him die, Lord.'

"They don't know yet; he's in ICU.... they got him stable...I'm here at Scripps now....I think you should be here."

".... OK, I'll get the next flight to San Diego... Mom, I love you...If Dad wakes up, tell him I love him and I'm on my way."

"Josh, I don't know how this is going to work out... you may have to be here a while."

"Mom, don't worry about that, just take care of Dad and yourself. What about Sarah?"

"She is staying with the Simmons; they said she can stay as long as we like."

"Good. Mom, we should pray," I gently suggested.

"... in Jesus' name, Amen." I felt a little calmer after the prayer.

"OK, I'll call you as soon as I land. Call me if anything changes, any news...I love you, Mom." I was already grabbing my duffle bag.

"I love you too, honey....Oh, Josh... what if..." she was breaking down.

"Everything will be OK, Scripps La Jolla is the best...And Dad is strong...Just pray and focus on getting through this. I'll be there as soon as I can."

"I'll try... Honey, I love you... get here soon." She hung up.

My next call was to check how fast Pi-squared could fly me to San Diego.

That was the last night I would spend at John Adams, the last time I would be a carefree student, and the last time my life was under my control, if it ever really had been.

As my dad recovered, it was clear that he could no longer run Prescience alone. Thank God his mind had not been affected; he was still sharp as ever. But he was in a wheelchair having suffered a stroke along with the heart attack. The doctors said that with daily physical therapy, he may walk but it would take time. So I was hired, over some of the board's objections, to be his assistant. I was his eyes, ears and legs. And while he had a professional nursing staff 24/7, I would often push him around in his chair as we went to visit the labs and programmers.

Once, I had prayed that I could have more time with my dad, and he had prayed the same prayer; The Lord had provided, just not exactly how we had planned it.

In some ways it was a blessing. I could learn so much from him. How he handled people, how he did business, his savvy but honest approach to "the deal" as he called it. He had taught me how to read people, their body language, eye movements, hand gestures and voice patterns. I studied harder than I ever had – browser technology, data security and encryption; and it was definitely on-the-job training. Dad was still deeply committed to his work, but now I was needed for him to fulfill that commitment. There was some downside; my dream of going to law school was probably over, at least for now, along with my somewhat carefree existence as a rich college student. I lived at home; and we did a lot of work out of his office, but he insisted on trips to the Apex building a couple of times a week.

One thing that was not affected was the work on the Vision and the CRIMSON plan. If anything it was enhance because now I was working on it more and doing a lot of leg work for Dad. We still showed up at the TPM in the new wheel chair adapted van. It had an automatic chair lift and everything including the kitchen sink, plus all the medical equipment Dad might require, even a defib machine; and I had been trained on all of it. Mom, Dad and I worked on the CRIMSON plan in the comfort of Dad's home office. After a few months things had settled into a routine.

There were a couple of other benefits to my new role. Hunter and I spent a lot of time together, and I was learning a lot about data security as well as some of the other skills that Hunter had picked up as a Ranger in the army. He still would not give me the details of his Iraq missions, but I got the feeling that I was glad he was on our side. I had put on another twenty pounds of muscle and a lot of bruises from our martial arts workouts, but it was worth it. And Hunter seemed to enjoy having me around; the younger brother he never had. And Dad had become the father that he never had.

Then there was my relationship (or lack there of) with the fair Miss Perez. Even before I left J.A. Cassandra had decided to treat me as if I had the plague, even though we had to be together for the team's sake. As far as she was concerned, I had never been good enough to have even made the team, and she was sure that my money and my father's influence had everything to do with it. Once I had hoped and prayed she would develop strong feelings for me, I guess I should have been more specific. Even after I had won a couple of crucial rounds on the way to another national championship, she would not acknowledge me. She had shown an unaccountable disregard for me most of the time, periodically sprinkled with seeming malice aforethought. I still had a hard time thinking about her: dancing the Tango, lacing up her skates, talking about what we wanted to do when we got out of law school, her voice, her walk, those golden green eyes. Those were the good memories, but they had been layered with a more recent set of vexing ones from J.A., and now it seemed unlikely I'd ever see her again. Farewell, M'Lady.

Chapter Three

The Breach

_*"The moment the idea is admitted into society that property
is not as sacred as the laws of God, and that there is not a
force of law and public justice to protect it, anarchy and
tyranny commence. If `Thou shalt not covet' and `Thou
shalt not steal' were not commandments of Heaven, they
must be made inviolable precepts in every society before it
can be civilized or made free."*
– John Adams, Defense of the American Constitution 1787

**"Mr. Reinhart, when did you become aware that Prescience
security systems had been compromised?"**
"About a year ago, in April," I replied, coming back to the real
world.
"And who first found the security breach?"
"Ms. May Li."
"Is Ms. *Li* a U.S. citizen?" The Senator's emphasis on M's last
name forced heat to the top my collar.

"Yes, she was born and raised in San Diego. Masters degree from UCSD, applied mathematics and computer science. Father and mother are *also* U.S. citizens." Where's your degree from, you blowhard; look at your own background checks for once. M probably had more on him than he knew himself, having run a deep Anticip8 search on the senators.

****

"Josh, its M. Just listen." I answered my cell out of a deep sleep. "We need to meet, now. Your mother's birthday, remember the place?"

"Yeah." I was wide awake after "...Just listen..."

"Twenty minutes, secure." The phone went dead, and I looked at the time, 1:10 a.m. typical working hours for M. I was pretty sure she was a vampire. If Hunter was the father of Prescience's data encryption and security system, she was its mother. I really had no idea when she slept, but she cared for the entire computer system like it was her offspring, 24/7. Dad, Hunter and I trusted her implicitly. She was completely dedicated to Prescience, and she could play the Anticip8 keyboard like Horowitz on a Steinway. She adopted the nickname of "M" because she ended all emails and texts with it, but I think it was also her love of the old James Bond movie character of the same name.

I put the Glock 26 sub-compact into its shoulder holster and strapped it in place, M's last word made me cautious. I slipped on a loose jacket and stepped out into a cool misty California night. My trusty old Beemer cruised up the 5 South onramp; I decided against my new Audi R8; that would have drawn nothing but attention. The radio came on, Phil Collin's insistent "I can feel it coming in the air tonight...."

I pulled into the La Jolla restaurant parking lot, my mind flashing back to the birthday dinner. My mom had enjoyed a great time with just a few close friends: Hunter, the Simmons, the McClarens and the Millers. I could hardly take my eyes off of Rebekah that Saturday night; Dad had flown her out from Harvard Law just for the weekend, (I was pretty sure it was Mom's idea), well, no complaints here. She was about to graduate first in her class, Constitutional law her specialty.

That Sunday I had joined the Millers for church at HGCF. I had to admit my motivation was not entirely spiritual. Rebekah was flying back to Cambridge that night; and I wanted, perhaps a better word was I "needed" to see her. Over the last couple of years we had conducted a long distance courtship. Our schedules allowed us little time, and we were the proverbial "ships passing in the night." In the Christian homeschool vernacular, "courtship" implied much more than just dating, as there was an honorable, serious intent toward marriage. High school and even college dating just seemed to be practice for divorce, "Let's date, and if it doesn't work out, oh well, we'll split up (get distraught perhaps) and move on." Most homeschoolers associated in co-ed groups, often through college, and knew each other well before any intentions were undertaken.

I loved hearing her clear soprano voice sing the popular worship songs. I did lose my place in worship a few times, but I figured God would forgive me for my avid appreciation of His perfectly created five foot four sculpture of brilliance and beauty. Mrs. Miller smiled discretely a couple of times as she caught me appraising her daughter. No secret, romance was evident, and I gladly accepted Mrs. Miller's early supper invitation.

One advantage of the older neighborhoods was the size of the yards versus the houses. Perhaps the developers felt the families back then would be bigger and there was a need for a large back yard, and of course the smaller houses took up less of the lot. The Miller's back yard was a good example, stretching back, crisscrossed with flower beds, grass islands and walking paths around fruit trees that led to a secluded gazebo. It had been a favorite spot for Rebekah growing up, and she seemed more relaxed there.

"Just stay put," she said as she got up from her chair and I started to rise. "I've got something to show you."

I turned in my seat so I could watch her dance out of sight toward the house. Her mood was very light; I wondered what she was up to. A few minutes passed, and I heard her clear high voice command, "Close your eyes and keep them closed."

I was tempted to see what she placed on the table in front of me, but did as ordered.

"No peeking," she cautioned.

Then I could feel her standing behind me as she put her hands over my eyes.

"Just making sure," she whispered as I smelled her perfume and felt her sweet breath so close on my ear. She definitely had my attention. My pulse ramped up.

I loved her like this... the playful side of Rebekah, not often seen, but more desirable because of it.

"OK," she moved her hands down to rest on my shoulders as I opened my eyes.

I saw myself looking back at me. On the table was a sketch book, and the first page was a black and white sketch of a slightly younger Josh Reinhart. But it was unlike any drawing I had ever seen, as it was essentially a black and white photograph. The detail was astounding, and the image was flawless. Speechless, I looked back up at Rebekah, she was smiling but her bright blue eyes were glistening.

"I never wanted to forget you, Josh," she almost whispered and then,

"I did that one my first week in China," she swallowed hard.

I looked closer at the sketch; there was a small date and two ℛ s overlapped in the corner. There was also a couple of tear stains dropped there nearly ten years ago.

The realization hit me like a thunderbolt; my heart felt like it would burst through my ribs. This sketch was not the product of a schoolgirl crush, and she was no schoolgirl now (if she had ever been). A fundamental truth launched from my head, piercing my heart, *exploding* – Rebekah's love was pure and true, steadfast all these years. She had given me her heart from the beginning, and I had not been the best of guardians, taking it much too lightly back then. The tear drops were proof enough of that. Her love was beyond my heart's desire, (and she cared nothing about the money or the power). She was unique and brilliant, a flawless jewel. I knew I loved her, but now it had just gone much deeper.

It happened much too easily, I turned and pulled Rebekah to me and into my arms. I held her, her eyes cobalt with anticipation began to close as her lips slightly parted. We kissed, at first with some caution, but then with more abandon. Her arms were still around my neck, fingers in my hair. The Miller's yard faded away and for a while my whole reality was Rebekah. Minutes, hours …. my internal clock had stopped. The sensation of Rebekah was all that mattered. I would need her with me forever, and I thanked God for her. Could I be good enough to deserve her? I would try with all my heart.

We pulled away enough to look in each other's eyes. I had never seen a more brilliant blue and she smiled as a little tear fell down her cheek; both of us somewhat breathless.

"Rebekah, you *know* I love you. You'll never have to doubt, I'm *yours*, heart and soul. Your eyes are my whole universe," I whispered to her. Searching into the brilliant blue abyss, I held her tight.

She pulled me in and kissed me, and I could feel the smile in her kiss, a private joy that she was sharing with herself as she moved her lips up to my ear and whispered.

"Don't worry; I've always been yours, just *never* let me go. Keep me safe in your arms." I knew what she meant; through all the years of turmoil and interruptions, difficulties and miss-understandings, she was relentless, driven by a love that I might only hope to understand. Yet she wanted, *needed* me to protect her from the world that would never understand her.

"I'll never fail you," I whispered.

I wiped the tears from her cheek and we laughed in relief... at the release of years of pent-up tensions, anxieties and dreams. Ten years of a mating dance. Finally we could relax, secure in our love for each other, dreaming of our lives together. My heart filled me entirely.

"Can I show you the others?" she asked as she stood up.

"Only if you let me hold you close." I wasn't ready to end the intimacy.

I held her in front of me as she flipped through the sketches, smelling her hair, kissing her ear, as she giggled...

"Josh, I'm...I'm having a hard time concentrating."

(That was saying something.) "Good." I kissed her on the back of her neck. "Did you do these from pictures?" I asked.

She looked up a little hurt. "Only in my mind. Do you like them?"

She was a little hesitant, but I held her closer and she relaxed.

"I love them. They're extraordinary. I've never seen anything like them."

I bent down to kiss her cheek, but she anticipated me and turned to meet me with her lips. This could become very addicting .... time began to dilate again....

"Rebekah...Josh....dinner's served," Mrs. Miller called from the house.

"Be right there," Rebekah called back, and frowned playfully.

We had a final embrace, and then she whispered, "We'll have to continue *this* later," as her eyes glittered and she gave me that wonderful high laugh.

I don't recall much about the dinner or the conversation, but I do remember I had never seen a more beautiful woman in my life than Rebekah that evening.

****

I came out of my trance as I saw the Hummer's lights, and then M's black Carerra rolled in. Clear your mind Josh; you need to be on your game. I got out, and Hunter followed me to see why M had called. She held up her hand, and we walked over to an empty corner of the lot away from the light and the cars before she would speak.

"We've been hacked. I didn't want to discuss it over the phone. We need to do something about it before work tomorrow."

"Hacked?! Are you sure?" I exclaimed. Dumb question, M was always sure.

"We'll need to bring down the system and mount a new master key, but before we do, we need to determine how it was done." Hunter's mind was already working on these two things.

"M, could you see what was compromised, any trace?" I asked.

"I went to lockdown, so all external accesses were blocked, as soon as I realized and saved all contexts. We can run some traces and 'fingerprinting' to figure out how they got in," M's voice was excited.

The Prescience computer facility was in the basement of the older Apex building. I had been there many times before, but seldom at 2:00 a.m. I decided to let Hunter and M be my guides. And as we went through security, M explained we had been out for some pizza, but she wanted to show us something she was working on. For anyone else, the guard would have questioned; but for M and Hunter, this was relatively normal working hours. I was just a tag-along.

When we got in, the quiet was eerie; just a few lights, and the sound of the server farm.

M went to the supervisory console, and she and Hunter got to work. I was a spectator at this point, but I might be needed to make a couple of important calls.

Fortunately, only one section of the entire system memory was accessed by the hacker, as Hunter had segmented the system with separate high security encryption domains. *Un*fortunately, the area that was hacked was project development.

This was good and bad. The good news was that the Anticip8 users, all 370 million of them worldwide, would not need to lose any sleep over lost or stolen personal information, it had not been touched. The bad thing was that a number of highly sensitive Prescience projects were compromised, including the CRIMSON plan and references to the gray flag and perhaps even the Vision itself. I probably looked concerned as I pondered the consequences, and Hunter asked, "Are you OK?"

"Yeah, I guess I'm just ticked because it would have to be my area," I replied, partially true.

"Hey, look at the bright side. No user's data was compromised. We could have been sued for billions, or worse, shut down until the government monkeys were satisfied with our data integrity." Hunter was right, this was the lesser of two evils for Prescience and many of the six hundred plus projects were pipe dreams with no real value. But the CRIMSON plan would stick out. I would have to let Dad know.

Chapter Four

A Tango in Paris

"Keep your friends close and your enemies closer."
                    – Sun-tzu, The Art of War. 400 B.C.

"Mr. Reinhart, is it true that no user's data or information was released or compromised in anyway by the breach in security?"
"Yes, Senator, that is true.   No user data was compromised. Anticip8 users have nothing to worry about.   We go to great length to secure our user data, and of course, it is kept completely separate from any of the development operations at Prescience.   It was   some   of   the   development   project   files   that   were compromised.   I can assure you Sir, that there was no loss or compromise of user data by the security breach." I wanted to be as clear as possible on this point.

"When did it become clear that there was some connection between the breach of security, the hacking at Prescience, and some employees at Markos Media?" a new Senator wanted some photo-op time.

"July of this year, Senator; it's in the written deposition. Mr. Erickson and I went to evaluate the trial proceedings of the hackers in Paris. It was there that we first made the connection between Markos Media and the hackers." Just the facts, Josh.

****

Landing in Charles de Gaulle Airport, Hunter and I were sent by Dad to determine who was behind these small-time hackers. Dad was convinced that there was more to it than just a simple pair of hackers out for some information to sell. Something didn't seem right; so here we were waiting to get through customs.

We quietly stepped into the Paris courtroom and sat in the back row of seats. The two defendants and their counsel were up front being questioned by the judge as the prosecutor stood by his desk. The attendance was sparse; perhaps a dozen people up front, some small time press and family. A woman in the third row caught my eye. I could only see spectacular black hair and part of her profile. Without a multitude of images engraved in my memory, I wouldn't have been sure.

"Stay here and get the trial info," I whispered to Hunter, "but try to avoid being seen by the woman in the maroon suit. I've got to leave. I'll catch up with you later at the hotel; but for now, you don't know me."
He looked a little puzzled, but then slowly nodded once as I stepped out of the courtroom. Fortunately, the defendant's lawyer was in full argument with the judge keeping everyone's focus.

My mind raced as I left the court building and hailed a taxi to my hotel. What was *she* doing in that courtroom? What could she *possibly* have to do with the two hackers? I needed to know more, and I needed to know now.

Back at the hotel room, I went immediately to my bag, pulled out my laptop and stroked the fingerprint bar. Starting the Apex secure encryption channel newly revised since the breach, I entered the authentication code and stroked the finger bar again, this time with my right thumb and then the left ring finger, and fired off a message.

M, Give me everything on Cassandra Perez, early address Aliso Viejo, CA. Attended John Adams. Attorney. ASAP. JR.

OK, M. came back after about 10 seconds.

A long five minutes later the file showed up. I had already made a list in my head of what I knew about Cassandra and it was surprisingly short. Scrolling through the file brought me up to date:

Perez, Cassandra Maria

Marital Status: Single

Age: 29

Education: Juris Doctor, John Adams University.

Member of the Bar, NY, NJ, Virginia.

Current Address: 245 Park Avenue South, Apt. 304

Employer: Markos Media

Occupation: Special Counsel.....And a number of other details.

Finally, at the bottom of the screen, a recent photo at a black tie party with a middle aged couple smiling for the cameraman. I got an odd feeling in the pit of my stomach. I hadn't seen her since J.A., and she had only improved in the last eight years. She was more stunning than ever. I shook my head. Josh, for what you have in mind, you are going to have to be on your game; there was no time for this. Not to mention Rebekah.

I came back to reality and typed:

M,. deep dive on Markos Media, ASAP, JR.

OK. M. came back.

I needed to know as much as possible going into this and sensed there wasn't much time. While waiting for the background on Markos, I decided to call and send up a few sandwiches and a salad, and then opened the mini-bar for a soda.

I placed a mental bet on M. vs. room service.

Too bad there was no one to place the bet with; one thousand mental dollars to Josh as my screen started to scroll with page after page on Dimitri Markos and Markos Media.

I started reading and the food arrived. I absentmindedly made quick work of the food while pouring over the pages. I had heard of Markos, everyone had, but had no idea the extent of his empire. He had holdings in TV news and media programming, internet news feeds, and even a couple of the last major dailies. But that was just the more public face. He owned a number of small banks, mostly in the Caribbean, and two investment firms in Europe. He held a large interest in a number of major U.S. and European corporations, perhaps enough to actually control them by his swing vote in case of a power struggle. There were major real estate holdings all over the world, from mainland China to downtown Manhattan. I checked down the list and sure enough, *245 Park Avenue South.* I smile sardonically; some pretty good perks.

Then the political stuff: campaign contributions, PAC donations, influence and king making... this guy had his finger on the pulse of a dozen major nations, and he was pulling the strings on a myriad of politicians and policy makers, all the way to presidents and prime ministers. He held radically liberal views and was a prominent member of WorldWon, an organization of wealthy and influential people who wanted to see a one world order become reality. He had been instrumental in the forming of the European Union. Now he was focusing his formidable resources to make the North American Alliance a reality. Like the E.U, it would merge the United States, Canada, and Mexico into one commercial region with one currency, ultimately destroying the sovereignty of each nation. The image of the gray flag passed through my mind as I continued to read.

At sixty seven, he looked more like mid fifties. Divorced twice and currently unmarried, four children and one grandchild. Constantly seen at fundraisers (both political and for causes like global warming, etc.) and with the 'beautiful people.' A paparazzi favorite, he seemed to like spending time and throwing parties on his huge yacht, The Gaia. Toward the upper end of the Forbes Billionaire list, Markos was a global mover and shaker extraordinaire.

But how did this all fit together? My mind was jumping to a number of outrageous conclusions. I could hear my dad, 'point by point.' So let's try to connect the points.

Two small time hackers break into the staging projects server at Prescience. We now knew that it was actually an inside job by a disgruntled ex-programmer who had placed a backdoor into an obsolete server that kept a bunch of back up email files. Somehow this information was acquired by the hackers, and they actually used it to hack into one of the Prescience server domains. That ex-employee, Rich Sheldon, had disappeared, and he had not surface for the last eight months. Our private detectives and other enforcement agencies had lost him in Eastern Europe. The two hackers were refugees from the Middle East and had come to France as students. There was no doubt of their guilt; their computer disks had been confiscated, and they had not been capable of covering their tracks. Modern disk drives make multiple copies of data for maintenance and data integrity sake. So even though they thought they had erased their files, all the incriminating information was still on the disk in hidden recovery partitions. They now faced many years in prison and large fines, so perhaps there would be some way to get information out of them.

But *what* did Cassandra have to do with these two? It must be work related, something for Markos Media. Was it possible that there was a connection all the way to Markos?

After all, Cassandra was on staff as part of Dimitri Markos' special counsel. Had she gotten high enough in the Markos organization to have access to the man himself? Had her multiple talents already caught the attention of the mogul; and only after a few years? She was good, but was she that good?   Too many questions, not enough answers.

It was almost five. I took my laptop briefcase and headed down to the lobby. Checking for messages, the desk clerk handed me a small sealed envelope. Spotting a secluded alcove, I entered it and checked my little gift from Hunter – two plastic magnetic keys and a small note.

Key to the Raphael Hotel, room 335 in case you need it, the other is a locker in the Gare du Nord train station. Go out for a walk, I'll pick you up. Burn the note,   H.

I put the note in an ashtray, lit it with the plastic lighter I had bought in the souvenir shop, and walked out into the early evening air.

There was a reasonable amount of foot traffic and I just strolled, window shopping with my briefcase in hand. I turned down a side street, and a BMW mini pulled up alongside. Hunter pushed the passenger door open, "Get in."

He wasn't smiling; I sat down as he accelerated.

"I tailed the woman after she left. Who is she?" Hunter asked. I opened my laptop and showed him the picture,

"Cassandra Perez."

"That's the woman. She can stop traffic, no doubt about it. How do you know her?"

"I once dated and debated the fair Miss Perez several years ago; she went to John Adams. She works for Markos Media now."

"Dated? How serious?" Hunter gave me a sideways glance as he drove around the side streets of Paris.

"I guess you could say we were more adversaries than friends, pretty much all on her side. She's very smart and ambitious. She's even more seductive in person and knows how to use it to her advantage; been manipulating men since she was out of pigtails." I filled in the basics.

"You didn't answer my question, how do you feel about her? … Do you have feelings for her?" Hunter's serious attitude raised the hair on my neck and the color in my face.

"Well, I guess you could say that when I was sixteen I was infatuated with her, but now I'm more interested in how she fits into the hacker's puzzle. I can be objective now if that's what you're asking," I replied trying to sound convincing.

"It may require much more than that. I got an idea, so just hear me out." He was trying out his scheme on me as he drove.

"She's involved, no doubt about it. She talked with their lawyer, and then I had to leave to avoid being seen. I followed her to her office; she puts Markos Media right in the middle of it," Hunter stated it as fact, I wasn't so sure.

"And you want to know if I will bring her down. The answer is 'yes', *if* she is guilty," I said it calmly, but my stomach churned as I hoped it would not come to that.

"Good, because you'll probably get an invitation soon," Hunter replied.

"An invitation?"

"After I tailed Miss Perez, a rather pleasant way to spend an afternoon I might add, I stopped off to see a friend of mine at the U.S. Embassy. I let it be known that you were in town for the week and also picked up a few toys," he grinned finally.

"Anyone who is anyone will be at Chloe Arneau's fundraiser this Friday. I figured you'll get an invite and it's likely Ms. Perez already has one."

He finished explaining his plan as we drove back to our hotel.

To add to the plan, I brought up the file on Marcos Media on my PC. Hunter whistled. "Pretty big fish, I hope you used my new secure channel to get that deep dive. From M., right?"

"How did you know?" I asked.

"She'd be the only one available at 5:00 a.m. P.S.T." He headed back on some familiar streets, now.

"Why the keys?" I asked.

"Just in case...you can't be too careful. Like I told you, if you're wrong, it doesn't matter; if you're right, it could save your life."

****

Hunter looked back at me in the rearview mirror of the black Mercedes. He was dressed in a black suit and drivers cap, and I was in full 'black tie.'

"You set?" he inquired.

"Ready as I'll ever be." That was the truth as I would never really be ready for what he had in mind.

"Remember, I can hear you, but I won't be able to tell you anything without giving you a call."

"Only if you need to. I need to look like I'm just out for a nice evening," I replied.

We pulled up to the front of an imposing 18th century chateau. The doorman opened my door, and I stepped out into a warm starlit Paris evening. Hunter in his driver's role pulled the Benz away as another limo pulled up. A general underlying murmur of the ball was laced with occasional ladies laughter. I handed my invitation to the guard; he checked his list and handed it back.

"Mr. Reinhart, you're seated at table seventeen. I hope you enjoy yourself tonight." I thought about that. Another time, perhaps.

I walked into the main room, it was very large and ornate, high ceilings with murals, ancestral paintings, and enormous crystal chandeliers. Virtually all the guests were in black, except some of the women with enough confidence to show off a colorful designer gown. I snared a Champagne flute and took a sip. 'Reinhart, Josh Reinhart' I chucked to myself. I was here to get vital information from a woman who had intrigued, no, let's be honest, *beguiled* me since high school. But that was then and this was now. She was involved in some way with the security breach at Prescience and I had a job to do. I strolled slowly through the crowd, lots of French and English with heavy French accents, some American and British, and a little Italian and German. I was definitely one of the younger men, but there was certainly no shortage of beautiful young women, many in the company of their older benefactors. Perhaps it was my age or the slightly lost look I was trying to hide, but a very well preserved woman of *that certain age* broke from her group's conversation.

"Mr. Reinhart, so glad you could come to my little gathering. I'm Madam Arneau. Call me Chloe," she introduced herself with a soft French accent, "Let me introduce you to a few of my guests." She took my arm and guided me through the crowd, somehow making me feel like we were just old friends. That skill must take years of practice, I thought. 'Chloe' introduced

me to a group of relatively younger guests: A father-daughter pair
from Norway, evidently in shipping. A couple of formula 1
drivers and their dates. A senior marketing guy for some
multinational firm. Nearly everyone picked up on the Prescience
connection causing a brief flurry of questions but soon that was
too mundane for this crowd. Race horses, power boats, yachts
and films were the topics for this evening. We were then all
ushered into another huge room set for dining. A fantastic ice
sculpture of a bear and cubs was by the grand staircase. The band
was playing some light jazz for background noise. Exquisitely
set tables surrounding the dance floor were filling up with guests.
The dinner was five thousand a plate to assist in arctic animal
rescue due to 'global warming' damage to their habitat. I
couldn't have cared less, but it was a cheap admission ticket to
catch Cassandra on neutral turf, and hopefully off her guard.

I still hadn't seen her as I finished a wonderful Beef Wellington
with a little red wine – 'Superb' according to the marketing guy.
He and the shipping magnate were in an animated discussion over
the contents of their respective wine cellars. The meal was a full
set of courses and I had to thank all those years at cotillion,
managing to avoid making a 'faux pas' with the silver. I drank
sparingly, except for water, wanting to stay sharp for the evening
ahead. I stood when the two dates got up to powder their noses
and no doubt discuss the target rich environment for wealthy
partners. Then, sitting down, I asked the Norwegian Danielle to
point out anyone of real interest. Again this afforded me an
opportunity to scan the room, but no luck.

The band, just ending some pop/rock number, was nestled under
the staircase that led to anterooms off the second floor gallery
that encircled the hall. Deciding to change things up, they began

a waltz that caused a rather comical line change as the younger guests cleared and the older ones took the floor. Still no sight of her, I decided to make the best of the evening and asked Danielle if she would like to dance. We got to the floor and my waltz came back to me like riding a bicycle. We exercised our small talk skills. She was a very lovely dance partner, blond and tall, no doubt a product of the finest Norwegian finishing schools; but I was somewhat distracted, still scanning the hall. The waltz ended and I escorted her back to our table.

I was about to sit down to my dessert when a party of four came down the staircase. The three men were led by an impossibly graceful woman descending in a black gown that reinforced the desired affect, while still maintaining the mystery and allowing for imagination. Even though I had been steeling myself for this moment, the adrenaline rush was unnerving. I had about ten seconds to chill out and hear the inevitable musical voice. At least my outward appearance remained calm as I crossed the dance floor. A knowing smile crossed her lips on recognition and she made a small comment to her escorts, who moved off to find their table. She glided forward, fabulous black hair falling in loose waves to her bare shoulders, an emerald necklace gracing her throat. But it was no match for her large green eyes in that gold speckle mode that opened wide as she leveled her signature knock-out smile. I shot a little prayer skyward, 'Lord, help me stay focused on Your plan.'

We met on the edge of the dance floor, she took my hands. Her warmth hit me.

"Josh Reinhart. Back from the Crusades. You do show up in the *most* unexpected places," that musical voice and warm smile set my pulse up. If anything she had become more devastating in the last several years. *Steady*.

"I had the night off, and a friend suggested I'd find this interesting; so far I've not been disappointed." Playing it as cool as I could under the circumstances, I gave her an appraising look and took a sip of my Champagne. The silk haltered gown touched the floor, but was slit on one side for dancing. I wondered if it was "designer" or perhaps custom just for her. Given the necklace and the gown, she must be doing very well, or being very well kept.

"Dinner with a couple hundred of Chloe's closest friends?" she smiled, very at ease with this sort of banter.

"I hear the wine cellar is very good. What brings M'lady to Paris?" I quipped back.

"My work; I'm doing a little job for Markos."

Markos Media or Dimitri Markos, I wondered. "You work for Markos Media?" let her think you haven't got an inch thick dossier on her.

"I work for *Dimitri*. I'm part of his special projects legal team," she said it proudly, as you might discuss a gold medal or a championship ring.

I put on an impressed look; working for Markos on a first name basis was not my idea of greatness, but in the fast lane of money and power her accomplishment was astounding.

"Your friends?" I cast a look over at the three suits at her table; they were trying hard not look at us and failing badly. I dropped my glass on a passing tray.

"Viktor's boys. Part of our European team, co-workers." Her shrug made it clear she was unencumbered for the evening. Who was Viktor? I decided to let it go and focus on her.

The band began the stirrings of a Tango.

"They're playing our song," I gave her a grin and offered my hand inviting her to the dance floor.

I put my hand around her bare back; she was warm and close. 'Focus on the job, Josh,' as her perfume carried my thoughts, 'no cotillion rules tonight.'

"Sir, you haven't lost a step," she smiled and her hazel eyes widened as I led her strongly through the half a dozen or so couples on the floor. Having difficulty concentrating on my steps, I was under no illusion that Cassandra was enjoying putting pressure on me emotionally as well as physically. She knew how sensual she was and how to get to me. It was an odd sensation, a struggle, really. There was an all too human part of me that would have let my imagination and emotions run unchecked with the exquisite woman in my arms, but that would only lead to disaster. On the other hand, there was my integrity; I had a job to do tonight, *and* there was Rebekah. Thankfully, my higher mind maintained control, keeping the lower one in check..

"Your Latin style is still quite enchanting, M'lady," I replied as we separated for a moment. Finishing with a flourish, it seemed I might have gotten more than just the three men's attention as the space around us had cleared. She gave me an odd look of admiration and determination, a little breathless, as she met my gaze.

"Does your work bring you to Paris often?" I still needed to keep it light until I felt I had the situation under some control. The Tango sure had not helped in that respect.

"Occasionally. I usually work out of our New York offices. But when I can, I take travel assignments, especially Paris. It's so beautiful, and I get to go to some amazing parties." I got the feeling she didn't actually get a choice of her assignments.

"Yeah, case in point," I glanced around for emphasis.

"Have you seen the gardens?" she asked.

"No... would you like to get some air?" She took my arm with an "mmmm," and I took that as a 'yes.' Just like old times, leaving her knights at the table to walk me out of the castle. This time would be different.

We walked through a set of huge double doors that let out onto a veranda overlooking acres of formal gardens, dimly lit. She turned to lean back on the ornate rail as I stood admiring the view. The band and crowd noise fell off as we were met by a slight fragrant breeze coming up off the flowers below. It played with her black tresses, and the light from the ballroom reflected in the gold flecks of her eyes.

"Quite a view," she used the full musical voice this time, very warm, inviting.

"Spectacular," I said as I focused directly on her. This was going to be a tough game to play, and she had all her skills and was in post-season form. I, on the other hand, was in need of practice, spending too many hours at Prescience.

She gave me a warm smile and that low chuckle, shaking her head just a little.

"It's been a long time, Josh. When did we first meet? Was it at cotillion?"

"Actually, we met briefly at a debate tournament in San Diego," I corrected her and then realized she had just scored a point, as I obviously would never forget when we first met. She was good.

"How nice of you to remember; you had just moved to California, as I recall," she replied; translation, Score: Queen of the Ball - One, Josh trying to be cool - Zero.

"It was my first debate on the CRIMSON team, and you were leading...?"

"REASON," she filled in the blank. "That seems like a lifetime ago. Have you kept track of CRIMSON?"

"Not much since my sister graduated," I replied, now we might be getting somewhere. Why bring up CRIMSON? Nice romantic topic, homeschool debate teams of the past. Just what a guy wants to discuss with a drop dead gorgeous lady on a warm starry night in Paris. But for me, this was exactly what I wanted to hear. Let's find out just how much you do know.

The breeze picked up for a second, her perfume still chipping away at my resolve.

"It seems that just about the time you joined CRIMSON, they really took off. They have dominated Nats for years now. Many of the alumni have gone on to some very prestigious law schools. It's almost as if it were *deliberately* orchestrated." 'Orchestrated!' This was much too close to the truth. What did she know or was she just fishing; and more importantly why did she care?

"Nothing succeeds like success I guess, and the team has grown considerably, you would expect that many of the members would head off to law school," I casually replied, wondering if I sounded convincing.

"Yes, but it defies reason. Did you know that J.A.'s debate team is made up of over sixty percent CRIMSON?" she offered.

Who *else* keeps stats on this kind of thing? I thought, smiling to myself.

"Well J.A. *is* very homeschool friendly," I countered.

"But it takes more than that to get in; it's nearly fifty grand a year. I did hear a rumor about a private benefactor....And that's not all, several ex-CRIMSON students are interning with some very influential congressmen and senators. It's just *weird*, I thought you might have noticed?"

Noticed. Dad and I had spent hundreds of hours, and over six million dollars, not to mention the countless dinners to further the CRIMSON plan. *Private benefactor.* – what could she possibly know about CHAF, it was buried deep in Dad's personal finances, not mentioned in any TPM documents. Her intuition was remarkable.

"I know you once said you kept track of your competition, but I would think after ten years out of Nats it would be time to *relax*." I grinned, trying to soften the remark.
"I guess it does seem a little obsessive. ...Old habits die hard," she feigned embarrassment, looking for sympathy as if she sat at home alone nights, keeping up files on Moot Court tournaments. The old Cassandra would have come back with some sharp witty reply, but tonight she was looking for any advantage, working it from all angles.

Then warm and natural, gazing up at the Paris night, "Those were some pretty good memories; you know our J.A. team took Moot Court three years running. Too bad we lost to Harvard in my senior year." Full lips pouting slightly at the loss. Then with a shake of her tresses she flashed me golden specs as her eyes narrowed, "That Miller girl sure has a talent for getting in my way."

Wow, all in one comment: An attempt to sweeten our time at J.A. with '*our*' team, then a play for sympathy about the loss to Harvard, and topping it off with a veiled threat to Rebekah. The *new* Cassandra was breathtakingly treacherous; how many members of the CRIMSON plan was she monitoring? I had this image of spreadsheets with all the data on the plan. And why bring up Rebekah? She still couldn't accept that "that Miller girl" had bested her at every turn. Did she know about us? She probably had seen me in the photo at the Harvard Law graduation. I decided not to take the bait.

"I really haven't been keeping track of the J.A team since I left, been too busy helping Dad run Prescience." *Let's see if she suspects Dad and Prescience, or what.*

"I heard about what happened; it must have been tough to quit your dream of becoming an attorney. It would have *killed* me." *She was giving me the opening.*

"I was disappointed at first, but now I realize I've learned a lot more about business, the real world, and how to run a company working with my dad than I ever would have at any law school."

"No regrets, then."

"I just wish Dad hadn't been hurt," I lowered my tone.

"I was sorry to hear about your dad. That must have been a very difficult time. Then you just dropped out of my life; I wondered if I would ever hear from you again," she sounded sincerely disappointed. *Was she playing me; "Dropped out of her life"? She did everything this side of bribery to keep me off the team, and then treated me like a leper when I final got in. Who was she kidding? She must be under enormous pressure, attempting to convince me she was sorry I left J.A.*

"Not by design, I assure you. But you have no idea how all consuming my life has been, being brought in over the board's objections. I had to ramp up fast on everything. Failure was not an option. For my dad's sake, I had to become completely knowledgeable about Prescience and prove his faith in me was not just nepotism. Tonight is one of the rare occasions I haven't been Prescience 24/7."

Tonight's battle of wits was important work, too. I smiled as she looked over my shoulder for just a brief moment, and then focused those fantastic eyes back on me. Checking on her team; she was definitely working as well. I had to constantly keep that in mind, as opposed to some other ideas streaming through.

"Hmmm....All work and no play?   Perhaps someone up there wanted us to meet again.   When I saw you tonight I couldn't believe it.   I thought you were forever buried in some office in California," she flashed me a warm smile, and she moved in a little.   She knew how to get my attention.   Forget the polar bears, Cassandra was providing her own global warming spike right here.   I smiled sadly at the thought, if it were only sincere.

"You were surprised.   I figured I would never see you again after J.A. given how you felt about me....   And it looks like your court doesn't need another knight," I nodded back at the three men that she had come in with.   It seemed that they were always keeping an eye on Cassandra.   I would sure like to know what was going on with them.

"Are you still tilting at windmills?   Gallant Knight-errant?" She raised an eyebrow.

I decided to cut this cute banter short.   I really needed to get some answers and this might be my only opportunity.

"Cassandra, I'm not the same Josh Reinhart you *thought* you knew back at J.A."   Not even close, I hoped she would find that intriguing.   "But you look like you've kept business as usual. Three suitors at a time, but not letting anyone get too close. ...Doesn't it get old?" Time to try to provoke her a bit.   Use a little Sun Tzu.

Her eyes flashed.   Then she let out her low chuckle and a sly smile I hadn't seen before.   Man, she still held a fascination for me, my pulse was racing.   Was my gambit going to work?

"You're right; you're not the same Josh I knew.   He would have never been so.. ah..direct.   ..To answer your question: I have a *great* life, prestigious, exciting job, Park Avenue apartment, travel, parties.   Got here a lot faster than I thought.   And men are not a problem, at least *most*." I had hit a nerve; but she covered up with bravado, pointing out her mercurial rise up the corporate ladder at Marcos. I just wondered what price she had paid for it. The Cassandra I once knew would have played the game aggressively but not past *that certain* point. She took a sip of Champagne and looked back at me with a little defiance, and then gave a knowing smile.

"What is it you actually do for Markos? I'm sure he must be a demanding boss," I inquired. How far *does* your work cause you to bend the rules?

"When difficult legal issues come up, our team is called in to sort it out; we're called the '*fixers*' by corporate."

"So what are you doing here in Paris, besides saving the polar bears?" I hoped my casual smile hid my anxiety, this was the question I had been at all night.

"Oh, I'm just here to help train some of the staff. It's like a vacation considering what I am usually up to, trying to clear some sticky legal hurdle. Sometimes it's as simple as finding a way around fine print in a contract or representing some middle aged V.P. who got caught in a compromising position," she answered.

Well, Josh, you really didn't expect her to tell you she was here to 'fix' a problem with the Prescience hackers.

"What about you? Your Dad must be hard on you just to make it look like he's not playing favorites. What exactly does the 'First Born' do at Prescience?" Her cross-ex skills hadn't diminished, emphasizing her question with a raised eyebrow, and a slight tilt of the head.

'First Born', does she ever miss a trick? "I work in project staging. It's pretty interesting work, new ideas, new products." 'Along with investigating mysterious dark haired beauties,' I thought to myself with a smile. Man, she was all that....*Focus Josh.*

"No more 'Save the world, change the direction of the country back to more fundamental values?" She was laughing at my supposed younger naiveté. If she only knew. Fine, let her think I am now just a corporate drone, easier for me.

"Too busy at Prescience. It's a full time job," I replied.

"So, no leading a band of merry CRIMSON alumns crusading for truth and justice?" she laughed, but it was strained. Back to CRIMSON. There it was! She *must* know the details of the plan. She dropped her eyes for a moment, knowing she may have overplayed it, but then came up with that dazzling smile; her weapon of choice.

"That's so far back for me... I'd rather not dig up ancient history. As I remember the reception wasn't always this warm." I decided to try and change the subject. Let's see where this leads. I had gotten what I came for...She knew something about the CRIMSON plan, at the very least.

"It does seem like there were always...*difficulties. I* never really wanted it to be that way. Why do you think I kept track of you, hoping one day we'd somehow...?" She looked away. Was this possible, could she really feel this way?

She looked back up and there was a slight resignation to her voice, but her eyes... her eyes never looked more golden, tantalizing. "Why can't we just let our guard down for once and enjoy each other this evening." I searched those eyes... Why indeed, because you know about a plan that is so important it must be protected at all costs.

"I have to admit sparring with you is self-defense on my part."
That was certainly true.

She pushed off the rail and took a step forward; the breeze caught her hair and her perfume was intoxicating.

"What are you afraid of?" she whispered, stepping in much too close.

My mind had just started to form a response as our lips met. I had no time to brace for the smoldering freight train that hit me. My hands held her at her waist as she caressed my neck and entwined her fingers in my hair. I felt her heart beat. Cassandra? Cassandra, what are you up to? Do you really think I am this vulnerable? A few heartbeats slipped passed....

I gently pushed her away as I tried to reason this out. 'You can't trust her.' a high clear voice in my head intervened..... She sensed it and pulled away a little breathless as she looked into my eyes, searching....

"What's wrong? Isn't this what you've *always* wanted?" she whispered.

"I told you, I'm not the Josh you once knew," I answered, looking for some truth in her eyes, but finding only golden fire. Cassandra was right; in an earlier time and with a much younger Josh, it may well have worked, I would have been hers, captured body and soul. But now, I was completely committed to my mission *and* Rebekah, and between the two women, there was no comparison. If this was her assignment, she had played her cards well. If not, she still knew too much about the CRIMSON plan in any case.

"Oh, Josh, what we have hasn't changed. We're *good* together... you feel it, I *know* you do. Just let go for once, for *us*," she paused letting the 'us' hang in the air, trying to permeate my thoughts.....then stepping in again with all her allure in a low, breathy whisper, deliciously toxic...

"I want to share your dreams... *together*... I want to *know*, be part of your plans, part of.... *CRIMSON*..." she breathed the last word like it was an ancient spell and looked away, burying her head in my chest. She had played her ace. She was good, no doubt about it, a consummate actress. All those years of training, debate and persuasion, it was almost believable, but for a pair of brilliant blue eyes... 'all she cares about is winning.'

Moments passed, my mind was working through various possibilities, and it reached only one conclusion.

"Cassandra, what have you gotten yourself into?... Whatever it is... I can help." Why I said it, perhaps it was an old distorted memory of her, warm and stunning, or... It didn't matter, I said it, gave my word.

"You can help me by telling me...*letting* me in." She looked up offering her lips, eyes pleading now.

"I don't know what you want me to tell you .... but I *can* help you." I held back from her enticing invitation, forcing my mind to assess the situation.

"You don't understand... *no one* can help." She looked back with a little distain this time. She probably thought, as she always had, that I was the clueless rich kid.

"CRIMSON is just a homeschool deba ...."

"This isn't a *game*, Josh," she cut me off. No more smiles. "Can't you just give a little on your *precious* integrity, your commitments? It's such a small thing for you, but it's *everything* to me." Her eyes were very green now, and glistening, pleading. Her voice was no longer musical, but with hints of distress.

She whispered, "Unless I can deliver...I can't save myself ... or you. You have to give me something, *anything* ..." She pressed in close, *"help me,"* she breathed, looking up more urgently. But her allure had vanished; my mind was focused on her last plea. 'I can't save myself ...or you.'

"Cassandra, there is always a way back, *always*. If you want my help call this number and say you need to talk to the 'Florida Hoopster.' Markos isn't the only one with contacts and resources." I wrote a number on my invite and pressed it into her hand.

"You don't know who you're dealing with, you have *no* idea..." She dropped her head and just rested it on my chest. She had done her best, exhausted, now resigned.

"What about those three, are you OK tonight?" It wasn't hard to sound sincere, she obviously was in very deep and as much as I knew she was deceitful, I still felt they could be real trouble.

"My team? They're no problem," she said, too offhand. Had all this been a show for them?

I tried to give her a little lift, some hope. "Call the number, I'll do all I can." She looked up as I said it. And for once I thought I saw the real Cassandra, so vulnerable, warm, a little scared and sadly beautiful. Constantly striving so long, she hardly knew who she was when she paused.

"I wish I'd *never* met you,... never heard of CRIMSON." She shook her head slowly against my chest.

Her fear caused me to ask, "One more dance?... A show for your team." I glanced over my shoulder at the three men still intent on us. The band was starting up "Bésame Mucho" slow and sultry. Her eyes narrowed, then....

"Sure.... Why not?" Head up, she turned on her signature smile and with impossible poise led me to the dance floor. Grace under pressure, no one would suspect she'd lost.

As we slowly moved to the music, I felt her warmth and her sadness throughout the dance, not knowing if she would call, make her way back. She had made choices, and they had led to this... but there was still one left to be made. As the last notes were strummed, "Call the number, you have my word." I looked straight into those hazel eyes, only a glimmer of gold embers left.

"No promises.... Goodbye, Josh." No banter now, as we locked gazes and then she gave me a light kiss on the cheek, smiled and gave a musical laugh as I followed her back to her "team."
"M'Lady, Thank you for a most extraordinary evening." All for show.

Chapter Five

The Best Laid Plans

"Be courteous to all, but intimate with few, and let those few be well tried before you give them your confidence.
– George Washington

I walked out of the Chateau and down to where Hunter was waiting. It felt good to be back in the Benz as he drove off a ways, but then stopped.

"Why are you stopping?" I said laying back and loosening my tie, thinking about a beautiful, vulnerable woman in serious trouble....and a guy who had once again given his word.

"I want to see where your lovely lady and her court head to after the party." He looked in the mirror and grinned at me.

"So you heard?" I said, now remembering all that had gone on.

"Sometimes it was muffled, which could only mean she was covering the mike in your shirt. Not much talking but some pretty fast heartbeats," he chuckled and shook his head. "With adversaries like that who needs lovers."

"Seriously, she is in way over her head. I don't know how we can help her, but she's definitely knows about the hacking and that connects Markos Media at some level, maybe even Markos himself," I frowned, trying to redirect the conversation to a more serious tone.

"Help her? She knows what was hacked, she is guilty as sin. And what's this obsession with CRIMSON?" he asked.

"I don't know, I've told you about my old high school debate team, CRIMSON, I have a lot of friends that were on that team." I had to stick to my story, even though Hunter was my closest friend.

"Well, for a guy who doesn't get out in the field much, you did all right tonight," he glanced in the mirror. Then, "here they come." Hunter pulled the limo out leaving some distance.

"Oh, by the way. After the "I can't save you" comment she made, you are going to the alternate hotel tonight. I'll stake out your old room. Could get interesting," he stated.

"Need some company? The adrenaline will keep me awake all night anyway." It was true. I had played my part tonight and gotten what I came for and I was pumped, even if it had been a difficult test for 'the first born.' I shook my head; ultimately I had made it through. I prayed a prayer of thanks to God for His help and for Rebekah's words at just the right time.

"I guess you could help me stake out, but you got to follow my lead." That was a given, Hunter had probably forgotten more than I'll ever know about these things.

"And as far as helping Ms. Perez, let's see if she calls the number," there was doubt in his voice.

Cassandra and her "team" stopped in front of an upper class hotel, all glass on the lobby floor, well lit. One of the men got out and opened Cassandra's door. She headed toward the elevators as the limo drove away. We headed back to our old hotel.

"Ten to one we see someone we recognize tonight," Hunter quipped as we drove slowly past our hotel. He parked down the street a ways and pulled out his laptop and cell link.

"Not taking that bet," I replied. Question was, who?

"You got to love these Skype systems," he booted it up and opened a few windows. The split screen showed two still life videos: one of the hall outside my room and the other inside my hotel room. I had helped Hunter set the tiny WiFi cameras up and configured another laptop that looked in hibernate mode on the desk, power adapter plugged in since this afternoon.

"In the darkened room the bed does look like someone is in it," I said peering over at the laptop screen.

"Too bad about the bet, I didn't even get paid my regular driver's fee tonight." He looked back and motioned with his head.

A taxi pulled up in front of the hotel and Cassandra, in trench coat and hat, headed into the lobby.

"Looks like Cassandra might be paying you a late night visit... Man, she even looks good on these cheap cameras." The hall showed a figure in a trench coat and dark hair under a hat.

"What is she doing?" I realize I asked out loud.

"One more shot at you to get information, I suspect. Sorry Ms. Perez, nobody's home," Hunter replied.

After no answer to her multiple efforts to knock, she finally slipped a note under the door and left.

"You stay here, I'm going to check out the room before anyone else comes." He got out of the car. A few minutes later I saw him in the room, picking up the note and checking the bed with "me" sleeping in it. He also checked the computer and then left.

"I think this is intended for you." He handed me the note as he shut the driver's door, her perfume filled the back seat compartment. I broke the deep red wax seal embossed with a **C** and opened the handwritten note.

Josh,

I wish things could have been different between us, but now it's too late.

I know I will never see you again, so please be careful. You'll never know how sorry I am, about Everything.

Cassandra

"Earth to Josh, heads up, we got company," Hunter brought me out of my thoughts as the three suits entered my hotel. It was past 2:00 a.m. and I was starting to come down off the rush of the evening. Still trying to sort out 'Everything', as Cassandra put it. I had been praying silently in the back seat. I prayed that somehow Cassandra would come out of this safe and that no harm would be done to the CRIMSON plan. I also started to wonder if I had made one of those irreversible errors in life, accepting her invitation to cotillion and then asking her out. It seemed incredibly innocent and simple at the time, but I still remember how Rebekah took me to task. "It's how it looks,... How could you betray the team?" She had been right, I had not put CRIMSON first; I had put myself and my desires first. She also had been jealous. I smiled at that, at least that was going well. Rebekah was so much more to me now. She had helped me get through tonight; she had crept into my thoughts, deflecting the few wild impulses lead by adolescent dreams that in the cool early morning seemed not only reckless, but so obviously self-destructive. I said a prayer again thanking God for bringing Rebekah into my life.

"Well, this ought to be entertaining," Hunter broke through, my eyes on the laptop as the three men came down the corridor to stop in front of my hotel room. After a couple of knocks, one of them got some tools out of a small case he was carrying and had the door open in less than a minute.

"Have to give the hotel a black mark on their service questionnaire about security," I quipped nervously; looks like this could be open season on Josh Reinhart.

The three stepped into the room and shut the door; one man moved swiftly to my bed and stuck a syringe about where my lower back would have been. But all he got was pillow.

"These guys are not happy. Well, let's see if they trash the room or just leave," Hunter chuckled.

"Nice to have all this captured on my hard drive in case you need to explain how your room got damaged." Hunter was enjoying this, but I wasn't. 'Viktor's boys' were playing pretty rough. If I had been there, I don't think I would be laughing. 'Just my team' she had said, *Right*. 'The fixers' were certainly not your typical lawyers, but they probably lived up to their nickname. They went through everything and finally left with the laptop, at which time our video feed ceased.

"You owe me a new one," Hunter grinned as he started the engine. All my important documents were in the Benz's trunk with my laptop.

"Let's get you to your new hotel and then I'll book our flight back to California. I think with what we have seen tonight and what you nuzzled out of Ms. Perez, we have what we need," he smiled in the mirror as I frowned back at him.

"'Oh, Josh, what are you afraid of?'" he mimicked her sultry voice and laughed.

We pulled up to a non-descript but clean hotel after swapping vehicles back to the little Mini. Parking in the underground and using the stairs to get to the 3rd floor.

I was completely drained as I hit the bed. Hunter was next door, having booked adjoining rooms under his name. We had taken time to set up another camera so he could watch my room. I would have to find a way to make up for all his sleepless nights. A new laptop just didn't seem like enough.

My mind kept coming back to the image of Cassandra, the real Cassandra, vulnerable and scared, looking up at me, knowing she was in far too deep and knowing that all her scheming had come to nothing. Knowing that she was going to have to make the hard choice to come completely clean or risk falling deeper down the hole that she (and others) had dug. But as I finally dozed off, the last image was of Rebekah walking out of my pool back home, slicking her hair back from her face, brilliant blue eyes competing with her shimmering one piece. Lord, help me make the right choices.

****

Back in San Diego. things just got busier. I briefed Dad about what had happened in Paris, minus a couple of moments with Cassandra. If he really wanted the whole story he would have to listen to the recording. The disturbing truth was that the TPM database was known at some very high level inside Marcos Media and perhaps even by Marcos himself. At the TPM we had gone over the fact that the database had been compromised and that it could become public. The good news was that we had used aliases as a simple precaution, but Cassandra could certainly decipher the initials. The other piece of good news was that according to Mr. Stanton we had not broken any laws and this could not be construed as conspiracy. He had spent the last two weeks scrutinizing the database, and since he had been the moderator for the database all these years, I was not concerned from a legal point of view. Certainly, to some liberal causes, it could look suspicious, but there was nothing illegal in investing in a child's future and guiding them through decisions or even internship placement.

That was the beauty of the CRIMSON plan. It worked because it operated within the bounds of what people were interested in anyway...what they wanted and were called to do. We just provide a little help... in some cases a lot of help, but always in line with the person's general career objectives. And it also worked because it was from God, I was convinced of this. So many miracles, some small and some large, had happened as we walked in His will, working on the CRIMSON plan.

To say that the thirteen members of the TPM were very disturbed about the database hacking was an understatement. Dad had claimed infallibility and now had to somehow reassure them. "I thought it was encrypted and secure" was the main theme. Dad and I had to explain what had happened and that the server was now made impregnable, but we met with many skeptics. So we simply said that we needed to be more diligent and that I personally would see to it that constant database movement and variable encryption would be used to secure our database. This would require about an hour out of my week but if it would keep everyone involved and feeling secure, it would be worth it.

On a positive note, the unaware members of the CRIMSON plan had just topped one hundred, and we finally had our first judgeship. John Petersen had become a superior court judge in Virginia. This was our first major milestone. It was a desperately needed shot in the arm for the TPM. We prayed and thanked The Lord for all His blessings, including CRIMSON's first judgeship. It had taken ten years of planning and prayer, hard work and millions of dollars, but the seeds sown had started to sprout and even bear fruit. There was great expectation that within a few years more judgeships would be secured.

Then there was the public policy arm of the plan. This had become the second effort for the CRIMSON alumni. Many had gone on to work in the State Department and other organizations as policy makers. Having our strong Christian brothers and sisters working to shape public policy was a serious weapon to be used against the gray flag. I prayed that somehow the security breach would not derail all our progress. With God's help we had made it this far, and now the CRIMSON plan was on the verge of making real impact... Pastor Miller had been right so many years ago when he said it would take decades, perhaps a lifetime. But the only way was to plan and execute the best we could and step out in faith each day. So far the commitment had been difficult, but worth it.

****

My family had leased a beach house down in Del Mar, a nice place right on the sand. After three weeks of nearly 24/7 work at Prescience and on the CRIMSON plan, I needed some down time. So this long weekend I had secured the place for a small group of my friends: Hunter, M, Robert and his fiancé, and Rebekah and I. The girls took up quarters in the upstairs bedrooms and the guys sacked out downstairs. This worked out great because the men were close to the kitchen, plenty of late night snacking, and the ladies got an extra bathroom.

The girls had opted to go shopping one afternoon and Robert went along, mostly to be with Debra, his intended; they were inseparable.

"How are you holding up?" Hunter asked while we sat out on the deck watching the surf as the afternoon faded.

"How do you mean? Work-wise or otherwise?" I countered.

"Both, but let's start with 'otherwise.' I figured you were doing this for Rebekah, but you needed a chaperone of sorts, so you invited the rest of us. You know it's no secret, you two are quite the item," Hunter grinned.

"Is it that obvious?" I replied. He just arched his eyebrows.

"I invited you all because she wouldn't have stayed with me alone, and I wouldn't ask her to. But she is *The* most amazing woman on the planet," I smiled as he shook his head.

"Man, you can pick 'em, that's for sure. First that stunning Latin femme fatale complete with three henchmen, and now a walking Encyclopedia Britannica with the extended law library bonus package. She *is* beautiful, I'll give you that. And those *eyes*, I could see how you could get lost. But it is just a little weird how much she knows, about *everything*. For instance, I heard Rebekah talking to M today *in Chinese*. ... And she's how old?" Hunter queried.

"She's twenty five, just out of Harvard Law," I replied,
"I supposed she finished ..." "...First in her class and editor of
the Law Review," I filled it in. Hunter just shook his head.

"Well... does she know about Cassandra?" Hunter asked.

"You gossip like an old woman," I chuckled. "What about M?"
two can play this game.

"Oh, she's a good friend. She's one of the few people I can have
a serious conversation with about security and encryption. I
mean, she cleans up real nice, but... just friends." I could see
there might be more there than he was willing to discuss.

"I saw you eying her in that little white suit she brought. I bet she
hasn't seen the sun in months. I was afraid I would have to order
a coffin for her to sleep in," I replied.

We both laughed. "Yeah, I haven't figured out when she sleeps
either," he had to admit and then continued.

"Nice try changing the subject, but we *were* talking about
Rebekah, so what's your plan?" He wasn't going to be put off.

"I guess you could say that I can think of no one else I would
rather be with, even if she can be a little difficult at times. We've
been through a lot of trials and she has always been there. She is
unique and brilliant. And don't think it's about the money, it's
not. I trust her completely."

"I guess it's a good thing Ms. Perez is out of the picture." This is
what he really wanted to get at.

"Look, if you're asking me to compare, there *is* no comparison.
Rebekah is on a whole different plane than "Ms. Perez." You
probably don't know this but they have met in debate, and while I
didn't see it I understand it was no contest. Cassandra may be
smart and driven, but she is no match for Rebekah, mentally,
morally or spiritually...." I was getting a little worked up,
surprising myself.

"Ok, Ok... I see how it is. And I really am happy you've found *"The One"* because I can't imagine what the next girl would have been like...some *alien*," he grinned, separating the two fingers of his right hand like Spock. I had to laugh, but then fell silent.

"I love her; I have for a long time..." I finally said. It felt good to say it out loud, to acknowledge it to a good friend.

Rebekah and Debra seemed to hit it off, and for a short time I was alone with my old friend Robert. I hadn't seen much of him lately. He had been working for the NCLC, National Christian Law Center as one of their senior attorneys taking cases that would impact the rights of Christians. He was on a fast track, and had even argued in front of the Supreme Court once. He was steady and even-tempered as ever.

"Rebekah tells me you've been seeing each other," he came out in his direct manner.

"Where have you been? This is pretty old news, but yes, I'm courting your sister," I said formally.

"Don't get me wrong, Josh, I am very happy about it. She has always cared deeply for you and I have never seen her happier, and by the looks of it the feeling's mutual," he replied in his defense.

"Yeah, it is... So, how did you meet Debra?" I thought I ought to get to know more about her, as there was a good chance we would become in-laws.

"She works for a pro-bono law office in D.C., helping clients who cannot pay; the only way she gets paid is when she wins a case. She seems to get paid well enough," he smiled with pride.

Man, I was going to be surrounded by attorneys. Of course, what did I expect, given I ran a gang of lawyers and law students, pulling strings and orchestrating their lives unbeknownst to them.

I smiled, bemused, what an amazing journey it had been, and we were really only at the beginning.

"Robert, you seem very happy, and Debra's a great gal, I never doubted you'd make good.   Something about your steady personality, people feel comfortable with you.   They like you right off, know they can trust you."   ....A hint of an idea was playing on the edge of my imagination and I had to let it grow till I grasped it, as I had a feeling it was important.....

"I do like my work and sometimes our team at NCLC makes an impact," he replied, but I wasn't really listening to him, I was concentrating, trying to hold on to the hint.

"That's great.   Could you excuse me, I'll be back in a few minutes," I replied already getting up to go, I needed to write this down.

I went into my room and took out a notebook and pen and started writing a list.

> - Robert needs to run for office. He's a natural. I need to talk to Dad.
> - But I think he may need to know about the Vision to be convinced.
> That could be a problem; he may not like the fact that we helped him without his knowledge.
> - then if he knew….
> - Debra will need to know. So we need to run background checks on her.
> - We need to run background checks on everyone in the plan and any wives / girlfriends.
> - Will this be ethical? Is this the right thing?
> - No wonder Dad never wanted to release the details to the plan members.

I added a few more bullets and then reread it. After a while I decided to flush it down the toilet. It was a very interesting idea and it had to be looked at from all angles carefully for all the consequences, but I didn't need it written down for someone to accidentally find.

The sun was throwing long shadows on the beach. Rebekah was relating a story about a crippled little boy in China that came to know The Lord, and then his testimony had brought his parents to Christ as well. She recalled every little detail, some would say too much detail, but I didn't care. I just loved hearing her, seeing how happy she was. I could have sat on the beach with her forever, scanning her loveliness, my heart was full.

"Josh, phone call for you." It was M yelling from the beach house.

"Tell them I'll call them back," I replied.

"I think you'll want to take this," M stood there, phone in the air.

"I'll be right back; this should only take a minute," I grimaced. Boy, was I wrong about that.

I took the phone from M and walked into the house.

"Yes." I was terse. This better be important.

"I have a call for the Florida Hoopster," the other party said and hung up.

I frowned into the receiver and set it on the counter. Then I went to my bedroom and picked up the old fashion land line phone and dialed. The phone and the service were completely secure; it was something Hunter had arranged in my office, here and at my house. And now his paranoia was about to pay off. The party trying to contact me would have been asked to go to a payphone in a public place if possible before I even got the call. And they were told not to use my name, any names. The conversation would be recorded on my end for review purposes.

"Florida Hoopster," I spoke into the receiver; waited for the three tones.

"Emily.   8247," I spoke again, a code for clearance and encryption.

"Go ahead." I heard the electronic voice on the line, then some dead air time.....

"Florida Hoopster?" She was scared and uncertain, but I would know that voice anywhere, even with the hash from all the encryption.

"M'lady, how can I help?" I said hoping to ease her anxiety.

"I'm in trouble....You said to call, and so I'm calling. I need to get out of this. You know you're the last person... but I need your ...You were right...."

She was talking fast and almost in a whisper, she was also breaking down. Perhaps she couldn't talk much or loudly on her end, or maybe it was something else.

"Where can I be *sure* to meet you and when?" I asked. I needed to just get the facts, and then perhaps I would try to reassure her.

"Ah... They watch me constantly, so it doesn't matter. ... I guess my apartment. 245 Park Avenue South...   Third floor number 304...any weekday early, before 9:00. But *soon*, I don't know how much time I have," she was starting to sound a little better, more in control.

"OK.   Be ready this Wednesday, 6:30 a.m.   You got it? Wednesday, 6:30," I replied, calculating in my head if Hunter and I could put it together that fast.

"Got it," she replied.

"How many are watching you, who do I need to deal with?" next big question.

"My old team, those three men in Paris. ... I think they killed a man.... they're probably watching me *now*...I got to go."

"OK, be ready, but try to act normal. Don't call again unless you absolutely have to," I replied, my mind racing, already starting to plan.

"OK…I don't know why you're doing this… but… just *hurry*."

The line went dead for a few seconds then an electronic voice came on the line… "8-2-4-7 Secure. Complete."

Well, this will sure put a dent in the rest of my weekend. I tried to calm myself and went down stairs to see if Hunter was around. I saw him with M and so he knew, he could add two plus two pretty fast. I went outside just in time to see Rebekah, packing up from the beach as it was starting to get a little cool.

"Coming in?" I tried to be nonchalant, my mind still in planning mode.

She nodded, "No one to keep me company," she teased giving me a very inviting pout.

I walked over and wrapped a towel and my arms around her shoulders, and gave her a hug and a light kiss, wanting more.

"I'm sorry; I needed to take that call. Work," I said. It wasn't exactly a lie, as one of the benefits of bringing Cassandra "in from the cold" was that she would testify against those who were responsible for the breach at Prescience. At least that was the plan.

"Why don't you just quit, and we can be beach bums?" she reciprocated with a hug looking up at me. A very attractive offer at this particular moment.

"Then who would keep track of Hunter and M," I grinned, giving Hunter a sideways glance.

"Speaking of that, we're all out of ice cream, and I promised to make my famous 'banana split ala Hunter' for everyone tonight. You comin', Josh?"

Hunter was getting his jacket.

"Yeah, get the Hummer started, I'll be there in a minute." I still held her. I never wanted to let her go or even think about another woman, but that was what I would have to do for the next seventy two hours.

"So she finally called. I was hoping she wouldn't," Hunter began as we pulled out of the drive.

"She's in real trouble, she sounded very scared," I replied.

"OK, what's the situation?" He knew there was nothing to do but go get her.

"We need to get her away from "her team", those three suits in Paris. And then she has to give herself up to authorities for questioning."

"Where and when?" Hunter was in Ranger mode again, planning an "op."

"Her New York apartment. Wednesday morning… I told her to be ready at 6:30 a.m. She says they watch her constantly," I replied.

"Doesn't give me much time, but I think I can get a little help from a guy I know in Justice." Hunter seemed to always have a "guy he knew."

"And one other thing, she thinks her team killed someone."

"She thinks, or she knows?" he gave me a sideways glance.

"She said 'I think they killed a man,'" I repeated.

"OK,… that will definitely get my friend's attention," Hunter exhaled, mental gears meshing.

"When we get back, I need to use the secure phone. We don't have much time, so we'll have to improvise a little. Taking no chances. We're wearing the ballistics, and going in locked and loaded, plus some hardware," he was planning out loud.

"Tomorrow, I need the afternoon off. OK boss?" Hunter grinned.

I nodded and then "Pi-squared is at Lindberg. I'll make sure she's prepped."

"If there are no hitches, you'll be back in time for the patent review meeting Wednesday afternoon." Hunter loved using the private jet.

"There are always hitches, but it'll work out," I said as I shook my head. Plan as thoroughly as possible, pray and let God handle the rest.

"For instance, morning traffic in Manhattan will be a mess," I gave him an example.

"I'm counting on it," Hunter said as we pulled into Trader Joe's.

I needed to cut the long weekend short, so I asked Rebekah to please bear with me but urgent business has caused me to get back into work on Monday morning. In reality, Hunter and I had a lot of planning and equipment procurement to do before Wednesday morning. I suggested she, M and Debra go on a shopping spree, courtesy of Prescience (actually me) to try and sooth her mood (and my conscience).

"I am perfectly capable of buying my own clothes, and if I wanted to be with a bunch of women I can do that at D.C. tea parties!" Her lasers blazed.

I guess I should have been flattered, but she was not buying my weak excuse. She would not be bought off with a few trinkets from the Mall; she wanted my time, jealous of it. I had once again added to her tally in the "mysteries Josh is still keeping from me" column. A column I couldn't erase.

"Please, just get me back to the airport; I'll see if I can get an earlier flight," she seethed.

I guess I couldn't blame her. Here I was, obviously courting her, and I'm sure she knew how I felt about her. Yet I was still keeping secrets and she just couldn't accept that, not in the long run.

Chapter Six

In from the Cold

"I love the man that can smile in trouble, that can gather strength from distress, and grow brave by reflection. 'Tis the business of little minds to shrink; but he whose heart is firm, and whose conscience approves his conduct, will pursue his principles unto death." – Thomas Paine 1776.

The plain white panel van was waiting on the tarmac in the private charter section of Kennedy as the Pi-squared landed. It would stand out like a taxi cab in New York City and that was the idea. The fact that there was a Ducati streetbike and two full sets of leathers, helmets, boots and some unrelated gear under a tarp in the back was due to a few phone calls by Hunter.

As far as American Airlines was concerned I was booked on a flight scheduled to land at Kennedy at 8:06 a.m., about two hours from now.
At least the weather had cooperated, it was cool and sunny. A beautiful autumn day for saving damsels in distress, I thought to myself as I stepped out of the jet.

In the van, Hunter and I went over the equipment in the duffle. We put on the type VI rated ballistic vests. They were heavier than just the Kevlar due to the ceramic composite inserts. The transceiver/GPS units were next. Then I snapped the striker bar into its leather forearm guard. The bar was nine inches of stainless steel almost an inch in diameter. I put my white shirt on, my cufflinks just closing around the striker on the inside of my wrist. Then the requisite old school tie. Finally, I slipped the tiny LCR .38 into its ankle holster. I would rather it had been my Glock, but it would do in close quarters, the weapon of last resort. With the leather bomber jacket over my shirt and tie and donning a Yankees baseball cap we headed into the city, about an hour away.

Traffic was getting heavy as we turned onto Park Avenue. We both pulled on a pair of disposable latex gloves as we went over the plan one more time. This could be relatively easy or it could become complicated and difficult. Hunter and I had worked through a lot of scenarios and contingencies over the last two days. I prayed that it would be easy and no one would get hurt. Just pick up Cassandra and take her to Hunter's friend in Justice.

We passed 245 South and there he was, casually standing near the entrance, dark suit, one of "my team" she had said. So much for easy. I marked him as we drove the van into the underground lot. Now where were the other two? We parked so that the back of the van was clear. No one was in the parking lot when Hunter, with Elevator Service Specialists stenciled on the back of his overalls, jumped out of the van carrying his tool bag. He stepped through the door, marked '245 Entrance.' Suit number one lit up a cigarette as he stepped into the parking lot. He looked up as I headed toward him and the building entrance. His eyes widened

as he finally recognized me under my ball cap. His hand went to his coat, but then he slumped as Hunter hit him hard from behind with the striker bar. I quickly stepped forward and helped Hunter drag him behind the dumpster in the back of the underground lot. Hunter took a small syringe from his tool bag and injected the back of his neck under his hair. "Sweet dreams," he muttered.
We dowsed him with a half a bottle of vodka, before dropping the rest by his side. Then covering him with an old raincoat, threw his shoes in the dumpster. Taking his passport from his coat, Hunter put it under the owners chin and snapped a picture with a pocket camera. I found his radio and tossed it to Hunter as I headed toward the stairwell and the third floor. Reaching the landing at the third floor stairs I took off my jacket and ball cap. Now looking like a few million other men in Manhattan, I peaked into the hall through a little window. My transceiver went off in my ear. "Set."

I took a deep breath and prayed, then opened the door and stepped into the hall. The guy outside Cassandra's apartment immediately turned and started walking toward me. On recognition he opened his coat showing me a holstered gun. Hunter had his back to the man, "repairing" the open elevator. As the "fixer" walked by him, Hunter swept the man's legs out from under him, and I cracked him across the side of the head with my striker as he fell forward into me. He was still barely conscience and tried to get his footing, but his legs would not hold him. I held him up as Hunter relieved him of a very nice Beretta and pocketed it. Hunter had his Kimber out immediately; and as we supported our charge to Cassandra's door, he was keenly aware of the cold barrel under his chin. I put the radio up to his head and told him to ask to be let in as if the door would not open. He was in no shape or position to argue as we heard the door bolts unlock.

Hunter nodded toward the door, and cracked the man on the side of his head, then we both shoved him hard into the room. The next few seconds seem to unfold in slow motion and extreme clarity for me, undoubtedly due to the surge of adrenaline.

The third man was not entirely unprepared for the attack. Perhaps he was more experienced or just on his guard. Our human projectile burst into the room landing flat on the marble entry; but his partner had backed up quickly, his pistol with silencer drawn from beneath his coat. I rushed past the fallen man expecting the gun to be turned on me, but following the line of the silencer it was clear that the first shot was intended for someone else. Standing by the couch, Cassandra's eyes were wide in horror and realization; her mouth opened, "No!" her hands going up to shield her face.

In the next fraction of a second I can't say exactly what was going through my mind, but I launched myself and felt the kick of a mule in my chest. "UUFFF" was my insightful, if brief, commentary on the events as all the air was knocked out of my lungs. I fell onto the couch in intense pain, but conscience enough to hear a coincident crack and grunt as Hunter took out the gunman with his striker. I rolled over to view Hunter pocketing the gun and sitting Cassandra down in a chair. "Josh!" she looked at me in astonishment.

Hunter opened my shirt and checked the vest to make sure I would have nothing more than a painful bruise. He dropped a piece of lead into my pocket, "A souvenir," he said flatly.

I sat up on the couch gaining some air and winced as every movement was accompanied by deep muscle pain in my upper chest, focused in my left shoulder area. "Josh Reinhart, at your service," I managed with a pained grin, as I appraised Cassandra. She was safe, shook up, but safe.

I saw Hunter turn the shooter over and then with two deliberate chops break his kneecaps with sickening cracks of the striker. "You won't be dancing for a while," Hunter stated coldly, then the syringe to the neck, and another nice picture with his passport. Same for the guy we had launched through the door, but Hunter spared his knees. He found the spent casing and pocketed it. Cassandra watched silently with wide eyes, her hand to her mouth.

I took another painful breath, "Do whatever this man tells you without hesitation, and you will most likely live to tell your side of the story, otherwise…" I just nodded at the man crippled on the floor.

Hunter pulled out some leathers from his tool bag. "Put these on *now*, Ms. Perez," he spoke with authority. Cassandra pulled the leather jumpsuit over her slacks and zipped it up. She looked over at me and spoke, calmer now.

"A little while ago a call came in, and I overheard. He said, 'I see, …no-show. OK, then come back here, you may be needed,'" nodding at the shooter.

"Sounds like we could have some company," I grimaced, the ballistic vest might be bulletproof, but certainly was not pain proof. I found I could stand, partly due to the adrenaline rush.

"You gonna be OK?" Hunter asked as Cassandra grabbed my right arm to steady me. She had a strange look, one I had never seen before.

"Yeah, I'm good." Josh Reinhart, human shield, faster than a speeding bullet. I managed a brave grin.

"The idea is to *avoid* the line of fire, not dive *into* it," he shook his head. "Here, take a couple of these, and keep a couple for later." Hunter passed me four plain yellow tablets, the fact that he joked indicated he was very relieved. I just put two of them in my mouth but couldn't swallow them, too dry. Cassandra and I moved to the bar for a glass of water. After I swallowed the pills, I was able to speak.

"I trust this man with my life, and you *must* trust him too. Call him ah... Eric." I smiled slightly at the irony.

"'Eric' will take you directly to the Justice Department, and you must tell them everything you know about Markos, about the hacking, about the killing you think happened. *Everything*....and if you have documents, bring them." It was painful to breath and speak, but this was all important. She nodded.

"You'll likely be given immunity as long as you're straight with Justice; so for your own sake, don't try to 'play' these guys." I gave her a hard look.

"OK, ...I need to go to the bedroom and get some things out of the safe," she asked. I nodded.

She left the room, and Hunter followed her just in case. I stood there, my right hand on the bar, steadying myself. She came back in with a slim briefcase and a small travel case strapped over her shoulder. Hunter finished gathering information on the men, including a skin sample from each. He took the Beretta out of his bag and shoved it back into its unconscious owner's holster. Then he put the silenced pistol back into the shooter's hand, firing a round into the couch, making Cassandra jump.

"Let's go," Hunter commanded as he picked up his tool bag, all business.

Cassandra steadied me as Hunter opened the door and walked out into the corridor cautiously, one hand on the Kimber inside his coat. Cassandra held me close to her. "Josh, I don't understand ..., you risked your life for me. I'd be dead back there...and I tried to bring you down, why'd you..."

"I gave you my word." I looked at her hard, straight into those stunning green eyes with shining specks of gold, that were wide, glistening now.

"You really are that knight... and once... I ...I could have been..." She shook her head and wiped her eyes. "... Stupid, *stupid* pride," she uttered under her breath. After a moment or two she seemed to collect herself, even flashed her signature smile.

We stepped into the corridor, and Hunter was already holding the door to the stairs, having retrieved my jacket and cap. We stepped past him, and he shut the door behind us. I took the stairs a little slower, and Hunter got out first and checked the garage. No sign of police or any other visitors – God was in on this one, I shot a 'thank you' skyward.

I straightened up the best I could and told Cassandra to go with 'Eric.' He handed her a pair of thin latex gloves. "Put these on now, please." Hunter was almost civil.

I walked out into the garage and she and Hunter were already at the van.

Looking at my watch, I was amazed to find the whole episode had taken less than fifteen minutes. It had seemed like an hour. I got to the van and stepped up into the driver's seat, with an audible grunt. Hunter came over to check me once again and then helped me with my bomber jacket and hat. "You good to drive?" he asked.

I nodded.

"See you back in San Diego," he grinned and went back to un-tether the Ducati. Cassandra was about to put her helmet on, but came up front between the seats and bent to give me a kiss on the cheek, raven hair falling.

"For my Knight-errant," she whispered in my ear, and for a second I was distracted from the ache in my shoulder. Then turned and put her helmet on as she walked to the back of the van, "I'm ready."

Hunter had stripped off his overalls, leathers underneath. He put on his helmet and gloves and rolled the bike out of the van, then pushed the ramp back up and shut the doors. I heard the engine start; and then he, with Cassandra holding on tight, rolled past me and headed out of the garage weaving into the stop and go traffic on Park Avenue. I knew I would never see her again, and that was probably for the best. Hunter would have her at Justice in no time, cutting through the traffic like a hot knife through butter. I started the van and pulled it cautiously out of the garage joining all the taxis, just another service vehicle. Thankfully, the pain was beginning to dull due to the pills. It would be more than an hour to get back to Kennedy and Pi-squared; I just needed to make it there. I saw a NYPD squad car pass the other way on Park Avenue, then double back to 245. Maybe we had made a little too much noise for the gentile residents of Park Avenue. 'Praises to You, Lord,' I thought, 'Your timing is perfect.' Cassandra was safe and no one got killed. But a couple of us got hurt, thinking of the shooter; he would need a year or two of rehab on those knees, and even then he would have to find another line of work. Welcome to the unemployment line.

I drove for another twenty minutes, then my transceiver went off "All is well," Hunter's voice in my ear. All is well; she was safely in the hands of the U.S. Department of Justice. And she had a story that they would be *very* interested in. If she played ball, who knows, she might even be allowed to practice law again some day. "All is well," I replied.

The Pi-squared sat on the tarmac, fueled and ready for boarding when I drove up. I just left the van there; the owner would retrieve it later this morning. Picking up the duffle bag with Hunter's overalls, I checked to see that there was nothing left in the van except the ramp and the straps that had tied the Ducati down. Hunter probably loved dodging the traffic in the city on that bike as he tied up a few loose ends. He had a flight back to San Diego tomorrow and a date with some old friends tonight. I would have to think of something I could do for him when we got back.

Hank came down the stairs of the jet and relieved me of the duffle. He noticed I walked kind of gingerly, but didn't say a thing. I gave him a smile and a 'thumbs up.' He smiled back and shook his head. Once aboard, I stripped off my shirt and the ballistic vest that had saved my life. I was already starting to turn very interesting shades of blue, yellow and red in my upper left chest area under my t-shirt. The pain from the impact was starting to get worse again so I swallowed one of the yellow pills plus a sleeping pill and settled into the large lounge recliner. The adrenaline rush was starting to subside, and sleep would come eventually. I heard the muffled whine of Pi-squared's engines lift us skyward and toward home; it was 8:47 a.m. and Hunter had been right; I would be back in time for the patent meeting this afternoon. I debated canceling and decided to see how I felt when I woke up. 'Reinhart, Josh Reinhart,' I chuckled to myself and winced, recalling the mule kick. I just shook my head, "What was I thinking?" Drifting off, the image of those green eyes with flecks of gold, so wide with disbelief; maybe this time she would finally turn it around.

I woke up somewhere over Arizona, took another look at my chest as it seemed to be a little less tender, but my mood had darkened just like the bruise. What had started out as a relaxing and romantic three day weekend had been ruined by that one phone call. The secret of the Vision and all its other mysteries was definitely taking its toll on my personal life. I had often paid the price for my commitment to it, and I saw no end to that as I was obviously called to lead this mission. I frowned. It was a cruel taskmaster, causing me to discourage my steadfast and loving Rebekah to fly across the country to take a bullet for a woman who had never been straight with me, not to mention the untold damage she had done to the CRIMSON plan.

In addition, the Vision had now taken on a new dimension. What had been a seemingly general evil symbolized by the gray flag had become a flesh and blood adversary. How high up the source of the evil went was anyone's guess, but there was definitely a group of people inside Markos' organization that were willing to kill to cover up their activities. What the true nature of those activities entailed was hard to say, but someone thought it was worth killing for. At least Cassandra was safe at Justice; and with all the evidence she had and her testimony, the evil would be starting to feel some heat of their own for a change. But the fact that people who were willing to kill knew those involved in the CRIMSON plan was of grave concern to me. Was it right that they were kept in the dark when there lives could presumably be in danger? What about the ultimate goal of the plan, placing godly people in important positions within the judicial and policy systems? What if I told them about the plan and the Vision, would they be willing to continue to go along? Or be incensed by the enormous arrogance of those who were manipulating their lives, refusing to take part in the struggle against the gray flag. It was a huge gamble. On one hand, they might be in danger, and I would be holding back information that they could use to defend themselves. On the other hand, it could set the plan back years, or even destroy it from within.

I would talk to Dad when I got back, but I was pretty sure what he would say. 'Keep the secret, there is very little to be gained by telling anyone, and much to be lost.' From the beginning, he had not wanted to reveal the Vision and our plans to anyone. It had been hard enough for him to realize he must allow the wives in on it, let alone about a hundred people. We had invested untold hours and millions of dollars into these 'Vision Warriors', each one of them a valuable, if unknowing, participant in the plan. But how could I live with myself if one of them was hurt or killed because of my silence? Was I responsible for them all now that I knew about Markos? My head started to ache nearly as much as my chest. I wasn't going to solve this right now and I needed rest, so I swallowed the remaining painkiller and tried to ignore all my demanding demons. As I drifted off to sleep, a terrible dark thought crept into my head - How would Rebekah feel about my plan to secretly manipulate hundreds of lives? It might be abhorrent to her sense of integrity and trust. I had kept it from her all these years, but I knew someday I must tell her, and I might lose her in the process.

****

I met Hunter that Friday at the beach house after work. It had started to become my residence when I was not at Prescience. We had some debriefing to do. He rolled up in his Hummer and I met him at the door. He suggested we go out for a walk on the beach, harder to be bugged. His paranoia was showing more lately, but after what we'd been through on Wednesday, I couldn't blame him.

"How's your shoulder?" he inquired.

"I'll live. But no workouts for a week or two, Doctor's orders," I replied.

"Ms. Perez will never understand why you took a bullet for her," he mused.

"How is she, did it go OK at Justice?" This was the most important thing; after all we had done, had it been worth it?

"OK?! They *loved* her at Justice. She gave them all the files, and then some correspondence from inside Markos Media. And then spilled what she knew about the cover-up of the Prescience hacking, even a possible murder." He shook his head and whistled.

"Some heads are gonna roll, you can bet on that." Hunter slapped my back

"Ouch! Take it easy will ya!" I winced.

"Sorry. Anyway, you will probably have some inquiries to deal with about the hacking and the Prescience database, but nothing our lawyers can't handle," he continued.

"What about roughing up her *friends* from Paris?" I asked.

"Are you kidding, after Cassandra told them about being held hostage against her will by those three goons and then being shot at. There won't be any issue with how we dealt with 'her team,'" he smiled.

"How is she holding up?" I asked again.

"Man, she sure got under your skin," he gave me a sideways glance. "She is one tough babe, I'll give her that, handled all the questioning like a pro. But when they told her that it might be five or six years before she could practice law again, she broke down. She cried saying she wished she'd never met you," he said it without humor.

"She once said if she couldn't be an attorney it would kill her." I recalled a starlit Paris evening; it seemed a long time ago.

"Yeah, well if it wasn't for you, she *would* be dead *because* she was a lawyer," he retorted.

I guess that was true. I had saved her life, and I felt responsible for her now somehow.

"She's going to be kept in protective custody for a while, and then they will see if they need to put her in a witness protection program."

"Will they change her looks?" I really had no idea except from movies and T.V.

"You mean plastic surgery? No, maybe a new hairdo and some colored contacts and she might be relocated to Texas or something. It depends on how much danger they think she's actually in," he explained.

"Not a bad deal I guess, all things considered." She would be gone from my life, and considering everything, that was probably a blessing.

"How about the loose ends? Did you enjoy seeing some of your friends in New York?" I asked.

"Fine, no problems. And that Ducati! Sweet bike. I considered buying it from the guy, but I knew he wouldn't go for it. That was the best part about the op, cutting through Manhattan traffic on the Ducati with the leather clad Ms. Perez holding on for dear life." He grinned, and then put up his hands in defense, as I gave him a dirty look.

"And one more thing, just because you strap on one of those vests doesn't mean you have to use it. You nearly gave me a *heart attack*. How could I face your dad if you had been killed? And believe me, if that bullet had found your head instead of your shoulder, we wouldn't be talking. Next time let Ms. Perez take her own chances." He was serious.

I had only dwelled slightly on what could have been. Hunter was right that it had been a reckless move on my part, but it had worked out.

"I don't think there will be a next time," I replied, thinking of her.

"I'm serious, first rule of staying alive, don't jump in front of trains or bullets." He gave me that teacher to student look.

"Glad you're back. It's been kind of boring at the office, just a bunch of patents disclosures to review," I smiled.

"Uggh! How about we find ourselves another damsel in distress?" he chuckled.

****

"Mr. Reinhart, the Senate would like to thank you for taking time out of your schedule and being so forthcoming with your answers to the panel's questions.

For the record, this concludes the Senate hearing on the Prescience, Inc. security breach...." As the formalities of wrapping up the hearings continued, I felt nothing but relief, revealing as little as possible about the events, but reliving the experience all over again in my mind, much of it I would just as soon forget.

Chapter Seven

A Blessing and a Curse

*"It is yet to be decided whether the Revolution must
ultimately be considered as a blessing or a curse: a blessing
or a curse, not to the present age alone, for with our fate
will the destiny of unborn millions be involved."*
　　　　　　　– George Washington, Circular to the States, 1783

Three a.m. and my cell woke me up. I was getting used to it. It seemed about every other week I would get a call about some panic in our European office. However, this time it was the "007 theme", my ringtone for M.

"Josh, it's M. My 'Sheldon alert' finally went off. Rich is dead. Found washed up on shore near Athens. Piraeus police calling it an accident. Not much to go on, seems Rich has been fish food for about a month, had to use dental records to ID," M was all business. Not much sympathy for the guy who messed with her "baby."

"Sounds too tidy. No other details?"

"No, I did a little digging but I'd say someone is covering their tracks," M replied.

"Yeah, if I were those two guys in jail for the hacking, I'd be nervous," I mused, "Have you called Hunter?"

"Just about to; by the way… Who is Cassandra Perez?" M was much too smart to miss the tenuous link between Cassandra, the two hackers and Rich.

"Someone I once knew back when things were a lot simpler. Remind me to tell you about it sometime," I figured that might be enough to hold M off for a while.

"You want me to keep digging?" M was a pitbull armed with experimental Anticip8 tools and administrative rights to a supercomputer/server; she would undoubtedly find something, something that probably shouldn't be found for Cassandra's sake.

"No, she's just extra counsel brought in after the fact." I hoped she bought it.

"Whatever you say, Boss." I knew when she called me "Boss" she didn't agree entirely with my point of view. But she would drop it for now.

"Thanks for the call, and can you try to keep these alerts from occurring in the dead of night?" I checked the clock.

"Just regular hours for me…and the Piraeus police. 'night Josh."

"Vampire," I muttered; as she hung up I heard her laugh.

I laid back and let my mind try to see if there was anything more than the obvious. "… I think they killed a man," she had said. Yeah, Rich had thought it was just an easy way to make a quick buck. After all, who cared about a bunch of Prescience science projects, most of which were never going to see the light of day. Sell the back door key to the highest bidder and retire, travel the world. Bad choices and bad luck makes for a short retirement. So now there was proof, a murder had been committed. Not enough to take to court, but plenty for me. I was sure Cassandra would have told Justice about the late Mr. Sheldon, so maybe they would get Interpol involved. My cell went off again, Hunter, of course.

"I figured you'd still be awake," he didn't apologize for the hour.

"Yeah, now we have our first confirmed murder, can't say I was completely surprised." My mood was going south.

"He was stupid. Sometimes 'stupid' gets you killed," he continued, "So shall I book some flights to Athens?" Sounded like Hunter was tired of working on the latest encryption algorithm.

"Call me at a more civilized hour and I'll let you know," I hung up.

I was tired; maybe tomorrow I'd see things more clearly. It would be time enough to worry about a murder that I had expected. But it was confirmation of my assumption that anyone who got in the way of this evil had to watch their back. I had Hunter to watch mine, but what was I going to do about the others. I still hadn't come up with a good solution to this problem. And Dad had reacted as expected, saying in the strongest terms we should maintain secrecy. Surely God did not intend for His children to die for the CRIMSON plan, or maybe I just didn't have enough faith in His ability to keep us all safe. But something needed to be done. I had to completely defeat an enemy that, frankly, I knew very little about, or somehow protect the unsuspecting "Vision Warriors." Both tasks seemed impossible right now.

Turning out the light, I turned over and tried to put the problem out of my mind. Well, there was someone I could protect, the one person that meant the most to me. I could start the planning tomorrow. A little peace settled in my heart as I imagined her brilliant blue eyes with me in the dark. How I longed to tell her my secret, lift off this huge burden for a while and share it.

"God, please let her accept what I have done. Please let her accept *me*. How will I be able to serve You if I can't be with her?" I prayed.

I finally fell into a deep sleep and dreamed of Rebekah, running toward me out of a clear blue-green sea, her golden hair flowing behind her forever and her incredible eyes shining bright blue, just for me. But no matter how we tried to close the gap between us, it remained the same. The longing was acute, unbearable. The dream ended with a start as my alarm went off. I had gotten three hours of fitful sleep, but I had an idea and the makings of a plan.

The week was almost over, and Rebekah had flown into Lindberg Field surprising me at my office Friday afternoon. They called up from security, and I met her as she stepped off the elevator. She was all smiles and ease today; we were looking forward to a relaxing weekend; it was her mom's birthday on Saturday. Robert was going to try to make it down. As she came into my office, she spied the matting, frames and one of her sketches on the desk. "What's all this?"

"I'm going to have one of your sketches framed. I think it would look nice in my office," I replied. I saw her head shake and her eyes narrow.
"What's wrong, it's not like it's a secret that we're seeing each other?" I questioned.
"I really wished you wouldn't; those sketches are private, just between us." She took my hands in hers, "I poured my heart out on those sketches," she almost whispered, blue eyes shining up at me. Once again I had stepped in it.

"OK. Bad idea." I looked at the topic of conversation; it still seemed impossible that anyone could produce such a prefect image from memory.

"I never ceased to be amazed each time I look at them. I've always been intrigued by your abilities. I think it was what originally attracted you to me, your extraordinary skills." I smiled down at her. This was not just idle flattery, it was simply the truth. She glanced down a little embarrassed by the praise.

I lifted her face and kissed her lightly.

"I do have a secret you know," she demurred.

"You're actually a direct descendent of Da Vinci, right?" I chuckled, "Seriously, how do you do it?"

"Take me to my favorite restaurant and I *might just* tell you." She gave me a sideways glance and a shy smile.

Never had I looked forward so much to a dinner. I couldn't believe she would really let me in on it. After dessert, she asked to walk along the beach.

She was very quiet while we walked, listening to the waves breaking.

There was a little gazebo off a small boardwalk from the restaurant. We had it to ourselves. "Will this do?" I asked, and she nodded engrossed in her thoughts.

We sat; I put my coat over her shoulders and put my arm around her. After a moment she began.

"There are only three people that know this, and I trust them implicitly. You must promise me you will *never* tell anyone, ever." She drilled me with her lasers.

"Scout's Honor," I held up three fingers and a grin, bad idea – the second of the day.

"No, really Josh. I'm serious." She held my hands and continued to hold me with her eyes. I could see she was *very* serious.

"OK, I swear on my love for you." I kissed her lightly and then, "I won't tell a soul, your secret's safe with me." No smiles this time – serious.

"I love you too, and that's why I've wanted to tell you for a long time," she may have had an edge on her voice, but perhaps she was just a little nervous. She knew I still kept something from *her*, but she was not going to play a game of 'quid pro quo.'

"Have you ever heard of 'eidetic memory?'" she asked.

"Is it like 'photographic memory?'" I attempted, I had never heard of 'eidetic.'

"Not exactly, but some people miss-use the term," she began, "Children with eidetic memory can look at a picture and then later draw or reproduce the picture perfectly from memory. I started to show signs of eidetic memory when I was three; my dad had it, too."

She continued, "Most people grow out of it by their early teens. Some think the loss of the ability has something to do with puberty. But even so, most adults still exhibit highly developed memory capabilities." This would explain Pastor Miller's talents, his ability to quote large passages of the Bible at will, or remember everyone's name in CHESS.

"OK, you have eidetic memory." That would explain a lot. What a skill for debate. "So, let me understand, you look at a page and it appears like a picture in your mind." The secret weapon!

"It's a little more complex, but you are essentially correct – when I read a document and then look at it, concentrating, I can recall it and my comprehension of the contents of the page perfectly, at a later time." she explained.

"But you said that people lose this ability in their teens," it was more of a question than a statement.

"That was a terrible time for me; I had hoped for and dreaded the loss of my ability when I was thirteen, just about the time we met. I was very emotional and apprehensive."

"Oh, I think I can vouch for that." I smiled, recalling our rocky beginnings. "You wished to lose your gift?" I asked in disbelief.

"Do you have any idea what it's like to remember *everything* perfectly, vividly, all the mean things people say, all the junk visible in our society, TV, the internet. Mom and Dad started shielding me as soon as they realized I had it. No TV, carefully screened videos, movies, books, magazines etc."

"You didn't lose it, did you?" I guessed.

"Actually, according to Mrs. Simmons, I did change, but … no, I didn't lose it. That's *very* unusual, almost unheard of," she stated, no pride in her voice.

"So, you can still look at a picture and reproduce it?" I was amazed.

"Yes, but now I have to concentrate; before I could just see it. Like I had a video camera running all the time in my head," she corrected.

"It's a great relief to be able to shut the camera off, suppress it," she smiled.

"I remember once you said you never wanted to forget me. How could that be possible given your memory?" I recalled.

"I was thirteen and I thought I might lose it, so compared to what I was used to, remembering you in the inaccurate manner like everyone else would almost be like forgetting," she explained, "I thought I might never see you again and I couldn't stand the thought that I would '*forget*' you."

Man, my head was swelling by the minute. This incredible woman, gifted far beyond anyone I knew, had cared for me for over ten years....loved me enough to reveal her most closely guarded secret.

"I knew somehow we had to meet again... in my heart," was all I could say.

She leaned against me, and I kissed her hair. It was very enticing, but I had one more question.

"Why keep it a secret? It's an incredible ability," I asked. But she pulled back from me and was very serious and a little sad.

"It's my blessing and my curse – it made me the reclusive, odd little girl; the sheltered, know-it-all genius. No friends, no one to talk to, or share. Just my books, my parents and my shrink," she frowned and fell silent. Moments passed.

She looked up with shining eyes. "Then you called me that day. I'll never forget; I couldn't believe it. Josh Reinhart wanted to come over, to be with *me*. All my so-called girlfriends were shocked. I heard things like: (She mimicked a tween girl) 'That new guy...Josh. He's so *cool* and she's *such* a nerd' or 'Oh. My. Gosh. What's *with* him? Come *on* – 'Bekah?- *Not*.' It hurt – a lot. But they were right; you had the money, the looks, the car. And I was the little freak, in braces no less. Why would you have anything to do with *me*? But you weren't what I expected. You were really nice and funny and always treated me like I was special, like you cared about me..." she trailed off and I held her close, kissed her, and after a while...

"From the beginning, I did find you intriguing. I knew you were something special, even then, I told you as much. But you *were* only thirteen," smiling, I recalled an interrogation at the ice rink under the blue lasers.

"Only *Chronologically*. I can't tell you how messed up I was about you. Even after our first debate. I know you had no clue... but somehow I got the courage to ask you for your Aff.

Remember? It gave me an excuse to have something to share with you." She blushed and I nodded. "And then you sent the private jet and the limo for me and I could hardly think, afraid I'd wake up. No one had ever done anything like *that* for me, I was completely caught up. And that crooked smile, *laughing* at me didn't help," she paused, smiling, remembering some private moment. Then with a blast of her lasers, "But you were so cryptic, so frustrating, your secrets drove me *crazy*," and then …. "They still do," she whispered, searching me.

I tried to get back on course from that last phrase. "I remember you shredding me a few times in debate, especially at your folks and all those notes…I couldn't tell if you liked me or just liked the target practice." I hoped that would do the trick.

"It was mostly because you wouldn't tell me what you were up to, but I don't want to get into that now. I wrote notes because… well, because sometimes when I started talking to you up close, I would lose my train of thought, my concentration. I even told you that once," she stopped and shook her head… and then seriously powering up the lasers. "Now you know my secret, only Mom, Dad and Mrs. Simmons know, even Robert doesn't know exactly."

"It's safe with me, no matter what. I do love you very much, you know that?" I felt a little overwhelmed. She had been truly in love with me since we met, and I remember disregarding that as a ridiculous notion till I had seen her, back from China and even then, not fully accepting it. And she still wants to know my secret, but that would have to wait.
She smiled and looked up with those brilliant eyes. "Yes, Josh. I know."

I drove her back to her parent's house. Pastor and Mrs. Miller were up and informed us that Robert would not be making it. That was too bad. I would have really enjoyed seeing him. I had grown very close to the Miller family. I had great respect for Pastor Miller – he not only talked the talk, but walked the walk. And Mrs. Miller was impossible not to like. She always made me feel so comfortable and I know she wanted nothing more than to see Rebekah happy and married. Out on the porch, I finally said goodnight and kissed Rebekah, "I'll never forget this evening, you are simply amazing. I feel like the luckiest guy on the planet….." was all I could say.

Her eyes shone, "I am *so* glad I finally told you, it's like a great weight lifted off me. I let my parents know and they're OK with it, they understand," then, "I love you, Josh," as she looked up for a kiss I was happy to supply. After time began again, "Oh, don't forget tomorrow for dinner. I'm cooking," she smiled as I looked astonished. Of course, her mom, a renowned baker, was not going to cook on her birthday. This would be interesting; I could get an idea of what kind of cook Rebekah was.

"See you tomorrow," I said as I headed for my R8. Cruising back to the beach house; what an amazing evening. She had finally told me, I could hardly believe it. I wondered if she felt she was due a similar admission by yours truly. If so it would be a while coming. I hope she could wait just a bit longer… I was working on a plan that would allow that, and make Mrs. Miller very pleased as well.

Chapter Eight

Trust

"Character, not circumstances, makes the man"
— Booker T. Washington

The setting was perfect. The moon shone through some wispy clouds off the surf. The stars seemed close in the dark blue sky. The Del had kept the area private, and so I stood frozen, watching her golden hair swing back and forth as she walked away, straight backed, hands balled in fists. And then she finally broke into a run toward the hotel, I thought I heard her sob out a single word, "Fool!"

I finally remembered to breath, amazed I still had organs in my chest. I was certain my heart at a minimum was mingled with the sand at my feet, but somehow I still had a pulse. My heart had gone from elated anticipation, soaring, lifted by her voice, her smile, her brilliance, only to be speared mid-flight by her blue lasers and her answer. "I could *never* marry you, I can't trust you! And now I have *this* stuck in my head, *forever!*"

It had started out just as planned, I had arranged for Rebekah to fly down for the weekend and on Sunday to spend the afternoon at a spa that Mom had recommended. I thought this was a good idea; I wanted Rebekah to be as relaxed and pampered as possible, topped off with a designer dress for the evening. Then Raymond picked her up and brought her to the Del Coronado. I was out in a private patio on the beach, a covered gazebo with a love seat and a small table for two; chilled Champagne and her favorite flowers. Harry Winston was considerably richer; and I was in the possession of a flawless, blue-white diamond and sapphire ring, custom cut and made for the world's most unique woman.

She came toward me from the hotel with a waiter showing her part of the way. As she came closer, she couldn't have been more beautiful in my eyes, but she seemed a little apprehensive and on edge. I waved to her, but she did not wave back.

"What are you up to, Josh?" was how she started out addressing the most important night of our lives.

"Come into my palace for two," I grinned giving a wave of my arm over the table. "I thought we could have dinner out here by ourselves. Private."

She sat down on the love seat beside me and I poured some Champagne.

Still not much smiling. Well, I guess she had a hard week. I was determined to do this.

"Raymond wouldn't give me any answers, so I don't know what's going on," she said without much enthusiasm, a little edge in her voice.

"You know you look incredible tonight, and I wanted to make it special," I gave her a once over. She was a knockout in that dress. My heart soared.

"Special? Did I miss one of our anniversaries?" She frowned, referring to a few special dates that were milestones in our relationship. She was getting something out of her clutch. Rebekah forget, not likely.

"You could say that." I had to get this done now. I took her free hand in mine, it felt cold.

I got off the love seat, and knelt down on one knee, my tux trousers a little sandy.

She stood up. "Josh!..." her blue eyes very big.

"Rebekah, I love you with all my heart and soul. I can't imagine living without you. Will you marry me and share your life with me, forever?" I looked up into that beautiful face, into those incredibly blue eyes that burned back down at me. I waited for my salvation, one word, just one word.

Her face turned bright red and the lasers flared more intense than I had ever seen them, boring through me, piercing my heart.

"I could *never* marry you, I can't trust you! And now I have *this* stuck in my head, *forever!*" she cried, slamming down a page from a glossy magazine. The picture of a stylish couple, spot lit; the graceful woman's back arched, raven black tresses nearly touching the marble floor, one bare leg extended. The man in a tux, leaning over her, one hand supporting her back, the other above his head. A perfect ending to a perfect Tango, shattering my dreams, my life.

I stood up, "Rebekah, *please*, you have to trust me. I can explain." But it was too late.

"*Damn* you, Josh, Damn your *secrets!*" her eyes glistened and tears were starting as she left me, marching back up the beach.

I had to admit, the timing was exquisite. Rebekah had picked up a society magazine to browse while getting a pedicure, just before being asked to make the most important decision of her life, and there I was big as life at Madam Arneau's 'little gathering.'

The next twenty-four hours should have been filled with joy and congratulations, a meeting with her father to secure his blessing, topped with a dinner with our families and discussions about venues and colors. Instead I was looking at the Pacific praying the surf would drowned out her last words – 'damn your secrets!'

They had cut through me, but by then the major organs had already been removed by her refusal. I had walked back up the beach to the hotel, the waiter ask if I wanted dinner, I don't recall my reply. As I went to the valet for my R8, there was a note waiting for me, a couple of tear stains and four words.

Don't Call. Don't Come.

I was pretty numb, driving the R8 on autopilot back to the beach house, to sit on the back deck and stare at the ocean lit by the same moon that just an hour ago had held such promise.....

....

....

.... The dark clouds finally gave way to the hint of sunrise and I still had no answers. I had prayed for wisdom and a solution, then just wisdom, and finally just for His mercy to take away the burning in my head and repair the gaping hole in my chest. But no apparent answers. I would have to simply continue on faith. Faith that somehow this would work out for the good.... somehow.

I got into my wetsuit and dove into the surf. Swimming out, I finally gave up thinking. I don't know how long I was out there but I finally crawled out of the surf, exhausted. I walked back up the beach and took a long hot shower. There had to be a solution. I would try to call her today, but I needed something, some answer. Maybe I could at least explain the picture, it would be a start. But how could I explain the recent events with Cassandra without divulging more evidence of the CRIMSON plan.

I had considered not going into work but I figured perhaps a major panic might have occurred offering to distract my mind if only for a short while. Best to just continue the routine, hoping some distraction would take away the actual physical pain in my chest.

Coming up the five freeway, I was surprised that somehow the world was going along pretty much the same as it had before last night. Same traffic jams at the usual spots, same line up at the Starbucks coffee drive-thru, same inane morning news reports. In a way it was comforting to know that the earth-shattering events of last night had gone unnoticed by the good people of San Diego. You would think there would have been a civic alert siren or at the very least an Amber Alert on the freeway info signs –

MALE HEART ABDUCTED – BE ON LOOK OUT FOR PETITE BLOND IN BLACK LIMO – LICENSE PI LIMO 1

Nope. Not a thing. Probably just as well, it would be pretty hard to take the sympathetic looks from everyone; that would no doubt come soon enough.

I can just hear it now. '*Poor* Josh. …Is she insane? Turning him down – All that money, and they seemed so in love.' It would look that way, like Rebekah's genius had finally crossed over into madness.

What a cruel joke. They knew nothing. It wasn't about money, it wasn't even about love. It was about trust. Trust and integrity; and as far as Rebekah was concerned, she couldn't marry someone she couldn't trust or felt lacked integrity. And I had no way to defend myself, nor could I defend her actions to others. I had to figure away around this for her sake (and for mine).

I got to my office and asked not to be disturbed. As I sat down at my desk, the frame and matting were still in the corner reminding me of the incredible night she had poured out her precious secret to me. Her marvelous gift and merciless curse – her memory. I had been the source for an abundant gallery of mental pictures, some wonderful and some terribly painful for her to view and review forever. I closed my eyes and thought about her, what she must be going through. She had played it as honest and straight as she could. While from her point of view, I had been a duplicitous adulterer, falling under Cassandra's spell even as I asked Rebekah to marry me, and all I could say in my defense was 'trust me.' I prayed "Lord, help her to somehow find peace in the gift You have bestowed upon her, a peace that transcends all understanding."

I turned my cell phone on about 11:00 a.m. It had three messages; I decided to call Mom back.

"Josh, are you all right? I thought you said you were going to call last night," as she answered the phone.

Was I all right, well let's see, how should I answer this. You remember that brilliant beautiful girl that we all knew was 'The One', she told me she couldn't trust me and would never marry me. Or how about – I think if I had an MRI right now they would find me shy a few major organs. Perhaps simple was best.

"No Mom, I'm not all right. I asked Rebekah to marry me last night, and she turned me down because she can't trust a man who keeps secrets."

"Oh, Josh. Oh honey, I'm so sorry. I know she loves you. What did you say?"

"What could I say? I just asked her to trust me and I could explain, but she wouldn't listen. I guess I've disappointed her too many times." This was not what I needed to be doing.

"Josh, I know it's hard, terribly hard. But God will honor you for keeping your commitment to Him. You have to believe that," she replied. She would never discuss the Vision or the CRIMSON plan over the phone, but I know that was what she meant.

"I've told myself that, but what if keeping my commitment means I must lose Rebekah? I don't know if I can do that...." This was what really scared me. Could it be possible that God wanted me to serve him alone, no Rebekah, no one to love but Him?

"Have you tried to call her?" Mom asked after a while.

"Not yet, I really don't have anything to say, any solution to the problem." Until I came up with something, it would be an untenable position.

"Call her; even if she won't talk to you, she needs to know you still are trying. Still fighting to save it," she insisted, and I needed some sound advice from a good source.

"I will Mom. I just don't know what more I can offer."

"Just call her, Josh. Don't wait on this. I know what I'm talking about," she was definite.

"All right, I'll call her today. I'm sorry I couldn't have provided you with a joyous occasion."

"Don't worry about that; you'll find a way to talk to her. She still loves you, of that I am sure, and that will make the difference. I love you Honey; are you going to be OK?"

"Sure Mom, I'll survive." At least I would for now.

"Why don't you come by for dinner? Marissa is planning Chili Rellenos tonight. And I'm sure your Dad would love to see you," she offered.

"I don't know, Mom. I'll have to see how things go today." I wouldn't commit. Who knows what will happen from now till then.

"Please try. I love you. Bye." She knew when not to push.

It would be 10:00 p.m. in D.C., and I had spent the last half hour praying. I dialed the number and close my eyes. It rang four times and then a generic voice, 'you have reached the Miller residence, leave a message.....'(beep). "Rebekah, it's Josh, please pick up. I need to talk with you. You have to believe me, I love you; and if you will at least listen, I'll try to explain some things. I don't have all the answers for you, but you have to understand I have not betrayed your trust. I know it looks like I have, but it's just not the case. Please pick up." I waited, but nothing.

"OK. I hope you're hearing this. Remember I had told you about a hacking of some project files at work. Well, Dad sent Hunter and me on an assignment for Prescience, to discover what we could about the hacking. We went to Paris to see the hackers as they appeared before the French authorities. In the court room, to my amazement, Cassandra Perez was talking to the hacker's attorney. I got out of there without her seeing me, and formulated a plan, with Hunter's help, to attempt to find out what she knew about the Prescience hacking. To do this"(beep)...Stupid answer machine. I dialed again. I needed to get this explanation out ...

"To do this, I got invited to a charity dinner where we expected Cassandra to show. I was on assignment to get information and, in order to do so, I had to act friendly. We dance and talked about old times and what we were doing now, catching up on the last eight years. Turned out she was trying to get detailed information out of me about files that were stolen from Prescience. They were in the staging projects area, my department. She seemed to be involved in some way, and she really pressed hard to get information from me. I didn't tell her anything, but she let a couple of things slip, and I was certain that she had seen the stolen files. So what you saw in the magazine were two people trying hard to get information out of each other. Please know that you were in my thoughts the whole time and helped me do my job.

Rebekah, I thank God everyday for bringing you into my life, I don't really know what I will do if you won't see me. Please...."
(Beep). I wondered how long it would record. I dialed again....
"Rebekah, Please picture me as I say this. I love you and only you; please let me talk to you. If you're there please pick up and let me hear your voice." .... nothing. I held the phone till the beep. Nothing. I could just see her, boring holes in the answer machine.

A few emails from Asia started filling my inbox; reviewing them, I sent a few replies. Finally, I had to admit to myself that I probably shouldn't try to pull back-to-back all-nighters. I started to head out of my office when a knock on the door startled me. "Come in."

M poked her head around the door, "Hey, kind of late for.... Josh, you look terrible, are you OK?"

I hadn't actually looked at myself today, except for a quick glance in the mirror in my bathroom. "Just working a little later than usual, and I didn't get much sleep last night."

"You should go home, you look like death warmed over," M scolded.

"Yes, *Mom*," I tried to make light of it. I know the gossip of my failed proposal would spread like a wildfire fanned by Santa Ana winds once known, but I didn't have to toss the lighted match tonight.

"Really Josh, go home and get some sleep. Prescience can run without you for a little while." M held the door for me.

"What about you?" I countered.

"You know me Boss, I can run all night on Starbucks," M replied with a grin.

"OK, hold down the fort." I gave her a salute as I stepped into the corridor, heading toward the elevators.

"Anything new? Anything you want me to look into?" She called after me. M was always looking for an excuse to exercise her amazing skills with Anticip8.

"Not tonight, thanks." That solicited a pout.

"'Night Boss and drive careful," she said as the elevator doors closed.

'Drive careful.' Exactly right, the R8 was easily capable of doing 180, and in my condition I could wrap it and myself around a pole. I had to actually concentrate on driving conservatively, anything to keep my mind off my situation.

As I pulled into the beach house garage, the fatigue started to set in, and the dread. Here there were no distractions, alone with my mind going a mile a minute. I did determine not to stay up all night watching the surf, so I laid there, mulling it over and over in my mind; looking for a way, and praying that even if I couldn't find a way that God would make a way. Somewhere between praying and thinking, I finally dozed off with "Damn your secrets!" ringing in my ears. Waking up the next morning, I called the airlines and Raymond. Then I called work to say I would not be in.

It was dark, drizzly and cold as I stepped out of the cab. D.C. was no match for San Diego, weather-wise, but it did have one thing that San Diego lacked.

The doorman let me into the building. "Mr. Reinhart, nice to see you." Well at least she hadn't instructed Jonathan to keep me out. "Hi Jonathan, have you seen Ms. Miller tonight?"

"Yes, but she seemed in one of her moods, I'd tread lightly," Jonathan winked. As many times as I had visited Rebekah, Jonathan and I had formed a conspiratorial relationship, he letting me know in advance how she was that day. I passed him a twenty and got a small formal bow and "Thank you, sir." Sometimes information can be priceless, but not tonight.

On the plane I had already prayerfully determined that I was going to tell her as much of the truth as I could. My secrets were destroying us both.

The chimes went off and I heard the intercom click, "Yes," terse and sharp.

"It's Josh, I need to see you. Talk to you," I replied.

"Didn't you get my note? I *told* you not to come," was her strained retort. I ignored it, her mood was pitch black, what did I expect?

"Look, I love you, you *know* that. I can explain a lot of things if you will just let me in."

"I can't Josh. I just can't…. do this right now. I *told* you not to come." Her voice was breaking up, I heard a sob. My heart ached to comfort her, tell her everything, how much I loved her, hold her.

"I need to see you, please just open the door. I won't even try to come in. Just open the door... *for me*." I took a step back.

After a few desperate heartbeats, I heard the deadbolts click off and the door slowly opened part way. There she stood; the tears had barely stopped streaming past deep dark circles under her red rimmed cobalt eyes. She was trying to hold her composure.

I just stared, if I had looked bad last night, it was nothing compared to what I saw before me. I could only remember once when I had seen her this distraught, and that was at a distance in a minivan, hands over her face, her body wracking forward, some ten years ago. I had been the caused of that, too....

Then she exploded.

"Explain to me, Josh!.. Explain to me about Cassandra Perez!" she spat out the words. "There are more photos on the net of you and her that night, particularly one of you standing very close out on a secluded veranda. How *could* ...?" her voice started to crack.

"I was trying to get information about the security breach, and she was trying to get information out of me," same old excuse.

"And just how *far* did you both go to get your *precious* information?" Her eyes bore into me as she stepped forward. I knew I had to tell her, my secrets were killing her.

"She kissed me. I..." The sound and the sting of the slap reached my brain simultaneously, but were overshadowed by the pain in my heart from the look on her face.

Rebekah's heart wrenching cry was punctuated by the slam of her door and the click of the deadbolts.

"Rebekah, *please*. I love you," was all I could say.

"*Go away!* I can't see you. Just *go!*" were the last words that registered in my brain that night. I don't even remember seeing Jonathan on my way out, but somehow I was in a cab back to the airport. On the red-eye back to San Diego, dead tired but unable to sleep, my heart was forcing my mind to search for an answer.

Raymond fought the morning rush hour as he drove me back to the beach house. As I dropped the carry-on in the entry and headed for bed, praying for some peace and sleep, I couldn't get passed the image of my Rebekah's face, her fabulous eyes so distorted, distraught. "Heavenly Father, please help her, give her some peace and a night's rest. Protect her Lord, and help me to find a way."

My cell went off, it was Hunter. "Hey, got time for a workout?"
"Whut….What time is it?"
"Come on, Man. It's four in the afternoon. Had a rough night, you party animal?" I could imagine his big grin. If he only knew I had been across the country trying to hold my life together. And I felt like my head was going to explode, but mostly I was famished.
"Workout, huh? Yeah, all right, and then I need to eat," was my semi-coherent reply.
"You sound a little rough? You sure?"
"Yeah. Come on over." I had to find a way to live while I was dealing with this.
"Great, I'll be by in about thirty minutes. Afterwards, you can pick up the tab at Antonio's," he chuckled.

"If you charge me again, I'll put this where the sun don't shine." Hunter pointed to his right shoe, as he got up off the court floor.

"That last hoop was no good. No ref in the league would let you get away with that." He shook it off, and I passed the ball to him. Completing what was a bruising game of one-on-one, we went to the mats for some martial arts work.

"Josh, what's eating you? M said you looked like hell the other night, and I don't think you've improved much." He grabbed a towel and rubbed his crew cut as we sat on the benches.

"I'll tell you, but I don't want this all over Prescience, so keep it to yourself and maybe M, that's it. Can you do that?" I really needed to talk to someone about it, other than Mom.

"Sure, OK. Scout's honor and all that," he smiled.

"Seriously, I don't need a bunch of gossip about this." I looked at him straight, and he nodded. I took a deep breath...

"OK, you know how I feel about Rebekah? Well, last Sunday I asked her to marry me, and she turned me down." There, it felt good to get it out there where someone else could see it.

"I can't believe that, you two couldn't take your eyes off each other last time I saw you. What happened? Did she turn you down flat or was it a 'I need time to think about it' turn down?" Hunter shook his head.

"She won't see me or talk to me. She's not just upset, she's off the chart." I let that sink in.

"Why? That's just crazy. You two are both a little bent, but perfectly matched in an odd sort of way. Did something happen?" He was intrigued but concerned.

"You could say that. .... Remember the night in Paris when I danced with Cassandra? Well, some society rag ran a photo of our Tango. Rebekah saw it the day I asked her, if you can believe it. I tried to explain but she's not buying it." I just shook my head and looked at the court.

"Oh, Man. Good luck with that. No amount of explaining is going to convince any girl that "Miss Perez" is just a casual thing.

I think you had better just throw yourself on the mercy of the court." Hunter was only half kidding.

"But I was on assignment, trying to get information about the hacking. You know that, you heard the whole thing," I retorted.

"Yes – the *whole* thing, and would you believe it was all just a work assignment with no feelings involved, if you were Rebekah and heard that recording?" He had me. The truth was that I did *care* about Cassandra, but I didn't *love* her. It was Rebekah who had stolen my heart and now I may never see her again.

"What can I do then? I already told Rebekah about that night."

"Like I said, throw yourself on the mercy of the court," he shook his head, then, "Let's hit the showers and go eat, you'll feel better after *I've* had a great veal cutlet." He slapped me on the back.

It was helpful to have a true friend I could talk to. I wondered how Rebekah could stand it, no one to talk it out with. Please watch over her, Lord.

****

I finally gave up calling after a couple of weeks; it was probably causing more harm than good at this point. Not once had she picked up or called back. She had made it clear I wasn't to see her, that one attempt ending in disaster. I remember the night I decided not to call; it was like I had overcome an obsession. Talking to the machine, I felt like I was really talking to her, and that she could hear me, but maybe she had just deleted my messages. I had held onto an unfulfilled hope for too long, no longer knowing what to say to the machine, hating that (beep) signaling another failed attempt.

Now all I did was pray that somehow The Lord would restore her to me. It was in His hands now.

Chapter Nine

Just Dinner

"God grants liberty only to those who love it, and are always ready to guard and defend it." – Daniel Webster

It was surprising what a desire to keep ones mind occupied can do for productivity. An exhaustive swim in the morning, Prescience and work on the CRIMSON plan, plus a heavy work out afterward, coming home late, ready to sleep. I had done this for the last several weeks, and people had started to get used to my new schedule. By the time I got home, there was usually just time enough for a snack and then go to bed. It actually did help to keep me from *constantly* thinking of her, but it was when I was alone, in my R8 or trying to fall asleep, that I was haunted by brilliant blue eyes, her shy smile and 'I've always been yours, just never let me go,' or sometimes burning lasers and 'I could never marry you, I can't trust you!' it was hard to say which was worse now.

Hunter stuck his head in the door of my office, "Got a minute?"
"Sure, what's up?" I replied.

"I don't want you to take this the wrong way, but you know there *are* other smart, attractive women residing on this planet," he smiled and lifted his eyebrows.

"What are you and M cooking up now?" I couldn't help but smile.

"It was mostly M's idea. See, she has this friend, I think she's in marketing. Anyway, she's been hearing about you, and would really like to meet the great Josh Reinhart, man of mystery," he grinned. "Seriously, this girl is spectacular looking, smart, and....M got a peak at her calendar and she even goes to a Bible study on Wednesdays." He gave me another anticipatory glance. "We're just talking about dinner....with me and M," he added the last bit as he saw my hesitation.

"I don't know, I don't think I'd be decent company right now," I offered my excuse. I really did appreciate Hunter's attempt to drag me up out of my funk.

"You haven't seen Monica, she could grace the cover of Sports Illustrated, definitely could give Ms. Perez a run for her money," he added.

"What if it gets back to Rebekah?" I tried a new deterrent.

"So what if it does. Maybe it would get her attention. I'll never understand her, if I were her I'd have said 'yes.'" He shook his head.

"T.M.I., Man. Now I'm scarred for life," I chuckled. Thank God for Hunter, he always found a way to bring me out of my self-imposed depression. He was still expectant. It was hard to disappoint him, I finally gave in.

"O.K., but just dinner. I'll check my calendar." I went for my cell phone.

"Already checked. You're free this Tuesday night. How about City Lights, in La Jolla. Your treat."

"So you already had this all planned out..." I frowned.

"Of course, like I always say, the secret to a good op is preparation," Hunter grinned wide, "Besides, I was tired of seeing you like this. And if your mood got any worse, I was going to have to wear body armor during our workouts."

"Sorry. And thanks, I think it might be fun. And tell M thanks, too." It might not be too bad. If nothing else, I would have a nice dinner with a couple of great friends.

"Don't thank me till you get the tab for a table for four at City Lights," he chuckled and rubbed his forefinger and thumb together.

****

I pulled up to Monica's high rise in downtown San Diego. Hunter had given me some lame excuse about a security update he had to get out, so he and M would have to meet us at the restaurant. I suspected an ulterior motive, but no proof.

My R8 stood out from the BMWs and Mercedes, as its engine under glass rumbled off the parking structure walls. Walking over to the elevator, I punched in 1208, and pressed the security button. A sweet voice answered, "Come on up, ah... Mr. Reinhart; I'm still getting ready, so make yourself at home."

Her 12th floor apartment provided the living/dining room with a view of the ocean a mile away. I stood looking at the panoramic view through the wall of glass and frowned, why had I agreed to this? Hunter had made it seem like no big thing and I had acquiesced, mostly because he had asked. 'Just dinner' – well that's about all I was up for.

"Hi," same sweet voice behind me. I turned and instantly wished I hadn't accepted.

She was just too beautiful. Tall, blond... perfect. Clad in a deep blue mini accentuating her long legs. She smiled shyly and no doubt saw my hesitation I tried to hide with, "Hi, … and it's just Josh. My father is Mr. Reinhart."

She looked at me uncertain.   I must have made her uncomfortable, not my intent.

I gave her my most disarming, honest smile, "You look great." That was no lie. "Are you ready to go?" Let's get this over with.

"Ah … sure, let me get my coat," she headed back into the other room as I tried unsuccessfully to relax. 'Last time, Hunter' I thought with a frown.

'Beep-beep', and the lights inside my R8 lit up as the security system released the locks, while the Xenon headlights lit up the parking garage.

"Oh, Wow," she gave out a little laugh as she looked sideways at me.

The R8 had that affect on people.

I got to my car and held the passenger door for her.

"This is an Audi R8 with the carbon fiber panels. Right?" she inquired. Not possible…she knows exotic cars. Great, just what I need, gorgeous, smart and can talk intelligently about cars.

"Yeah, they call the panel a 'side blade.' So, you know about the R8 Quattro? I hope it meets with your approval."

"Are you kidding…it's awesome. Red line at about 7500?"

"Close… 8250. She's a screamer. But most people have only heard of Ferraris or Lambos, not many know the R8, that's why I chose it. Too much hype and commonality today, I'll go with originality."   Man, did *that* sound pretentious; are you trying to impress her? What are you doing?

"I know what you mean. I read about it in Road and Track, there's a V10 version out, too," she replied as she slipped herself into the passenger seat as modestly as possible given the circumstances.   "Thanks," she smiled up at me as I slightly delayed shutting the door, catching me staring as I was caught off guard by the V10 comment. 'Great, *just* great,' I thought as I got to the driver's door.

So, she reads Road and Track. What next, maybe she'll pull a Glock 9mm out of her purse for show and tell. I had to hand it to Hunter, he knew what I liked; but this was without a doubt the worst timing for this, and I knew it. I'd just have to get through the dinner and chalk it up to experience. Just another test for me to pass.

"What got you interested in cars?" I asked as I pulled the R8 out of the garage, dropped it into a lower gear just to hear the exhaust notes mix with Sade's 'Smooth Operator' from the sound system. 'Hardly,' I thought to myself, glancing at Monica.

She smiled as the Gs pushed her back in the seat. "I paid my way through college working the auto shows; you've seen those girls they have pitching the new concept cars, etc? Well, we're not all dumb blonds, and you have to study up on the car's features. I found it interesting, and so I still keep up on them."

Monica turned toward me, and we talked about our favorite cars and where some of the best scenic drives were. She knew her stuff, and the scenery wasn't bad either. She had a disarming, easy way about her, for all her looks. I started to let down the drawbridge just a little.

The valet grinned wide as I handed him the key and then drove the R8 about twenty feet to be on display between an Aston Martin Vantage and a Porsche Turbo all shouting to the world, 'We have high end clientele!' I smiled sardonically. Monica probably got taken to the best places routinely, just by the very nature of the world. Tall and leggy, beautiful women were taken care of, highly valued by our secular society. It made me think of Rebekah, while she was very beautiful, she would never be a model, and her value to society would always need to be proven. I was supposed to be her stronghold, and tonight's activities were definitely not part of that job description.

We waited a few moments for the hostess to come up.
"I can seat you now, Mr. Reinhart," she smiled, another beauty.
"We are expecting two more, a Mr. Erickson ….and his guest." I said, not quite knowing how else to describe Hunter and M.
"Would you like to wait?" she inquired.
I looked at Monica, trying to put myself in her place. "No, we're ready now."
I saw her smile to herself out of the corner of my eye.
The high backed booth was facing the glass wall and overlooked the water and a curved string of lights created by the San Diego skyline. The restaurant was aptly named.
She slid in and I followed her, stopping a distance apart that I felt was reasonable considering we had known each other less than an hour.
"Nice view." She sipped her drink, and then eyed me over the rim of her glass. "Have you been here before?" she asked.
"No, but I couldn't agree more about the view," glancing at her.

She flashed me a smile, blushing a little, but otherwise let the comment pass. Hunter hadn't exaggerated; she could be on the cover of a dozen magazines. Any guy would be crazy not to enjoy an evening with her. And I was trying hard to relax, to simply let the conversation unfold, 'enjoy the view,' as it were. Trying to forget about the terminal damage to my heart lying in its dungeon, its role reduced to operating as a pump, I had to move on – somehow still live.
The shrimp cocktail was great, but no Hunter or M. We were off on her college days at UCSD, and my time at J.A. She was easy

to talk to and had a laugh that was genuine. Then the hostess
came up.

"Mr. Reinhart, I have a note for you, from a Ms. Li."

"Thank you." I opened it.

Hunter and I are held up at work,

Won't be able to make it.

Enjoy your Dinner. M.

"Friends," I muttered, frowning.

"Anything wrong?" Monica asked

"Looks like Hunter and M can't make it, held up at work. I hope
you don't mind," I smiled erasing the crease between my eyes.

"Sounds like M. Workaholic. And I'm more than OK with it,"
she blushed a little.

'More than OK.' Hunter - you never had planned on showing, I
shook my head at this. And Monica took it the wrong way.

"What?" she asked not smiling.

"Oh, nothing, really.   I'm kind of glad it's just the two of us. I
see Hunter and M all the time," I finally stated, smiled my best
appreciative grin, but my mind was back in the Miller's back
yard. 'I'll never fail you.'

"M said you were secretive, always jetting off to Europe or
Washington, something about some great plan you have." She let
it hang there; I took a sip and let my mind formulate the response,
making a mental note to keep an eye on M.

"M's got an over-active imagination. But she is partly right, I do
have a lot on my mind and I would love to ignore it all if only for
this evening." Ignore the ever-present pain; ignore the burden of
the Vision; ignore the responsibility of executing the CRIMSON

plan. Just be a regular guy out to dinner with an incredibly beautiful girl.

"Sounds like a good excuse to go dancing, take your mind off it. I know a good club that's not far from here, legit' band and fun people," she suggested, raising her eyebrows, seeing the burdens in my expression.

"Ah...Sure... I'd like that actually... First, though, what can I order for you?" I asked looking at her menu and then up to that flawless face. She really was a terrific girl.

The meal had been superb and from my point of view the company had surpassed it. Monica caught nearly all my humor, and we had a number of similar interests. By dessert I was actually starting to feel somewhat human again, momentarily forgetting the demons. Maybe Hunter had been right.

So much for 'just getting through dinner.' I smiled to myself as I drove into the club parking lot. I opened the car door for her, offering my hand as she stood up out of the R8.

"I *definitely* like arriving in this." She flashed a perfect smiled and took my arm as we entered the club and I felt a twinge of guilt. She was bright, gorgeous and sweet; looking for her 'Mr. Right' and I sure wasn't him. On the surface, maybe, but once you started peeling back the layers.... But tonight, we could have some fun and I could forget about it all.

We got on the dance floor and moved pretty well together to a couple of numbers off the bands current playlist. She laughed a lot and I appreciated her beauty and her relaxed nature. The crowd was having fun, gyrating in unison to the bass, blowing off the steam of the workday.

Finally, the band slowed it down, and she came in close. Monica was tall and in heels she easily put her lips to my ear. "This is nice," she whispered. The scent of her perfume really doing its job.

"Monica, I should tell you..."

"Shhhh ...Just dance," she breathed.

I held her, trying to execute her simple request and not feel I was somehow betraying something or someone (after all, *she* had turned me down). Finally, I started to relax a little and became more aware of my partner. She was a heart stopper, no doubt, and she seemed to be enjoying herself as well. My emotions were pretty conflicted.

The band took a break.

"Can I get you something to drink?" I motioned to the bar. Monica smiled with a nod and led me off the dance floor.

"I'm glad you suggested this. And the band is *'legit,'*" I emphasized the slang.

She laughed at that, "You don't go to clubs much, I take it."

"No, but I might have to add it to my list...You really dance well." Complementing the obvious.

"So do you," and then we both said it in unison, "Cotillion." We laughed and discussed the trials of cotillion; she put her hand on mine. "I'll be right back, I need to freshen up."

I waited at the bar as Monica went to 'freshen up.' She seemed perfect as it was, but what did I know. So this is what the smart twenty-somethings did in San Diego on an odd Tuesday. I might have to try it sometime. I watched the crowd as the band started up again.

"Josh Reinhart, right?" He had moved up beside me at the bar and looked vaguely familiar. I had met him somewhere before, just couldn't quite place him.

"Yes...I'm sorry..." I started, looking a little puzzled.

"John Hall, we debated once back in high school? ...I was on the REASON team."

"Oh, right... Good to see you," I shook his hand. "That was a long time ago."

"Sure was. Listen, I don't want to disturb your evening, but I have a message from a mutual acquaintance." The club was pretty loud, so he didn't have to do more than lower his voice to make this a very private conversation.

"She asked if things were going well with Rebekah and if she would be forced to wish you joy soon." He slipped a folded note into my hand.

"Got to go. Nice car by the way, hard to keep up with."

I stared at his back as he faded into the crowd, then I started to open the note, but saw Monica returning. I slipped it into my jacket pocket just as she came up.

"See someone you know?" she asked as I turned back to reality.

"Just an old acquaintance from high school." I put on a good smile.

"How about another dance," her eyes expectant, hard to refuse.

Driving back to Monica's, my mind was working overtime. On the surface, I was trying to pay some semblance of attention to the lovely woman sitting next to me, her inviting perfume filling the R8's cockpit. But sometimes the conversation slipped into silence as I was trying to work out the message just delivered in the bar and deal with my curiosity about the unopened note. And always there was Rebekah, creeping in, demanding attention from my heart.

"Josh, is something wrong?" She could sense it.

"No…just thinking," I lied.

"You seemed a thousand miles away. M said you were like that, always planning, and recently you had a lot on your mind," she replied, putting her hand on mine as I let the R8's transmission go into automatic mode. I held her long fingers, very warm, she was very hard to ignore.

"What else did M tell you?"

"Just that, for the founder's son, you work way too hard and sometimes you're off on special assignments all over the world. Sounds exciting." She squeezed a little. I used to think so too, 'Reinhart, Josh Reinhart, secret agent;' but now it had just become a burden.

"If M thinks I'm working too hard, I know I better cut back," I chuckled, and then, "I'm pretty sure she's a vampire." I showed my eye teeth like Dracula. That brought a laugh.

"Maybe you're right. She's always been a night owl, ever since college," she played along.

"Yeah, I bought her a coffin for her office." Monica laughed and then sighed, settling back into the two tone leather, relaxing. The R8's V8 rumbled behind us, providing a subtle massage for the occupants, mingled with perfume and warm hands, creating a pretty intoxicating environment.

I walked her to number 1208, and she turned expectantly, waiting for a response.

"Monica, I wanted to thank you; I needed a break from all that's going on."

"And that's what tonight's been about, a break?" Her smile faded, disappointment obvious.

"No, tonight was about a casual dinner that turned into something else, …a lot more than I bargained for, and more than I should even consider," I admitted. Certainly not fair to her.

"You weren't what I expected either, not just a rich guy out for a good time. You're real and funny, and just a *little* mysterious." She flashed that perfect smile with a casual laugh, she was breathtaking. I was sure she had had her fill of the rich guys looking for a trophy to be on their arm, but I was far worse. I had liked her instantly, and cared about her even after just a few hours, more than I should or had a right to. But she was not Rebekah; no one could be.

"And drive an R8," I tried to lighten it up, but that only made it worse. She sighed and then stepped in closer, and took my hands, her sweet voice dropping a little.

"Look, M did tell me one more thing. Someone hurt you recently, and you're not over her. But I wanted to meet you anyway, and I want you to know that she's a fool." She dropped my hands, then closed the gap and kissed me, it was warm and genuine. I responded slightly and held her, enjoying how she felt, her perfume and her warmth. She pulled back, bright eyes and a sly smile. She got her answer.

"And if she's careless enough to let you get away, you know where I live." Yes, Monica could be someone I could consider being with, more than almost anyone I'd met, but 'almost' was the problem. My heart ached, knowing Rebekah was still "The One," even as she refused to have anything to do with me, she was still in control.

"It's been an unforgettable evening. …. And you deserve much more than who I am right now," I said, and her hand closed on mine, still very warm.

"Josh, I'm a big girl, I know where I stand. Call me, even if it's just to talk." She put her key in and opened the door, and turned,

"Good night," giving me that spectacular smile to remember her by.

I turned back to the elevator and the image of a pair of once brilliant blue eyes, bloodshot and dark rimmed filled my thoughts. Somehow, someway I needed to bring her back to me.

The note read:

There are still many fowlers out there. William C. Bryant

C.

As the elevator opened at the garage level, I used my cell phone to access Google and searched for "Bryant Fowler Crimson." A few hits came back. All famous quote and verse sites.

Vainly the fowler's eye
Might mark thy distant flight to do thee wrong.
As darkly painted on the crimson sky,
Thy figure floats along.

-William C. Bryant

I got to my car and looked again at the ominous quote, and remembered the message: 'She asked if things were going well with Rebekah and if she would be forced to wish you joy soon.' *Forced?* - Cassandra, your green eyes are showing. What were you up to? Shoving the note back into my bomber jacket I frowned into the rearview mirror as I backed out. Who knew where she was, but she had John Hall still doing errands for her, tracking me down. *Amazing.* And there are many more fowlers to 'Mark thy distant flight to do thee wrong.' Monica, you have no idea the trouble you've just sidestepped.

It was late as I flew up the 5, wanting to get back to the beach house, my mind like a pinball bouncing off three disturbing quandaries, with a beautiful woman at the center of each one. How did I get myself into these situations? I just shook my head. You'd think I went out looking for them.

Cassandra's note played on my mind. She was out there somewhere still 'keeping track of the competition.' ('*forced* to wish me joy'?) It was amazing to me that even though she might be in a relocation program or had gone underground, she still was able to keep tabs on me and even get that ominous message to me via 'a mutual acquaintance.' What was John Hall doing acting as her agent? Note to self: Tomorrow have M do a deep backgrounder on John Hall. Ask Hunter to find out what was happening with Cassandra these days. And then there was the verse - obviously a warning. So there were more than just the three suits from Paris, this was bad news indeed. It meant that I still had to watch my back and continue to feel the great weight of responsibility for the safety of the Vision Warriors. Was Cassandra capable of personally interfering? I wouldn't put anything past her. Finally, she knew about Rebekah, and by her comment she was less than thrilled at our recent marriage plans. I smiled at this, just like her senior year in high school, couldn't be satisfied with a full ride debate scholarship to J.A., she had to attempt to avenge her losses and win at Nats. This level of competitive nature was a sickness. But evidently for all her resources, she did not know about Rebekah's refusal. Whether,

John Hall would divulge details of tonight, like "unless Rebekah has grown another six inches, Josh was out with someone else," I would have no idea.   And what effect that would have on Cassandra was also a mystery. But it was just too late, and I was too tired to try and sort out the web Cassandra was weaving.

Pulling into my garage, I began considering the other two focal points, trying to sort out my true feelings toward Monica. First, I had only met her this evening, although it seemed I had known her longer. I had liked her from the start, probably too much, and I seemed to be more relaxed around her than many women I'd been acquainted with for years. I replayed the evening in my mind as I got ready for bed. Finally laying there looking at the ceiling I could honestly assess what happened.   Monica was terrific therapy, actually that did not do her justice, she was more than that, much more and I would be calling her tomorrow morning if not for *her*.

She had absconded with a number of my vital organs plus my soul and continued to hold them for ransom, slowly destroying my ability to allow anyone to get close to me. Although I had to admit a few cracks had appeared in my dungeon tonight, if only momentarily.   The whole roadmap of my life depended upon whether I had really lost...

I could hardly make myself go there. I actually was physically impacted by the thought that I might never hold...

What would happen to me if I truly had lost ..."Rebekah?" I said it out loud, and it shot through me, no ballistic vest could keep these projectiles from finding their mark.   Insidious, they operated from within and were already formed waiting to be laser guided to their target, a target that still pumped blood, but was otherwise useless.   Finally, my mind hoped it would be a dreamless night, but my heart longed to see her in my dreams.

Just before I fell off to a fitful sleep, I prayed, "Heavenly Father, I am really at the end. I will still serve You and bless Your name, Lord, all my days. Will You find a way?...Just find a way... I will wait on You, Lord."

Waking, she had not been in my dreams, my mind was clearer, but my heart was sullen. I needed to focus – assess the new facts about the threat to the CRIMSON plan. I reached into my bomber jacket for the note, and my fingers could feel something else, hard, metal – a key. A small flat key with 1809 stamped on it, seemed like it was for a safe deposit box. Replaying the evening I couldn't figure how it could have gotten there. Maybe it had been there a while. I thought back to the last time I wore the jacket; I had been driving a white panel van in Manhattan. Cassandra! How she had placed it there was not that difficult to imagine. I remember Hunter helping me on with the jacket as my shoulder was badly bruised. Then...   .... 'For my Knight-errant' she had said with a kiss. Distracting me so as to drop the key in my pocket, unnoticed. I whistled low, I had to give her credit, she had the presence of mind to do that even as she was going to confess to the Feds, having just escaped certain death – The word that came to mind was 'unfathomable' – How she must be wired was beyond me.

****

"Hey, you doing anything for lunch?" Hunter all smiles, wanting to get the details on last night.
"Sure, give me about ten minutes to finish this; Toxic Taco sound good?" I might as well get the interrogation over with.
"See you in the lobby in ten." He shut my door.

Hashing out some of the unexpected events from last night needed to be done. I had purposefully stopped thinking about it all morning until now. It would be helpful to talked to Hunter about it, and at least take up some of the lunch hour; otherwise it would be a constant, "What did you think of Monica?"

Hunter showed uncharacteristic restraint and didn't ask anything until we were out of the lobby door and at his Hummer. "Well, was I right? Is she a *babe* or what?"

I could not resist giving him a hard time. "What babe are you referring to?"

"Monica. Come on, man. What did you think? She is gorgeous, right?" This could be entertaining, if real feelings were not involved.

"Look, I am not going to give you a play-by-play of last night's 'just dinner with me and M.' If you had wanted that you shouldn't have ditched me. I figured I was set up the minute you called with that lame excuse about installing a security update." I had to smile as he faked hanging his head.

"M and I figured you wouldn't go if it had just been a blind date without us, right? And it doesn't look like she did you any bodily harm," was his come back with a grin.

"She was everything you said and more. Did you know she knows a lot about cars, *exotic* cars? We had other things in common too, like cotillion, and she does attend a Bible study." I figured I had to give him something or he would just keep at it.

"Well, so how'd it go?"

"Dinner was great; City Lights was expensive, but the food was first rate, great view." I knew that wasn't what he meant, but I had to enjoy this a little.

"I don't want to know about the hors d'oeuvres. How did you get along?" Hunter inquired eagerly.

"Seriously, I know I will get no peace, so here is how it is. Monica was terrific, we had a great time at dinner, and then we went dancing. I had fun last night and I like her - a lot, and I think the feeling's mutual. But that doesn't change anything. If I had never met Rebekah, I would probably be calling her for another date tonight. But as it is...." 'What a mess,' I finished with a thought as I grimaced.

Last night had shown me that there could be 'life after Rebekah.' Not nearly the perfect, joyous union that could have been, but a pleasant, even happy life might still be possible. My heart ached in saying it; there was no doubt how it felt about my last thought. The difference between once-in-a-lifetime and once in a while.

"M and I thought it might help, I guess we should keep out of it." Hunter looked concerned. He and M had only been trying to help and in a small way they had. I didn't need to ruin his lunch.
"Don't get me wrong, I am very glad I went last night. You can tell M that I had a good time and thank her for trying to help." I attempted a smile.
"Why don't you call Monica and tell her yourself," Hunter suggested.
"Because it's not fair to her; she said some very brave and sweet things last night, but I can't take advantage of her, I can't do that," I shook my head. And I can't get another innocent bystander involved in the CRIMSON plan.
There was silence in the Hummer as we pulled into Takeout Taco. Hunter knew not to push it.
When we had ordered and took a booth, I thought I might let him in on the bit of intrigue at the club.
"Got a message from Cassandra last night," I figured I'd cut to the chase.

"*What?!* Cassandra? What did it say?"

"It wasn't an "it", it was an old high school debater that used to be on the same team as Cassandra. He followed me in my R8 and passed it on at the club," I explained.

"And…" he was interested now.

"It actually came in two parts. As you know, nothing's ever simple with her." I shook my head and then, "The first part was a comment about Rebekah. The other was a note indicating that there could be more trouble from others besides the guys we took out in Manhattan."

"Interesting. And this guy delivered it to you?" Hunter was all ears, except for the gears that were turning a mile a minute.

"Yeah, which reminds me, when we get back I want to run a deep backgrounder on a John Hall."

"What did the note say?" he asked.

"I have it right here." I showed him the note. "It refers to a poem about fowlers trying to harm a dark bird flying in a crimson sky," I explained as I passed him the note. I had decided to keep the discovery of the key to myself for now.

"She's not even supposed to contact anyone, let alone send threats. The guys at Justice will not be amused," Hunter frowned.

"I don't think we should let Justice know. Don't really want to cause her any trouble; besides, she could be trying to warn me; doing us a favor." I didn't want anymore contact with the Feds than was necessary; and yes, I didn't want to make any more trouble for Cassandra. I still hoped that someday she would turn it around.

"Ok, I guess I can pass on that, but this does make it pretty clear you are still in danger. I guess we will have to put you under better surveillance. Twenty four hour bodyguard. I know a tall beautiful blond who would be happy to take on that assignment," he grinned and I shot him a frown. "Seriously, you need to be more careful, and I'll have to be around more. We'll do some training on this. No more of this moping around by yourself. OK?" He was right, but I had no way of knowing who, what or when something would happen.

"Yeah, OK." I took a bite of my taco and then, "One thing Cassandra didn't seem to know about was Rebekah turning me down. So at least she is not all seeing and all knowing. In fact, her message implied she wasn't particularly thrilled with the idea of me getting married, especially to Rebekah," I explained.

"She is a piece of work, *that's* for sure," he chuckled. "Tries to get you killed…well, abducted at least, but then is jealous of your marriage plans with Rebekah." He shook his head. "It's probably good she's not loose, who knows what damage she could do?"

"So that was my night, pretty uneventful wouldn't you say?" I replied, deadpan.

"Man, you can pack more stunts into an evening than anyone I know," he grinned as we left Toxic Taco, "Maybe you should be the one in protective custody, or at least charge admission."

"I guess it's a good thing I don't get out much," I smiled, shaking my head.

"Well, think about calling Monica back. At least she's not a psychopath or an evil legal genius."

"Rebekah's *not* evil," I retorted, too strongly.

"I'm sorry, Man. I know she's got her hooks deep inside you, but really, you need to stop beating yourself up over it. She turned you down, and you act like it was your fault. You need to stop moping and start paying attention, be more alert to this threat, whatever it is. *And* you have to admit you had a good time last night." Hunter had said a mouthful, summarized the situation pretty succinctly, except for one little omission, The Vision.

****

How to turn off the pain? Really the only thing that helped was distraction. Work - I actually hoped there would be a crisis when I walked in every morning. And the workouts and time with Hunter, plus plotting and executing the details of the CRIMSON plan, all kept me seriously occupied.

Hunter and I signed up for the Safeguard Executive protection course. It involved aspects of personal security detail, evasive driving and convoy driving training, just for starters. This was an intensified group of courses which sole purpose was to keep you safe and alive in case of any kind of attack. It included counter-ambush driving, evasive driving, vehicle as a weapon, counter-surveillance, and disarming techniques; designed for corporate executives and military personnel operating in high risk areas of the world. It was no-nonsense and included real-life scenarios with trained instructors to simulate the bad guys. I could hardly wait, as the next session of classes began in about three weeks. We got all the written material and Hunter and I went over it preparing for the course. His training as a Ranger gave us a leg up, but this was specifically designed for what we were concerned about, my personal safety and his too, as he was going to have my back. All this activity also served the purpose of filling my days and evenings, driving me to an insane routine of work and workouts.

My mind had banished my heart to the lower depth, and left it there under a guard of detachment, this was how I would now have to operate. Perhaps in time, it might again be useful for something other than providing a pulse, but for now this was how it had to be; otherwise, the frustration and pain would debilitate me to the point of uselessness. I tried to stay occupied right up till the moment I hit the pillow, reading my Bible a little and praying I would dive immediately into a dreamless slumber until the alarm at five. Sometimes I was successful, but when I wasn't the 3:00 a.m. sessions were devastating. My mind let loose with a barrage of self-doubt, frustration, mercilessly allowing the memories to burst forth: her words, images of her face and worst of all her eyes, as I waited for the alarm, leaving me in a venomous mood for the next day or two. It was no way to live.

Chapter Ten

Know it All

*"Wisdom and knowledge, as well as virtue, diffused
generally among the body of the people, being necessary for
the preservation of their rights and liberties, and as these
depend on spreading the opportunities and advantages of
education in the various parts of the country, and among
the different orders of people, it shall be the duty of
legislators and magistrates ... to cherish the interest of
literature and the sciences, and all seminaries of them."*
– John Adams, 1776

It had been a little over a week since my "dinner" with Monica. I
had refrained from calling her for obvious reasons. It was a crisp
sunny Saturday morning, and keeping to my routine, I pulled on
my wetsuit, the water temperature being fifty-nine degrees. I had
allowed myself to sleep in after enduring a nightmare where
Rebekah had again slashed me wide open with her blue lasers, all
the while hearing her damn me for my secrets. I had experienced
that one before, but being a veteran didn't make it any easier. I
could hardly run fast enough to hit the surf and swim till my mind

was numb. As my muscles got warmed up in the surf I started to muse. No work today unless I just wanted to go in for show. Perhaps Hunter would be there, and we could go work out at lunch. The CRIMSON plan always needed work; maybe call Dad and see if he had time to discuss the threat from Cassandra or look over the backgrounder on John Hall, who evidently worked for the Justice Department. I could just drop by and see Mom and we could awkwardly dance around the "big elephant in the room": my relationship, or current lack there of, with Rebekah. Where was she right now? It would be about noon back in D.C. Perhaps she was shopping, or working on a brief. She might be at a charity event or out with a friend for lunch. ...OR maybe she was sitting at home, rocking back and forth, wracked with pain, cursing my name and doing more damage to her extraordinary blue eyes – I prayed it wasn't so. Should I call again, should I go there and risk more suffering on both sides? Would she pick up, would she even be there? Just keep swimming Josh, just keep swimming.

The surf dumped me onto the wet sand. I had stayed out too long this time; pushed it beyond my limits, totally exhausted, my mind started hallucinating.....

...... Everything I wanted in life was running toward me, blond hair swinging and cobalt lasers flashing, laughing. Her pure steadfast love shining from them, just for me; .... a vision in blue. Could my tormented mind conjure up anything worse to devastate my heart? The vision waved to me as I finally stood up out of the surf, pulling down my wetsuit to my waist. Detached, guarded, I watched as it got closer, pretty good detail for a mirage except for one flaw, as I had never seen the real Rebekah so excited, bare feet dancing through the sand. I hadn't seen or talked to her in nearly two month, not my choice but hers. Only in my subversive dreams did I see and sometimes hear her voice.

But that didn't matter now, this vision was simply too vivid.

My heart, which had been a sick recluse these many weeks, awoke in its self-imposed dungeon, peering out through the bars of my skepticism. I was afraid to hope, but something had happened; the stirrings of joy started to pulse. But I wasn't prepared to completely drop my guard, to let the exquisite pain that I had finally numbed down to a manageable, if acute ache, be re-animated. To allow my heart to take another serious blow would seal it in those dreary catacombs for good.
Yet I had prayed and prayed that she would somehow return to me, and now....

I heard her high laugh mingled with short sobs. She must be close enough to see my uncertainty, my wariness. My mind was frantically sorting through the possibilities, but my heart was straining to accept, to leap with faith at what could be. I expected to hear something to set my heart at ease, waiting for her clear high voice. True to her way, being so unpredictable, she had a much more direct communication in mind, launching herself, and by reflex I caught her, cradling her warm body as she threw her arms around my neck, tears mingled with kisses.
Finally some words came.
"Oh, *Josh*, Josh, I *know*, I know it *ALL* and I love you more than ever. Please say you still love me. *Please,* I'm so sure of us now....*forever*."

She looked into my face, begging for an answer. I had so longed for those eyes, haunting me day and night since she had left, wondering could I live without them. Seeing the truth of her words in her brilliant blues, my heart easily overpowered my head, bursting forth past all the defenses I had built up, holding her, kissing her, hearing her confession…It would *not* be denied. If this was a mirage, I would choose to live in my heart, letting my mind go insane, I *had* to have this.

"*Rebekah*, …my Rebekah, *I love you*, I'll *always* love you," my heart sang.

More kisses, more tears. Gradually, straining to be recognized, my mind with extreme effort had to inquire, "You know?" I whispered.

I set her down finally, but she would not release me, hands still around my neck, eyes locked on mine.

"The *Vision*, The CRIMSON plan, *all of it*. And I love you the *more* for it"….She paused seeing my concern. "Don't worry. I know how to keep a secret," she gave me that shy smile. The one I had seen so many years ago, after our first debate.

"But how did you find out?" My mind needed to know this. In a way I was relieved; it had brought her back to me, and my heart would not let me be angry about this severe breach. Faithfully, I had spent my entire adult life keeping the secret, ultimately sacrificing my one true love for its safety till now. But, somehow, I was at peace with her discovery, instinctively I knew it was God's timing.

"I received a package two days ago; it came by courier, but with no sender information. It was thousands of emails and database entries going back over ten years. It was fascinating, all about

CRIMSON and law schools and judgeships," she paused and frowned,

"And there was a note: *J.R, and the CRIMSON Plan*   in a distinctly *feminine* hand." She flashed her lasers, but then smiled, brilliantly.

'Cassandra' I thought. Why? Why send them to Rebekah, what ulterior motive was brewing in …but these were puzzles to be left for another time.

"But how do you know about The Vision?" I was starting to worry, maybe more people knew. Her explanation came in a torrent.

"Oh, The Vision…and the gray flag….It's so *amazing*. You once told me you were on a mission from God. If only I had trusted you then, I would have saved myself so much heartache all these years, I'm such a *fool*. I died a hundred deaths since you asked me and I turned…..I … I was so heartsick; but I couldn't find a way to trust you. I listened to your calls, but I just couldn't make myself believe, refusing to pick up, crying myself to sleep. It was literally *killing* me; and then you stopped calling, and that was worse. Not knowing, I imagined all sorts of things: that you had given up or worse that you found someone new. I barely slept, *searching* for a way. But I won't ever doubt you again, you *had* told me but I was *too* smart. I should have trusted you, but I was afraid of being hurt….Ultimately, I *was* hurt, terribly, and all I could see was my life without you, just dead inside…. except for all those *perfectly* vivid memories to torture me."

I held her close and wiped her tears, and kissed her forehead and then her closed eyes.

"Shhhh….It's all right…I can't imagine my life without you. I never gave up on us. My heart wouldn't let me. But I was afraid that if I told you about the Vision, I would lose you. You'd think I was crazy, or worst that I was a truly deceitful megalomaniac, manipulating people's lives, and hate me for it."

She looked up at me, and I could see she wanted more reassurance. I was glad to oblige, her kisses tasted warm and salty. I was overcome with my feelings for her. Finally, the curiosity brought me back to reality.

"You didn't tell me how you found out about The Vision," I inquired.

She paused… and looked down.

"Please, don't be angry… my dad. He felt that you had sacrificed too much, and he hated seeing me so distraught. He finally filled in the rest, giving in under my…ah…my insistence."

"And you're OK with what I have done? Leading a double life, scheming behind the scenes, steering peoples careers and lives… all my friends…*everyone* ….except you." I held my breath, searching her eyes.

"Josh, you didn't *control* their lives. They still made their own decisions. You helped them to reach their already existing dreams and aspirations. You helped them, secretly yes, but you were not misguided. I *know* you; and I now know the underlying motives, and they are important and honorable, *God given*. I can't believe you carried all this around inside you for so long, couldn't tell a soul. It must be killing you. And I've made it so difficult…caused you so much pain, I'm *so* sorry I hurt you," she dropped her head, "…. Why do you…bother with me?…." But I lifted it back up.

"Because I'm lost without your eyes," I said and smiled.

She laughed and flashed them at me. I just held her.

What a gift God had given me. I shot a prayer skyward, Heavenly Father, please always keep her safe and by my side, praises to You, Lord. You have blessed me forever.

I kissed her again and again; we laughed and sighed like teenage lovers we might have been in another place and time. She was all I could ever hope for, and this time I would not lose her to the Vision or anything else. I would tell her all my dreams, share it all with her. My Rebekah.

Chapter Eleven

Engagements and Arrangements

"The happy State of Matrimony is, undoubtedly, the surest and most lasting Foundation of Comfort and Love; the Source of all that endearing Tenderness and Affection which arises from Relation and Affinity; the grand Point of Property; the Cause of all good Order in the World, and what alone preserves it from the utmost Confusion; and, to sum up all, the Appointment of infinite Wisdom for these great and good Purposes." – Benjamin Franklin

It was the end of the holidays, but the decorations still lit up the Del as I arrived at the party early; Rebekah would be coming with her family. This was Mom's idea, an engagement party for us. I would have been fully satisfied with something much less extravagant, but I think she felt so happy and relieved that we were engaged and scheduled to be married next November that a serious fancy dress affair was called for. I couldn't wait to see how Hunter was going to be dressed, but right now I was trying to help with the preparations with little success.

"Just go relax somewhere; you'll just get in the way. Go see your dad," Mom made an attempt to shoo me out of the ballroom as she instructed the caterers and decorators.

"How *is* Dad doing, really? I saw him a couple of weeks ago, and he seemed like his old serious self," I queried.
"He's much better; he saw his doctors last week, and they are very pleased with his progress. They say all his vitals are almost normal. You should see him, most of the time he refuses to use that cane." It had been a long haul, but Dad had come nearly all the way back, and soon he might walk normally.

Sarah came up, "You still here?"
"I was thinking, why don't we just have the wedding tonight and be done with it. After all there will be a preacher on hand," I grinned as my comment brought the desired scowl from both Mom and Sarah.
"Because, my dear dense brother, Rebekah doesn't have a dress yet and there are a thousand things to do before we could possibly have a wedding. You men just want to skip the formalities and get to the honeymoon," Sarah retorted, she had grown up to be a polished young woman, looking very much like a younger version of Mom; but to me she was still my kid sister.
"OK, just trying to save everyone a lot of work." I left the room before I got hit with something.

I finally located Dad at the back of the hotel looking out at the surf. He had his silver handled cane firmly planted and cut quite the dashing figure in his tux. I came up from behind, and he didn't change his gaze. "You know, I love you and Rebekah. And I couldn't be happier that you two are finally getting married. She will be the best thing to happen to you." I was waiting for the "but" and wasn't disappointed.

"But, I am concerned that she knows so much about the Vision. I don't think Pastor Miller should have told her. I know that's water under the bridge now, but we *must* maintain secrecy if this is going to work. It's critical to the mission."

I really didn't want to get into this right now, and as he said, it was already done, so rather than argue about a dilemma that I was also struggling with, it seemed better to reassure.

"Dad, you don't have to worry about Rebekah, after all, in a few months she will be my wife and would have been informed anyway. Besides, there isn't a person I would trust more with the Vision than Rebekah, she is a master at keeping secrets."

He turned to look at me, serious resolve in his face.

"It was a breach in our security. What if the others decided that their son or daughter should be informed, now that the precedent has been set? We must be careful, Josh. Very careful," he held on strong to that position, over the last few years he had become more stubborn and controlling, as if it was his personal mission, as if he couldn't trust anyone with it. I could see this conversation could go no where but down hill, I tried a different tack.

"Anything new I should know about, work-wise?" I had been so busy I hadn't had a chance to just chat with him recently.

"As a matter of fact, there is, but I can't discuss it here. I've been working on a project that could be a game-changer, revolutionary. Come by and I'll show it to you, even though it's not quite finished." I could always count on Prescience to brighten up my dad's mood. I just nodded, smiling. He was always innovating.

"I think some of the guests are starting to show, Mom wants us to be available to meet and greet." I took his arm as we walked back to the ballroom; the last ten years had been a difficult journey for both of us. I thought back to that men's retreat and our basketball game, the last one I would have with him. He had been my guide and mentor, and now I would have to be there for him.

We got there just in time to see Hunter and M arrive. M was definitely turning heads in a little red silk number slit to the hip, (definitely not a member of CHESS). Behind her, looking much less comfortable and more like a chauffeur, Hunter grimaced. "I can't believe I have to do this again in November." I just chuckled while I gave him a slap on the back, and grinned, "No whining. Besides, we've had some pretty interesting times in tuxes."

He filed past with a pained expression, as a few more CHESS families started to trickle in, including the Simmons. Mrs. Simmons gave me a particularly warm hug and whispered, "You take care of that girl; she's *very* special."

"I know, and I will, and thank you for watching over her," I responded.

She let go with a knowing smile.

Many couples and families were arriving, and it appeared that Mom had invited all of CHESS. The ballroom began to fill, and my mom had succeeded in fulfilling a lifelong dream, cotillion on steroids.

The band was in background music mode, and nearly everyone had arrived, except the Millers. Probably Rebekah's fault, she really didn't go in for these things. Mom was starting to get nervous, when finally Robert and Debra came walking in chatting with Mrs. Miller. Pastor Miller and Rebekah came in arm-in-arm sharing a private conversation, Rebekah in a deep blue gown that flowed to the floor, hair up and wearing a necklace for the occasion matching her engagement ring courtesy of yours truly. She released her dad's arm and glided up to me, stopping both my heart and my thoughts.

"I know this is for your mom, but I'd much rather just be with you tonight, especially the way you look in your tux," she flashed her eyes and gave me a very enticing pout.

"Given that dress, I would second that motion, counselor," I gave her an appraising gaze. "But duty calls. Besides this is a great opportunity to check up on some of our Vision Warriors," I whispered.

"*Shhh.* I don't want you speaking in a public place about that," she was serious. I smiled to myself; Dad had nothing to worry about.

"OK, OK. Nice weather we're having Ms. Miller, love what you've done with your hair," I teased. It really was wonderful being able to share my plans with her, but I guess now was not the time. She just rolled her eyes and led me to the dance floor. The band was playing a nice waltz number, and we fell into step as many of the CHESS alumns and parents joined in.

"Josh, I've been thinking. How is this going to work? My job's in D.C. and yours is here. When we're married, I don't want to see you just on the weekends." She didn't want to talk about the Vision, but she was OK lobbing this domestic grenade as we danced.

"I don't know what we are going to do. We need to talk about it," I replied

"We *are* talking about it," her eyes flashed.

"How 'bout we just enjoy the evening, and I promise you we'll get to these types of issues sometime soon." It was a sticky problem, and there were others as well. But I didn't care as long as she was with me; I was sure they could be worked out. The band moved on to a slow dance.

"OK… for now…but we need to discuss it, and some other things too," she acquiesced, then she smiled up at me after a thoughtful pause.

"I used to fantasize about this day, engaged, soon to be *Mrs. Rebekah Reinhart*, but I never would have imagined all our trials *and the secrets*." Then she laughed and shook her head. "You looked so astonished on the beach."

'On the beach' had become to mean only one time and place between us.

"Well, I had just emerged from a forty minute swim," I offered in my defense.

"At first I didn't think you saw me even though you were looking right at me," she mused.

"I looked that confused?" I knew I had had a hard swim, but ….

"No… actually you looked very buff… and pretty *hot*, standing there in half a wetsuit." She blushed a little and looked down and then back up, "And then when you caught me in your arms…" she trailed off her mood reminiscent. "Josh, I know you love me, but I have loved *you* almost from the beginning," she stated, trying to make a point.

"Remember our first dance? You tried to cover up your embarrassment about dancing with me. Bet you didn't know I had worked out the exact position in the grand march beforehand so I would get paired up with you. I remember I was so nervous as you took my hand and held me, even at arms length, all I could do was chatter on about the history of the Waltz and Samba," she laughed lightly, and then frowned. "Then Jennifer Nichols cut in, and I just went to the bathroom and cried till it was time to go." She remembered every detail, of course.

"I wondered where you had gone after we danced. I looked for you; I was worried I had upset you, as usual." I reassured her kissing her hair, inhaling her perfume.

"It wasn't your fault. How were you to know I had my sights set on you from the first night I met you. I hated the thought of sharing you with anyone. That's why I even got upset with Elizabeth. I imagined all kinds of silly things," she blushed, and I felt awkward, even now. I was always amazed that she knew from the start, even at thirteen; and once Rebekah had acquired her target, there was no escape. My fate had been sealed after our first debate. I chuckled to myself, "stealth bomber."

"How could you have been so certain from the beginning? You were only thirteen."

"I know, it seems hard to believe, and it was very scary for me at the time, and yet wonderful," she recalled. "But it *is* what happened, maybe it had to do with my "gift," I don't know. That's why I was so hard on you at first, it was my defense mechanism trying to protect myself from the inevitable trauma when I would find out you already had a girlfriend, or just didn't like me, or you thought I was just too odd or young."

"That never happened," I declared, and she raised a questioning eyebrow.

"Well, at least I never thought you were too odd, and I didn't have another girlfriend." That brought a roll of the eyes and a pointed, "Really?"

"Oh, you mean Cassandra." Why is it that women want to discuss other women? "So I went out with her a couple of times, you can hardly call her my girlfriend; and did you know she tried hard to undermine me at J.A. So you see, you had nothing to worry about, after all, *you* will be Mrs. Reinhart."

"Humph!" But the crease between her eyes smoothed, and then a bright smile punctuated by her high lilting laugh and brilliant eyes. "I *do* like the sound of that, but it seems like a long time from now....all the preparations. And don't think I have forgotten a certain Tango in Paris," she gave me a glimpse of the lasers. I guess I would never live that down, I had hoped I was absolved of that incident; but evidently Rebekah wanted me to pay more attention to her on that account, and I was happy to balance the ledger.

I sighed and lifted her face to my mine. "You need to know about one other girl." She looked up, lasers acquiring their target, I held up my hand to keep her from launching into a discourse she might regret.

I began. "During the time after you turned me down, I went out on a blind date with what by the world's standards would be considered the perfect woman. She looked like a supermodel, was no dummy, and was easy to talk to and fun. She wanted me to call her back, get more involved, but I didn't. You know why?" She shook her head just slightly, her disturbing blue eyes big now, focused on me with a little crease between her brows.

"Because my heart wouldn't let me - she wasn't *you*, and could never be you. If I had asked God to create the perfect woman just for me, he would have said, 'I already have, it's Rebekah.' You can ask Hunter or M, and they will confirm my story, there is no one but you that completes me, no one I would rather be with, *no one*." I kissed her and she responded, a tear ruining her makeup a little. We finally separated as the song ended.

"Josh, you're all I've ever wanted; I really don't care what people think, the Vision, all the rest, it doesn't matter as long as I have you." I wiped her tears and smiled.

"I am yours, *completely*. And now we need to look like the happy couple-to-be." I led her off the floor and up to a table where our parents were. It was time for toasts and some food.

After dinner, I got a chance to mingle and talk with some of the point men and women of the CRIMSON plan.

"John, congratulations on your judgeship; so glad you could make it. Now I guess I need to address you as 'your honor.'"

I grasped his hand and Judge Petersen gave me his strong handshake and a warm greeting.

"Thanks Josh, I wanted to come, especially for your dad. I owe him a lot; he got me a great position out of law school, it was a tremendous springboard to my current success. And I think there have been some other workings behind the scenes, as well. I hear rumors of some influence coming out of San Diego, and I naturally think of him." Well, that's an interesting bit of trivia.

I wonder what other rumors were floating around.

"I think we owe you for all your hard work and dedication. Becoming a judge at your age is a real accomplishment," I countered.

"It's hard work and lots of hours for sure and much more to come, but I can't imagine doing anything else and I think I'm called to add a counterbalance to so much of the secular influence in our courtrooms today." You can say that again. It was as if I had written a script for him to say, his words assuaged my concerns about how people would feel if they knew they were Vision Warriors in a grand scheme to stop a catastrophe called the gray flag.

"Well, again it's great to see you; and make sure you find Dad, he'll be so happy you were able to come." I moved off in search of other Warriors, encouraged by the Judge's words, and only a little disturbed by his reference to the rumors of influence.

"Aaron, how's life in D.C.?" I said as I stepped up for another piece of cheesecake from the dessert table. Aaron was back in Southern California during the Congressional break for the holidays. He worked on policy positions for the White House and had become quite influential in Washington. Some of his papers were sited as the best to come out of the State Department in years. That bastion of liberal secularism didn't always like the conservative and often Christian undertone, but they had to admit Mr. Morris was brilliant. The fact that he had strong contacts into Harvard Law was also a plus.

"Crazy as always, you should know considering who you're engaged to." Aaron and Rebekah crossed paths on occasion, and sometimes he consulted with her on matters of Constitutional law.

"Yeah, she tells me some pretty astounding stories. But it's where the action is," I replied.

I knew it was going to be hard to extract Rebekah out of D.C. and I wasn't sure how that was going to be accomplished.

"On the outside it does appear to be the center of power in the world, but individually, most of them are just people. Can't say that about your fiancée; she is a true genius, one of a kind, in my experience." So she's already starting to make a name for herself, *Great.* That was just going to make it more difficult.

As I moved around the room, I saw Rebekah talking to Jeff Petersen. He had not become an attorney like his brother, but instead had gone into sales for a large sporting goods firm. By the looks of it, he had done pretty well; and I suspected he always wanted to be more than a friend to Rebekah, but she was never more than courteous to him. I always wondered if Jeff had tried to undermine my favor with her by divulging my dinner with Cassandra. Well, that was definitely ancient history.

"How's things going? I really need to get out of this monkey suit." Hunter broke my concentration as he walked up from behind. He had already lost the jacket and who knew where his tie was by now.

"Things are going great, and you have to stay reasonably dressed in order to escort M around. I think she's trying to get your attention," I chuckled; he always felt a little uncomfortable discussing M and I always enjoyed exploiting it.

"Can we not talk about that, I told her it was slit too high and fit too tight for this crowd," he explained.

"She's sending you a message, and if you can't translate it, maybe I can get Rebekah to help you interpret Chinese body language." I grinned and he gave me a frown in return.

"I can read her body language just fine, I just don't want to mess up our working relationship. You know, for the company's sake." He sounded like he was looking for an excuse to stay unattached, even while he wanted to be more than friends with M.

"So you're saying if you didn't work together you'd be asking her out. I can arrange that." This was too much fun, now. After all the drama I had been through, it was nice to be on the other side.

"No pulling rank, plus it's M whose bordering on sexual harassment tonight," he grinned.

"Look, it's your business; but if I were you, I wouldn't make her wait too long, not the way she looks. Just ask her out to dinner… Rebekah and I will come along too, if that helps," I offered with a grin as he scowled back at me.

"Hey, it's only fair that I offer you the same courtesy you afforded me with Monica." I could chuckle about that now.

"Hey, speaking of Monica, have you told Rebekah about her?" he was trying desperately to change the subject, but I was having none of it.

"Already told her and let her know that there was no contest; I never even called Monica back, and Rebekah is fine with it." I wanted to set his mind at ease on that account. "But that has nothing to do with you and M." I restored the flow of the original discussion. And it looked like the subject of the conversation had decided to zero in for a dance as the band came back from their break. I chuckled to myself; the way she looked tonight, Hunter was in big trouble.

Rebekah began to dance with her father, and I watched M and Hunter head for the dance floor and then looked for Mom, escorting her to the floor.

"Having a good time?" Mom asked as I was appraising Rebekah from across the dance floor.

"Yeah. Thanks Mom. It's a great party; you've really outdone yourself." I can just imagine what she expected the wedding to be like; but Rebekah and I wanted a much smaller, simpler affair. It should be an interesting negotiation.

"Your bride-to-be is simply stunning, Honey, and I'm *so* happy it worked out, it makes me cry every time I think about it; how God got into the details. You are truly blessed." She gave me a peck on the cheek.

"He does work miracles, no doubt in my mind." Cassandra's jealous malevolence, revealing the CRIMSON plan to Rebekah in hopes of derailing our courtship, God had used for good. Sort of like the story of Joseph, I thought to myself, and smiled. He was still watching over his children, confounding the clever.

"Where are you two going to live? I understand the beach house is up for lease soon and I thought maybe you might take it long term." Mom was already starting to put in her bid to have us stay close. Can't blame her for trying.

"Mom, we really haven't sorted that out yet, there's a lot of time before the wedding," I parried.

"I'll make sure David renews the lease just in case," she stated. Like I needed this help.

The band slowed down more and Rebekah cut in on Mom. "Hi stranger, how's the intelligence gathering going." She was bright and cheery, no doubt after dancing with her dad. I had come to understand that they had a very special relationship.

"Pretty good, I'll fill you in later. How's Jeff?" I gave her a smirk, and she frowned and flashed me with her blue lasers.

"He's just fine and doing quite well as VP of sales. I know he's not your favorite person, but he's harmless." She looked up for a kiss and wasn't disappointed.

"How about we just sneak out and let the party go on without us." Her offer was pretty tempting, I would certainly rather.

"How about dancing over to that exit for some fresh air and some *distraction*?" I grinned.

"Josh, there's too many people, but I will take you up on some fresh air." As she took my arm and we headed out of the room toward the back of the hotel, the cool ocean breeze mingled with her perfume.

"Do you remember the CRIMSON beach party where you told me about having to go to China?" I asked rhetorically. We had so much history, and she remembered every little detail.

"Of course I do, why?"

"Tonight kind of reminds me of that; it was the celebration at the end of the debate season, and you had won Nats, but you only showed up to see me. And you said you were afraid we would never see each other again and that I would forget you," I recalled.

"I remember all too painfully. What are you driving at?" she asked, eyes now locked on mine.

"I should have realized how you felt; I knew you were much more than thirteen inside, and I should have done something to make you more assured." I held her hands looking down into her beauty.

"You told me I was unique and that you would never forget me, it did help some, but it wasn't what I wanted to hear," she smiled thinking to herself.

"And what was that?" I could play this game, rather enjoyed it.

"That you were secretly madly in love with me and that if I left for China you would find a way to follow me, no matter where I led you," she laughed and looked up for a kiss.

"You *were* crazy back then. But I *am* madly in love with you." I laughed, and gave her her wish. What a joy I felt in my heart. Our lips parted, and she buried her head in my chest as I held her, and I looked out over the beach and the ocean reflecting the full moon's light.

I caught her out of the corner of my eye. Just for a moment. Her dark tresses moving in the breeze gave her away, her hazel eyes widened, staring, sparkled golden in the moonlight, full lips in a shape of a gasp. Clad in the trench coat I had seen outside a hotel in Paris, she disappeared behind a pillar perhaps twenty feet away, and I must have tensed up because Rebekah sensed it.

"What's wrong?" she whispered.

"Oh, I felt a chill. Someone just walked across my grave," I laughed tightly.

"Well, let's get you warmed up," she tightened her hug and kissed me warmly. I tried to respond, but my mind was in overdrive.

"I think they're going to start missing us." I wanted to get back to Hunter. What was *she* doing here?

Driving Rebekah to her house after the party, I felt I needed to tell her something about what was happening with Cassandra. No more secrets from Rebekah, or as little as possible. They had cost me dearly up till now.

"Cassandra was at the party tonight." I figured I might as well just come out with it.

"*Cassandra!?* How can *that* be?" Rebekah was now on full alert, coming out of the warm glow the evening had afforded her.

"I don't know; she's supposed to be in witness protection, but who knows what's going on. I caught a glimpse of her when we were outside looking at the ocean tonight. Just for a second, then she disappeared," I explained.

"Are you sure? It was pretty dark." Rebekah's mind was in analysis mode.

"I'm sure; I recognized her and the coat she was wearing. And *she* recognized us," I stated firmly.

"OK,… So now she's *spying* on us. I *know* she wasn't invited." Rebekah had asked Mom for the invite list.

"I think she wanted to confirm for herself that we were truly engaged and going to be married." This was one of a number of explanations, perhaps the simplest.

"What *business* is it of hers? How did she even *know* about the party? Have you talked with her recently or something?" Her eye's narrowed, flashing as the questions came fast and furious. She found nothing amusing about this.

"No, I haven't seen her since last summer," I said a little defensively, "but I think she would love to disrupt our plans."

"Josh, let me be crystal clear about this. I don't want you to have *anything* to do with Cassandra Perez. She is *psychotic*… and vengeful, in fact, I think she hates me ….for a number of reasons." She drilled me with her lasers as I glanced at her.

I was silent, trying to decide if I should let her in on it, then…

"You do know she is why we're back together?" I had to tell her.
"What are you talking about?!" Rebekah's voice higher and louder than normal, incredulous.
"Remember the package you received last month with all the information about the CRIMSON plan?"
"Yesss," Rebekah hissed hesitantly.
Josh, I sure hope you know what you're doing.
"It came from Cassandra. I'm pretty sure she meant it to end or at least damage our courtship, to cause you to distrust or hate me. But she didn't know you had already turned me down *because* of my secrets – like the CRIMSON plan."
"Unbelievable!" Rebekah shook her head, and after that she was speechless.
"So you see, we are getting married, in part, because Cassandra wanted to stop us. Isn't God awesome, taking something meant for harm and turning it into something wonderful?" I smiled smugly hoping I didn't have to discuss it much further.

We arrived at the Miller's in silence. I was contemplating other reasons for Cassandra's unannounced visit. I had no idea what extraordinary mental gymnastics Rebekah's mind was performing, as she had been silent since our discussion of Cassandra.
We walked up to the door, and she let us in. I stood in the living room of the small house. Memories flashing: studying for the tournaments, dinner after our first kiss. Mrs. Miller's knowing smile as she watched me come by to court her daughter. It was late, past midnight, and the house was dark and quiet.
Rebekah turned to me and threw herself into my arms. She kissed me like that first time in the gazebo. I was caught off

guard, but certainly willing to return her passion. The room started to go out of focus, and time did that dilation trick it had done before. Finally, she pulled back, breathless.

"I will not lose you, Josh Reinhart. I will fight for you till my last heartbeat," she whispered with serious conviction. "No Cassandra, no Vision, nothing or no one will come between us, *ever*," she proclaimed.

Then firmly as her eye's blazed up at me,

"I want the date moved up. If I could marry you tonight, I would. I don't care what people think. *Please,* Josh. I want it to be as soon as possible, for *me*," she pleaded. I thought for a moment about Mom and her plans, but the answer came easily.

"OK, some people will be disappointed, but I think it can be done; after all, your dad can marry us at HGCF anytime." I could see she was deadly serious. For her it had been a very difficult twelve year test of her will and love for me.

The thank you came in the form of another embrace and a few grateful tears.

Chapter Twelve

Changing of the Guard

"The tree of liberty must be refreshed from time to time with the blood of patriots and tyrants." – Thomas Jefferson

Of one thing I had been right about, some people were disappointed; but we managed to move the date up to the 12th of February. So about five weeks to get the invitations out, the dresses found, the flowers ordered, and the reception arranged; but I realized that with enough prayer, effort and money, almost anything was possible.

It wasn't going to be the extravaganza Mom wanted; but this was about Rebekah's desires, and I had promised her. Mom would just have to understand.

I told Mom the alternative was Vegas next week, so as the lesser of two evils, she put her considerable talents to work arranging the "Valentine" wedding.

****

Hunter adjusted my tie and chuckled, "Man, I've never seen you so nervous. You have no problems jumping in front of bullets, but this has got you as tight as a drum."

"Marriage is a once-in-a-lifetime commitment, I only get one shot at it," I replied.

"You'll be fine. You told me yourself, she's your soul-mate, *'The One.'* After the hell you've been through, I'd think you'd be anxious to finally be done with it. I know I will," he gave me a big grin.

"You got the ring?" I asked with an anxious look, not amused.

"Right here," he showed me the simple ring that completed the setting of the elaborate engagement ring. "Time to go," he patted me on the back trying to drain some of the tension.

I looked out over the HGCF chapel, it was packed. It seemed like all of CHESS past and present were here, not to mention half of the employees from Prescience. On the bride's side, a few of Rebekah's D.C. friends had flown out; and even the Dean of Harvard Law had shown, a favorite of Rebekah's.

Pastor Miller was not up here in front yet as he would be escorting his daughter down the isle. Mom and Dad were seated in the front row as Robert brought his mother down the isle, she was all smiles and wiping an occasional tear. Then he took his place beside Hunter and next to Dan Jr., Steve, Ben and Judge Petersen.

They matched up with Elizabeth, Debra, Leah, M, Sarah and Sharon, Rebekah's friend from D.C. The ladies were all in long gowns, sky blue and white.

I stood nervously and prayed I would relax a little. The wonderful conclusion to our long and winding courtship was just ahead, and

I couldn't help think that something crazy would keep it from happening. Just in case, I had put on extra security and asked that they pay additional attention to Rebekah's safety, *and* to look out for a particular black haired beauty (you just couldn't underestimate her).

The organ began the traditional processional music. I turned to gaze down the isle at Rebekah on her dad's arm, entering the chapel. The wedding dress had been the most difficult thing to arrange in the short time. Finally they had found it, and she had gone to New York City for the fitting. Whatever amount of effort, money and tears that had been spent, it had been worth it. All in satin with intricately beaded bodice and sleeves, the veil shimmered and flowed back six feet against the fifteen foot satin train. The crowd literally gasped in awe. My heart nearly burst from my chest.

Even Hunter gave out a "Wow" from under his breath. The sunlight through the stain glass windows layered muted colors onto the train and lit her veil giving it an effervescent glow.
At last Rebekah Miller was the main focus of our universe, as she had frequently deserved to be but instead had shunned the attention. She slowly proceeded down the isle with her father who was completely overshadowed by his incandescent daughter. He had a very contented smile on his face, as he knew he had made the right choice revealing the Vision.

Finally, my precious Rebekah stood with me, and Pastor Miller moved up to the podium to secure our future.
"Dearly Beloved, my dear friends and family, we are gathered here in the sight of our Heavenly Father..." my future father-in-law began.

"Rebekah Erin Miller, do you take Josh to be your husband, to love and respect, in all circumstances, forever."

"I do!" was the high clear certain reply.

"Joshua David Reinhart, do you take Rebekah to be your wife, to love, cherish and protect, in all circumstances, forever."

"I do," I replied as I exhaled realizing I had been holding my breath.

"Therefore, by the power vested in me by the State of California, I now pronounce you Man and Wife. Josh, you may kiss your bride."

I lifted the sparkling veil to reveal truly the most beautiful woman I had ever seen. Her spectacular eyes were a deep cobalt blue and shone brilliantly. I bent to give her the kiss, and she threw her arms around my neck and just before our lips met she whispered "forever." Then time stopped and things went out of focus for a while.

The crowd cheered as the kiss lasted a little longer than propriety generally allowed. It seemed fitting, given how long we had waited. The little, reclusive genius in braces with disturbing blue eyes, and the earnest "First born," trying to save the nation one debater at a time, had finally become one in God, completing each other.

"Ladies and Gentlemen, I am very pleased to present Mr. and Mrs. Josh Reinhart."

She took my arm, and after her three attendants adjusted the dress and the train, we proceeded down the isle and exited the Chapel. Smiles and tears abounded.

There would be plenty of photos and video, but that was just back up for Rebekah, whose unique memory had captured all of it in minute detail. It would be with her as a permanent reminder that God had found a way to bring us together.

Raymond pulled the limo up to the Del, how Mom had managed to secure the reception there on such short notice I'll never know. Debra and M had removed the train and veil and we entered the reception. The party was already well under way, and we interrupted it as Hunter announced us. Our friends gathered around, and there was lots of, " 'Bekah, you look gorgeous. ... Incredible dress, where did you find it?..." "What a beautiful ceremony... your dad was so cute." to "Josh, you looked a little nervous up there, but redeemed yourself with that kiss." The dance floor had remained empty, anticipating our arrival. The band began a waltz and we led off in traditional style.

"You know the Waltz was originally an 18th century folk dance called the 'Lander,'" I quipped. And she laughed that delightful high laugh that I now heard more frequently. "'And that came from the waltzer or volver,'" she could have recited the entire conversation. I hadn't actually considered it until now, but I wonder what it would be like to be married to her as I would never be able to dispute any recollection. I decided it just relieved me of an extra burden; no sense in arguing with Rebekah about the past, undoubtedly wasted effort.

As the party headed late into the evening, I was getting anxious to be alone with her. She said she wanted one more dance, and walked over to the band. I stood by the dance floor waiting as she approached and then signaled the band. A Tango.
"I wanted to show you what you have been missing." Her eyes flashed, but she was smiling. She must have been practicing, because I was hard pressed to keep up with her alluring moves.

She was captivating and undoubtedly surprised some of our more conservative guests. When we came together for the crescendo, she whispered, "I will not be second to any woman where you're concerned, especially in *this*" As she dipped till her long blond hair swept the floor, I leaned over her, our lips an inch apart, breathless, she had my full attention. The guests cheered and clapped with more than a few "Bekah!"s and "Go Josh!" to be heard from our friends. It was a fitting ending to a perfect day.

****

The pond shone like a frozen mirror reflecting the moonlight as we arrived at the Chalet, a secluded New Hampshire bed and breakfast with room for six couples; but not this week. The proprietors, a nice older couple, had been surprised when I called and told them I wanted to rent the entire place, and yes, only my new bride and I would be staying. But after the credit card cleared they could not do enough for us. I couldn't think of a better escape, alone with our own private ice skating pond. I wanted this honeymoon to be just the two of us, nothing or no one to distract us from each other. "No Distractions," I smiled at the private joke. I loved how Rebekah transformed into a graceful joyous fairy as she flew across the ice. Now we would finally have some time to enjoy and discover ourselves "as one," like our vows had said.

The next morning after a marvelous breakfast, thanks to Mrs. Kristofson, Rebekah couldn't wait to go skating. She had chosen a new dark blue and white outfit for the occasion, and I was looking forward to trying to catch my fairy bride.
I had my hockey pants on and a lined windbreaker over a knit shirt as I walked out to enjoy the view. The pond was much

larger than I had first envisioned; one could just make out individual trees in the stand off in the distance on the other side, perhaps a mile. I imagined there could be skaters on that side, but we would essentially have our own skating rink all to ourselves. Trying out a few moves on the ice, Rebekah's laughter rang through the crisp still morning air mixed with a few bird calls. As I sat down on a small log pile to put on my skates, Mr. Kristofson came up and addressed me in a very serious tone, "I already told your wife and I'll tell you, the ice is pretty thin. It's only three inches thick in some spots, very unusual for this time of year, five to six ordinarily. You can go skating but watch yourselves." He eyed me, and then, "How much do you weigh, Son?" I had to smile at his tone. He was certainly old enough to be my dad.

"About two-ten." I had put on a few pounds with all the food and celebrating lately.
He poked his thumb out at the lake, "Your wife's no problem, but you should be careful." Then he set down the ice axe and a large coil of rope, "I'll leave these here just in case."

I thanked him and continued lacing up my skates. I watched Rebekah do a jump and then a scratch spin punctuated by high laugher. I smiled, she was happy, *finally*, and I would make it my goal to keep her that way. She shone like the spectrum from a faceted jewel, and I promised myself I would never do anything that would cause her light to dim.
As I finished the lacing, my head was brought up by a muffled whine. It was hard to locate but it was there, getting louder, closer. It had my full attention now.
Then came the answer - bursting out of the trees on the left side of the pond, birds erupting from their perch, a snowmobile

screamed, racing straight toward me. Rebekah had skated further away, and I saw her stop as she had heard the noise. Standing up I yelled at her and gestured to skate away but she did not appear to hear or see me.

A piece of splintered wood stung my face, and I saw the fresh divot in the log, then a puff of snow erupted at my feet. I started to move, grabbing the axe and dashed onto the ice, with only one thought in mind, *Rebekah!* "Go!" I yelled, and that time she got the message. As she turned from me, I skated head-on toward my assailants.

I could see that there were two of them as adrenaline pumped my legs and carried my attack to the raging machine that sent up a plume of ice shavings in its wake. I was focused on the shooter, struggling to steady his aim behind the driver. I caught sight of an elongated laser dot on the ice in front of me, then my pant leg, but it lasted only an instant as I skated in an erratic pattern, praying Rebekah was still skating away from me. A bullet dug into the ice where the laser had directed it.

The distance closed faster than I had gauged as I sped toward the two men. My heart was pounding and my legs pumped as my skates slashed across the ice. Inside my head, the whine of the snowmobile was drowned out by only one thought, "take out the shooter, save Rebekah." His eyes went wide with astonishment through his ski mask as I turned the ice axe pick-side out. Time dilated, slowing to a crawl as I dove at the shooter, a flash from the silenced gun, and the impact occurred in a fraction of a second. I felt a twinge in my shoulder, but mostly the satisfying crunch. My would-be killer providing the cushion as we smashed into the ice, his head snapping back hard. Then the sickening gurgle as his eyes focused on mine for a moment and went blank, a pool of crimson expanding under his ski mask, his life poured out on the hard white surface.

I lay on him, barely able to breathe, but turned to see the snowmobile heading for a small blue and white figure. "My God, save her!" I prayed aloud with all that was left in my lungs.

The snowmobile closed in as it chased Rebekah to the middle of the pond, the high pitch of its engine screaming with rage to kill its prey. She was skating wildly, zigzagging, trying to somehow escape the deadly machine in relentless pursuit, closing the gap. Just as it appeared that she would be run over, slammed to the ice and shredded under the whirring treads, eighteen years of training took over. Rebekah executed a perfect axel, taking all her forward energy and transforming it into vertical height and twist. The murderous machine sped past, the driver's head within inches of her spinning blades. After what seemed an eternity, gravity took hold and she landed; now racing back toward me. There was nothing that could maneuver like Rebekah on the ice; but in his fury to catch her, the driver pulled the snowmobile in an overly tight U-turn, gunned the engine, and the treads dug deep into the ice. I heard the distant crack over the pulse pounding in my ears as Rebekah was flying across the ice. But somehow the snowmobile was no longer in pursuit, even as its exhaust muffled, and Rebekah turned to look back at the sound, the machine, tail first, and its driver disappeared from view, sinking into the freezing water. Evidently, the driver was caught somehow, the machine and his watery demise sealed together. I watched with an odd sense of satisfaction as steam rose from the place where the snowmobile had been moments ago; then only the sound of her skates cutting the ice and my harried breath remained as I lay exhausted, motionless on top of the dead man. She was safe. I silently prayed a prayer of ultimate thanks.

"Josh! Oh God, *No!*" Rebekah screamed at my apparent lifeless form atop the man and the spreading pool of blood. I finally moved and got to my hands and knees as she reached me. "Josh!" grabbing my arm to help me up. "Ahhh!" I winced and saw a dark red stain on my windbreaker - blood - and it didn't belong to the shooter.

****

Lying in the hospital bed, my shoulder bandaged and under some painkiller, I had slept for most of the day. I gazed over at Rebekah; she was sleeping, breathing softly in the reclining chair in the corner. I imagine she had not left my side since the attack, and she probably was given a sedative. I prayed a prayer of praise and thanks that she had not been hurt. I could handle anything but that, anything but losing her now. It was my left shoulder again, but not just bruises from a ballistic vest. I remember being loaded onto a gurney and seeing her wide eyes, cobalt with concern, mouth set in that tight line. I also remember the blank stare of the man who had put two bullets into me and the pool of blood spreading on the ice under his ski mask as I lay on top of him. "Bastard," I muttered. Well, he wouldn't be bothering anyone, and neither would his partner. The ice had taken care of both of them; in one case it had been thick and hard enough to crack a man's skull, and in the other it had been too thin to support the weight of a raging snowmobile and driver. I felt no remorse for either man, they had dared to try and kill Rebekah (not to mention me). I suppose there would be a ream of paperwork to fill out and statements to be made about how an ice axe got buried in a dead man's chest, but for now I just thanked God we were alive.

I looked at the clock on the wall, 3:17 p.m. Grunting in pain, I raised my bed up to a sitting position as the nurse came in and wanted to check my vitals. She said I was lucky that the bullets had not hit any bone and exited cleanly. She checked the dressings and gave me another pain killer to take when I felt I needed it, and left.

Rebekah continued to sleep, she must be exhausted. My cell phone rang on the table. I reached to get it and groaned again,

"Josh Reinhart," I stated, a little slurred.

"Josh, it's Hunter. You Ok? They said you took two in the shoulder, I talked to Rebekah."

"Yeah, I'll survive." I was more awake, Hunter didn't sound normal. "What's wrong?"

"Josh, I don't know how to tell you this. Your dad...."

"What about Dad?!" My heart rate ramping. The monitors started to get agitated.

"Your dad had another heart attack…"

"…..How is he?!..." Oh, Please God, *please.*

"I'm sorry Josh, your dad's…. dead. They couldn't save him; they did *everything*…but…"

"……*DEAD?!* …. when,….where was he?"

"I'm sorry, Man… I'm so sorry…. he was in D.C. this morning for a hearing. He collapsed in an elevator."

"Where was Mike?" I almost shouted.

"He was right there, in the elevator. He performed CPR. The paramedics got to him right a way. It didn't matter, he was gone."

I had to think… My mind seemed to be operating in slow motion….

"How's Mom? Where is she?" How will she live through this?
"She's at home; they have her sedated for now. The Miller's are there and so is Mrs. Simmons. She wanted to talk to you as soon as you were awake, but she just heard ... You need to call home for more details."

The nurse rushed in to see why my vitals were going off the charts. She said something to me, but it didn't register. She went for a syringe, and I held up my right hand stopping her. "*Wait!*" She backed off and stood there watching my monitors start to give some signs of normalcy. I had to force my mind to think. I felt a cold numbing of emotion and a terrible anger I had never experienced override everything. An amazing clarity came over me.

"Josh, *Josh...* are you there?" I guess I had paused longer than I thought.

"OK, here's what I want you to do." A voice I didn't recognize came from inside.

"Get a 24/7 guard on Mom and the Millers, the best. Cost is no object. Then I want all the information they have on Dad's... death." I could hardly say the word but it came out monotone, robotic.

"If there was a camera in that elevator, and the hallways leading to that elevator, I want the tapes. I don't care how you get them, and I want them now, sent here to me. If the police interviewed anyone, I want the transcripts; I want to see any video of the hearing. I want to talk to Mike, Now!"

"I'll see what..." he started to reply.

"Hunter, Just do it! I don't care how, or how much it costs. Am I clear?" I had never spoken to Hunter like that.

"O.K. Man, it's done." He got the message.

"Finally, I need security here, right now. Get someone you trust and get them here fast until you can get here yourself."

"Already on that, Jared Martinez should be there any time now. He'll have ID, but he's about my height, little stockier build with a three inch scar over his right eye; Hispanic, 36 years old, good man, ex-ranger."

"OK, call me back when you know something. I want those tapes. First secure Mom and the Millers. And get Mike on the phone." Too many questions, but there was only one answer.

"Roger that. I'll be there as soon as I get the intel." Hunter was back in full military ops mode.

"And Hunter, ...thank you," I started to calm down.

"I'm on it, Josh. ... And I'm sorry, Man.... *so* sorry." I could hear the loss in his voice; I had forgotten for a moment what Dad had meant to Hunter.

"Yeah, I'm sorry, too." I hung up the phone, and waited for Mike to call. A cold emptiness had taken over; my mind would not stop... too many things to do, responsibilities, no time to dwell on the sudden gaping void in my life, maybe later. Although part of me wanted to, I refused to weep.

Dad was with Our Lord now, and we were left down here to carry on the struggle. 'Lucky' the nurse had said, but I knew better.

****

The certificate stated Dad's death was due to a second massive heart attack, 'Cardiac Arrest,' perfectly logical and acceptable. I was still looking at the video on my laptop, and Rebekah was going over the written statements. Hunter was on his way, and Jared had taken a great load off my mind. He had an easy smile and manner, and took to Rebekah instantly. I had no doubt that this man could take care of business if the need arose. I asked him about the scar, he said he took some shrapnel from an IED in Iraq. He said that was the part that showed. I didn't pry any further.

The camera angle was from the ceiling and behind in a corner, I could see Dad with Mike in front of him, holding Dad's briefcase. I had questioned Mike, but he said it seemed like Dad had been fine that day, the hearing went well, and Dad was excited about being in Washington and back into the swing of things. I could see Dad's cane in his left hand. The camera image detail was pretty good, picking up Dad's wedding ring design. There was a woman to the right of Mike and two men behind Dad, both dark haired and shorter than Dad's 6'3" height. Five people in the elevator as it departed from the 6th floor going down. The woman had pushed the 2nd floor button, and Mike had pushed the button for the first floor.

As the elevator started, everything seemed normal; the man directly behind Dad had what appeared to be a camera bag, probably a photographer. He accessed something in a small pocket of his bag and then stood there, adjusting his gloves a little, preparing to go out into the D.C. winter.

The elevator came to a jerky stop on the 2nd floor, and Dad had to grab the metal railing with his right hand, so did the man behind him and the woman next to Mike. The next seconds were hard to watch; Dad jerked and then slumped down. Mike turned and caught him under the arms and laid him carefully on the elevator floor as the doors opened. The woman's right hand let go of the rail, and her left hand went to her mouth as she stood there looking at Dad. Mike said something to the two men, and the one without the bag grabbed his cell, presumably dialing 911. The man with the bag helped Mike to pull Dad out of the elevator and into the corridor, as the other man was speaking into his cell.

Switching to the hall camera image, I saw the woman run down the corridor to find help. The man with the bag walked the other way and pushed into a door, an exit, stairs.

Mike and the man on the cell stayed with Dad, as Mike performed CPR. A security guard showed up with the woman, and from there it was about eight minutes before the paramedics came. Mike said they worked on Dad for over an hour, but he never responded.

I had reviewed the tapes for the second time, and I saw nothing really out of the ordinary. Except that there had to be something, I was as sure of that as I was of my own name. I started to watch the elevator video again, slowing it down further, frame by frame. I zoomed in and look at each person. I decided to focus on the men behind Dad, because the woman seemed the least likely. As the frames stepped along, the man with the bag directly behind Dad had grabbed the rail and his left hand had moved down under where Dad's left hand grasped the top of his cane.

There it was. A tiny flash of light, just as the man's gloved left hand touched the stem of the cane's silver handle for about twenty frames. I jogged the few frames back and forth. At first I thought it was just a reflection, but zooming in, the glove had a shiny pad on the inside of the middle finger. A metal pad. Dad jerked.

"You Bastards!" I muttered. "You *murdering Bastards!*" I felt the cold numbing and mental clarity again. Cardiac Arrest, *Induced by Electrocution*. Shocked right across his heart from the metal railing to the silver cane handle. The bag carrying the charge, probably disguised as a camera flash battery pack. Not as spectacular as a snowmobile drive-by, but more subtle ...and for Dad, more deadly.

The full force of Cassandra's warning hit me, "still many Fowlers." They were coordinated, organized and lethal. They had attempted two murders within minutes of each other, knowing that if the attempts were not simultaneous, the other intended victim would be warned and go on high alert. So as I lay on the ice this morning, Dad laid in an elevator. There was one more thing to confirm, and I found it now that I knew what to look for. As the man bent down to help move Dad, I zoomed in on the black camera bag, and the light caught the embossed image on the side of the bag, MM. Markos Media.

I showed Rebekah my heinous discovery, murder plain and simple; well not quite simple, but there was no doubt someone had taken Dad's life in a premeditated act. I could see her mind working behind a look I had seen only once before, at a debate tournament after I had lost to Cassandra, but much more intense. She had jumped way ahead, past my cold rage.

"We have to warn them, Josh. We have to tell them *all*."

Chapter Thirteen

The Revelation

"I am well aware of the Toil and Blood and Treasure, that it will cost us to maintain this Declaration, and support and defend these States. Yet through all the Gloom I can see the Rays of ravishing Light and Glory. I can see that the End is more than worth all the Means. And that Posterity will triumph in that Days Transaction, even although we should rue it, which I trust in God we shall not."

– John Adams, July 3, 1976

The conference room at HGFC was full, and security was tight. I had asked Jared and Hunter to make certain that the room held only those I wanted. I had decided Hunter would be in the room during my speech. It was time he understood what was going on, as he had risked his life for the CRIMSON plan, unknowingly.

Many of those in the room had stayed over from Dad's funeral and reception. My mind had suppressed the task of dealing with my grief and loss, hardening my heart. I had prayed that someday it would be normal again, whatever that meant. But for now, I had a job to do and my personal problems, regardless of their severity, were relegated to the back burner. How this affected my relationship with my new bride was hard to tell, she was putting on a strong show of support and resilience, and I thanked God continually for her.

I had modified my suit coat so that my left sleeve was attached. This allowed my left arm some support for my shoulder. I wanted to look as normal as possible even though many knew I had been shot.

The crowd settled down when Pastor Miller took the podium.
"I would like to begin this meeting with a prayer, but before I do, please take your seats and stay in the room until Mr. Reinhart is finished speaking. So let us pray.
"Our Father, Our King, please bless this gathering and we ask that Your Holy Spirit put Your words in the heart of Josh tonight…….."
The crowd repeated the "Amen," and Pastor Miller sat down at the head table between Rebekah and Mrs. Miller.

I stood up and took the podium; the many faces in the crowd were focused on me. It was an odd feeling; twelve years ago I had been given a revelation that the CRIMSON students were the answer to the Vision, and I had worked behind the scenes continually to secure all their futures. I knew them all. Some were my closest friends, like Robert, Ben and Dan Jr. The others, point men and women like John Petersen and Jillian Holladay, the past CRIMSON students, now attorneys and policy makers such as Aaron Morris, law students soon to be attorneys; all were more than just acquaintances as I had been involved in their lives for many years. They were the flesh and blood of the CRIMSON plan. I shot a prayer up to God, 'Please Lord, give me the words to continue Your plans, in Jesus name, Amen.' I looked over at Rebekah, she looked so proud, so sure of me, and then I began the most important speech of my life.

"Tonight I will not lean on my own understanding, but I will completely trust in The Lord to supply me with the words to tell you a secret revealed.

For too long our nation has gone its own way, asking for its inheritance early and foregoing the basic tenants on which it was founded; squandering the great miracles and blessings of its creation and early accomplishments to sink into the state of ungodliness that exists today. Gradually distaining the great heritage of its Fathers, proudly proclaiming its accomplishments and forgetting to be humble and thankful to Our Creator for all the blessings bestowed upon us. And now, it has descended into a condition where God is shut out from our schools and out of public service, where to pray in the name of Jesus before we go to fight our battles is discouraged. Many powerful people of this nation have chosen to honor the creation above God the Creator and to flaunt our own supposed wisdom, choosing to live sinfully rather than striving to be more like Our Savior. For too long we have wallowed in a pigsty of post-modern relativism, allowing all things to be accepted in our society except one: Our God in heaven, His Holy Spirit and great commandments, and His Holy Son's sacrifice."

"But it is not too late. Our loving God waits, looking out into the distance, longing for our return. He has made a way for us. Tonight I am asking you to join me and those at this table on a mission from God to save this great nation from its current self-destructive course and turn it back to its original God-given virtues. We are asking you to serve in a cause that was conceived more than twelve years ago, a vision that spawned a plan that has been hidden from you until now."

This set up a stir in the audience.

"Please allow me to finish, and I will be happy to answer all your questions." I shot a small prayer up to God. This was the pivotal moment. Either I would be allowed to continue God's mission for my life, or be disdained by those in this room, many I considered close friends.

"Since the time that most of you were in high school, a plan to support your careers has been in operation. This plan is based on the simple premise that all of you here tonight are strong Christian men and women, sold out to Our Savior, Jesus Christ. And that you have the strong desire to serve His cause as attorneys and government policy makers." At this, the crowd stirred with affirmation.

"The plan's purpose was to assist and provide the underlying means to allow you to reach tremendous goals. To provide monetary support and personal influence to assist each of you as you advanced in your careers. But the plan had a goal as well, and that was to place godly men and women into positions of influence and power, in order to help turn this country back to God. That goal was to fill as many judgeships and governmental policy positions as possible with the men and women in this room and to change the course of our nation and realign it with the unerring fundamental truths we hold dear. Here is the CRIMSON plan."

The huge screen behind me flashed up the CRIMSON plan, with the names of those in the room on the left and the possible goals of judgeships and policy making positions on the right. In between were hundreds of lines and dots representing the milestones achieved and the steps taken along the way. CHAF funding, visits to Senators and Congressmen, a detailed map of everyone's career.

The room erupted with discussion. I let it go for a few moments before raising my hands for quiet, causing a sharp pain in my left shoulder.

"Ladies and gentlemen, please let me continue. I have promised to answer all of your questions and I will."

The room quieted down again with a low level of murmur remaining.

"As you can see, each of you has been carefully supported by the CRIMSON plan, helping you achieve your already existing career goals. The fact that it was done in a well thought out and orchestrated manner is testament to the men and women up at this table. We have met faithfully over the last dozen years, prayerfully making decisions, providing underlying support for you as you succeed in your careers. Many of the steps in the plan you are already aware of and some of them you are not. The scholarship program, CHAF, that allowed most of you to attend the best law schools was funded by my late father's personal estate, and that funding will continue. The influence and career support will continue as well."

The crowd murmur rose considerably, and then settled.

"Tonight, I am asking you to continue your efforts and your career achievements as you have been, except with one crucial difference. Work with us on God's mission to save our nation.

Join us in the fight to turn this country back to God and His commandments, so that our children and grandchildren can live in a nation that will prosper and hold tight to our God-given truths. I will not deceive you; it will not be easy or safe. There are many who oppose our efforts, and they will go to great lengths and use any means to see us fail. I want you to decide this without any misunderstanding. I stand here with two bullet holes in my shoulder as proof that there are forces at work who will try to destroy what we have begun to accomplish. But we have been called by God to do this and as long as we are faithful and follow His plan, we will prevail. We shall not be deterred by these despicable men; I am resolved, *committed* to continue to fight with all my resources to accomplish the work that God has set before me. I ask you tonight to join us in this mission, knowing full well its dangers, but also in the knowledge that we are being called by God to lead our nation out of its bondage of unrighteousness. Will you say, 'Here I am'?"

The crowd sat for just a moment. And then the room erupted in a standing ovation with His Honor, Judge Petersen leading the chorus of, "Here I am!"

I stood, holding tight to the podium, emotion overwhelming me; I sent a prayer skyward, "All the Glory to You, Lord."

The Vision Warriors had been awakened.

Epilogue

The risk had been monumental, and I now understood why Dad had always counseled to maintain secrecy. It was only natural not to trust your fellow man. But I had been conditioned for the last dozen years to trust in the inherent nature of the Vision Warriors, and ultimately, God's faithfulness, for without it the CRIMSON plan would not exist nor would it continue to succeed.

I had walked from the podium back to an ante room to let my adrenaline subside. God deserved all the Glory and I was sitting praying to Him, thanking Him for His steadfast direction in my life, enabling me to make it this far. The CRIMSON plan and the Vision Warriors had just entered a new phase. I prayed now for Him to guide my path; show me how I was to continue. I had begun to see the beginnings of how to proceed, like the path into a forest, you could see how it entered the trees, but only so far, and then you had to follow the path to see more. God would reveal it in His time, not mine. I prayed for His words to come from my mouth as I attempted to persuade the Vision Warriors to follow His plan. Why my father's death was necessary, I could not understand and certainly not justify, only accept and take some solace that he was with Our Lord now. My mother was completely heartbroken, and as far as she knew he had died as the coroner had stated, a second cardiac arrest. I saw little value in revealing the murderous truth to her. In fact, only Rebekah and I knew the real truth and the reasons behind it. It was a secret card that might yet need to be played. It had little value now, but like all things, each has its appointed time and place.

I also could not forget that I was still a target and so was Rebekah, by simply being my wife. But somehow I felt that as long as we were following God's plan for our lives, we had a purpose and therefore would survive. That didn't mean we should make it easy for the "fowlers." As I pondered our future, where was Cassandra in all this? Could she be behind any of the murders or attempted murders? Somehow I just couldn't bring myself to believe she was involved in those evil acts. Certainly she was not to be trusted, but aside from some harsh comments about Rebekah, she had provided me with warnings and a key that I had yet to decipher.

Markos Media was my only real concrete adversary; if there were other fowlers, I could only guess. But this much I was certain, someone or group inside Markos Media was trying to stop the CRIMSON plan. They were well organized, well trained ...deadly. Without God's intervention, they would have succeeded already, and I would not be planning the next stage, and my precious Rebekah with her near-supernatural gift would have been lost to the world. How to attack them, or at the very least, neutralize their efforts was a major part of the next stage. It would require a large and elaborate expansion of the current activities of the CRIMSON plan.

The door opened, and Hunter stepped in; my mind shifted back to the present as I stood to meet him. I had wondered how long he would wait, but patience was not Hunter's strong suit. I could see his jaw line tighten as he looked me straight in the eyes.

"You know, when I was in Iraq, my ops were the most successful, and I lost the fewest men; it was not because of my intellect, but because I trusted my men with all the information I had.   Sometimes, seemingly unrelated intel saved them from injuries and death." Then with a particular edge to his voice, "I don't appreciate being asked to operate in the dark." He did not blink.

I really wanted to say something to diffuse the situation, but nothing seemed adequate.

"Hunter, if I could have told you, I would have. I was bound to secrecy. If it had been just up to me, I would have let you in on it." I knew it wasn't good enough but it was the truth.

"I'll take your word for it. But I want you to know, the secrets stop here, or I walk. You're like a brother to me, and I would hate myself if something happened to you that I could have prevented if I had *all* the intel. So it's up to you." He couldn't have been more serious.

"OK, you're due it anyway, just for always being there for me. And I need you for what I have planned, so how about tomorrow at the beach house," I replied. I saw the tension drain from his eyes, and the curiosity glimmer.

"Great, but I plan better on a full stomach; how about Antonio's first, and then we talk," he grinned, and slapped me on my good shoulder. I breathed a sigh of relief; what would I do without him?

As he left the room, Rebekah entered, exchanging glances. She came to me with tears in her brilliant blues. "I'm *so* proud of you; no one could have done what you did tonight. You don't need a law degree; you just convinced a room full of lawyers and a judge to follow the plan."

Then, after the kiss, "I married the most amazing man in the world," she whispered, arms around me. Smiling, I shook my head.

"I wished that were true, but all the Glory belongs to God. I just happened to be willing to follow Him." I couldn't have been more certain of that, as I wondered what He had in store for me next.

"All of us who were engaged in the struggle must have observed frequent instances of superintending providence in our favor. To that kind providence we owe this happy opportunity of consulting in peace on the means of establishing our future national felicity. And have we now forgotten that powerful friend? Or do we imagine that we no longer need his assistance? I have lived, Sir, a long time, and the longer I live, the more convincing proofs I see of this truth-that God governs in the affairs of men. And if a sparrow cannot fall to the Ground without his Notice, is it probable that an Empire can rise without his Aid? "

– Benjamin Franklin 1787.

To My Readers:

I want to thank all of you who have read C.R.I.M.S.O.N.

I began writing C.R.I.M.S.O.N. for my own enjoyment, but the story soon took on a purpose of its own. I determined to publish it after I received so many encouraging responses from those who read my early manuscripts. Now I hope to continue to earn my readership's trust and loyalty as I complete the next novel in the C.R.I.M.S.O.N. series – The Vision Warriors.

– R. H. Krebs

About the Author

R. H. Krebs (Bob to his friends) lives with his wife Renée and daughters Rachelle and Kimberly in Southern California. He and his wife have homeschooled their daughters from preschool through high school. Homeschooling has been a very rewarding and challenging experience involving prayerful consideration in the day-to-day efforts of both the parents and the children. The Krebs family got involved in Christian homeschool speech and debate activities and became inspired by what they heard and saw. As committed Christians, they are concerned about maintaining the religious freedoms inherent in the founding of the United States and feel the best way to defend these freedoms is by educating the next generation so that they understand the principles used to establish this great nation. Mr. Krebs feels strongly that the life skills learned through speech and debate are essential in everyday life and business activities. When he is not judging speech and debate, Bob enjoys writing, reading historical novels, listening to music and spending time with his family and friends. He holds a Master of Science degree in electrical engineering from U.C. Irvine and currently works as a microchip architect for a computer electronics firm.

Visit: http://www.crimsonthebook.com

The Official C.R.I.M.S.O.N. Website

On the website you can find ordering information,
become informed of upcoming C.R.I.M.S.O.N. events,
find out more about **The Vision Warriors**, the next
novel in the C.R.I.M.S.O.N. series and
discuss C.R.I.M.S.O.N. with others.

C.R.I.M.S.O.N. ordering information can be found at:

http://www.crimsonthebook.com

C.R.I.M.S.O.N. may also be ordered from Amazon.com

C.R.I.M.S.O.N. is also available at booksellers everywhere.